O

Linda Nagata

Mythic Island Press LLC
www.MythicIslandPress.com

INVERTED FRONTIER

BOOK 1

EDGES

LINDA NAGATA

Mythic Island Press LLC
Kula, Hawaii

First edition: April 2019

ISBN 978-1-937197-26-1

Cover art copyright © 2019 by Sarah Anne Langton

Mythic Island Press LLC
P.O. Box 1293
Kula, HI 96790-1293
MythicIslandPress.com

EDGES

PRELUDE: ARRIVAL

AGAINST A STARSCAPE, a smudge of white light. A faint gleam, devoid of detail. Notable, because it had not been present when that sector of the Near Vicinity had last been surveyed by the array of telescopes in orbit around the Deception Well star system.

So it was something new, although not unknown.

A Dull Intelligence, assigned to analyze astronomical data, had observed such phenomena five times before during its twelve hundred years of existence. Knowing what that gleam portended, the DI tagged the object with a unique identifier: Transient Hazard 6 or TH-6.

The DI felt no excitement, no fear—it was capable of neither—only a simple, satisfying sense of duty as it confirmed its initial assessment by formally comparing the object's spectral signature with database records. This exercise produced multiple matches of both luminosity and the spectrum of emitted light, providing unassailable confirmation of the object's identity as a Chenzeme courser: an ancient robotic warship of alien origin.

"Chenzeme" was a human-coined term. No data existed on who or what the Chenzeme had been. They had originated—and likely vanished from existence—long before the human species evolved. But their robotic ships continued on, an autonomous fleet with genocide its singular purpose. For thirty million years, Chenzeme warships had patrolled this region of the galaxy, hunting for newly emerged technological lifeforms—and wiping them out.

The Dull Intelligence directed two telescopes to monitor the courser and determine its heading. It did not expect the courser to enter the Deception Well system.

The Well was a trap for such starships. It was a highly engineered star system consisting of only the central sun , a single planet, and an enveloping nebula. The nebula was artificial: a vast-and-slow thinking machine operating on a molecular scale. A weapon. One developed long before the beginning of human history, its purpose to infect the deadly Chenzeme starships, rewrite their motives, and quell the violent instinct that drove them.

The Chenzeme ships knew this—at least their behavior suggested they did. They were autonomous machines capable of learning and of communicating what they learned to one another—and not one of the five prior ships sighted by the DI had dared to enter the nebula despite obvious signs of technological life thriving on and around the solitary planet.

Still, the discretion shown by those past warships was not to be relied upon. This courser might choose to attack. If it did, the mechanism of the nebula would operate too slowly to ensure the safety of the Well's human inhabitants.

The DI acted according to both instinct and its instruction set, sending out emergency notifications to the security council and to the Defense Force stations.

The people of the Well had not suffered a Chenzeme attack in the fifteen hundred years since they'd settled in the system—but they had not forgotten their history. They'd emigrated to the Well only after a massive Chenzeme assault left their beloved home world of Heyertori uninhabitable and their people on the edge of extinction. So alongside the ancient, protective mechanism of the nebula, they maintained twin warships—*Long Watch* and *Silent Vigil*—stationed opposite each other on the nebula's periphery. Both ships were dark and stealthy and fearfully well-armed. If the courser made a sunward run, threatening the world of Deception Well, those ships would work together to blow it out of the sky.

CHAPTER ONE

RIFFAN NAJA RARELY thought of himself as a military commander. Really, he was an anthropologist. The study of human society was his specialty, his passion. It was the reason he'd sought a position aboard *Long Watch*.

Any position aboard either *Silent Vigil* or *Long Watch* required extensive Defense Force training—after all, the primary duty of both ships was to guard the Deception Well system against Chenzeme incursion—so Riffan was qualified as a military commander. He had just never expected to use his military training.

No one had expected him to use it because seven centuries had elapsed since the last time a Chenzeme ship was sighted. It had been even longer—twelve hundred years—since a human starship visited the system. Career Defense Force officers had long ago deemed duty aboard either ship too dull to endure.

So over time, *Silent Vigil* and *Long Watch* became scientific platforms as well as watch posts. Career officers were no longer posted to the remote duty. Instead, the position of commander rotated among each ship's senior scientific staff.

Riffan happened to be in command when the emergency notification arrived.

He was alone in the hexagonal chamber of his study, eyeing a complex display of charts and evolving schematics that described the observed orbital motion of debris around an abandoned planet in a distant star system. He hoped a thorough analysis of the data would reveal some anomaly that could be explained only through the presence of a technological lifeform—specifically, human survivors, finally recovering from an assault that had ravaged their system centuries ago.

The alert shattered his concentration with a triple warning-tone that bleated across his brain. His whole body recoiled, his bare foot kicking free of the loop that had anchored him in place in the zero-gravity environment of *Long Watch.*

He scrambled to catch a hand-hold as the display refreshed and the calm, familiar voice of the astronomical Dull Intelligence spoke into the artificial neural organ of his atrium: *Alert. Alert.*

His atrium's tendrils wound throughout his brain tissue, linking his senses to the ship's omnipresent network, allowing him to hear the DI, even though the workroom remained silent.

As the Dull Intelligence continued to speak, a text version of its words appeared on the display:

A newly sighted object, designated Transient Hazard 6, confirms as a Chenzeme courser. Approximate distance, nine light-hours beyond the periphery of the nebula.

Riffan finally caught a hand-hold. He squeezed it in a painful grip. "*No,*" he whispered as additional data posted to the display. "No, no, *no.* Love and Nature and the Cosmic First Light, this *can't* be right. This can't be happening. There has to be a mistake."

There is no mistake, the DI assured him in its calm way.

"Well then, damn it, why *now?*" he demanded. "Why *me?*"

The DI knew better than to attempt an answer and after a moment, Riffan settled the question for himself: "You fool, it had to be someone, didn't it?"

Seven hundred years was a long span on a human scale. The absence of sightings for all that time had led some to speculate that the ancient robotic warships had already won this latest phase of their endless war of extinction, that Deception Well, nestled within the weaponized nebula, was the last surviving human settlement. With no viable targets left to hit, the warships had withdrawn—so the theory went—to wait with machine patience for the emergence of some future technological species whose history they would subsequently cut short.

Riffan was aboard *Long Watch* to prove this theory false. He refused to believe Deception Well was the last refuge of human-kind. He'd aimed his studies at detecting signs of a surviving human presence, though he'd been unsuccessful, so far. A Chenzeme vessel appearing on his watch struck him as cruel irony. Its existence disproved the theory, without offering hope of other survivors.

"*Focus*, you idiot," he ordered himself.

Academic arguments didn't matter. Other worlds didn't matter. Not now. All that mattered now was the defense of Deception Well.

He closed his eyes a moment. Drew a deep, calming breath. Then another. Sliding into the role he'd trained for: Defense Force commander. If this Chenzeme courser approached the system, it was Riffan's duty to direct *Long Watch* against it.

He sent his first order out over the ship's network, his voice mostly steady: "All senior crew report to the bridge *now*. Everyone else, summon your external equipment and see that it's safely stowed. Secure your internal gear, and configure your quarters for acceleration."

Then he punched out through the gel membrane that served as the door of his study, shooting into a round-walled passage. Two worried-looking students and a maintenance drone scrambled to get out of his way as he launched himself toward the bridge.

Deception Well was the farthest outpost of the human frontier in the direction known as *swan*, named for the still-distant supergiant star, Alpha Cygni, brightest light in the constellation of the swan as seen from old Earth.

The first Chenzeme ships ever sighted had come out of the swan, probably originating from somewhere far beyond Alpha Cygni. This newest courser had come from that direction too.

The luminosity of a Chenzeme warship's hull was a known factor that allowed the astronomical DI to work out the courser's distance from *Long Watch*, while the Doppler shift provided a rough estimate of its relative velocity. The implication was ominous.

Riffan reached the bridge just behind the ship's senior astronomer, Enzo Hui. "You've seen the numbers?" Enzo asked in a low voice.

"They don't look good," Riffan murmured.

He kicked off the wall, shot through a detailed holographic projection of the Near Vicinity that filled the central volume of the chamber, and then arrested his glide at a workstation on the opposite side of the room.

In its current configuration, the bridge held four workstations evenly spaced in a ring around the plane of the designated floor. Enzo took the station on his right. Exobiologist Pasha Andern already occupied the station to his left.

Without looking up, Pasha said, "I'm going over the historical record. Transient-Hazard 6 is closer to the periphery of the nebula than any previously recorded Chenzeme ship."

"Understood," Riffan said as he shoved his bare feet into stirrups that would hold him in place at his workstation. "Its velocity relative to the system also appears significantly slower than past sightings."

The door drew open again. Past the holographic projection, Riffan saw the ship's engineer, Zira Lin, glance around the chamber, her eyes wide, lips slightly parted.

Riffan sensed her fear and shared it. His heart raced. His hands trembled, though he strove not to show it. He had a role to play. The amateur acting he'd done helped him to keep his voice steady as he addressed his companions.

"This is serious, friends," he told them, watching Zira take her place at the station opposite him. "In our sixteen-hundred-year history at Deception Well, no Chenzeme ship has ever tried to enter the nebula. I hope TH-6 will pass on too, but right now it is not behaving like any courser we've observed before."

"Its behavior is frankly ominous," Pasha interjected, a hard edge to her voice. The exobiologist had spoken without looking up, her right hand moving in steady rhythm as she scrolled a display on the slanted surface of her workstation. "Why would its velocity be so low, unless it intends to come in? We know that *can* happen. It's happened at least once before."

Riffan grunted agreement. The evidence of that long-ago incursion haunted Deception Well's night sky. Caught in the planet's gravity well was the dead dark hulk of a swan burster—a gigantic, ring-shaped Chenzeme warship far larger than a courser—easily visible despite its high orbit.

Like all swan bursters, this one had once carried a gamma-ray gun capable of boiling oceans and burning off planetary atmospheres. It was harmless now, but in some long-gone, pre-human era it had penetrated the nebula and reached Deception Well intact.

Riffan said, "If TH-6 tries to come in, we'll work with *Silent Vigil* and do what's necessary to stop it."

"We've got time to work out what it's doing," Enzo said. "Maybe days. The courser is slow, but it's not slow enough to survive the nebula. It'll have to dump velocity if its target is Deception Well."

That was true. If the courser entered the nebula at its current speed, its mass would be quickly eroded by continuous microcollisions with the nebula's tiny grains of debris, and eventually it would be destroyed. That was the good news. The bad news, Riffan thought with a sinking feeling, was that this awful encounter could stretch on for days.

"It might not slow down," Zira said in a trembling voice. "Not if this is a kamikaze mission. Depending on its angle of entry, it might be able to survive long enough to deploy its gamma-ray gun against the space elevator, or worse, aim its mass at the planet. With enough momentum, a collision could shatter the crust and destroy the atmosphere. One courser is a small sacrifice if it means wiping out the last surviving settlement anywhere on the frontier."

Love and Nature! Leave it to an engineer to find the worst-case scenario.

"We are *not* the last surviving settlement," Riffan said. "There are others out there, somewhere, and someday we are going to find them. And there is *no* historical record of Chenzeme ships ever employing a suicide attack."

"Because they've never had to?" Pasha wondered. "Our situation here is unique. Chenzeme tactics might prove unique too."

"I agree," Enzo said, eyes half-closed as he communed with the ship's information system.

Riffan nodded. "We'll keep that possibility in mind, but right now, Enzo, we need you to calculate the courser's trajectory. That will tell us if we've got a fight coming."

"I'm working on it," the astronomer assured him. "But it's going to take time."

"Understood."

To work out the courser's trajectory, Enzo had to map its relative motion against background stars—and at its present distance many minutes would have to elapse to detect any motion at all.

Riffan looked across the holographic projection to the engineer. "Zira, I want you to reconfirm all systems. Ensure everything's in peak condition. But keep us silent. Don't give our position away."

She sniffed a little, and nodded. "All systems *are* in peak condition, but I'll run the checks again."

"Thank you." He turned to his left. "Pasha—"

"I've already run system checks on the gamma-ray gun," she said crisply. "All nominal."

In ordinary circumstances, Pasha spent her hours studying the tiny artificial lifeforms that inhabited the nebula, but for the extent of this emergency, she would serve as weapons officer. Cool and unruffled, she appeared particularly well-suited to the task—though she'd never had an opportunity to fire the weapon. Over the centuries, the laser had been test-fired only three times. The security council feared the weapon would be a beacon to draw the Chenzeme—but they would use it if they had to.

Riffan sighed, now that the first panicked flurry of activity was past. His gaze drifted over the holographic projection, really seeing it for the first time since he'd entered the bridge. It was a high-resolution, three-dimensional model of the Near Vicinity. At the center, a tiny bright sphere represented Kheth, Deception Well's star. The vast scale of the projection gave an illusory impression that the solitary planet was nestled very close to its sun. The blue-green orb was shown as a dot, far smaller than Kheth, but still exaggerated in size to make it visible on this scale. A silver wisp represented the column of the space elevator that linked the planet's surface to the orbital construction yards. The city of Silk, mounted on the elevator column, was indicated by a glint of golden light. Extending far beyond the orbit of the planet was the artificial nebula, its outer boundary represented by a translucent, spherical green shell. A blue flag at the edge of the nebula marked the position of *Long Watch*. Another indicated *Silent Vigil*, on the opposite side of the sun.

Vastly farther out, the Chenzeme courser. A red flag marked its position, making it clear that *Long Watch* was situated to encounter it first—*if* it was bound in-system.

And if it was inbound? He worried it was not alone.

Warships like this one were known to run in pairs, with one ship dark. Cold and dark and therefore invisible, its propulsion reef quiet as it coasted through the void on a pre-planned trajectory designed to bring its gun into position to deliver maximum destruction. A trajectory detectable only if it chanced to eclipse some background object while the narrow eye of a telescope was turned its way.

He linked to the astronomical DI. *Re-examine all survey imagery. Look for any indication of a second ship, running dark.*

A re-examination is already underway.

Good.

He turned to the astronomer. "Enzo? We really need that trajectory. A rough estimate, at least."

Enzo shook his head. "Not yet. Not for a while. But if we put another telescope on it—"

"No, I don't want to do that," Riffan said. "We know where the courser is. What we don't know is whether or not it's alone. Now more than ever, we need to continue the standard full-sky scan."

Pasha must have picked up on his worry, because she spoke in a voice so firmly determined Riffan knew it was a play to shore up his confidence. "If there is a second ship, we'll find it and we'll hit it—or *Silent Vigil* will—before it knows we're here. It doesn't know we're here, Riffan. We're dark, too."

Not entirely true. *Long Watch* had a heat signature. It was unavoidable given that the ship had to provide an environment warm enough to sustain biological lifeforms. And they potentially advertised their position every time they engaged in bursts of laser communications with the head office in the city of Silk—although such communications took place over a narrow beam unlikely to be detected even with some scattering from the nebula's dust and debris.

"We need to get this right," Riffan said quietly, speaking as much to himself as to the bridge crew. He did not feel adequate to the task but that didn't matter. The task was his.

"*Oh*," Enzo said. A soft solitary syllable, dull with fear. His head was cocked, his eyes unfocused as he contemplated some newly arrived data visible only to him. "Oh," he repeated. "This is *not* good."

He looked up, looked around, looked at Riffan. "I put a DI to the task of analyzing recent data from the gravitational sensors. It's found a series of perturbations. Faint. Very faint. But real. A swarm of them, each with a signature that suggests a propulsion reef."

"A swarm?" Riffan asked, his stomach knotting painfully. "Does that mean multiple objects?"

Enzo's lip stuck out. He scowled, he shrugged, then finally he nodded, conceding the distasteful truth: "Six discrete sources of perturbations. I'm assuming six distinct objects."

By the Pure First Light!

"Do you have locations?" Pasha snapped. If she felt any fear, she kept it firmly locked away.

In contrast, Enzo's voice shook when he answered her: "There's data enough to triangulate, to chart their recent movement. All six objects appear to be following roughly parallel paths, separated by intervals between one and two light-hours. I'm going to show you estimated trajectories. Posting on the display . . . *now*."

Six thin lines, bright orange in color, popped into existence on the projection of the Near Vicinity. The lines curved, suggesting paths that dipped slightly toward the sun. In his mind, Riffan imagined another curved line, one that connected the still-unseen objects in the swarm. Extended outward, that line pointed in the general direction of the courser.

In a subdued voice, Enzo said, "Note that less than a light-hour separates *Long Watch* from the closest object in the swarm."

Pasha spoke aloud the obvious conclusion. "That proximity can't be coincidence. It knows we're here."

Clemantine woke from her latest sojourn in cold sleep, brought slowly to awareness by the ministrations of her body's complement of Makers—complex nanomachines programmed to sustain her at peak physical condition and to defend her body at a microscopic level.

She did not allow her Makers to affect her mood, so they did nothing to ease the anxiety that arrived with awareness.

Her first thought: *How much time has gone by?* Impossible to know if days had passed, or years—or centuries?

She'd left a personal Dull Intelligence on watch, charged with overseeing the integrity of her cold-sleep chamber and instructed to awaken her only for a short list of explicit reasons:

If her personal security was threatened.

If there was an existential threat to Deception Well.

If ever there was a visitor or news of events from beyond the system.

She did not try to guess between these reasons. As her thoughts quickened, she assumed the cause of her waking encompassed all three.

The transparent mucilaginous tissue of her cold-sleep cocoon pulled away, retreating in shimmering streams along the ribbons of its anchoring umbilicals, leaving her adrift in the zero-gee of her tiny chamber aboard *Long Watch*.

Clemantine was not part of the ship's small crew. She was but an elder legend, an artifact of a tumultuous past, a hero to her people, and as such she was granted certain privileges—like the privilege of maintaining a private sanctuary here on the edge of the system. Forgotten by most as she was ferried forward in time through the routine of cold sleep, always awaiting some word, some echo of salvation from those who'd left long ago on a quest to find the source of the Chenzeme warships. They'd been just a small company of adventurers. She'd been one of them, once, and an avatar might be one of them still in an alternate life. A better life than this one? Or a worse life? A life already ended? No way to know.

"How long?" she asked, speaking aloud to the empty chamber.

The DI that had wakened her answered in its familiar voice, speaking through her atrium:

Seven hundred twenty-three years, one hundred twelve days, two hours, thirty-two minutes.

"By the Unknown God," she whispered, taken aback at such a span of time. Far longer than any she'd ever spent in cold sleep before.

The Dull Intelligence made no response to this comment, commencing instead on a status report as its instructions dictated it should do, brief line items spoken in a nurturing masculine voice audible only to her, summarizing the centuries so as to orient her in this age:

Deception Well's active population had slowly increased, tripling in size. Many still lived in the capital city of Silk, built around the column of a space elevator, 320 kilometers above the planet's surface. Many more now lived on the planet, in scattered villages.

The inactive population had grown as well: more people in cold sleep, and many kept only as library records.

The orbital construction yards remained dormant, their last products the twin warships, now more than eight centuries old.

A long untroubled time.

But the DI would not have wakened her only to say that all was well.

"Get to it," she said, wiping the last of the mucus off her smooth brown skin. "What's gone wrong?"

The DI told her of the Chenzeme courser. In its reassuring voice it said:

The warship's heading is still being determined. It is not yet known if it will enter the Deception Well system. But there is an additional threat. Gravitational sensors have detected faint perturbations approaching this sector of the system periphery. These signals are consistent with known effects generated by propulsion reefs, suggesting the presence of an inbound swarm of artificial objects, estimated six in number.

Fear shot through her, bitter cold. "Give me details. What kind of objects are we talking about?"

*Unknown. The telescopes have been unable to resolve an object in any wavelength.

So the objects were stealthed. They had to be weapons. What else could they be? Running silent and dark.

"Has there been an order for a radar sweep?" she asked, knowing her revival would have required nearly half an hour following the initial alert. Time enough for the bridge crew to take action.

*Negative. That strategy is presently under discussion.

Despite her lack of any official position, Clemantine intended to be part of that discussion. Caution had always been the guiding principle of their little civilization at Deception Well. Caution, always—and they were a long-lived people. Change came slowly. She didn't doubt that even now someone on the bridge was insisting that using radar was a mistake, that the courser would detect it, and interpret it as confirmation that some fragment of a technological civilization still existed in the Well, while passive observation would give away nothing.

But we are not hidden from any who bother to look!

Clemantine intended to argue for aggressive action. Every Chenzeme encounter recorded in their broken and fragmented histories—whether with courser or swan burster or plague—was a testament to the ruthless nature of the Chenzeme killing machines. It must be assumed the stealthed objects were associated with the courser—and anything associated with the courser had to be a weapon aimed against them.

It was up to the crew of *Long Watch* to locate and destroy the intruding swarm before it could deliver its payload in-system.

Clemantine looked around to find freshly compiled clothing budding off the walls. Puffs of air propelled the clothes toward her.

She dressed quickly in a gray-green shirt with a patterned weave and dark-gray leggings—surprised and grateful at the return of such a simple, practical fashion. She ran her palms over her scalp, smoothing black hair that had been modified at the roots to never grow to more than a stubble. Then she kicked at the wall, propelling her muscular body toward the door.

"Open an audio channel to the bridge," she told the DI. "I want to hear what's going on."

CHAPTER TWO

LIKE *LONG WATCH,* Deception Well's array of telescopes orbited on the periphery of the system, beyond the nebula's obscuring dust. They formed a great circle, so far from the central star a single orbit required two and a half centuries to complete.

Riffan had pursued his position aboard *Long Watch* to gain access to those telescopes. He'd undertaken the requisite two years of Defense Force training to earn time on them and he'd used every minute he'd been allotted.

Half his telescope time had gone to searching the stellar frontier. The other half he'd used to look much farther back along the route of human migration, turning the lenses toward that distant region of space known as the Hallowed Vasties, where the human species had begun.

Great civilizations had once existed there, but all observational evidence suggested those civilizations were gone, lost in a catastrophic collapse centuries ago, though they were so far away no one knew what had happened or what might be left. No one had gone back to look because the resources of the frontier had been consumed in the long defensive struggle against the Chenzeme's robotic ships.

Riffan, gazing at the projected line of unidentified objects on track to enter the nebula, could no longer doubt he was about to engage in an action in that war.

His gaze shifted to take in the span separating *Long Watch* from Deception Well. Nearly six light-hours lay between them. It would be hours more before the security council even knew there was a threat. Riffan could not receive timely orders or advice. Whatever action he took he would take under his own authority, and the fate of his people could very well depend on the choices he made over the next few hours.

He ought to be frantic under that burden, on the edge of meltdown, yet he felt strangely detached. In shock, he supposed. He was aware of being afraid—muscles taut, heart running in a giddy beat, his breathing a little ragged—but as he weighed the array of threats they faced his mind felt clear.

Despite the known hazard of the luminous courser and the potential threat of a hypothetical dark twin, the line of six undefined objects worried him most.

The Defense Force training they'd all undergone had covered every known means of Chenzeme attack, but had failed to describe an attack like this one. Pasha had searched the library, seeking any mention, any hint of such a phenomenon, but she'd found nothing so far.

"Working hypothesis," Riffan said aloud, his voice trembling only a little. He gestured at the orange lines marking the widely separated paths of the anomalies. "These objects originated with the courser but are now independent of it, powered by their own zero-point propulsion reefs. They are likely small, stealthed, designed to penetrate the nebula while carrying some specialized weapon of unknown capabilities."

"That 'unknown' aspect," Pasha said heavily. "That part's brutal. Is it unknown because it's new? Never been used against anyone in our branch of history? Or is it unknown because no one survived the encounter?"

"Right," Riffan said.

History was understood to branch. Given the distances between settled worlds there had never been much trade in information and after the war with the Chenzeme had gotten underway there had been none. So the history they possessed was only that branch lived by their ancestors. Distant worlds around the frontier would have their own legacies—if those worlds still survived.

Many worlds had not—a stark fact that compelled Riffan to

say, "It doesn't matter which it is. Either way, we do what is necessary—*whatever* is necessary—to prevent the devices from reaching the nebula."

He looked across the chamber to Zira. "If you could get a DI working on navigational options. Develop a course that will bring us within effective range of the intruding devices, optimized so we can hit all of them over the smallest possible span of time. I don't want to have to chase them down."

She drew back, looking horrified at this request. "Riffan, if we move the ship while the courser is in position to observe us, that could give it incentive to come in-system."

"Right," Riffan said again. "I understand that and I agree it's a risk." He realized he was responding as an academic rather than a military officer, but given Zira's obvious emotional fragility he thought that might be best. "We are a warship," he reminded her. "We have fire power. We were designed to take on the Chenzeme." He called on his acting skills again, making sure to sound confident—though neither *Long Watch* nor *Silent Vigil* had ever been tested in battle. "Anyway," he added quietly, "if there's a dark courser already in-system, we need to draw it out."

"I agree," Pasha snapped. "We need to act. But let's remember that this projection is showing us estimated positions. Until we know what's out there and exactly where it is, we've got nothing to shoot at. Right now, what we need more than anything is data. We can get that by using active radar. If we illuminate the unknown devices, we can pinpoint their locations, map trajectories and velocities. And maybe expose the dark courser, if one is out there."

"*No*," Zira said, hovering over her workstation with fist clenched. "Active radar is too much of a risk. It will expose *us*. It will pinpoint *our* position."

"We'll have moved position long before the signal reaches the courser," Pasha countered.

Riffan considered it, considered what he knew of Pasha. He'd known her all his life. They were a similar age. They'd gone to school together. Even so, she had never been more than a casual friend, someone to say hello to. The truth was, Riffan had always found her uncomfortably blunt, even acerbic. Intimidating, too. But he'd never seen her rattled, and he was glad to have her on the bridge.

He said, "Pasha, I think you're right. We've got too many unknowns. Zira, I want you to plot that course, and Pasha, I'm authorizing the radar scan."

"On it," she said, cool and professional.

Riffan hoped it was the right decision. Every order he gave was automatically relayed in-system. Any order he gave could be countermanded by the Defense Force chief, but if that happened, he wouldn't know about it for twelve hours.

To Riffan's surprise, the bridge door snapped open, the luminous white material of the flesh-soft wall retracting to create an oval entrance.

Apart from the bridge crew—already present—there were only six students aboard *Long Watch*. All should have known to stay clear of the bridge during this emergency. Riffan opened his mouth, ready to remind the transgressor of that, but then he caught sight of the intruder and realized she was not one of the students.

The gentle reprimand he'd intended died on his tongue as an unknown woman glided in. She was tall and muscular, her skin golden-brown, her hair black and very short, her features bold, strong. Tiny gold tattoos glinted on her earlobes. She reached back for a hand-hold that sprouted from the wall just in time for her to grasp it, arresting her momentum with expert grace.

He cocked his head, trying to puzzle out how she had come to be there. They were isolated. On the edge of the system. Visitors did not just drop in.

Gasps and astonished protests greeted her entrance:

"*Whoa.*"

"What?"

"Where did she—?"

Riffan's atrium automatically queried hers for an identity, but he didn't need its help. "I know you," he said, pushing away from his workstation to get a better look at her past the projection of the nebula. "At least . . . I know *of* you." He'd never seen her before, not in the flesh, but he knew who she was. Everyone did. She was a figure out of history, out of mythology. "You're Clemantine," he concluded in astonishment.

Clemantine had been part of Deception Well's founding generation and later she'd ventured into Chenzeme space, part of the Null Boundary Expedition. She'd been the only one of a four-person company of adventurers to return home. The zero-point propulsion reef had been exclusively a Chenzeme technology until Clemantine brought it back with her, giving the people of Deception Well the means to defend themselves—giving them the technology to build warships of their own.

He'd had no idea Clemantine kept an avatar on this ship.

Clemantine had followed the conversation on the bridge through an open audio channel, so she knew where things stood. Gambling her celebrity would give her some measure of authority, she said, "Get that radar sweep underway. We need to know what's out there—and given the distance, it's going to take hours to get any returns."

"Yes, ma'am."

This response came from a woman, identified by Clemantine's DI as Pasha Andern, an exobiologist. Short, white-blond hair floated in a layered halo around Pasha's alert face. She had the slim, slight body type of those who favored efficiency over raw physical strength, an impression reinforced by the beige tunic and pale-green leggings she wore: simple, pragmatic clothing. Pasha added, "It's an honor to have you here, ma'am."

In contrast to Pasha, the ship's commander-of-the-moment, Riffan Naja, had some size to him—well-muscled and emphatically male without being pretentious. Riffan agreed, "It *is* an honor. But why are you here? How long have you been here? Oh . . ." His confusion gave way to realization. "You were waiting for this day, weren't you?"

"For the day the Chenzeme returned?" Clemantine asked him, startled at the bitterness she heard in her own voice. "*Yes.*"

"Then you knew they'd come again." This was spoken by the engineer, Zira Lin. Each syllable sharp with anger, her words an accusation.

"Of course," Clemantine answered. "Did you let yourself believe otherwise?"

A warm flush rose in Zira's cheeks. She looked away, rolling a shoulder as if to deny such a naive thought. But truth was in her words. "We hoped," she said. "Some of us dared to hope, anyway. It's been more than seven centuries since the last sighting."

Clemantine had no patience for such a limited perspective. "What are seven centuries," she asked, "when the Chenzeme have waged their autonomous war for thirty million years? A war of that duration won't end in your lifetime or in mine, however many centuries we might survive."

"At least we *have* survived," Zira answered, though she sounded chastened. "Here in the Well. Some say we're the last to survive. That between the Chenzeme and the collapse of the Hallowed Vasties, the human age has come to an end."

She paused as if to give Clemantine an opening to argue, but Clemantine did not. Riffan spoke up instead, "I don't believe that."

"Do *you* believe that?" Zira pressed as if Clemantine owed her an answer.

Clemantine consented, giving all the answer there was: "No way to know."

The truth was, hunkered down as they were in the shelter of the nebula, not daring to venture beyond it, not since the Null Boundary Expedition anyway, they were abysmally ignorant of the status of other star systems. Still, Clemantine did not hold much hope.

Deception Well survived because of the nebula's ancient inhuman technology. No other reason. And no one knew how far the robotic Chenzeme ships had ventured in their war of extermination. They might have pushed past the frontier, in among the star systems of the Hallowed Vasties. If so, had they found anything left there to destroy?

"It doesn't matter if we're the last or not," Clemantine concluded. "Our duty is the same—to survive."

For Zira, this was answer enough. Tears shone briefly in her eyes, crystalline, trembling in the zero gravity until she wiped them away.

Forty-nine minutes later Riffan had an update on the courser's relative velocity and a solid estimate of its trajectory. Together, those figures assured him that it would bypass the Well. At closest approach, TH-6 would still be light-hours beyond the measurable edge of the nebula with a velocity too high to be captured by the system's gravity or to survive passage through the nebula's debris field.

It might still try to dump that velocity. Turn about and return. But such a maneuver would require months, maybe years. Someone else would be designated as commander of *Long Watch* by then. So Riffan put the courser out of his mind, focusing instead on the suspected weapons swarm.

He watched and he waited, enduring the slow unfolding of time as radar waves propagated outward, moving at the speed of light but still requiring most of an hour to reach the nearest target, and an equivalent time for the reflected waves to return to *Long Watch*.

At last the first faint signals arrived. A DI compiled them into a blurry image, revealing the shape and size of the leading object in the swarm. They all studied it—Riffan and Pasha, Enzo and Zira, and Clemantine.

Zira spoke first: "It looks too small to be well armed."

The object was like a dart, thin and elongated, only seventy meters from bow to stern and just a few meters in breadth.

Zira said, "It's large enough to house a zero-point propulsion reef and enough bio-mechanical tissue to insulate a thin core of computational strata—but not much more than that."

"Maybe it's a plague ship," Enzo suggested grimly.

Pasha proposed another possibility. "Maybe the swarm is meant to scout the system, chart our defenses and our weaknesses."

Both suggestions sounded plausible to Riffan. He turned to Clemantine, wanting her interpretation, knowing that she'd endured a more harrowing experience of the Chenzeme than anyone else alive. He was taken aback by the shock he saw on her face. "Do you know what it is?" he asked her.

She bit her lip. He heard a hoarse tremor in her words as she said, "I've seen the form before."

Pasha, eyes half closed in mad linkage with the library, said, "It's the same dimensions as the ship that brought you home!"

"Oh, *hey!*" Enzo shouted in excitement, one hand tapping and stroking his control panel. "Riffan, I've got a radio transmission."

"Radio?" Riffan echoed in confusion. Communications out of Deception Well came by laser relay—and it was far too soon for that.

Enzo said, "It's a repeating segment. Voice. *Human* voice. Not encoded. Here, listen." He touched a finger to the screen of his workstation and a man's voice emanated from hidden speakers: *Don't shoot. Don't shoot.* A repeated phrase spoken in the language of Deception Well, but with an accent like Clemantine's, only heard among the older generations:

Don't shoot. I mean no harm. My name is Urban, formerly of the starship Null Boundary. *Like Clemantine before me, I've come home.* Then he laughed and added, *Are you listening to this, Clemantine? I know you made it home, that you brought them the zero-point reef because I've detected its signature here. We* won, *Clemantine. We learned how to beat the Chenzeme. This courser you see? It's mine. I took it. I hijacked it and made it my own. So don't shoot. I've sent small out-rider ships in-system as a communications relay. They're harmless, but through them I can send you the history of the Null Boundary Expedi-tion. You'll want that. Respond to this. Open a data gate. And set up a resurrection pod. I'm sending my pattern through. Do it quickly. I won't be in range for long.*

A tonal signal followed, indicating a break, and then the mes-sage started to repeat: *Don't shoot. Don't shoot. . . .*

Riffan's heart hammered in shock, in suspicion, in a desperate hope that it was all true.

He had not been born when Clemantine returned from the Null Boundary Expedition. In those days the Well had possessed only paltry defenses, but even so, Clemantine had approached cautiously in the tiny ship *Messenger*.

Excitement cut across this line of thought. The object picked up by radar had the same dimensions as *Messenger*—corroborating evidence that the radio transmission *was* true. Only someone familiar with the Null Boundary Expedition could have known what those dimensions were.

Clemantine had made her presence known months before she came into range of Deception Well's orbital guns. Her ghost—an electronic version of her persona—had preceded the ship itself and a physical avatar had been grown for her. She'd testified to the history of the expedition up to the point she'd left it, she'd delivered a library of data, and she'd brought the propulsion reef that powered both *Long Watch* and *Silent Vigil*.

She'd been accepted for who she was, but Clemantine had not come back in the company of a Chenzeme courser.

Riffan turned to her as the voice continued to speak its repeated message. "Is it a trick?" he demanded.

Her eyes were closed, her lashes trembling against the pressure of a flood of emotion. "It is probably a trick," she said in a husky murmur just audible over the recorded laugh. Her head tilted back as she drew a gasping breath like a swimmer surfacing after some long time underwater. "But it *is* his voice, his inflections, his attitude." Her eyes opened. She listened—they all listened—until the message finished again.

As the tonal interlude began, she turned to Riffan. In words now sharp and sure she said, "Reply to him. Quickly. As quickly as you can. He can't be allowed into Silk, not yet. Not until we're sure. But we can bring him here. Give him the access code to a data gate, accept his pattern. We can examine it while his avatar is assembled. If there's anything suspicious in it . . ."

A slight hesitation, that Pasha filled. "Then we end the process," she said. "And wipe the avatar before he's live."

Clemantine's gaze fixed on Pasha, as if really seeing her for the first time. Riffan thought she must be angry, but after a few seconds she acknowledged Pasha's words with a slow nod. "Yes. Exactly." Stern approval in her voice.

Then she turned again to Riffan. "In the meantime I suggest

you adjust this ship's course, take it closer to the swarm, and find the best angle for the guns." She kicked off the wall and glided toward the still-open doorway.

Before she passed through it, Pasha spoke again. "This is why you're really here, isn't it? This is why you've spent centuries in cold sleep at this remote post. You were waiting for him, or them . . ."

Riffan hissed at her, appalled at the impertinence of such a question. Too late. Clemantine caught the edge of the doorway and turned back. Riffan braced for an outburst, a reprimand.

But Clemantine sounded only downcast, not angry. "Not knowing what became of them has been hard," she confessed to Pasha. "If it is him, I will be grateful to hear his story. But to come here after so long, after all he must have seen, and in such circumstance—" She gestured at the projection. "Who is he now? Not the man I knew."

With that she went out, and the sides of the door swept in, sealing shut behind her.

The message continued to repeat as Riffan turned to Enzo. "Do as she said," he instructed. "Reply to him, and send him the key to a data gate."

"On it."

"We'll need to isolate all data that comes in," Riffan added. "Create a new library for it, separate from ship's systems."

Zira said, "I'll set that up."

"Thank you, Zira," Riffan told her. "I'll work on our trajectory."

He was grateful they had time to prepare. Given the light-speed delay, it would be nearly two hours before the pattern that defined Urban's physical incarnation came through—if it was him at all, and not some Chenzeme trick.

This thought cast a shadow on his mind. Even so, he recalled a subset of the words Urban had spoken: *We learned how to beat them.*

By the Pure First Light, Riffan hoped it was true.

CHAPTER THREE

FOR NEARLY SIX hundred years Urban had existed as a pattern of data, an electronic ghost, a virtual entity, a complex ever-changing simulacrum of his biological self that ran on a web of computational tissue grown within the Chenzeme courser. An army of highly evolved defensive Makers guarded the perimeter of his holdings, preventing all attempts at incursion by aggressive Chenzeme nanomachines.

This ghost could imagine itself as the inhabitant of a physical body, or as pure mind, or it could adopt the senses of the courser.

Urban had secured his control over the warship by replicating his ghost over and over again and then editing and pruning each electronic avatar to create a new, machinelike personality incapable of distraction or boredom. These artificial ghosts became his staff, his crew, each designed to embrace a specific task—navigation, calculation, astronomy, library research, Chenzeme biomechanics, and engineering, including the propulsion and weapon systems.

He named these assistant personalities the Apparatchiks, an ancient term whose connotation of blind devotion to assigned duty he found amusing.

Urban had synthesized an army of Dull Intelligences too, to assist the Apparatchiks and to handle all the simple, repetitive tasks each day required—not that he experienced night and day, but he held tight to the tradition of measuring time according to the days and years of Earth though millennia had passed since any news had come from there and maybe, most likely, humanity's birth world was gone to dust.

He'd like to know if that was true.

Urban had also created small outrider ships, based on the design of *Messenger*, the little ship that had taken Clemantine's ghost back to Deception Well. He'd named his outriders after ancient gods and guiding spirits: *Khonsu, Artemis, Lam Lha, Pytheas, Elepaio,* and *Fortuna*. None were armed, but they extended the reach of his senses and his communications.

He'd grown the fleet of six from raw materials carried by the massive warship, matter originally intended for the ship's own biomechanical reproduction.

For most of their existence, the outriders had run ahead of the courser in a long, staggered line, spaced ninety light-minutes apart. All were equipped with small telescopes enabling them to observe across the spectrum. Combining the data they collected gave Urban a detailed view of distant objects. And each outrider held backup copies of his library, and archived copies of his ghost.

Replication was a form of insurance. Even in the void of deep space there was a potential for collision with some bit of rubble. The courser, with all its mass, might be able to survive the huge energies of a high-speed impact, but the tiny outriders could not. Over the centuries, two of them—*Khonsu* and *Artemis*—had been destroyed.

Urban had grown new ships to replace them, giving them the same names.

He did what was needed to survive and he endured, but he did not let himself forget who and what he was. He took care to guard his core persona, that most-human version of himself. To endure the years, he modified his time sense, ensuring that neither the events of his past nor his hopes for the future ever seemed too far off as the ship coasted in a centuries-long passage through the vastness between stars.

As he finally drew near to Deception Well, he copied his core persona: one version to stay aboard the courser, another to replicate through the chain of outriders, establish communication, and eventually pass through a data gate aboard the warship stationed at the periphery of the nebula.

If all went well, these two ghosts would ultimately recombine into one. Until then, they operated independently, separated by light-hours from one another.

For the first time since he had hijacked the courser and made it his own, Urban rose to consciousness inside a physical body. His eyes snapped open. He heard the beat of his heart. Felt the touch of cool air against newly made skin and a faint electrostatic charge lofting the sparse black hair on his forearms.

He stretched the arms, legs, neck, back, even the feet of this avatar, newly grown aboard the warship, *Long Watch*. A fully rendered version of himself. Sleek and lean and comfortingly familiar. He curled long-fingered hands into fists, unfolded them again. Relishing the details of mass and resistance, of existence itself. So many years spent in simulated reality he'd forgotten how different it felt to be alive. How glorious. A pleasure just to breathe again, to feel the rumble of his stomach.

Hungry. Not just for food. Instinct stirred, sending blood towards his groin in an ancient tide. Desire as a homecoming rite, an affirmation of place. He'd been alone so long.

Was he still alone?

He shifted his focus outward. Found himself adrift in a zero-gravity environment, nude, confined within a transparent membrane just large enough to contain him. Strokes of light curved across the membrane's shifting surface and across his dark-skinned body.

What was the membrane for? It might be just a gel cocoon left over from his resurrection, although in his experience those were designed to dissolve and drizzle away.

It might be meant to confine him.

Beyond the membrane, a dark undefined space.

His atrium sought a network connection. Found none. Not a surprise. Still, his isolation made him uneasy.

He peered past the cocoon. Was someone there?

Certainly there would be cameras on him, watching, evaluating. And his body would have been studied in detail as it was grown and assembled, confirming he was truly human. He expected no less.

The people of Deception Well—whoever they were in this era—were taking a chance by communicating with him at all. It was a risk on his side too. So much time had passed since he'd left the Well he could not claim to know his people anymore. His heart beat faster as he wondered: *Have I made a mistake?*

Aloud, he asked, "Why the darkness, the silence?"

No answer, but beyond the gel membrane darkness yielded to a barely perceptible blue light emanating from the walls of a small spherical chamber. As the light brightened, it picked out the edges and curves of a woman's drifting figure. A familiar silhouette.

"Clemantine," he growled in a low, victorious voice. The light became whiter, revealing the woman he'd come to find.

She had not changed, not physically. They'd been lovers once and he remembered every curve of that long, strong, well-muscled body, the feel of full breasts in his hands, the spicy scent of her skin. Her face was the same too: a broad, beautiful, balanced face with a flat nose and full lips. Serious in its expression, even now.

His heart hammered as he gazed at her; his hands shook. The joy of meeting her again almost overwhelming. He longed to reach for her, ached for her physical reality, skin to skin. He held back only because he did not see any similar joy on her face.

Instead, she looked distraught and defensive. "Who are you?" she asked. A demand phrased as a question. The chill in her words froze him.

"You know me," he answered.

"I did once. But who are you now? Did they turn you?"

"They?" he asked. "There is no *they*. The Chenzeme—whatever they were—they're gone. We found remnants. Artifacts. That's all. But we learned. Like I told you in the radio message, we won. We learned how to beat their ships."

"If you won, where are the others? You said 'I've come home.' Not *we*. What happened to them?"

The fear and suspicion in her eyes was more than he'd expected. "They stayed behind," he told her. He made no effort to hide the bitterness these words brought him, but she was unmoved by it.

"Why?" she insisted.

He shook his head. "I'm not going to tell you that story, Clementine. It's in the library files that I've transferred over. I haven't hidden any part of it. Not from you. Relive it there if you want to. I don't want to. I want to talk about you. I came here to find you."

Raising a hand, he probed at the membrane, pressing his fingers through what proved to be delicate tissue. Tore it open.

She watched him, unmoving. He didn't doubt that she'd left instructions to disassemble them both down to their constituent atoms if something went wrong and he proved to be a Chenzeme weapon after all.

"How did you get here so soon?" he asked her. Then he held up a palm to stop her reply. "No, I already know. You *were* here. Do you keep an avatar aboard the second warship too? Waiting on the system's periphery for some word from us, for someone to come back. I think you hoped it would be someone else, and not me."

Her golden-brown cheeks warmed with a flush. "*No.* Urban . . ." Her eyes glistened. "I never thought to see him again. I never thought I'd see any of you. But if I'd ever considered that only one of you might make it back, I would have guessed it'd be you." Her voice shifted, becoming low and feral: "But a Chenzeme warship, Urban. No one else—"

"That's right," he interrupted. "No one else dared to do it, to come all this way in a Chenzeme ship. Not even that other version of you. But here you are on a different timeline." He reached out a hand to her. "Maybe you'll make a different choice."

To his surprise, she took his hand, pulled him into a tight embrace. He reciprocated, the warm scent of her an aphrodisiac exploding across his brain. He kissed her neck, her face. He remembered the pretty chains of tiny gold irises tattooed on the edges of her small ears; he found them and kissed those too. Glittering tears broke free and writhed in the cool air.

"This avatar is not really you, is it?" she asked.

"No. It *is* me. This is the core." He got his hand up under her shirt, kissed the corner of her mouth. "*Please*," he whispered. "Have mercy for once. It's been a thousand years."

Her throaty chuckle jacked him even harder than he'd been before. Unbearable.

The chamber shrank around them, squeezing out the glint of camera eyes, leaving them enclosed in a hollow just large enough to contain them. No way out. No way in.

Clemantine helped him peel off the thin layer of her clothing and then they locked together, his fingers embedded like claws in the soft wall to hold their position, her fingers hard against his back. Reminding one another of what it was to be physical beings, man and woman. To be alive.

Later, but still too soon, he told her, "I've got only hours before I have to go."

He held her close, her body against his, a physical connection unbroken since they'd begun.

She leaned back in his arms and eyed him sleepily. "You have forever," she countered. "You're home. This avatar, anyway. This is your home."

"No. I won't stay." Her body tensed in his arms, her embrace tightened as if she would hold him there. "I made that decision long ago," he reminded her. "I'm here now for you—and to trade information. I've already transferred the full history of our expedition. Now I need data from Silk's library. Everything known about the Hallowed Vasties. Their history, and current observations. I've got only hours to make the exchange. You're tracking the courser so you know this is a fly-by. I wish it could be longer, but it would have taken years to dump enough velocity to achieve orbit—and if I'd tried it, this warship or the other one would have blown me up."

"You sent the swarm ships instead," she mused. "We thought they were some kind of weapon, plague ships maybe."

"Just communications relays to extend my reach, give me more hours here."

She shook her head. Sighed deeply. "*Damn* you, Urban. After so many centuries, to have no time. And you don't stay, you won't leave even a ghost. Because no version of you wants to be trapped here?"

"Sooth," he agreed.

Bitter now: "Some things never change."

"You know me, Clemantine. I'm in possession of an immensely fast and powerful starship. What version of me would ever give that up? "

She sighed again. "No version I know. So you're going there? To the Hallowed Vasties?"

He nodded, wanting her to share his excitement. "Our origin lies in the Hallowed Vasties. Our beginning, our earliest days. But it's all changed. All of it unknown now. That makes it a new frontier, an inverted frontier, because the unexplored region lies inward from the edge of settled space. I want to see what's there, what's left, voyage all the way to Earth if I can."

The outward migration from Earth had unfolded over thousands of years. Robotic probes went first, exploring and mapping tens of thousands of stellar systems, looking for those with sterile worlds orbiting within habitable zones. Those worlds were re-engineered, made viable and beautiful for the people who came to possess them.

It was as if the galaxy had been given to humankind by an unknown god, theirs to nurture and to slowly fill with new generations.

Frontier populations were never great in number, but they were enough that an innate restlessness drove some portion of them onward to still newer worlds. Always, they were the individuals who made a choice to engage in life, in the reality of physical existence.

That choice served as a filter in a selection process dividing them from those who chose to stay.

And when they looked back across space and time, they wondered what they'd left behind as megastructures enclosed the stars of the earliest inhabited systems.

On the frontier, those distant star systems came to be known as the Hallowed Vasties. Frightening rumors crossed the void, describing a behavioral virus run wild, one that spurred massive population growth and an evolutionary leap to a group mind, a Communion that was more than human.

Too far away to worry about. That was the consensus on the frontier and people pushed on—until the Chenzeme warships found them.

In those tumultuous centuries as the frontier collapsed, the Hallowed Vasties too began to fail. The stars that had been hidden within cordons of matter emerged again, and no one knew why.

Urban wanted to know why. It was the goal he had set for himself: to learn what had happened to the Hallowed Vasties and what was left. If there were only remnants and ruins, he wanted to see them. If something had grown up from the ruins, he wanted to see that too. He wanted to see it all with his own eyes.

"I've watched the Vasties for centuries," he told Clemantine. "Every star ever known to have been mantled by a Dyson swarm is visible again. We thought that meant failure. Civilizational collapse on a massive scale. Death. But there are signs of life. Transmission spectra confirm the presence of oxygen, water, organic molecules. I want to know what was there, what happened, and what's come after. And I don't want to go alone. I want you to come with me."

She closed her eyes, giving him no answer. He nuzzled her neck. "What are you thinking?"

"The past and the future," she whispered. "Both are so very far away. That last time I saw you—you and him—a thousand years ago. And another thousand years to Earth, even in that great beast you've stolen."

"It *is* a great beast," he agreed. "And I've named it after a great beast. I call it *Dragon*. And time doesn't matter to us. So what if it takes a thousand years to reach the Hallowed Vasties? If the time drags, we sleep."

"How peacefully can we sleep aboard a Chenzeme courser?" she asked him.

He told her, "Don't think of it that way. It's a hybrid ship. Its neural structure is heavily modified. It's under my control. And I want you with me again. *You*. After all those years we spent together, you are part of me ... and I am so hungry for human company. Don't abandon me again."

Her eyes narrowed. "I think that other version of me made a smart choice to stay behind."

"No. I think she regrets her choice. Because you're her. You're the same. You haven't changed. You don't have another life, do you? No new lover, no children. All you've done is wait. You've skipped over these years, passed them in cold sleep, waiting for us to come back."

"I needed to know," she said defensively. "But you—you seem the same too. That's on purpose, isn't it? You want me to believe you're still that same smart-ass pirate, but Urban, you can't be. Not if you've grafted yourself on to that alien killing machine."

A tremor of guilt. A shrug. A confession: "This is me. My human core. I keep this persona because I want to remember who I am and what matters. But I'm not alone. I remade myself multiple times. My Apparatchiks are highly edited, each with a different technical skill. They're based on me, but they're not me anymore. Some of them are insufferable and sometimes we argue among ourselves, but no mutiny so far."

"All ghosts?"

"Yes."

"And what is it like to be the master of an alien killing machine?"

He tapped his chest and told her the blunt truth: "For me, this version of me, it's fucking miserable. Soul-annihilating loneliness. Out there, coasting in the void between stars, awake and aware and so far from anywhere or anything, any *human* thing, knowing with utter certainty that I'm alone and not even the mind of the Unknown God could find me. It's terrifying."

"That's not a very persuasive argument if you're trying to convince me to come with you."

"I need you."

"I don't want to live as a ghost."

"We don't have to. It's a big ship. There's room. There are

resources. We can be physical when we want it—and *god*, I want it. I want *you*. And when time becomes unbearable we can retreat into cold sleep to speed the transit, like we did before. Think about it. Please."

"I am thinking about it," she admitted. She stroked his arm, his cheek, considering what he'd offered. "An inverted frontier?"

"Yes. That's how I think of it."

"I like that."

Curiosity was awake within her—an almost forgotten feeling. And he was right that she had no attachments, no obligations of honor. She'd spent three-quarters of a millennium asleep, waiting for some word.

She told him, "It was unbearable not knowing what had happened out there. I would have turned around and gone back after you, but I was afraid that no matter how long I looked, I would never find a sign of you. That seemed the likeliest outcome."

"This time we'll be together. No doubt about what happens. We'll know."

She nodded her tentative agreement. "I want to send a ghost to your ship, *now*, to verify what you're telling me."

"Due diligence," he agreed. "You've got the address."

She shifted her focus inward, using her atrium to create the ghost, and then she sent it on its way. If this turned out to be a trap, the ghost could dissolve itself. If it didn't return, she would know.

"It's a long round trip," he warned her.

"I can wait."

"I want you to go over the library files too," he said. "Make sure they're legitimate, consistent, human."

"I've got a DI working on it," she assured him.

He nodded shortly, then confessed, "I've sequestered some of the data. Nothing critical. Just some of the raw details. Things too personal to share in full—mostly at the end. That cache is open to you, but no one else."

"All right." Her voice, suddenly hoarse. She feared what she might find when she accessed that privileged data. It might be enough for her—it might be best—to know in only a general way what had happened.

She allowed herself one question: "We lost him in the end, didn't we?"

"Yes."

A soft sigh. She had always known it.

"Nineteen hours," Urban warned, "before we lose data coherence."

"Okay."

Time enough. If he was lying, if this was subterfuge, if his apparent sincerity was a false front for a Chenzeme weapon, the history he carried would surely reveal it.

He must have guessed her thoughts, because he looked at her with that pirate half-smile of his, so familiar, taunting her away from melancholy, and he asked, "You still don't trust me, do you?"

She replied very seriously, "In the madness of these hours I don't trust myself."

FIRST

You are confused, sure that you once were far more. Your mind feels as if it's been rolled and crushed in a landslide. You wander through wreckage: torn metal arteries, broken white ceramic housings, heavy glass plates marked with impact scars, and everywhere thin crystalline sheets, shattered and jumbled, oozing fluids, your thoughts and memories spilled out across the floor. So much unrecoverable.

You stoop to pick up a crystal fragment. With this action, you realize you have somehow contrived to reconstruct a physical avatar. You are *here*. You have hands. You drop the crystal and hold up your hands for your eyes to see. Large, masculine hands. You curl your hands into fists. A familiar gesture.

You look about, smell the air. There *is* air. Good. System integrity not entirely demolished. Lingering stink of burnt toxins. White light from a surviving ceiling panel. Most have fallen.

So quiet here.

Now that you are still, you can hear the fluids move in your body. You can't hear a heartbeat—but then you remember: You're not human anymore. This avatar you wear looks human, but you redesigned it, gave it thousands of little hearts to keep the fluids circulating. No longer that one heart muscle vulnerable to execution.

She tried to execute you.

The memory of that affront ambushes you.

She tried to execute me.

The details are hazy. Why she did it, how, that is lost to you in this moment. Perhaps you'll find the memory somewhere in the shattered strata of your mind but this much you know: She tried to execute you and—fear bubbles up from the dark depths of this avatar's ancestral instinct as you realize the truth—she has in some sense succeeded. You are broken. You will never again be what you were.

What was I?

Something other than this. The answer—you know though you don't know how you know—was once contained within the weeping crystalline fragments. Can it be recovered? It *has* to be.

You sniff the air again. The scent of your avatar lingers in the stillness. No one else about. There has never been anyone else here. You would not allow such a security vulnerability. Another fact that you know without knowing how you know.

You follow the fading scent trail through a corridor, retracing your steps though you don't remember coming this way. Sleepwalking? More likely the biological mind contained in this avatar was then still incomplete and unable to retain permanent memories.

You walk carefully, stepping over fallen strata, taking care not to stumble or to cut your feet. You are nude. Lean, wiry, male. Dark-brown skin. Hairless, which seems strange.

Every ten steps or so you pass a meter-wide circular plate in the otherwise featureless white floor. Each plate fitted so neatly that there is only a faint gray seam to indicate its perimeter. A handle lies flat, its shape a half-circle, but you don't try to lift the plates, not given the heavy debris that lies on top of them.

You notice a drizzle of clear gel, a few millimeters wide but over twenty centimeters long, moving past your feet in a shimmer of motion, disappearing beneath the crystalline wreckage. Another strand slithers around the sharp edge of a fallen block. A few steps farther on and you see many more, sliding as if in rapid inspection across the tumbled debris. One gel strand disappears into a thin gap between plates of crystal.

Do they come to feed on your broken mind, or to fuse the broken pieces of it back together?

You think, *I was no fool. I would have taken precautions, created backup systems, repair networks.*

This thought comforts you as you continue to backtrack, your scent almost impossible to follow now, but that's all right because now you can follow wet marks where you tracked gel across a section of floor.

One of the circular plates has been lifted on a hinge, exposing an opening in the floor. This is where your footprints originate. You crouch at the edge and peer in.

Cold, cold air. And darkness. A silver ladder descends. You count the rungs you can see: fifteen. Despite the ladder, you're sure this is not a shaft. Sparks and trails of light interrupt the otherwise velvet darkness below, suggesting a vast space. This, you know: It is an underground sea, but not filled with water. Another unsourced fact.

You descend the ladder. On the tenth rung your feet encounter a freezing gel. Drizzles of gel dart up your calves, circle your thighs, weave about your groin. You continue to descend, your skin puckering in the cold as the gel strands flow over your shoulders and veil your head. You give yourself up to it, releasing your grip on the ladder to subside into a gel ocean.

Tiny bright lights distract your mind as a slow current rolls your body. Consciousness fades ... though as it goes you wonder if this dull state of mind you've been enduring even deserves the word.

CHAPTER FOUR

A MESSAGE FROM Clemantine forestalled panic when the walls of the isolation chamber contracted, cutting off the cameras and eliminating all sight and sound of what was happening in that space.

Her message said:

Take no action. Give me time. Understood?

Too well understood. From his post on the bridge, Riffan glared at his workstation's screen, cursing the banality, the triviality of sexual desire. Against the wonder of Urban's return, his capture of a Chenzeme courser, the question of what he intended to do with that ship, of where he intended to take it . . . this tryst struck Riffan as both dull and dangerous. Clemantine had left him with an order to dissolve the chamber with herself in it if anything went wrong. But how was he to know?

Still, Riffan had done as she requested. He'd taken no action, using the time instead to send an army of DIs combing through the river of data that constituted the library Urban was transferring to *Long Watch*. Years would be needed to thoroughly analyze everything that library held. It was a task that would consume the working hours of hundreds of researchers and Riffan was certainly keen to learn of all that had been discovered among the star systems that lay *swan* of Deception Well.

And yet he was even more anxious to learn what Urban's future plans might be.

Riffan had come to *Long Watch* to search for surviving human civilizations, new human migrations, or a renewal of life among the Hallowed Vasties. But the telescope time he'd earned with his service had turned up no evidence of any life at all beyond the protective nebula of Deception Well.

This did not mean his studies had been a waste of time. A negative result was still useful data. It was proof he'd done all that could be done from the vicinity of the Well.

He had not confessed his plans to anyone, but it was his intention, when his time aboard *Long Watch* was done, to present the results of his studies to the security council and to challenge them to take the next step.

The crux of the argument he would make:

If anyone remains alive out there, they are alive because they stayed hidden, and they will not be found unless we, the people of the Well, screw up our courage and venture forth from our refuge here on the frontier's edge, to find them.

And now here was Urban, his presence testimony to the rewards of exploration.

An anxious sigh. A quick glance around the silent bridge confirming Pasha, Enzo, and Zira, all at their stations. They took no notice of him, enraptured as they were by the data from the new library posting to their screens.

Riffan turned back to his own screen, scanning the summaries gathered by a DI trained in information science. He found descriptions of terrifying encounters with robotic Chenzeme ships, of the discovery of great technologies eons old, of alien lifeforms devolved from sentience, of an encounter with a human settlement where none should be, and the conquest of the courser that Urban had named *Dragon*.

Life is long, he mused, *full of strange twists and imbued with wonder*. Urban had dared to venture *swan*, and by doing so he'd made discoveries that redefined human history. Riffan envied him that, and he regretted that he'd been born too late to be part of the Null Boundary Expedition.

A link flashed to life on his screen, interrupting these restless reflections. Anxious excitement shot through him as he realized the link was from Clementine.

A sharp gesture of acceptance and her image coalesced on screen, a head-and-shoulders view. Urban drifted behind her. He eyed Riffan with an arrogant half-smile while Clemantine appeared breathless, on edge, a ruddy heat in her brown cheeks. In a softly matter-of-fact voice she told him, "Urban is bound for the Hallowed Vasties, to discover what is left there. I'm going with him. There's nothing you need to do. No need to break quarantine. I've sent a ghost to confirm what he's told me. I'll stay where I am, here with Urban in the isolation chamber, until it returns. I can work from here, complete my survey of his library and gather the data we'll need to take with us. Once we upload, you can dissolve this chamber and everything in it. No need to take any risks of inadvertent contamination."

Riffan stared at her, stunned at this news, although he realized that on some level he'd been expecting it. "Truly?" he whispered past a dry throat. Jealousy burned in him. A bitter wonder. "The Hallowed Vasties?"

Misunderstanding the root of his shock, Clemantine sought to reassure him. "It will require an immense time to reach the Vasties. We understand that."

"Yes. Yes, of course," Riffan said, waving off any such concern as anxious words tumbled one after another. "Of course it will require time and it will be worth any amount of time that must be invested because the greatest mystery of our time, the unanswerable question of our age is: What happened? What happened to the Hallowed Vasties? And to answer this question we *must* venture beyond the sanctuary of the Well."

What a fool he felt! He had meant to use his unsuccessful surveys to lobby for just such an expedition, one that would follow in reverse their ancestors' migration route from Earth and *yes*. Yes, an expedition to the Hallowed Vasties would require an immense stretch of time. Centuries.

Given the distance and the risks it was unlikely anyone who signed on would ever return, but what did it matter? Those who wanted to go need not send their core selves. They could create avatars for the purpose. A version of themselves to stay, and one to go. The knowledge they gathered might be sent back to Deception Well in a series of robotic messenger ships propelled by the zero-point reef.

A grand project, truly. An inspirational project. A project Riffan had hoped to ignite and to take part in.

Others had lobbied for such a project in the past. The resources were within reach and there had never been a shortage of volunteers. But each time the idea had been proposed, the security council had withheld approval. Deception Well's founding generation remembered too well the perils and fraught choices of the past. They feared such an expedition would draw the attention of the Chenzeme, and that the trajectory of such a starship would be mapped back to the Well.

Riffan had been resolved to try the idea again, he'd invested years in preparation, but now here was Urban, embarked on the voyage Riffan had dreamed of undertaking, asking no one's permission. Seeking an answer to the unanswerable question.

Riffan's frustration was so acute it was all he could do not to pound his fist against the soft, fleshy structure of his console.

"I want to go with you," he blurted out before he quite knew what he was saying. But then, disoriented by his own boldness, he looked away—and discovered Pasha adrift beside him. The upwelling light of the console highlighted the fierce set of her brow, an expression suggesting he was not the only one with secret dreams. "And you?" he whispered.

She nodded.

But did it make sense when there was a chance of a well-planned, fully staffed expedition, launched under the authority of the security council, in a starship of human design?

Yes. It took only a moment of reflection to know he had to try for this. This was real and imminent, while there had only ever been the slightest chance that he could sway the council.

Resolved now, he turned again to the screen to find Clemantine regarding him with curious interest—but he saw only skepticism in Urban's gaze.

Convince him, you fool, he thought. *If you want this, it's now or never.*

He drew a deep breath. "I want to go with you," he repeated, this time in a calm, determined tone. "I want to be part of it. I've wanted this all my life. And I think Pasha wants this too."

"Yes," she said, leaning into the screen. "I want to go. I would not miss an opportunity like this. Not for anything. And I know there are others who would seize this chance too, if you offered it to them, to us. If you're willing to host an expedition like the great ships of old."

Urban traded an uneasy look with Clemantine. Riffan imagined a silent conversation bouncing back and forth between their atriums. Then Clemantine brought that conversation out into the open. Speaking aloud, she said to Urban, "It's true an expanded ship's company will complicate things. You'll need to consider the welfare and goals of others. But with the right people, you'll gain by their knowledge, their experience, their viewpoints. And a thousand years from now, when you're tired of me and yet you've found nothing human in all the Hallowed Vasties, you're going to be grateful to have others to talk to."

Urban scowled resentfully. "It's *you* who wants it." Words spoken like an accusation. If Clemantine made an answer, it wasn't out loud, but after a few seconds, Urban turned to the screen. "You understand that if you come, you'll only be sending a ghost." He gestured at Riffan and Pasha. "These versions of you will stay here."

"Of course," Riffan answered.

Urban went on, "You also need to understand that the ghost you send, that version of you, won't be coming back. Your timeline will split into two and you will never know what happens to that other version of yourself. Even if you do somehow make it back to Deception Well, millennia will have passed. Nothing will be the same."

"I understand all that," Riffan said, feeling hollow with fear but excited too. "And I'm still eager to do it." Eager to go, but also to stay. Two versions of him, soon to be bound to separate fates. No doubt each would be jealous of the other.

Pasha nodded her affirmation. "Yes, I understand all the implications too."

Urban turned again to Clemantine. She gave him an encouraging nod, but he still did not look convinced. He said, "No one needs to decide yet. No one goes until Clemantine's ghost reports back. So you'll have hours to reconsider."

Riffan suspected it was Urban who needed time to consider the wisdom of this move. Wanting to reassure him and ensure his place on the ship, he said, "I want you to know this is no sudden fancy. I've thought about this for years. I've had time to ponder the practical aspects—the slow pace of discovery, the unresolvable timelines, the . . . the . . ." He stammered as pain welled behind his eyes. "The heartbreaking reality of leaving everyone and everything I know. And I've made my peace with it. I'm not going to change my mind."

"Neither am I," Pasha said. "But will you make this a real expedition, with a ship's company larger than just Riffan and me? I can find the people for you. Good people."

Urban drew back, but before he could say no, Clemantine again intervened. "Can *Dragon* support more people?" she asked him. "Does it have the resources?"

"Sure," Urban answered reluctantly. "Given time to prepare."

Clemantine shrugged. "And we'll have plenty of time, once our ghosts transfer in. So there's no reason we can't expand the ship's company. I think we'll be better off with a larger group. It'll give us more options, more flexibility."

"More conflict," Urban groused.

"Conflicts can be worked out," Riffan said, determined to be helpful. "And I promise we won't be difficult company. I'm psychologically qualified for this. So is Pasha. We've both reached fifth level. We wouldn't have been posted to *Long Watch*, otherwise. You can make fifth a requirement. Reject anyone who doesn't have it. That way you'll know that none of us are going to break down or exhibit toxic behavior."

Urban cocked his head. His eyes narrowed. A crooked smile. "*I'm* not fifth level. You sure you want to take a chance?"

Pasha leaned closer to the screen and said, very firmly, "Yes, we're willing to risk it." In a more conciliatory tone she added,

"You're the ship's captain. On the old expeditions, the captain was the final authority. I recognize that. I'm sure Riffan, as acting commander of *Long Watch*, recognizes that too."

"Well actually," Riffan said, "our situation on *Long Watch* is different because our command rotates, and ultimate authority lies with the security council."

"We'll find a way to make it work," Clemantine said quickly. She looked at Pasha. "Ask if anyone else is interested. Qualified people, with diverse specialties. Let us know."

Urban looked ready to object, but the link cut out before Riffan could hear what he had to say.

CHAPTER FIVE

"IT'S BETTER THIS way," Clemantine said after the link closed.

"*Why* is it better?" Urban demanded. "Why do you want this?"

"I've told you my reasons."

"You think I'll get bored with you? I won't."

She rolled her eyes. "Of course you will and it won't be the first time."

"I'm not that kid anymore, Clemantine. We can make it work."

She said, "What I don't understand is why you're so against it."

"I didn't come here intending to pick up a roster of passengers. I don't want them. Each one represents a risk. A huge risk to the ship. A risk to *us*. Fifth level or not, we don't know who these people are."

He said this with sincerity, appeared to believe what he was saying, but Clemantine didn't believe it. "No. I don't think that's it. You've never been afraid to take a risk, and you're no introvert. You've always ruled your personal kingdom. So what's different this time?"

"*I'm* different."

"Different how?"

He turned half away. "I've lost people, Clemantine." He tapped his chest. "I don't like the way it feels. Friends and lovers, gone forever." He shook his head. "And you want me to take on *more* people?"

"Ah . . ." It was all she could manage past a painful knot in her throat. She understood now, too well. She touched his shoulder. Leaned in to kiss his cheek.

Urban said, "I hate him sometimes . . . that version of me I left back there in the cloud."

"He has what you don't."

"Sooth."

She narrowed her eyes, recalling their earlier conversation. "So there *was* a version of you who gave up your monstrous ship."

His crooked smile. "Wasn't really a choice for him. One of us had to stay. Can't have it all." His uncertain gaze sought hers. "Right?"

Not a rhetorical question, she realized. So she answered it. "It's never easy—and I'm not going to make it easy for you this time. We *need* more people, and the complexity and variety they'll bring."

"You need them. I don't."

She was done arguing. "How many can you safely take?" she asked, moving on to the practical details.

"I'd have to work it out."

"Twelve's a good number," she suggested.

Surprised: "You think that many will want to go?"

"I think it's more a question of how many will get the alert and get here in time. Can you give us more time?"

"I can slow the last ships of the outrider fleet. That'll allow a couple more hours for data transfer. But once we're out of range, it's done."

Clemantine raised an eyebrow. "No, that's when it starts. And there we'll be, locked up together for millennia. No possibility of escape or diversion while we come to despise one another and go mad in our souls."

This jest won her a rogue's grin. "That's not how I run my ship. When it starts to fall apart, everyone who irritates me is going to get shoved into cold sleep."

Clemantine laughed, not because she thought he was joking but because he was ruthless enough to carry out such an outrageous act.

There was only a little time.

Pasha's first priority was to get the word out about the expedition. Already she thought of it as a formal scientific expedition, which meant those aboard should have expertise across a variety of disciplines.

She returned to her workstation on the bridge and began to compose a group message:

By now you've heard of the Chenzeme courser, hijacked and brought home by one of our own . . .

She described what she knew, and the opportunity available to those who could make a quick decision. Clemantine messaged her to say that Urban was willing to accept up to twelve volunteers, so Pasha included that number. Then she went on to emphasize the points Urban had emphasized: that there would be no going back and that the version they left behind would never know what the venturing version had found.

After more thought, she added a cautionary closing: *This is a gamble beyond the dangers presented by any interstellar voyage. Clemantine has sent a ghost to the ship to affirm that what we've been told is true, but there are no guarantees.*

She addressed the message to only eight colleagues, wanting to respect the limit Clemantine had set. Her heart raced as she sent it off. Hours would elapse before it was received, hours more before she knew how her colleagues would react. Would they think she'd gone mad? Would anyone come?

She shook her head. It was all out of her hands now. She had her own preparations to make. "Riffan," she said, looking up at his workstation, "I need time—"

She broke off when she saw he was gone from the bridge. Zira and Enzo remained at their stations. Both looked at her, seeming worried and doubtful.

"He went to his quarters," Zira said quietly. "To prepare."

"I need to go too," Pasha said.

Enzo told her, "It's fine. There's no emergency. Not now."

For a moment, Pasha felt confused. Then she realized, "Neither of you are interested in going?"

"I couldn't bear it," Zira said simply.

And Enzo told her, "I could never leave my family. Not forever. No version of me could do that."

Pasha did not miss the accusation in his words, the implication that she *could* do that, that she was eager to do it—and that she should not feel that way.

She smiled a cold smile, defiant in the face of his quiet judgment. "How fortunate then, that we're each free to make our own choice."

She left the bridge, left that debate behind her. But as she returned to her quarters, she wondered how many of the colleagues she'd invited would feel the same as Zira and Enzo. What if none were willing to come? She should probably invite a few more, to ensure a reasonable number of volunteers. A few minutes of thought produced ten more names and she sent the invitation out again.

Then she needed to think on her own future. The question that troubled her was not whether she should go, but instead, if she should stay behind at all. Alone in her quarters, she pondered it, reflecting on Urban's words:

Your timeline will split into two and you will never know what happens to that other version of yourself.

Zira could not bear to be the one who goes. Pasha worried that she could not bear to be that version of herself who was left behind.

She was an exobiologist. No one could ask for a better place to train for that field of study than Deception Well, where eons of evolution—some of it directed evolution—had combined the clades of different worlds into a balanced, self-sustaining biological system.

Pasha had spent years on the planet, studying the weave of lifeforms there. The posting to *Long Watch* had let her extend her research to the microscopic life existing within the nebula—the so-called gnomes and governors—biomachines whose activities maintained the nebula and drove its defensive functions. She could see herself continuing that research for years to come, either aboard *Long Watch* or remotely, from her apartment in the city of Silk. And she might have been content with that, if Urban had not come.

From the short time she'd spent reviewing the summaries of the Null Boundary Expedition, she knew it had been wonderfully successful. Lifeforms had been discovered in varieties never before seen in known history, and stranger than she'd ever thought could be. The cleverness and adaptability of life fascinated her and forced the question: *What else might there be to discover?*

Her thoughts turned to the Hallowed Vasties. Surely some form of life remained there, re-forged in the cataclysms that had washed over the once-cordoned stars. That version of herself that would go with Urban, would have the chance to discover what was left.

She was fiercely determined to go.

She had never thought an opportunity would come to leave Deception Well. All past proposals to outfit a starship had been rejected by the council, but now her prospects were utterly changed. Such luck to be here aboard *Long Watch*! To have this chance.

She only feared to be that version of herself that stayed behind. *And I am that version.*

This consciousness—*me*—the mind thinking these thoughts aboard *Long Watch*, who was herself, Pasha Andern. She was trapped here. It was only a copy of herself who would go as a ghost to *Dragon* while she stayed behind . . . unless she chose not to stay at all, to leave no copy of herself behind.

Could she, in good conscience, make such a decision?

"Why *not*?" she growled aloud.

She had no spouse, no devoted lover. Her parents were alive and active, but she rarely saw either them or her thirteen siblings who all lived on the planet with families of their own.

Pasha was the loner of her parents' brood.

It was not that she was deficient in social skills, or that she didn't like people. She did. She enjoyed the company of others; she had many friendships. She just tended to get distracted by her work, and she didn't have the same need for close companionship that drove so many others. Her family was used to her disappearing from their lives for years at a time. Pasha did not think her absence would leave many scars.

But if she stayed? She imagined herself growing bitter, always wishing she'd been the one to go. She didn't want that.

So she composed another group message, this one addressed to her family. She embroidered an explanation to soften the blow, but at its core her message said, *I will leave an archived copy of myself in the city library against some extraordinary circumstance, but please do not petition to wake it up. My true self is now bound for the Hallowed Vasties.*

Urban passed the hours with Clemantine in sweet indolence and quiet conversation. She told him of her return to Deception Well. He told her of some of the things he'd seen after she'd left the Null Boundary Expedition and what he'd learned of the Chenzeme.

None of the hard details. Nothing on the people they'd both known and loved.

"It's there in the library files," he reminded her. And with a sly smile he asked, "Do you still think I'm a trick of the Chenzeme?"

She shrugged, beautifully, naked again, afloat and in indulgent ease within the little quarantine chamber. "When my ghost returns I'll know the truth."

He reached for her. She rolled against him. Another long kiss. "Not tired yet?" she asked, and he laughed.

They passed the time entangled in body and mind until Urban succumbed to sweet fatigue and vague dreams.

Sometime later, she roused him, her husky voice soft in his ear. "Wake up, son. Get dressed. We're going to break quarantine."

"What?" he asked groggily. "Why?"

She gathered loose clothing left to drift in their little chamber. Some of it hers, some assembled for him.

She pulled a shirt on, saying, "Kona's here. He's come to see you."

A frisson of shock. "He's still awake? Still aware?"

She shrugged, reaching to pull on gray leggings. "He might have been in cold sleep, but he'd wake up for this. *I* did."

Ancient guilt, resurfacing. "I wanted to see him," Urban confessed.

"Did you?"

"*Yes.* I didn't expect to." They had not parted on good terms.

"Get dressed," Clemantine repeated as the chamber expanded in size.

Urban obeyed, scrambling to pull on snug-fitting trousers and a long-sleeved shirt, heart racing, dreading this reunion would not go well.

A subtle air current warned him. He turned, to see a doorway retracting open, a still-familiar figure on the other side.

Clemantine spoke first, as if to ease the awkwardness of this encounter. "Hello, Kona," she said. "I wondered if you'd come."

He came in, but no farther than he needed to. He arrested his glide as soon as he cleared the door, revealing Pasha's slight figure behind him, and Riffan, looming protectively at her side. Both entered cautiously now that quarantine was broken.

Urban spared them only a quick glance before his gaze returned to Kona. He shared his father's dark complexion. Kona's eyes were dark too, his gaze as intense and intimidating as Urban remembered it. He had used to wear his black hair in a thick mass of tiny braids tied loosely together behind his neck, but this avatar had close-cropped hair, as Urban did. It made them look very much alike, though Kona's face and his features were broader, his body more muscular, his disposition far more stern.

Urban's taut smile was met by a stony gaze. The weight of centuries between them.

In a gruff voice Kona acknowledged what he must see as a most unlikely circumstance: "You lived."

"I *thrived*," Urban corrected—and immediately regretted the childish defiance in his voice. So much time had gone by. So much had changed. What could be gained by holding on to old animosities? He glided closer. "It's good to see you, Dad. I'm glad you came."

They talked.

Kona was proud to recount the history of Deception Well since Urban had left. Like Clemantine, he was part of the founding generation, born in another age, on another world, a witness to the brutal murder of that world by the Chenzeme's robotic warships. He'd made it his task, his duty, to ensure the survival of his people. He'd led them through all the harrowing early years at Deception Well, re-elected time and again as council chair.

But no more.

"I stepped down after the warships were built," he told Urban. "And I started passing the years in cold sleep." A knowing glance at Clemantine. "I woke every ten years to check on things—and I instructed a DI to wake me at any news of an outside threat. *Are you a threat?*"

Urban answered this with a half-smile, acknowledging the implicit menace of *Dragon*'s presence. "Not to anyone here," he said. "You know I'm not coming in-system? This is just a fly-by, trading information."

"I've been told." Kona hesitated then, seeming doubtful, uncertain. "This Chenzeme courser . . ." He trailed off, leaving the sentence unfinished.

What had he meant to say? Was it a question? A judgment? Maybe a plea for confirmation. "It's all true," Urban said. "It is a Chenzeme courser, and it's mine."

Kona sighed. His demeanor softened. "Urban, that's astonishing. It's an incredible triumph. It's something that's never been done before, not in any history we know. The knowledge you've gained—you must have mapped every vulnerability in that ship, learned to hack its communications. This could be a turning point in our self-defense strategy."

"I hope so," Urban said, his cheeks warm, thinking that all of this sounded like rare praise. It was good to hear, and he responded to it with enthusiasm. "All the details on how we did it, everything I've learned about the ship, are included in the files I transferred. The molecular libraries are complete. With that information you can modify *Long Watch* and take it out hunting for a Chenzeme courser."

Shocked silence met this proposition, followed by curt laughter from Kona, who interpreted it as a joke, and a simultaneous silent protest from Clemantine, *You're not serious?*

Urban shrugged. No need to frighten anyone. Not now.

Hiding behind an apologetic smile, he deftly shifted the conversation to his plans for the journey to come. He spoke with passion, he spoke from the heart, only gradually realizing he was seeking Kona's approval, striving to win that nod of assent he had never gotten when he left on the Null Boundary Expedition.

The thought silenced him. Engendered a thread of anger. *Some things never change.* But that was wrong. It was a child's complaint. Given time, everything changed. Growing up, he'd only ever thought of Kona as a stern parent. He'd never really known him as a person, and after today he never would, unless . . .

"You could come with me," he said.

As soon as the words were out, he wondered if it was a mistake. A raised eyebrow from Clemantine suggested it might be. Through his atrium she asked, *You sure that's a good idea?*

It was true that growing up, he'd chafed under his father's authority—but that was a long time ago.

I was a kid then, Urban reminded her.

Did she roll her eyes?

"You *should* come," he insisted aloud to Kona.

It felt suddenly critical to grasp this chance to know the man who had given him life, this man who had devoted his life to securing a future for his people. Urban could see now that as a kid he'd resented Kona's devotion to duty, and on some level he must have feared being trapped in a similar role.

A thousand years allowed for a hell of a perspective.

He said to Kona, "All your life, everything you've done has been out of duty, to see that our people survived. Maybe it's time for a change. This voyage is not about survival. It's a quest for knowledge. Who knows what we'll find? Aren't you curious?"

"The council has consistently voted against an expedition like this," Kona told him.

"Of course they have," Urban said dismissively.

The people of Silk were conservative, cautious—especially the founding generation, which included both Kona and Clemantine. That wasn't a bad thing. A stable culture had helped them to survive in a dangerous world. But Urban had festered in Silk, too restless and reckless to ever really belong. "The council doesn't have a say in it this time."

Riffan spoke in a tentative tone, reminding them of his presence. "I had been hoping to persuade the council to reconsider, although I admit it didn't seem likely."

This proved to be a wrong turn in the conversation. Kona's gaze hardened. His hand sliced the air in a gesture that took in Riffan, Pasha, Clemantine, but mostly Urban. "So you've dismissed their concerns and taken it on yourself—"

"Yes, I have," Urban interrupted. "And I'll be gone in a few hours."

"Do you really believe your control of the courser is absolute?"

"You don't need to worry about that."

"Of course I need to worry about it," Kona said. "If it's mapped our existence here, if it's designated us as a future target—"

"No," Urban said. He thrust his hand out, gesturing toward the faraway courser. "I'm there now, monitoring and directing the ship's mind. I won't let it draw a conclusion like that."

"Your control is that refined?"

"Yes."

"Then why haven't you taken it over completely? Phased out the Chenzeme aspects? Evolved the ship to be a purely human thing?"

Purely human.

Ancestral human.

Such things were important to Kona. Urban had let himself forget that. Now that he was reminded, he felt himself regressing into familiar patterns, taunting the old man. "I could do that, but then I'd make myself a target for other Chenzeme ships."

"It's camouflage, then?" Kona asked.

"It's an adaptation. A hybrid existence. The purely human won't survive out there. If you want to come with me, you need to accept that. You need to be willing to adapt." He tapped his own chest. "This is me, but this one persona wasn't enough to ensure survival, so I created a staff of assistant personalities based on me."

"Sentient assistants?" Kona asked suspiciously.

"Yes. My Apparatchiks are sentient and self-aware, but they're artificial. *Not* human. I still trust them to make decisions, to do what needs to be done."

Kona glanced at Riffan and Pasha, at Clemantine. "And if those needs conflict with the freedoms or even the existences of your companions on this voyage? Whose need takes priority?"

Urban's brows knit. He shook his head. "That's not realistic. Not given the resources I can command."

"But what will the status of your companions be?" Kona pressed. "Will they have a choice of where you go? What you risk?"

Urban aimed a resentful gaze at Riffan, whose request to accompany the expedition had initiated this kind of complication. "I've laid out my goal," Urban said. "The details can be worked out on the way."

This wasn't enough for Kona. "You are the master of the ship," he pressed. "Every decision is ultimately yours."

"Sooth," Urban conceded. This was true and he meant it to stay that way.

Clemantine spoke as a mediator. "This is no different from our situation on the Null Boundary expedition," she reminded them. "Like then, we'll work to achieve consensus."

Pasha waded in. "The voyage is a risk. Every voyage is. No one denies that."

"Agreed," Kona said. "But it's the nature of that risk that should be made clear." He looked again at Urban. "I want it understood that you are not as human as you appear. You *are* the ship, aren't you? You or some version of you, melded with the courser's Chenzeme mind and affected by it. Who knows what's changed with you in the centuries you've been locked up with that monstrous intelligence?"

"I know," Urban answered. "I know who I was, who I am, and I know what I will never allow myself to be." He let himself drift a little closer to Kona, their gazes locked. He said, "You're not actually arguing with *me*, are you? You're arguing with yourself, looking for some reason to stay behind, like it's your duty to stay here. But you don't have to stay. You've done your part. If you're bored with your existence here, admit it, dissolve whatever husks you have, and move on."

Clemantine's brows rose. "It's one thing to send a ghost, but you're suggesting Kona should abandon the Well? Leave our people? Leave nothing behind? That's not something he would ever—"

"No," Kona interrupted her. A brusque syllable. "Urban knows what he's saying. I won't split my existence. It's all or nothing."

Urban sensed imminent victory. He might come to regret this victory, but what the hell. If he could tear the old man loose from his past, from a duty that had weighed on him with the gravity of a dark star but that he'd carried anyway, carried for centuries, and set him instead on a new and hopeful venture—it would be worth it. "So you're coming?" he pressed.

Kona's expression remained stern, but after a few seconds he conceded with a nod. "I've lived this same life too long. It's time to begin again."

Kona withdrew to spend his final hours arranging his affairs and writing missives to explain his decision and to lay out his last thoughts on the possible futures of Deception Well.

Pasha and Riffan had their own concerns, so Urban and Clemantine were left alone as time wound down.

Urban still had no network access to *Long Watch*, but the data gate that linked him to his chain of outriders remained open. Subminds started to arrive through it—partial personas, derived from ghosts but requiring far less data to define them—finally completing the hours-long journey from *Dragon*.

Some of the subminds belonged to Urban, some to Clemantine. They brought memories from their ghosts aboard *Dragon*, so Urban knew the status of the ship and of Clemantine's reaction to it.

He grinned, knowing he had won her over. "You've seen it all now," he said to her. "You know it's real."

She nodded, not answering at first. To his dismay, he saw apprehension in this version of her. Rising fear, now that the moment had come. He worried she would change her mind, that she would delete her ghost from *Dragon*, leaving him alone again—but she extinguished that doubt, saying, "All right. Let's do this. I'll pass the access code to Pasha. You and I, with these final memories, can go on ahead."

Ghost patterns required vast complexes of data. Their transfer took time.

Urban departed first. He left his husk unconscious, with disintegration processes underway to ensure no one could revive that version of himself against his wishes.

Clemantine watched his consciousness leave his body, and then the swift decay process that followed, beginning with a clouding and then a blackening of the eyes. The sight disturbed her enough that she turned away.

Urban had not always regarded his physical self as something disposable. This was a new aspect of him. It troubled her how easily he had abandoned this incarnation of himself.

Still, there was no other way to reach the courser.

She drew a deep breath, preparing herself. The ghost she'd sent to inspect *Dragon* remained there, but its experiences had returned to her through the arriving subminds and were now integrated. She possessed a memory of visiting the ship and of affirming everything Urban had told her. She looked forward to her return—but she was despondent too.

All or nothing, Kona had said. Clemantine felt the truth of it.

She instructed her personal DI: "After my ghost has gone, dissolve whatever is left in this room. Dissolve my husk that is aboard *Silent Vigil*. Then dissolve yourself."

The DI acknowledged these instructions.

Clemantine created a new ghost—a final rendition of this phase of her life—and sent it to *Dragon*, but of course *she* still remained behind, the consciousness that abided in this body. For this version of herself there was no way out.

A flutter of panic, quickly suppressed.

Just one last act left to do.

Sleep. A command carried out through a biochemical reaction. This life was over.

CHAPTER SIX

URBAN'S GHOST LEFT *Long Watch* with transmission protocols set to ensure no copy would be left behind. The data that defined him passed first through a gate on *Khonsu*, the closest ship in the outrider fleet. From there, the ghost was relayed to *Lam Lha*, and then *Artemis*, and on up the chain until at last it reached the courser. There, it melded with the ghost Urban had left behind.

That moment did not produce a revelatory burst within his core persona; he experienced no high of enlightenment at the awareness of another life lived. Instead, the arrival of his ghost induced a sense of absentmindedness. Because its memories were already his own, receiving them was like waking from an artificial amnesia, the abrupt recovery of a history he'd always known, but had temporarily forgotten.

Two distinct timelines now accounted for his recent past: one in which he'd gone to find Clemantine and the other where he'd stayed aboard *Dragon*, waiting in suspense to learn if she would come.

She *had* come, and to his profound relief her visiting ghost had chosen to stay.

He turned to her, this version of her that had arrived through the data gate hours ago to undertake an inspection of *Dragon*. She'd sent subminds back to *Long Watch* bearing the memories of what she'd found, but she remained here, with him. The virtual environment of *Dragon's* library contained them in a simulation of physical existence, so that they appeared identical to their living avatars aboard *Long Watch*.

Clemantine watched him curiously, sensing the difference in him brought on by the melding of timelines.

"You're back," she said.

"Yes." He raised a hand, touched her cheek. The simulation conveyed a sense of gentle pressure, but not her warmth, or the faint spicy scent of her skin—a poverty of detail intrinsic to the library's virtual world.

She kissed his hand with dry, breathless lips before smiling a sly smile. This version of her bolder and more confident, already at home here.

Her first question upon arriving had been, "Is this library a copy of the one on *Null Boundary*?"

"Yes," he'd told her. "Though I've worked on it since. Organizing, indexing, adding new observations. And I modified the interface."

The baseline visual architecture was deceptively simple, just a bright white path crossing a boundless, blue-gradient plain that grew darker with distance. There appeared to be nothing there, but an extra sense available to their avatars allowed them to perceive the data embedded at every point.

Clemantine had adapted easily to the new system. After she'd mastered search functions and the summoning of windows, he'd briefly introduced her to his crew of Apparatchiks, all six of them derived from his persona but diversified into distinct individuals with machinelike natures that allowed them to focus obsessively on their specialties: the Engineer, the Bio-mechanic, the Pilot, the Astronomer, the Scholar, and the Mathematician.

"It's interesting," she had observed, "that you utilize both a swarm of outrider ships and a swarm of personas."

"A modular existence," he'd agreed. "Expanded senses and an expanded intellect, all supporting *my* intentions."

The Engineer was the only Apparatchik on deck now. He looked out at them from within a frameless two-dimensional window, standing with arms crossed, a flat brown background behind him. Superficially, the Engineer looked like Urban but his speech patterns, his expression, the way he carried himself, and the way he dressed—in dull brown coveralls—all distinguished him from the master copy. Within his frame he appeared at full scale, his intent gaze focused on a three-dimensional illustration of a new project, floating head-high above the library floor. The illustration depicted a small warren of tunnels and chambers that together would suffice as a simple physical habitation where a handful of people could live. Temporary quarters, quick to grow. Clemantine had taken on the task of overseeing the design.

"I like working with the Engineer," she mused, still eyeing Urban with that sly smile. "He's blunt, but so calm and efficient, and he answers questions in an instant." Her finely shaped eyebrows arched. "I wonder why you've always hidden this aspect of yourself?"

The Engineer snorted. "Other than my blunt speech, the qualities you've named are all artificial additions to my personality's original framework."

"Then he *isn't* you?" Clemantine asked in feigned innocence.

"No more than necessary," Urban agreed. He'd long ago grown accustomed to the incessant preening and self-regard of all the Apparatchiks, not just the Engineer, who was the most tolerable among them.

Their conceit derived from Urban's personality, he understood that. Within the tailored personas of the Apparatchiks, conceit had become distilled and concentrated, just like the qualities that let them acquire and sustain their essential skills. Each one of them a specialist, sentient and self-aware but focused obsessively on their subjects of interest and incapable of distraction or boredom. They made for deeply irritating company but they were his crew and they supported him in his position and his ambition.

Turning to the Engineer, Clemantine spoke with exaggerated regard, "It's clear to me now why you're so good at what you do."

"You'll get bored with him," Urban assured her. He gestured at the 3-D illustration. The actual warren was already under development, its initial growth phase begun hours earlier. "Let's see how far we've gotten."

The courser was, in some sense, a living thing—or more accurately, a mosaic of diverse lifeforms woven into one monstrous bio-mechanical organism. It had the shape of a long tapered cylinder. Deep in that cylinder's core, banks of active tissue worked to sort and store vast quantities of material that could be extracted when needed and then recombined to build nearly anything. Around the core, and comprising the bulk of the ship, was a layer of bio-mechanical tissue interleaved with Chenzeme computational strata. Another computational layer, this one composed of millions of Chenzeme philosopher cells, wrapped the outer hull.

The philosopher cells glowed with white light. Each was effectively a tiny mechanistic mind, neither conscious nor self-aware but adaptable, capable of thought, containing memory, and perpetually engaged in simultaneous machine-sharp debates that ran in currents across the cell field. The cells formed alliances and gambled opinions, the links between them made and shattered a thousand times a second as they tested the validity of ideas and intentions, and negotiated consensus. Together the philosopher cells formed the mind of the ship, an intellectual machine specialized for the ruthless pursuit and destruction of lifeforms not of their kind—except that Urban controlled them now.

He'd hijacked the ship by introducing a parasitic neural system into its structure. A molecular war had ensued as an army of Chenzeme nanomachines attempted to defend against the invasion, but the Makers Urban brought with him had proved capable of more rapid adaptation. He'd swiftly come to dominate the ship's Chenzeme mind.

His neural system had continued to expand, growing ever more intricate over centuries, reaching everywhere within the warship. He'd tested his control under demanding circumstances and concluded it was absolute—at least under the ship's current configuration.

The warren growing within Dragon's bio-mechanical tissue would change things. He'd never before tried to create a human-friendly inholding. The Engineer had consulted with the Bio-mechanic and they'd agreed it could be done and that for the first time, Urban could exist as a physical avatar aboard *Dragon*, alongside Clemantine and those volunteers, now inbound, who would comprise the ship's company.

Still, Urban regarded the project as an experiment, one that must advance with great care.

The illustration of the completed warren refreshed to show current progress. The first stage was complete: An enveloping barrier wall now enclosed the site. The wall's exterior was composed of Chenzeme tissue, with a neutral layer on the inside.

A barrier was essential. If human tissue mixed with Chenzeme, an immune response would be triggered, setting off a new molecular war.

Within the safety of that enclosed space, the warren was just beginning to take shape.

"A basic habitat to start with," Clemantine said.

Urban nodded. "I want to work out if it's possible to design a rotating deck, to give us at least a light simulated gravity. But there's time."

"Time is something we have in quantity," she agreed, her words spiced with dark humor.

"Sooth." A vast expanse of time stretching far ahead of *Dragon*.

A DI whispered to him that Clemantine's newest ghost had arrived after the hours-long transit from *Long Watch*. He watched her face, watched anxiety and worry take over her expression as this new ghost joined its memories to hers. She gazed at him and then looked around, her shoulders slowly relaxing as her two timelines poured into this singular moment.

"So it's done," she said. "And here we are." But whether she spoke in relief or resignation, he couldn't tell.

"You've been busy," he reminded her, nodding at the projection of the growing warren.

"Yes. We'll make this work."

"I hope so."

She cocked her head. "Are you still worried about our inbound company?"

"Why shouldn't I worry? These people of the Well—"

"They're *our* people," she reminded him.

He shrugged. "Maybe once. But they're not like us. The people I grew up with never spent time as ghosts—unless things have changed?"

"No. I think that's still the same."

He gestured at the projection. "The warren isn't ready yet. Even when this first phase is done, our living space is going to be small, cramped, dull. This is all an experiment. I can't risk expanding too quickly."

"Understood," she said cautiously. Then added, "This looks similar to the warren aboard *Long Watch* so it won't be unfamiliar."

"We're only getting two from *Long Watch*."

"Riffan Naja and Pasha Andern," she reminded him.

"Right. And maybe they can handle life in the warren for a time, but there will be others. How are they going to react when they're faced with the reality here? I don't want them falling apart because this warren is too small and cramped, while the library overwhelms them. So I'm thinking of holding them in the archive until—"

"*No*, Urban."

"Just until I get the ship fully modified. It'll be easier for them. Better, if they wake to a secure, comfortable, familiar environment. And they'll never miss the time away." He hesitated as a DI whispered another update. "Kona's here," he told her.

Kona winked into existence alongside them. He glanced their way, suspiciously eyed the Engineer within his frame, and then turned a swift circle, taking in the blue gradient of an otherwise featureless environment. "Where is this?"

"Ship's library," Urban said.

Clemantine continued their debate. "Let them at least instantiate as ghosts," she insisted. "Then let them *choose* to enter the archive if that's what they want. Don't treat them like toys that you can take out and play with when you get bored."

"What's under discussion?" Kona asked.

Clemantine summarized it. Urban, eyes narrowed, prepared his argument, sure that Kona would take her side. But he surprised them both by saying, "Urban is right. No one has been vetted for this company. There wasn't time. It's just whoever happened to be in the right place at the right time, in the right mood to make a life-changing decision. Some are going to wake up to what they did and wonder why. So let's make the transition as easy as—"

"A new ghost is coming in," Urban interrupted. "I'm shifting it to the archive." He raised two hands to forestall Clemantine's objection. "Where it will stay for as short a time as possible, okay?" He turned to Kona. "Could you figure out who these people are? Why they're here? And if we want them all?"

"Link me to their bios and I'll look, but it's been a long time since I was active. It's unlikely I'll know most of them."

"Pasha Andern did the recruiting," Clemantine reminded them. "She'll be able to vouch for them."

Urban gestured at the projection of the proposed habitation. "What I really need is another engineer. Someone experienced and ambitious who can work with my engineer. I want to construct a gee deck if we can."

Clemantine volunteered to introduce Kona to *Dragon* and its systems—the same tour she'd taken with Urban when her ghost first arrived to inspect the ship. Urban agreed, admiring how quickly she'd adapted.

After they left the library, the Engineer also withdrew, leaving Urban alone—but only for a moment. Two more Apparatchiks appeared—the Pilot and the Bio-mechanic—each locked in a virtual dimension contained within a frameless window.

Their uninvited appearance suggested trouble.

The Bio-mechanic wore dark green. He floated within a background of motile tissue, looking suspicious and short-tempered as he always did. He'd spent centuries delving into the structure and behavior of *Dragon's* bio-mechanical tissue and devising molecular triggers to control its behavior. Over time, his own behavior had taken on a veneer of contempt and hostility, as if echoing the Chenzeme attitude. He looked at Urban and announced, "She doesn't trust us."

Urban cocked his head, eyes narrowed combatively, unwilling to allow the Bio-mechanic to treat Clementine as an outsider or a threat. He said, "She wouldn't be here if she didn't trust me."

The Pilot shrugged dismissively. Within the frameless rectangle of his window he was a dark, nearly featureless silhouette standing within a detailed, three dimensional star map. "She *wants* to trust us," he said. "But within a simulated environment it's hard to be sure if the maps are real, or if they're complete."

Urban drew back, wary now.

The Pilot continued, "She will seek to prove to herself that everything we've shown her is real. She will consult with Kona, compare her perceptions to his, and look for inconsistencies that might indicate the absence of some knowledge or history that's been hidden from her."

The Bio-mechanic summed it up: "She wants to be very sure she has not been misled."

"I haven't misled her," Urban said.

The Bio-mechanic smiled coldly. "Not in any critical way."

Urban had shown Clementine the structure of the ship: its layers, its immense propulsion reef, its dual telescopes.

She'd questioned him on how well the ship could track activity in the region around it. He'd hidden nothing about the process, explaining, "The philosopher cells keep watch on the Near Vicinity. I can ride their senses, see what they see, but it's a general view. Minimal magnification. Long-range sight comes through the scopes. *Dragon's* instruments are good, but the seeing is exponentially better when I digitally integrate them with telescopes on the outriders. That lets me create a virtual lens light-hours in size."

The reason for her particular interest became clear when she'd asked her next question—the question he'd dreaded. "How often have you seen other Chenzeme ships?"

Long ago, Clementine had watched helplessly from a far orbital outpost as two Chenzeme swan bursters swept in from the void to destroy her home world of Heyertori, her family gone with it, and most of the people she'd ever known.

She hated the Chenzeme, feared any encounter with their robotic ships. Urban knew it had taken heroic courage for her to come to *Dragon*. He worried she would back out if she knew what was to come.

So he'd edited two ancient log files to conceal a few critical details of his return voyage, and he'd evaded her question, responding with a question of his own. "You looked over the library files . . . right?"

An ambiguous answer that had earned a sharp response: "I haven't had time to examine everything in detail."

But then in a softer tone she'd added, "A DI is analyzing the files, but for myself, I've only skimmed the summaries. I'm not sure how much I want to know about that life I never lived."

He understood her caution. The decisions, the actions, the experiences of her other self existed now only as historical events, over and done. She could not change any of it. And still, it was history she'd lived, witnessed, endured—been responsible for—and some of it was ugly. She would have guessed that from his silence. No wonder she was afraid.

"You're right," he told her. "There's no need to go back there. Better just to let it go."

Her sharp tone returned. "You think so? Why? Did I fail along the way? Do something to regret?"

Of *course* she would twist his words! He had wanted to divert the conversation but not in that direction.

"*No,*" he said. "You did all you could. We all did. Sometimes you just can't win. Not the whole game. Not the round that matters most. No one could have changed it, but in the end we learned to beat the Chenzeme." A vague gesture. "*Dragon* is proof of that."

"Was it worth it, then?" she asked. "Would you do it again?"

"Hell, yes, I would. You would too. We all would. What was the alternative? Hunker down at the Well for ten thousand years of cold sleep? We had our freedom at least, to change, to become what we needed to be. And we did. And you and me, we're both still out there living some other life. A good life. It looked like it would be a good life. You can't have everything."

But she was still circling around her fear of the timeline she'd never lived. "It got brutal at the end, didn't it?"

"Sooth. And I did what I had to do. It was the right thing to do, the only thing to do—but that last day will haunt me for the rest of my life."

He knew she hadn't accessed the privileged data cache that recorded the details of those last days because he'd assigned a DI to alert him if she did. So he'd braced himself, certain she would ask what had happened, how it had ended. But she didn't.

Instead she had returned to the other subject he did not want to discuss. "After I left you to return to the Well, I never saw a sign of the Chenzeme. I was running dark though, and I didn't have an array of telescopes. You've seen other ships, haven't you?"

"Sure," he'd said cautiously. Then added, "Not often." And that was true.

To his surprise and relief, she had accepted this answer. It was what she wanted to hear. She had assumed he would go dark and keep his distance if ever he sighted another Chenzeme ship—and she had pressed the issue no further.

Now, hours later, the Bio-mechanic said, "This ship is not a closed system. Eventually someone will think to ask how resources are renewed."

Urban shrugged.

The Bio-mechanic translated this vague response into words: "By then it will be too late. No going back."

"It's already too late," the Pilot informed them. "By the time a ghost could relay back through the chain of outriders, the link to *Long Watch* will be lost."

"She doesn't want to go back," Urban insisted. "She's made up her mind." Guilt tweaked his conscience. "I'll restore the modified log files. Later."

"Are we going to go through the Committee?" Kona asked when they were all back in the library again and Urban had introduced him to the Pilot.

The Committee was a cluster of neighboring stars easily visible in Deception Well's night sky, where there had once been several settled worlds.

Kona added, "I'd like to know if anyone is still there."

"I'd like to know too," Urban said. "And if I had more resources I'd send an outrider to investigate. But I don't want to take the courser there. Too many Chenzeme ships have visited those worlds. I've relived memories of it when I've been immersed in the hull cells' shared thoughts. If anyone is left, they'll stay silent. They'll see a courser and they won't respond except maybe to launch an automated attack. So why frighten them?"

"You'd frighten them less if you destroyed the hull cells and sculpted this ship into something human," Clemantine pointed out. Nothing in her manner suggested this was a joke.

"I don't want to look like something human—not while I'm still in Chenzeme space." His attention shifted as an update reached him.

"What is it?" Clemantine asked.

"We've got twelve ghosts in the archive and another coming through."

"That's all right, isn't it?"

"I was expecting ten or twelve."

"Word must have spread," Kona said. "Pasha picked up a few extra volunteers. I'm not surprised. It's an exciting project."

It was more than he'd expected.

The thirteenth ghost cycled into the archive. A fourteenth began to come in. He waved off the Pilot. Brought back the Engineer and the Bio-mechanic.

The Apparatchiks did not have access to Urban's thoughts and memories but they were derived from him, knew him well, and generally intuited what he was thinking. "You want to know how many individuals the new habitat can support," the Bio-mechanic said before Urban could present the problem.

"The warren is designed for a population of fifteen," the Engineer reported.

But the fifteenth ghost was now arriving. Add Urban, Clemantine, and Kona to that count, and the capacity of the warren was already exceeded.

It was far too late to send a stop order. Light-hours separated *Dragon* from *Khonsu*, the trailing ship in the outrider fleet.

"You could close the data gate," the Bio-mechanic suggested.

"No!" Clemantine snapped. "This is not just random data. We're talking about people. They could be expecting to meet friends, family. We're not going to erase them."

"Closing the gate is not an option," Urban conceded though he felt hollow as he said it, caught up in chaos, no longer in control.

With so many new people, everything would change.

He opened a window above the boundless blue plain of the library. Contained within its perimeter was a chart listing names and brief bios of each newly arrived ghost.

He watched in horrified fascination as the chart expanded to include sixteen, eighteen, twenty ghosts, the number continuing to climb.

Privately, he messaged the Engineer: *Is there a limit on how many fully realized ghosts the library can support?*

Yes, of course. Resolution is presently set to an efficient margin but as the number of simultaneous users grows, it will begin to drop.

Urban wasn't willing to endure the sensory deprivation of a low-res interface. *We need to expand capacity.*

Yes.

Clemantine had summoned a three-dimensional schematic of *Dragon's* structure. "This is a huge ship," she was saying. "Far larger than *Null Boundary*. It should be able to support large numbers—"

Urban stopped her. "No. You have to remember, *Dragon* is a hybrid ship." He reached into the projection. A thin gray filament embedded within the ship's tissue brightened at his touch. The silvery glow rapidly expanded, illuminating the structure of a branching network, the filaments densest beneath the hull cells, though they left no part of the ship untouched.

"You see this? This is *my* neural system. I inhabit it continuously. I'm there now. This is the bridge that translates between my mind and the Chenzeme mind. A neural bridge. It's how I monitor the ship, and guide the thoughts and temper of the philosopher cells.

But from the Chenzeme perspective, this bridge is still all alien tissue. Not integrated. Something to be purged from the ship's body, if possible.

"That first day, those first minutes when I breached the courser's defenses, there was a hot war on the molecular scale. My Makers evolved to meet the threat. I won, but it was close." His gaze shifted to acknowledge the Bio-mechanic. "There have been a few more skirmishes since then."

"You're still here," Kona said warily. "So you won those skirmishes. You're in control."

"That's what you said," Clemantine reminded him.

"I *am* in control."

"Thanks to my constant vigilance," the Bio-mechanic amended. Twenty-five ghosts.

"I'm in control," Urban repeated, "but I never let myself forget there's a quiet war ongoing at molecular scale across every square micron of the boundary between my neural bridge and the Chenzeme zones. Right now, the situation around the warren is stable. But if we push deeper, radically expand the surface area of our safe zones, the existing balance could be overthrown."

The Engineer expanded on this, saying, "Our challenge isn't just about the volume we inhabit. It's also the resources we require, the heat we produce."

Thirty.

"So we take it slowly," Clemantine said. "Expand carefully."

"Always," the Engineer agreed.

"Most of our people will choose cold sleep anyway," Kona said. "They understand it. When we first came to Deception Well, all but a handful of us were in cold sleep."

"And when we reach the Hallowed Vasties?" Urban asked.

"Even then," Kona said, "centuries between star systems."

"Centuries between now and then to make this an entirely human ship," Clemantine added.

Urban's gaze shot to the Bio-mechanic. The Apparatchik loomed dark, menacing, within the confining boundary of his window. Before he could speak, before he could object to this call to wipe out centuries of his work, Urban silenced him with a look. *Not now.*

*Not ever, the Bio-mechanic said, speaking through Urban's atrium.

*Agreed.

Clemantine wanted to believe it was possible to remake the ship, and on a theoretical level it might be, but Urban would never consent to it. The hull cells were in some sense sentient and together they contained tangled memories accumulated over millions of years—an overwhelming sweep of time that he'd hardly begun to understand.

But this wasn't the moment to explain that to her.

"We'll take it slowly," he agreed.

Thirty-five.

"And find me that engineer."

SECOND

You wake, cradled in a cocoon of warm gel with only your face exposed to cold night. Your chest rises as you breathe deeply, gratefully, of sweet, clean air. *Still alive.*

Glimmers of light play on the periphery of your vision. You recognize them as little bio-machines, existing to serve your purposes.

Your senses extend beyond this physical body you inhabit. You mentally map yourself in your surroundings: afloat in a subterranean ocean.

There is a layer above the ocean—still subterranean—where computational strata are distributed throughout a vast complex of fluid-cooled tunnels and chambers. This is the network of your existence, though your mind is not what it used to be. You have a tentative recollection of terrible, crushing acceleration, shattered strata, the components of your mind snapping loose, collapsing into dust.

Panic shoots through you. You flail upright, your head above the cloying gel, your feet thrashing, reaching a deeper, colder layer. A slant of pale light flicks on, reveals a ladder close at hand. You reach for it. The solid feel of it is soothing and calms your fear.

You climb through the half-light to a hatch that opens at your touch, admitting a brighter light and a puff of warmer air. You pause as your eyes adjust, pondering why you re-created yourself within this avatar with its limited abilities, its inefficient memory. But you trust yourself. There is a valid reason.

The hatch swings back to lie flat against a floor and you emerge into a clean corridor with rectangular leaves of crystal neatly arrayed in banks along the walls and ceiling.

Your skin prickles as you remember an earlier existence when you and everything around you was in ruins. You reach out with your mind, tentatively, to assess the memories gathered in the strata around you—recoiling at once from disconnected visions, ambitions, emotions, and swirling facts cut loose from all basis, all structure. *Chaos!*

The strata you see have been rebuilt but the memories within are useless. Broken in their disorder.

A thousand tiny hearts beat hard, flooding your mind with rage and frustration. You know now why you have been reduced to this pathetic avatar. It is a simple pattern, a first step to recovery. A surviving kernel, a seed crystal.

You wonder: *Is it enough?*

Can all that was, coalesce around you again?

Unlikely. You arose from the Communion, with the resources of quadrillions contributing to your ascension. No way to recover all that. Not here—you pause to sniff the air, scan your mental map—here, where you are utterly alone.

You think of her, of what she did to you.

She destroyed you.

Your fists clench. *You destroyed me!*

Even so, there is something of you left.

And you'd like your revenge.

CHAPTER SEVEN

THE FINAL COUNT of ghosts reached sixty-three. Urban looked at the list of names and bios in consternation, in dread. These were good people, serious people. Educated, experienced. Scientists, engineers, historians, journalists, storytellers, and even two planetary scouts. It wasn't the presence of any one of them that worried him; it was *all* of them, together.

Kona's early questions returned to haunt him: *What will their status be? Will they have a choice of where you go? What you risk?*

Urban did not want to submit his will to the choices of others, but that would happen now. He did not want to be responsible for so many lives, but now there was no choice in it.

Kona looked over the bios of all the newly archived ghosts, smiling as he encountered a scattering of familiar names. Over the years, he'd made the mistake of letting too many friendships fall away . . . but at least he hadn't left everyone behind.

"You know some of them?" Urban asked, approaching out of an unexpected and undefined distance.

Kona looked up, looked around in confusion. Though the library appeared much the same, his immediate surroundings had undergone a quiet transformation. Clemantine had receded. He was aware of her, not far off and yet only half sensed as she continued to work with the Engineer.

"Have I been shoved off into my own workspace?" he asked.

"Something like that," Urban agreed. "The library allows for privacy and strives to respond to a user's shifting focus."

"Huh."

"About the engineers," Urban said. "There are nine in the archive. You're a better judge of people than I am, so I want you to pick one."

Kona didn't have to think about it. "The one we need is Vytet Vahn-Renzani."

Urban puzzled over this. "Do I know that name?"

"Yes, you do. When you were a child, you knew Vytet."

"She—" He broke off with a frown. "He . . . ?"

A distracted moment as they both checked the bio. "*She,*" Kona confirmed. "For now, anyway. Vytet's a shifter."

Vytet had never kept a fixed gender. She chose sometimes to be a man, other times a woman, or other, rarer variations. Always experimenting. She would change surface features too: the shade of her skin, the color of her eyes, the structure of her face. Retaining only the basic dimensions of her body.

Urban nodded. "I remember."

"We're incredibly lucky to have her here. She's an exceptionally skilled engineer. Careful, determined, but daring, too."

Long, long ago, Vytet had led the effort to bring the city of Silk back to life in the desperate early days after their arrival, and she'd made it a better place in the years that followed. The extraordinary passage of time since that age had not diluted Kona's opinion of her. If Vytet had joined the expedition looking for new challenges, he could surely accommodate her.

"All right," Urban said. "Wake her. Give her the tour. Help her to feel at home."

Kona could not remember the last time he had talked to Vytet, or even heard her name mentioned. If pressed, he would have guessed her gone forever into cold sleep, as so many from that age were. Ruefully, he acknowledged to himself that Vytet might have assumed the same fate for him.

He sent a DI to fetch her ghost from the archive. An anxious moment later she instantiated beside him on the library's surreal blue plain.

Kona smiled in recognition.

Regardless of how Vytet might change the envelope of her appearance, he was sure he would know her by her gaunt height and by the ceaseless curiosity of her gaze. She turned her head, assessing her surroundings with dark eyes set in a sharp-featured face—not a face he remembered. The hair that covered her scalp was short, thick as a pelt, and startlingly white. She stood several centimeters taller than he did but carried far less weight—always too preoccupied to devote sufficient time for the drudgery of consuming each day's required calories. She'd dressed her ghost in a loose blue coverall and flexible foot gloves. Nothing in her face or figure strongly signaled a female identity but her bio made it clear that was how she chose to be seen—until she changed again.

"Hey, old friend," Kona said gently. "I was surprised to see your name in the inventory."

As Vytet's wandering gaze settled on him, her eyes widened in surprise. "*Kona.*" A disbelieving smile. "You're here."

"I am."

She started to reach out, using both hands. Hesitated as if unsure. Then she gripped his shoulders. He felt the pressure of her fingers, registered the confusion on her face. "Ah, this is so strange," she said. "You *look* the same as always—"

"And you, forever different."

"I *feel* different." She released him. Held her hands up, studying them, as if looking for a flaw. "We're ghosts, aren't we?"

"We are," Kona confirmed.

"Ghosts in an artificial matrix," she murmured, puzzling through the situation. She looked at him again and confessed, "I have not experienced this state before. I've rarely ghosted, and when I have, I always instantiated within someone's atrium, riding on their senses. This is different. Very different. By the Unknown God, it feels so *incomplete.*"

"Our natural senses are limited here," Kona affirmed. "But this state is temporary. We'll resume a physical existence once living space is assembled."

Something drew her attention. Her eyes narrowed as if to bring a distant object into focus. "I have a new sense," she realized. "I feel myself standing on the surface of a vast library." She turned in a circle, scanning the featureless blue plain. "I *feel* the presence of well-ordered data."

She reached out, and to Kona's surprise, a curving side path appeared in response to her beckoning gesture. Files sprang up on the path, each one a thin, vertical pane large enough to step into. The first file in the stack showed a branching map of the library with all its major sections neatly labeled.

"How did you do that?" Kona asked. He could sense the presence of data too, but Clemantine had taught him to use a DI to do his research.

Vytet was too absorbed in discovery to hear his question. "Wondrous," she whispered reverently as she stepped onto the side path. Then she stepped into a file, and disappeared.

Kona shouted in alarm. "Vytet!"

Corruption and chaos! Why was it possible to step into a file? Was there a flaw in the library's environment that allowed it? Could the data that was Vytet's ghost be lost within the data of the files?

No, he told himself. That was ridiculous. The library was surely designed to be used in such a way.

Gathering his courage, Kona followed Vytet's lead. He stepped into the file—

And emerged into a circular room walled in stacks of horizontal files, much smaller than the files that had appeared on the path. Some were labeled with characters from writing systems Kona did not recognize, but most had labels he could read.

Vytet was there, her face luminous with delight. "This interface is for browsing," she concluded as she surveyed the stacks. "Look."

She touched a file with the label *Planets*. Immediately, it expanded into a doorway that led into a second room walled in more stacked files. She gestured at the room. "Through here, I suspect, we could begin to browse more deeply into the topic of planets. No doubt a chain of rooms will open depending on the specific query. A real planet? A fantasy planet? A gas giant? A terrestrial world?"

But instead of entering, she tapped the side of the doorway. It reverted to its original configuration of stacked files. She brushed the stack, causing it to scroll up. Then she touched another file, seemingly at random. Kona saw that it was labeled *Plants*. The doorway opened again, but onto a different room, colored a different hue.

"Plants," Vytet mused. "Another vast topic. There must be tens of thousands of linked rooms beyond this starting point, no doubt cross-linked to many disciplines."

She closed the doorway again. "I could wander happily in here for ten thousand years!" She reached for another file.

"Vytet," Kona said, holding out a restraining hand. Urban had urged him to help Vytet feel at home, but clearly she was going to master this bizarre environment far faster than he. "Vytet, there will be time for all this. Right now, we've got a complex project to undertake, and we need your skills."

As the warren neared completion, Urban assembled resurrection pods in each of the four residential chambers. Soon after, he awoke, his newly grown body held close to the chamber's curving wall, prevented from drifting in the absence of gravity by luminous white, warm ribbons of wall-weed.

The flattened tendrils lined the entire chamber. Most were short, ten centimeters, their soft glow the only source of light. They swayed in concert: slow, beguiling patterns designed to stir the air as they absorbed pollutants and regenerated the oxygen content. For several seconds Urban made no move, content to watch the hypnotic motion, to breathe, to exist.

The wall-weed, this chamber, his living breathing avatar—all roused in him a sense of wonder. When he'd hijacked the courser, he had not imagined a day would come when he could exist aboard it as a physical being. He had thought it impossible to establish a human outpost amid the hostile alien tissue—but time had extended his ambition. Now his plans, his hopes for the future, were becoming actualized, real at last.

He stirred. The extended tendrils of wall-weed that held him sensed the intent in his muscles and retracted. He kicked free, brushing away the sticky remnants of his resurrection, grateful to be alive and even happier knowing this avatar's existence would not need to end in some short time.

A gap opened in the wall-weed, enough to allow clothing to bud from the wall's generative surface. He dressed quickly and hauled himself through the chamber's gel door, eager for company.

In her virtual existence, Clemantine could tap the ship's senses and perceive its mass, its relative motion, its ever-growing distance from Deception Well, its position among the stars—factors that assured her of the reality of her situation, as strange as that still seemed.

But when she woke into physical existence, that reality felt tenuous. Nothing in her tiny residential chamber anchored her to a specific place or time. She might have been aboard *Long Watch*, or even back on the Null Boundary Expedition—and wasn't either option more plausible than resurrection in a chamber stashed deep within the bio-mechanical tissue of a Chenzeme warship?

She entertained the possibility that she was caught within a strange corrosive dream born out of want and madness and information decay. A head game that made her heart beat a little faster.

Then her atrium connected to *Dragon*'s network. Immediately, she created a ghost and sent it to the library. That ghost sent a slow-pulse of subminds back to her, effectively linking her again to the ship's senses, affirming the reality of her existence aboard *Dragon*. She sighed in relief and then messaged Urban: *You there?*

Waiting for you, he answered with no perceptible delay.

She dressed in the simple clothing and quiet colors she preferred, then hurried to join him, speeding down the empty passage outside her residential chamber. A U-shaped turn brought her to a common area she called the forest room.

It was an expansive space, with room enough to play in, and nooks around its perimeter to contain cozier gatherings. "Up" was defined by a projection of a pergola entwined with a climbing camellia that became real wherever its branches descended; chips of bright blue sky glinted past dark glossy green leaves. "Down" was a floor of light-gray cushioned tiles imitating the look of sandstone, but with a soft texture. White panels rose halfway up the side walls—a visual cue to separate accessible space from the projection of a sunlit forest that lay beyond.

Clemantine had engineered the forest room so that the brightness and angle of simulated sunlight coincided with ship's time, now late afternoon. She was last to arrive, coming in just behind Kona. The relief of her renewed physical existence demanded contact so she touched his muscular shoulder. He turned to trade a quick hug.

"Thank you for this," he told her. "It's beautiful. A welcome respite from the library."

"A work in progress," she said.

When *Dragon* began to accelerate, they would have a sense of gravity. Until then, they had to put up with zero gee. So why not try to enjoy it? She kicked off to join Urban and Vytet, who were already bouncing and tumbling in the open space beneath the pergola.

Vytet had traded her ghost's coverall for silky soft-brown pantaloons and a creamy tunic with deep pockets, a contrast to Urban who was, as always, dressed in snug trousers and a long-sleeved shirt, both in utilitarian dark gray.

Happily, his mood was brighter than his clothing. He saw her coming and reached for a pendulous gray-barked camellia branch that snaked to meet his hand. The branch became rigid just long enough for him to pivot off it and launch himself toward her. They met in a whirling embrace. Traded a quick kiss before she pushed him away.

"Go make me breakfast," she ordered, baring her teeth in a fierce and playful grin. "I'm starving."

"Already done." He twisted to kick off the ceiling. "I've ordered breakfast for everyone."

They gathered in a large nook on the side of the forest room. Distant birdsong could be heard past the soft rustle of wind in the canopy. The light shifted as clouds drifted past the face of a simulated sun. Bulbs of water and sweet juices budded from the ceiling, low-hanging fruit, ready to pick.

Clemantine plucked a pink bulb. Sipped it as she hooked a foot through a stirrup. Guava, she decided—then pasted the bulb to a pedestal table, freeing her hands to accept a warm bun passed to her by Urban. She bit into it to find a spicy protein filling inside bread rich with calories.

Calories were the cost of physical existence. Though they had retained the look of ancestral humans, internally they were highly evolved. Hosts of Makers inhabited their bodies, continuously repairing damage to their cells and protecting them from infestation—and consuming energy to do it. Their atriums burned calories too, at a terrific rate. So they were burdened with more demanding metabolisms than their ancestors, making frequent large meals a necessity, and an important part of their social culture.

Clemantine took another bite of the bun, relishing the taste of spice and fatty oil. "You were always good with a fabricator," she told Urban, deliberately bumping up against him.

"Hey!" he objected as water squirted from the bulb in his hand.

A dart glided out of the forest, unfolding into orange and brown butterfly wings that swept forward to embrace the water globule, corralling the spill. The artificial creature released a jet of air that changed its trajectory, sending it to the pergola overhead where it shifted back to a virtual object, and then fluttered out of sight.

"Nice," Vytet said with admiration.

"Butterfly tenders," Clemantine told her. "I found the pattern in the library."

More buns emerged—an easy food to eat in zero gee—and fresh fruits in bite-sized pieces stacked in edible, transparent tubes. Colorful blocks of dense jellies too, packed with nutrients and calories.

Clemantine could not resist playing with the butterflies that swooped among them. By blocking the slow-moving creatures from their task of gathering escaping crumbs, she could induce more butterflies to emerge. Urban joined in, the nook fluttered with wings, and for a few minutes, laughter prevented eating.

"Let them do their job," Kona urged at last.

"All right," Clemantine conceded.

She grabbed another bun, just one more.

The air cleared. The last few butterflies fluttered away, their mass reabsorbed by the walls as they transited to virtual creatures.

Clemantine closed her eyes, allowing herself a sigh of contentment.

It turned out Urban was not familiar with such a benign emotion. He touched her shoulder. Asked, "Are you all right?"

She opened her eyes again. "I'm good, thank you. No, I'm good *thanks* to you. Thank you for not forgetting me."

He grinned. "Forget you? How could I? Anyway, I knew you'd be missing me."

"Smart ass."

Vytet raised her arms in an extravagant stretch that emphasized her height and the thinness of her body. "Ah," she sighed. "It feels good to be real, to exist in this space. I admire the efficiencies of a virtual existence, but I also love being alive."

"Sooth," Kona agreed. "This is a good first step. Still a lot of planning and assembly to do."

"A lot of people to get out of the archive," Clemantine added. "I think we should start. There's room. This warren was designed to accommodate twelve."

Silence, extending across awkward seconds. Frowning, she turned to Urban to find a distracted look on his face as if he'd checked out of the conversation, checked into some other reality. Vytet looked uneasy, twirling the translucent blue shell of an empty bulb in the air.

Only Kona met her gaze. "I want to do the right thing too," he rumbled. "But we can't wake everyone. So how do we choose who to wake? And how do we explain that choice later, to those who weren't chosen? We'd create a situation in which some are seen as privileged over others."

Clemantine reached out and caught the twirling bulb, annoyed at its carefree motion. "That's an easy problem to fix. We'll rotate. Each of us returns to cold sleep after an allotted time, with the choice to continue as a ghost in the library." She shoved the bulb against the wall, where it was swiftly absorbed.

"That's not going to work," Urban said quietly, his gaze still unfocused as if he was somewhere else. "Right now, the library doesn't have the capacity to support a high-res existence for everyone. The computational strata are being expanded, but—"

"But it will take *time*," Clemantine interrupted, anticipating what he would say because she'd heard it so many times already. "Just like everything else."

"Yes," Urban agreed. "This is no easy thing."

She wrestled her temper down. He was trying. She could not deny it. He was doing what he could, given the unexpected number of recruits. But it was crushing to know the archived ghosts would not even have the choice of a virtual existence.

Moderating her tone, she said, "We could still rotate. Take turns here and in the library. Let people participate in the life of the ship, in the decisions that will need to be made."

"And if someone refuses to return to cold sleep?" Kona asked her. "If people begin waking out of turn? Once they're given agency, they'll be able to do what they want."

"No," Urban said, his focus finally returning to the discussion. "I can enforce any restriction."

Vytet bit a thumbnail, looking worried.

Kona asked, "At what cost? Deprive people of agency and you sow resentment, and dissension."

Vytet slid her thumbnail out from between her teeth. "We're better than that," she argued. "Every archived individual is fifth level. Rational and cooperative. They'll grasp the necessity of rotation."

Clemantine sighed, feeling defeated. "I wish it was so," she said to Vytet. "But we can't be sure of that." The idea of further delay vexed her. It was inherently unfair to keep people locked up and helpless in the archive. But Kona had a point.

"I worked security for years," she reminded them. "Even normal, rational, cooperative people behave in unpredictable ways in extreme circumstances." She did not want to concede the argument. Still . . . "Waking in a cramped warren aboard an alien ship to face the consequences of a decision—made in haste—to leave behind loved ones and all that's familiar, with no way out and no way back, *is* an extreme circumstance. Who knows how anyone will react?"

Kona was a master politician; easy for him to cast his voice in a grim tone when he said, "All it would take to create a cascade of resentment is one person refusing to return to cold sleep." He shot a hard look at Urban. "Whether you force the issue or not."

"I'll do what's needed," Urban responded.

It sounded like a warning. Clemantine heard it that way and felt a need to intervene. "We don't want to reach that point."

"Agreed," Kona said. "Our best path forward is to treat everyone equally."

Vytet's fists were shoved deep into the pockets of her tunic. "It's too late for that. You and Clemantine are exceptions because you were invited by Urban. But I came with the rest. And I'm the only one awake, the only one who can take part in this discussion. It isn't fair."

"You're right," Kona told her. "It's not fair, but it's necessary, because you are the one I trust to design the gee deck." His gaze shifted to Clemantine and then to Urban. "Let's focus on that. Get the gee deck designed. Get it built. Then bring everyone out simultaneously into a comfortable environment, one they can begin to think of as home—and we'll all be better off in the end."

Urban looked irritated and a little puzzled. "You understand it could take years to finish the gee deck?" he asked.

"*Years?*" Clemantine echoed in disbelief.

He looked at her, the intensity of his gaze reminding her of the Engineer. "If we encroach too quickly into Chenzeme territory, we risk igniting a molecular war."

She turned to Kona. "*Years*," she said, the word feeling toxic in her mouth.

Kona looked disgruntled. "That's a disappointment," he admitted. "But it doesn't change the argument."

"You don't think so?"

"No. I don't. We'll be centuries on this voyage. A few initial years invested in setting up our infrastructure won't make any difference in the long run."

Logically, that was true. But it felt wrong. Clemantine looked around their small circle, still half-expecting someone else to voice an objection—but who would? Not Urban. He met her gaze with a stony, resentful stare. Vytet wouldn't look at her at all: hands still deep in her pockets, shoulders hunched, gaze averted, body language that declared she'd removed herself from this decision.

"Years," Clemantine said once more, this time in resignation.

"It'll be all right," Kona said. "People will understand."

Clemantine raised a skeptical eyebrow.

"It'll be all right," he said again.

CHAPTER EIGHT

URBAN KEPT WATCH from the high bridge, cognizant of the grandeur around him: distant blue suns, furiously bright, illuminating nebulas light years across; the perfect repeating rhythm of pulsars; streamers of cold dust longer than he could transit in ten thousand years; the remote electromagnetic cacophony of star death at the galactic center.

And always, he remained mindful of the nearest stars and of the ship's precise position among them.

Dragon had coasted as it left the vicinity of Deception Well, its velocity less than five percent light speed, allowing the fleet of outriders to catch up and then to move ahead into their customary formation: a long, staggered line around *Dragon's* vector of travel. *Khonsu* was now closest, then *Artemis*, *Lam Lha*, *Pytheas*, and *Elepaio*, with *Fortuna* in the lead. Ninety light-minutes between each ship: a vanguard to warn him of hazards to come.

Urban issued an advisory: *Five minutes until we commence acceleration.*

Ready, Clementine acknowledged. Kona and Vytet echoed her assurance.

At the scheduled hour he directed the philosopher cells to accelerate. They fed the propulsion reef with pulses of fierce ultraviolet radiation, enough to stimulate activity across its surface.

The reef was an aggregate entity, like a coral reef, made of billions of tiny cooperating organisms—polyps—layer upon layer of them, with those on the surface seeming most alive.

The polyps functioned in a manner so utterly alien Urban

speculated they had originated in some other Universe. Each was capable of synthesizing nanoscale particles of exotic matter from the zero point field—matter that decayed in an instant—but with a billion events per microsecond the cumulative effect was to tweak the structure of space-time. Not randomly.

The reef was positioned far forward, at the bow. The polyps worked in concert to create a steepening gradient aimed away from the slight gravitational distortion of the ship's mass. The reef accelerated along that gradient, and *Dragon* came with it, the ship's velocity slowly growing.

The outriders accelerated at the same time, each powered by its own propulsion reef and piloted by a DI. From the high bridge, the lateral lines of *Dragon's* gravitational sensor let Urban detect the signature of *Khonsu's* reef, and more faintly, that of *Artemis*. The other outriders were too far ahead to be seen or sensed.

As the rate of acceleration increased, that version of Urban within the warren drifted toward the designated floor and began to walk. The ship's company joined him—Clemantine, Kona, and Vytet. They sat together at a table, and ate and drank as if they were on a world. A convenient situation, but temporary.

Urban took the fleet to thirty-five percent light speed and then he dampened the activity of the reef, leaving *Dragon* to coast toward its faraway destination in the Hallowed Vasties. The reef could pull the ship to much higher velocities, but as *Dragon's* speed increased so did the risk of collision. Interstellar space was not empty, and even a tiny object could severely damage or destroy the ship if it impacted the hull at a significant percentage of light speed.

Even at this compromise velocity, molecules of dust and gas constantly bombarded the hull cells. The cells renewed themselves, but *Dragon* slowly bled mass. That mass would eventually need to be replaced.

"Is this what you wanted?" Clemantine asked one evening, not long after *Dragon* ceased to accelerate. The warren had returned to a zero-gravity configuration. Ribbons of faintly glowing wall-weed again lined the oval interior of her private chamber. She drifted in the cozy space, one arm around Urban, a leg hooked over his, skin to skin. Shared sweat, shared warmth. She gazed at his face, at the sheen of his eyes under half-closed lids. Shared tranquility, after a long session of deeply attentive love-making.

"Having you here?" he asked in a low, almost hoarse voice. "It's exactly what I wanted."

Clemantine wanted the truth.

She ran two fingers down the smooth skin of his chest and, with a sharp edge of accusation in her voice, she said, "I *trusted* you."

This induced an unmistakable tension in his body, an acceleration in his breathing—unwelcome evidence that her emerging suspicion was not misplaced.

"Look at me," she said.

He obeyed, turning his head until they gazed at one another. She read guilt in the worried set of his eyes, but his confused frown hinted he wasn't certain what he was being accused of.

Multiple options, then? Interesting. She would have to investigate further, but right now, she just wanted an honest answer on the status of the gee deck.

She said, "I talked to the Bio-mechanic today. The Engineer was there too."

"Uh-huh?" Low, puzzled syllables rising from deep in his throat. He clearly had no idea what she was getting at—and that surprised her.

She said, "The basic structure of the gee deck has been designed. A site's been determined. A construction plan is in place."

Still no hint of enlightenment breaking through his perplexed expression, so she expanded on her complaint. "Construction should have begun as soon as we ceased acceleration. But nothing's been done. I asked the Apparatchiks why. Both were irked. They said they were ready to begin. They would have begun already, but *you'd* withheld permission—"

"No, wait." He grasped her concern at last. "That's not what's going on."

"Then you did give them permission to proceed?"

"No."

Anger flared. She started to untangle herself from him.

"Wait," he insisted, his arm tightening around her. "*Listen* to me. Vytet asked for more time, that's all. She's concerned. She and the Engineer can cross-check each other's work, but no one has ever cross-checked the Bio-mechanic's knowledge base. Vytet wants time to confirm his studies, his experiments, his conclusions. That makes sense, doesn't it? It makes sense to take the time to confirm our knowledge base before launching a major, invasive project."

Her hand slid back up his chest, came to rest beside his throat. "You're saying you want to confirm six hundred *years* of studies and experiments?"

"It's not me," he protested. "Vytet asked for more time. That's all."

"And you gave it to her because you don't trust the Bio-mechanic?"

"I *do* trust the Bio-mechanic. I wouldn't be alive if the Bio-mechanic made mistakes."

"Then why are you doing this?" Her fingers pressed a little too hard into his flesh.

"Vytet asked for more time," he repeated, wriggling to escape her grip. She let him go. Even gave him a little push. "She just wants to make sure there are no mistakes," he explained.

Clemantine said, "It feels like you're trying to delay the project."

A dark scowl. "And end up with your hand at my throat?"

She held up her hand, palm out. "Tell the Apparatchiks they can start the project. If it's going to take years, we need to get started."

"Fine," he snapped. "It's done. Whatever you want."

"Thank you."

He had drifted against the opposite wall of the little chamber, where fresh trousers had already budded. He tugged them on. A shirt appeared next. He grabbed it, put it on.

She felt a little guilty. She'd been wrong about him. He wasn't trying to delay the project. He'd just been accommodating Vytet's obsessive concerns. And still, she'd shaken him up with that line, *I trusted you.* She'd seen a flash of guilt—but whatever weighed on his conscience had nothing to do with the construction of the gee deck.

"I *do* trust you," she said aloud, just to see how he would react.

This time he was ready, his signature half-smile, taunting her. "It's not like you have a choice."

She hissed. His grin widened—a dangerous delay before he darted for the gel door. She dove, intercepting him before he could make his escape, slamming him against the waving wall-weed. "Ah, son," she crooned, biting at his earlobe as they bounced back across the chamber, "don't ever underestimate me."

He laughed and protested, "I was joking. *Ow!*"

"Of course you were joking."

"I *was.*"

Even so, it was true she had no choice but to trust him—which put the obligation on her to verify that trust.

Clemantine sent a ghost to the library to confirm that the process of construction had truly started. The Engineer and the Bio-mechanic surprised her by appearing within their frames a moment after she arrived. Always before, they'd come only when summoned.

She cocked her head, looked from one to the other, wondering if Urban had ordered them to be there. "You've begun?" she asked.

The Engineer gestured. A huge, translucent, three-dimensional model of the ship appeared, with the planned gee deck ghosted in. Dashed ribbons, brightly colored and branching like tributaries, linked the construction site to the stored matter at the ship's core. "We've begun," the Engineer confirmed.

The Bio-mechanic explained, "I've initiated the growth of matter channels to transport required material to the construction site, and carry undifferentiated tissue away."

She nodded, eyeing the ribbons. "This is the easy part."

"Easy for me," the Bio-mechanic agreed acidly. "Easy now, after the centuries I've spent studying this system."

Clemantine gritted her teeth. "I meant that this phase uses only Chenzeme biotechnology, so you don't need to be so careful. The dangerous part comes when you begin defining human spaces."

"Ah," the Bio-mechanic said. "I will keep that in mind. Do you have other advice? I do so value the advice of those wholly lacking in expertise."

Clemantine rolled her eyes. "You're a sensitive flower, aren't you?" she asked.

The Bio-mechanic's eyes narrowed. His image changed, fading into the complex background of his frame—removing himself from the conversation in a fit of pique?

She shrugged, offering no apology, making no plea for him to stay. A flicker of surprise on his part and in moments he restored himself. In a crisp voice he informed her, "I know what I'm doing."

"I'm confident of that," Clemantine answered. "And I won't insult you with amateur advice, but I do have an instruction."

"Any change in the basic structure will slow the process," the Engineer warned.

"Exactly," she said. "That's my instruction—or call it a request if the idea of an instruction exceeds whatever authority I might have. Allow no changes in the basic design. Nothing that will delay completion of the project. *If* someone attempts to introduce such a change, let me know."

"All actions and relevant discussions are recorded in a log file," the Engineer informed her. "Including this one."

"Good," she said. "I'll set a DI to monitor that log—and all the others."

She should have done it before, but she'd been lax, overwhelmed during the early days of the voyage by newness, and by the immediate demands of creating a home within the hostile body of this alien starship.

No more surprises, she resolved. She needed to comprehend her environment, understand the operation of the ship, know when tasks shifted, and when orders changed.

And she needed to discover whatever sordid detail it was that Urban didn't want her to know, even though she suspected she'd be happier *not* knowing.

She left the library, leaving the Apparatchiks to their work, but she did not return to her atrium. Instead, she entered the complex of *Dragon*'s neural bridge, intent on continuing her mission of verification.

The bridge was a cross-linked web of neural filaments extending throughout the ship, studded with cardinal nanosites—tiny processing nodes that tracked and monitored the surrounding tissue. The cardinals supported a limited virtual environment that allowed Clemantine to access the data they'd collected, in numeric and text form and also visually, so that she could see the structure of the tissue surrounding each node.

But the cardinals offered no representation of Clemantine's physical presence. She existed only as a mote of awareness, a disembodied will. It was a state she heartily loathed. Although the cardinals were easy to instruct and she had no trouble moving between them, the absence of even an illusion of physical existence left her plagued by an underlying panic, in quiet terror of being trapped in that disembodied state.

She thought of Urban. She could not sense the presence of his ghost but she knew he was somewhere on the bridge. He was always on the bridge. It dismayed her to think he endured this state all the time. She wondered if he'd edited his psyche to do it, or if his brash confidence was enough to fend off the doubt that haunted her.

Despite her doubt, her fear, her aversion to that mode of existence, she continued her inspection, moving from cardinal to cardinal, assessing the function and status of the ship's diverse array of bio-mechanical tissues, sensing its metabolic heat, aware of the incessant probing of Chenzeme nanomachines, and the firm push-back of the defensive Makers that guarded the bridge. She let herself feel it all, and she began to fit it all within a mental map, verifying what she'd been told about the structure of the ship.

It would be so easy to retreat, to leave it all in Urban's hands, to trust him in his role as master of *Dragon*—but she kept going. She had to.

It's not like you have a choice.

A teasing, taunting challenge. A dare. Asking her to look more closely.

If Urban had a guilty secret, it surely involved either their shared past or the functioning of this ship. Clemantine was still wary of immersing herself in that other life, so instead of accessing the data cache he'd set aside for her, she'd come here. Resolved to inspect the ship first, face the truth of her past later.

Nowhere among the cardinals did she encounter anything to suggest forged data in the library files, or a critical truth, hidden.

She kept at it until she could find no path she had not already explored. Then she fled, retreating directly to her atrium where her ghost memories merged with the memories of her physical avatar—alone within her chamber, just waking up, tension and fatigue tangled up together as if she'd only just escaped the grip of a bad dream.

She sighed and stretched, grateful her inspection of the cardinals was over. She did not want to go back there again.

Only as she relaxed, as her tension eased, did it occur to her she'd found no pathway leading to the philosopher cells.

CHAPTER NINE

FROM HIS POST within the restricted span of the high bridge, Urban monitored Clementine's tour of the lower cardinals. He logged the time she stayed at each node and the data she perused.

I trusted you. Past tense. She'd said it to shake him up and it had worked. She'd seen his concern and now she was looking for a discrepancy. A difference between what was and what ought to be. She wouldn't find an answer out among the cardinals, but eventually she would work it out, or Vytet would. One of them would think to run the equations on *Dragon's* immense mass.

In all likelihood, Clementine would never forgive him.

Vytet spoke to him in the library—another version of him, but he heard that conversation:

"You can't assume this pre-construction phase is safe just because it uses all Chenzeme elements," she argued, her brows knitting in frustration. "It is *not* a Chenzeme process. It will not be using elements in a way known to Chenzeme instinct."

The Bio-mechanic answered her, though from within his frame he aimed his impatient glare at the Engineer, not at Vytet. "It *is* using elements in a known way," he insisted.

The Engineer amended this claim, "To a point."

Most of the courser's mass was bio-mechanical tissue and stored material, but it was organized around a structural frame— the bones of the ship. The plan was to synthesize sheets of this framing material, shaping them into a huge cylinder surrounding a short segment of the core. The cylinder would be stationary, anchored to the ship's frame. A second cylinder within the first would rotate on magnetic tracks, just fast enough to provide a small pseudo-gravity.

Urban—that version of him in the library—said, "All we've done is to adapt the processes that we used when we grew the outriders. It'll be fine." At the same time, the version of him on the high bridge continued to track the passage of Clementine's ghost as she transited the last of the cardinals.

In the library, Vytet remained uneasy. "I'm confident the design of the gee deck will serve our purpose, *if* it's presence doesn't trigger a defensive reaction in the surrounding tissue—but it's such a large structure, it's hard to see how it could fail to be recognized as an artificial and invasive growth."

"Barrier issues are my responsibility," the Bio-mechanic said brusquely. "And I have already taken these concerns into account. The outer cylinder will have a reactive surface using Chenzeme molecular signaling to mimic the hull of an ancillary ship under construction."

"Is that a permanent solution?" Vytet asked.

"Of course," the Bio-mechanic said. "So long as the correct molecular signals are produced, the cylinder will not trigger a defensive response."

"That's not the only factor," Urban said. "It matters how fast we consume resources. The first outrider we tried to grow was lost because we went too fast. Looked like uncontrolled growth, a runaway event. The entire mass of the half-formed ship was ejected."

On the high bridge, a mental twinge. He had not meant to bring up the topic of *Dragon's* mass.

For a moment, Vytet looked distracted, her brow wrinkled as if chasing an elusive thought, but the Bio-mechanic reclaimed her attention with an acerbic dismissal of Urban's cautionary story. "Not a relevant issue," he said, waving away any concern with a sweep of his hand. "Acceptable growth rates are now well understood." He fixed his cold gaze on Vytet. "Focus your concern on your own responsibility. Leave me to mine."

From the high bridge, Urban watched Clementine's ghost depart from the last cardinal, returning to her atrium, where it vanished from his perception.

Alone in her chamber, Clemantine studied a schematic of *Dragon*'s structure, made visible through the augmented reality generated by her atrium. Glowing silver threads mapped the filaments of the neural bridge. Wherever the threads intersected, a tiny bead indicated the presence of a cardinal node.

The schematic showed tens of thousands of filaments linking to the ship's outer skin of philosopher cells, which together comprised the ship's composite mind. Those filaments were separate from the rest of the bridge. They led back to a spiraling trunkline of bridge tissue that linked to the lower threads at only a handful of points.

Clemantine was sure she must have passed those points during her inspection, but she had not perceived them. They'd been hidden from her. Her access had been limited to the lower threads only.

The message was clear. The philosopher cells were off-limits to her. Urban didn't want her interacting with them. He didn't want her tempted to interact.

Why?

She pondered this question, understood there could be many reasons. None boded well.

No doubt he was jealous of his command. *Dragon* was his pride as well as an avatar of his existence. He guarded its structure just as he guarded the structure of his own body, protecting the ship's Chenzeme elements, resisting any suggestion of re-making the courser into a human ship.

But what if the reason was some fault of hers?

I do trust you, she'd said.

He had not responded with any similar assurance, an omission that now made her suspicious of her unknown past. Had she, in that other timeline, given him reason not to trust her? Made a fatal mistake or failed at some critical juncture?

He had denied it, but could she believe him?

Easy to find out. All she had to do was access the data cache that held the details of her other life. She'd resisted because she was sure grief waited for her there. Regret too, and maybe jealousy for a life she hadn't lived.

Even so, it was weakness to hide from the truth. She'd succumbed to a failure of nerve. Shame brushed her, knowing she needed to review those records regardless of what they held.

She could confront Urban only when they stood on equal ground.

An alert reached Urban on the high bridge. A DI whispered the news. Clemantine had accessed the data cache he'd set aside for her.

Fear flushed through the architecture of his ghost, defying its limited capacity for emotion. A dangerous fear because on the high bridge his emotions and his intentions were shared across a hundred thousand connections with *Dragon*'s vast field of philosopher cells.

Fear among the cells implied an enemy unexpectedly close at hand. Casual debate gave way to immediate consensus:

<attack!>

Energy flowed to the gamma-ray gun. It began to deploy, while the Near Vicinity was re-scanned for a target. The closest object out there was the outrider, *Khonsu*.

Urban set his will against the consensus to attack—

– *hold* –

– *calm* –

—issuing this command simultaneously from his hundred thousand connections, a coordinated response that flooded the field, forcing a new consensus.

At the same time, he edited his ghost, numbing its capacity to feel fear, tension, anger, boredom. Creating the personality he thought of as the Sentinel, not really a personality at all.

A submind brought the memory of this incident to his ghost in the library. Emotions too dangerous to be experienced on the high bridge now became his. He reacted by abandoning the squabbling discussion still going on between Vytet and the Bio-mechanic. He withdrew into a different reality, a private space within the library, where he set his will against the turmoil of these emotions:

– *hold* –

– *calm* –

He had wanted Clemantine to open the cache, he'd wanted her to understand what had happened, but he feared her judgment. He feared she'd hate him for what he'd done.

I couldn't save him!

Things had gone too far. He'd had to end it. He'd had no choice—but a last accusation still echoed in his mind: *You are the courser now.*

Bitter truth.

He had only just joined himself to the courser, his control over it tenuous but real when he chose to use *Dragon's* gun for the first time, destroying what he loved and feared.

Stop! he told himself. *Don't go back there.*

That era was over and he would not revisit it. He pushed the memories away and waited for her judgment to fall.

Subminds shunted between the library and the high bridge, syncing thoughts between the dual versions of himself—the one anxious and regretful, the other artificially calm. He kept watch over the stars of the Near Vicinity as hours slipped past. Enough hours to allow her to go through everything the cache contained, his own memories part of it.

Surely she would contact him soon? Say something. He needed her to say something. Anything?

Nothing.

She didn't stir from her chamber. His fear grew. He was afraid of what she would do. Afraid she would hide herself away in cold sleep, depriving him of any chance to win her forgiveness.

He checked the ship's log, assured himself she had not retreated into cold sleep yet.

Without thinking too hard about whether or not it was a good idea, he messaged her:

Hey.

No answer. Not for ominous seconds. Then finally, a single husky syllable: *Hey.*

Enough to give him hope. *Are we okay?* he asked her.

Heh, she scoffed. *You were monitoring the cache?*

Yes, he admitted. He held his breath, waiting for her to say something more. Waiting. More seconds ticking past. Too many of them. When she finally did speak, her voice was hoarse, syllables catching in her throat:

You want to know how I feel?

He didn't answer. She knew the answer.

She said:

I don't blame you for it. That's what you want to hear, right? And it's true. You did what you had to do. You did what I hope I would have done.

Another long pause—his gratitude made this one easier to endure—before she added, *I didn't think you had it in you.*

She might have meant that as an insult or a compliment, he didn't care. He only wanted to know, *Are we okay?*

We will be, she assured him. *Now go. I need to grieve.*

CHAPTER TEN

KONA GHOSTED IN the library, afloat within a virtual space that showed him the cosmos outside, as if the ship's substance had all gone transparent, leaving him adrift in the void, surrounded by two hundred billion stars and the dark streamers of molecular clouds that would someday forge more suns, more worlds, more potential for life.

They were a year out from Deception Well.

Looking back—looking *swan*—the brilliant beacon of faraway Alpha Cygni was still easy to pick out, but he could no longer distinguish Kheth, the Well's sun, from the scattered stars beyond it. He could ask a Dull Intelligence to find Kheth for him, to draw a circle around it or artificially increase its apparent magnitude, but on his own, he'd lost track of it.

Back there somewhere lay his past. Centuries of joy and grief, terror and hope, struggle and disappointment—and quiet triumph because his people had survived. They *would* survive, Kona was confident of that, but the burden wasn't his anymore and with every passing day, he felt the weight of those years slowly lifting. As the distance separating him from Deception Well accumulated, he felt himself renewed, reinvigorated, gifted with new purpose.

He turned to look ahead. He was no astronomer, but he knew enough to pick out some of the closer stars of the Hallowed Vasties. There was Ryo, and Tanjiri, Quin-ken, Bengali. Somewhere farther, the Sun.

Did Earth still exist? Did it still rotate to a twenty-four hour day? Still revolve in a three hundred sixty-five day year? Did it still harbor some vestige of the life that had arisen there, miraculous result of a long chain of incredibly unlikely circumstances?

Up until a year ago, he had never even entertained the thought that he might someday find out. Now, he dared to imagine that in some future century he might voyage there, come to see it for himself. If so, he would come there in stages, with many stops along the way, passing the intervals between worlds primarily in cold sleep.

With the busy first year over, and the planning and design phase done, he wanted to hurry on.

He closed the virtual bubble. His ghost migrated back to his atrium, melding with his core persona, reaffirming his determination to leap forward in time. His skills were people skills. His real work would start when the ship's company was resurrected.

Now, alone in his chamber, he generated a new ghost and sent it to the archive. From there it would waken at intervals to review the progress of the ship and the status of those aboard, before returning to stasis. He also instructed a Dull Intelligence to keep watch, charging it to alert his ghost if ever there was an event, anything out of the ordinary.

After his ghost was away, he summoned a cold-sleep cocoon, closing his eyes as the cocoon's transparent mucilaginous tissue enshrouded him.

He looked forward to the future, and he'd already said his goodbyes.

Late afternoon in the forest room:

The weather algorithm had summoned gray clouds into the projected sky beyond the pergola. Clemantine appreciated the muted light as she floated in tandem with a curved screen displaying the tabular genetic data of an ornamental descendant of an ancient line of maple trees. Genetic sculpting was an art form she enjoyed, modifying not just the appearance of plants, but their life cycle as well, in this case seeking a perfect balance of autumn leaf coloration. Through her atrium, she ordered the screen to refresh, to display an accelerated simulation of the tiny tree's seasonal life cycle.

Green leaves had just begun to unfold when a DI brought her news of a course change.

Startled, Clemantine froze the simulation and sent a ghost into the library to investigate. Then, turning her gaze skyward, she sought a point of reference, settling on a white camellia blossom just above her nose. Slowly, as seconds ticked past, she watched herself and her free-floating screen drift away from the flower, scant centimeters toward the side of the room—motion so subtle she couldn't be sure of the cause until a submind returned, informing her *Dragon* was undertaking a navigational correction, using a slow, subtle lateral force to nudge the ship's immense mass. *Why?*

She waited to find out and at the end of the extended maneuver confirmed their course to be fixed a little more closely on the future position of the Tanjiri star system.

A reasonable action, then. A responsible action. And yet the incident troubled her. She should have known the adjustment was necessary. She should have known it was coming. But she wouldn't have known about it at all if she hadn't been monitoring the logs.

She thought about the process behind that correction, wondering if Urban had ordered it, or if it had been triggered by the Pilot, operating independently.

A chiding inner voice scolded: *I should know that.*

Heat rose in her cheeks, a flush of shame. More than a year had passed since her ghost had transited from cardinal to cardinal, exploring the neural bridge. She had meant to go back. She wanted to look again for the pathways leading to the spiraling trunkline and its hundred thousand filaments reaching outward to meet and link and control the vast field of philosopher cells. She wanted to confirm that she had not just missed those pathways, but that they had been hidden from her.

And yet, day after day, she'd put off the task.

At first, after opening the cache of privileged files, she had needed time to come to terms with her other existence. She felt no shame for the actions taken by her other self, but her grief ran deep. Comfort came to her through the belief that this expedition was different, that the disastrous past lay behind them, that they were embarked on a new age of discovery—or re-discovery—and that they would ultimately find evidence of vibrant, tenacious life blossoming among the ruins.

At the same time, she worried this benign outlook was fragile, that it would disintegrate if she asked too many questions. So she curbed her questions and kept busy: working with Vytet to develop a plan for the interior of the gee deck, devising a housing scheme and a landscape, and then working out the chained sequences of assembly that would bring her vision into existence.

All of that was done now. She was out of excuses.

So get on with it!

She wiped the screen she'd been using. Pulled up a schematic of the neural bridge. Reviewed its intricate, branching structure, and plotted every path that led to the trunkline. There weren't many, just thirteen. She identified the sequence of cardinal nanosites she would have to pass through to reach each one. Then, despite her aversion to the sense of disembodiment she would face among the cardinals, she sent a ghost to investigate.

Very soon, the ghost returned. It affirmed what she'd inferred over a year ago: The paths to the trunkline were not visible to her. She had no access to them.

A deep breath to gather her courage. The philosopher cells were on the other side of those hidden paths. Once she crossed over, she would be in contact with them, plunged into unfiltered communication with the ship's murderous composite mind.

She dreaded it. The Chenzeme had murdered her family, her people, her world. She wanted no intimacy with the minds behind those deeds. And still, she held it to be her duty, her responsibility, to learn all aspects of the ship. At the very least, she needed to know why Urban had closed the paths to the high bridge.

So she messaged him: *Hey. We need to talk.*

He woke his avatar and, still stretching and yawning, came to her in the forest room. She observed the moment he caught up on her recent activity, a wary look taking over his face.

She said, "You know I've visited the neural bridge."

He shrugged, as if to dismiss the topic as anything that might cause him concern. "You've been there before."

"I have. And just like before, I found that part of the bridge is not open to me. The spiral trunkline and all those filaments that link to the philosopher cells—"

"That's the high bridge," he interrupted.

"The paths to it aren't just closed," she said. "You've hidden them. Why?"

"Because I don't want you there. It would be dangerous."

She raised her eyebrows, though she gave him credit for the blunt honesty of this answer. "Dangerous for who?" she asked.

"For you, and for all of us."

"You go there."

"I'm used to it. I understand it."

"I want to understand it."

"No, you don't. You don't want to be immersed in Chenzeme thoughts, Chenzeme conversation, millennia of memories, the murder of worlds."

"You've seen that?" she asked, her gut clenching.

"Yes. And you don't want to experience it. You don't want it to touch you."

Clementine let out a slow breath. "You don't need to protect me."

"I'm not sure that's true."

"Trust me when I tell you that it is. You're right that I don't *want* to interface with a Chenzeme mind. But I do want to learn this ship, to understand how it operates, how you integrate with it. I want to learn from you what it takes to pilot *Dragon*—and if the cost of that is intimacy with the philosopher cells, so be it. I'll take it on."

His jaw clenched in frustration; he shook his head. "*Why?* Why do you feel you need to do this?"

"Because it's dangerous for me, for you, for everyone, if you're the only one capable of handling this ship. If something happens to you—"

"Nothing is going to happen to me."

"I believe you, and still, you shouldn't be the only one to know."

Intimacy, she'd called it, and Urban found that it was a strange intimacy to feel her ghostly presence overlaid against his own in the branching fibers of the high bridge.

He didn't want her there. He knew her history, and understood the horror she must feel at interacting so directly with the philosopher cells. He also worried her presence would change the temper of the cells, feeding their suspicions, making it harder to bring them to consensus. Mostly, he resented her implication that he was vulnerable, that he might someday be separated from his ship, that someone else might need to take over.

But none of these objections were sufficient grounds to refuse her request. Clemantine believed she could handle the experience. It would be petty and paternalistic to deny her—and besides, she would never forgive him.

So he'd opened the high bridge to her.

Before her first visit, they'd met in the library. He'd warned her, "If you feel overwhelmed, if you can't suppress an emotional reaction, I need you to retreat. If you stay, you'll destabilize the cell field."

"All right. I understand."

Clemantine kept her voice level, but even a ghost existence could not mute her escalating anxiety. She closed her eyes, took a few seconds to gather herself. Then she departed for the neural bridge, leaving behind all illusion of physical existence.

A mapped path brought her to the trunkline. From there, a brief, terrifying moment as her awareness flowed to fill the great network of branching fibers. Then she was plunged into the swirling, combative conversation of the philosopher cells. The bridge translated their intent, their emotion, the bite of their hateful aggression.

She recoiled.

Careful, Urban messaged her, much too late.

Her revulsion and fear spilled across a hundred thousand connections, flooding the cell field. The cells re-echoed her emotions, amplified them, sought the cause behind them as they debated in a complex language she comprehended but could not effectively translate so that she "heard" it only in primitive phrases:

<revulsion: all that is not chenzeme>

<we are strong>

<locate target: identify>

<all that is not chenzeme: kill it>

<target: not found>

<kill it!>

By the Unknown God, she whispered to Urban—and then she withdrew.

Just like the cells, he had been hit by the force of her fear and revulsion. It left him shaken, but he suppressed that and worked to soothe the philosopher cells.

Simultaneously, he awaited her in the library.

She appeared before him, wild-eyed, lips parted. "You're there all the time," she whispered in horror. "Some version of you."

"Some of the time I use an edited version," he admitted. "I call it the Sentinel. Low empathy. Emotionally numb." He tapped his chest. "But it's still my core persona that makes all the decisions. You could do that too."

Eyes half-closed, she nodded, visibly recovering her composure. "Right now I need to be able to handle it as me. I'm going back in."

She shifted from the library to the high bridge. Again, she became a disembodied presence that dispersed to fill the network of fibers, Urban there with her, everywhere. No breath to hold or she would have held her breath against the vicious, tumultuous conversation that engulfed her. Sadistic longings. Frustrated hates. The philosopher cells still restless, still seeking a target that would let them satisfy an instinct to burn/kill/sterilize.

Revolted again, she slipped away, back into the library.

Urban met her there. Saw the shudder run through her. "You don't have to do this."

Her fist closed. "I *can* do this."

She shifted out of the library, but not to the high bridge. She needed to breathe, so she returned to her core persona. Alone in her chamber, she shivered and gasped, her heart raced, tears escaped to drift in the air around her, reflecting light like precious gems. "I *can* do this," she growled aloud. "I can. I *can*."

More than ninety minutes slipped past before Urban again felt her join him on the high bridge. This time, she came knowing what to expect; she had prepared herself. He felt her as a calm, glassy presence that allowed the endless conversations of the philosopher cells to pass through her, without touching her.

She stayed there with him, far longer than she'd stayed before.

After a time, she messaged him: *This conversation ... it's like mindless, poisonous froth riding on the surface of an ocean of memory.*

Not mindless, he replied. *The cells are a composite mind operating as minds do.*

Later, in the library, he explained it in more detail:

"Each cell has its own senses, a particular awareness, a cache of memories, and a measure of influence in the cell field. That influence waxes and wanes depending on the success of the hypotheses and ideas that it supports. That's what most of the chatter is: discussion and argument on the meaning of sensory input evaluated against known data. You can enter that debate. The bridge gives you enough influence to command consensus—but you will always need to be careful that the field doesn't coerce a consensus out of you."

Clemantine hated the philosopher cells, hated interacting with them, but the strength of her hate made them amenable to her will.

She learned to perceive as they did, through the senses of the ship: the carefully nurtured vitality of the reef; the burn of dust against the hull field; the slight gravitational perturbation generated by the closest outrider and the occasional incoming bursts of laser communications that marked its position; the population of stars in the Near Vicinity; the chaotic radio chatter of background radiation.

She sensed the link to the gamma-ray gun. Explored a memory of a time—she guessed it was long ago—when the gun had been used against another ship, one vastly larger even than *Dragon*. She felt the excitement of the philosopher cells, their frantic demand to

<*kill it*>

Suppressing a mental shudder, she diverted the cells from the violence of that memory by giving them a task. A simple task, but it was the first time she exerted her will on them.

She asked them to push *Dragon*'s velocity a little higher, just to do it, to know that she could.

She thought: – *go* –

Lightly, easily.

In response, a spike of awareness: Urban shadowing her, his concern for what she was doing. But he said nothing, nor tried to interfere.

Again, she thought: – *go* –

The cells responded, commanding just a tiny pull of acceleration from the reef. She felt it as a shift, a sense of falling forward, so slight she wondered if it would even be noticed in the warren. But then she suppressed that thought, not wanting to distract the cells.

Enough, she decreed.

The acceleration ceased, but *Dragon*'s velocity was now slightly higher. Urban issued an order to the outriders to boost their velocity to match.

Clementine visited the high bridge often during the second year of the voyage, but never alone. "You're always there," she mused, lying entwined with Urban one morning. "Your ghost, always present. You must get tired of it. You have to find it . . ." She groped for the right words. "Emotionally exhausting," she decided.

"Did you want to take over?" he asked with that familiar taunting smile. "Hijack my ship?"

"Mind reader."

He chuckled. "You've learned everything I know."

"No, that's not true."

Still, she'd learned a lot. She'd skimmed the ship's history, delved into its systems, interviewed the Apparatchiks, and refined her control of the philosopher cells.

She had needed to verify all those systems to truly trust him. *And I do.*

She kissed his cheek and sniggered.

"What?" he demanded.

"Just remembering what an asshole you used to be when you were younger."

He chuckled some more. "Come on. You found me entertaining."

"Always," she agreed.

A comfortable silence followed, one she eventually interrupted with a softly spoken promise, "We'll have years together."

"Sooth," he agreed, sounding half asleep. But then his eyelids fluttered, his brows knit in a suspicious scowl.

She said, "I'm going into cold sleep."

His eyes snapped open. "*No.*"

"Yes. I'm going to skip ahead to when the engineering phase of the gee deck is done. The Engineer estimates two more years to finish the assembly of the inner cylinder, the rotational mechanism, the permanent supply lines, the heat sinks. Then it'll be my turn to assemble the interior landscape."

The Bio-mechanic had warned her it would take an additional year to complete the interior and lay in material reserves. After that, they would finally be able to waken their company of archived ghosts.

She said, "I'm looking forward to the future, Urban. I'm eager to start my project. So I'm going to jump to that point in time."

"But what am I supposed to do while you're down?"

She rolled her eyes. "It's just two years. Aren't you the one who voyaged alone across six centuries?"

He sighed a heartfelt sigh. "I was younger, then."

"You'll get by," she assured him. "You'll be there on the high bridge whether I'm awake or not, whether I'm *there* or not. Nothing will change. And if you need to, you'll adjust your time sense so the years don't burden you. I know you've done it before."

He sighed again, gazing at her unhappily. "The times in between matter too."

"We'll have time," she insisted. "We'll be okay."

THIRD

Time heals all.

It is an ancient aphorism that surfaces in your mind as if by chance.

You are aware that a billion seconds have gone by since you resolved to take revenge. A billion seconds spent in reconstruction of your ravaged memories.

A billion seconds.

More than enough to know that time does *not* heal all, that it cannot, because the circumstances that created you will not exist again in any future you can foresee.

Judged strictly, the aphorism is false.

You understand though that the aphorism is not meant as a binary true/false statement. Instead, it is intended as encouragement in the process of recovering from grievous emotional wounds. That you are aware of this distinction reflects the progress of your own slow recovery.

You walk the tunnels that honeycomb the cold crust of your world; miles of tunnels restored or rebuilt. Thousands of miles more lie still in ruins but you will get to them in time, if time allows. At this time, you focus your mind on what you've accomplished, not what remains to be done.

Re-grown in ordered ranks on walls and ceiling, are the thin, crystalline leaves of your computational strata. Now, as always, your mind works to gather scraps of data and memories from the ruins.

You organize what you find, analyzing and testing as you do so, seeking to place it all again into proper context although with no outside means to cross-check results, you know there will be errors.

Still, you do your best and second by second your mind recovers. You remember more and more. You are capable of more and more.

Another billion seconds, and you have used resources stored in the subterranean ocean to grow telescopes, and subsurface silos to house them. When the silos open, you look out on the cosmos for the first time since she destroyed you. You map the position of your world and realize: *There is not time enough.*

You are light years from anywhere. No star holds you within its gravity well. She has cast you away, flung your world into the void. You are alone, alone, alone. Stranded, with no way back.

Terror stirs deep within the biological structure of your ancestral mind. You experience it and then the sense of shame that follows it—shame of both your fear and your defeat.

You could cut both fear and shame from your persona but why would you? The old passions sustain you. They give you all the reason you need to go on. So you remind yourself that her cruelty, her jealousy, her fury, marooned you here.

This helps to focus your mind.

You continue your observations. You hunt through your shattered memories, seeking astronomical data and eventually you are able to recognize the closest stars, map their relative positions, and determine your precise location in both space and time.

Quite a lot of time has passed, but less than you would have guessed.

In the course of your astronomical survey you observe a hint, a glint, a tiny reflection where you are sure no reflection should be. For eight and a half million seconds you watch it as it moves against the background stars.

Does she regret her fury? Has she sent some monstrous servant to look for you, to fetch you back? *No.* Wishful thinking, that.

More likely some other entity observed your defeat, your disgrace, and is coming now to pick over your bones.

You ponder this as you walk the corridors of your wounded mind—and you prepare. You hide your presence, disguising the telescopes so that the surface of your world once again appears to be that of a dead and airless rogue world.

There will still be an infrared signature, but that will be attributed to the subterranean ocean cooling only very slowly with the passage of time.

Another aphorism: *The best defense is a good offense.*

You begin to prepare.

You will never be more than a shadow of your former presence. Still, you remain formidable.

CHAPTER ELEVEN

THREE POINT SIX years out of Deception Well:

From his solitary post on the high bridge, Urban observed an anomalous flash of pale blue light. He saw it through the composite mind of the philosopher cells. A brief, bright flare ahead of the courser, slightly offset from its trajectory.

Furious speculation erupted among the hull cells. The memory of a similar incident circulated among them, a familiar memory, one that Urban shared. Like the cells, he'd seen that same spectrum of light flare and die before. He knew what it meant.

He replicated into the library, sending the rage and frustration rising within him safely away from the cell field, while the copy of his ghost that remained on the high bridge reconfigured, taking the form of the imperturbable Sentinel.

In that form, he sensed the alarm winding through every cross-threaded conversation among the philosopher cells, and their growing awareness of impending danger. He entered the conversation. Determined to soothe the field, he introduced the same argument at a hundred thousand points:

– *hold* –

– *calm* –

The composite mind of the philosopher cells had recognized the flash of light as the visible energy emitted by the explosion of an outrider. Urban didn't know yet which one.

A faction of cells wanted to interpret the incident as a hostile attack, but a far larger number sought consensus for the proposition that what had happened was a fluke, an accident, the result of a collision with a high-speed fragment of matter—a conclusion Urban encouraged.

No reason to believe otherwise. No evidence of another hostile presence anywhere in the Near Vicinity.

Even so, the cells were correct. The hazard was not ended. The danger they anticipated would come from secondary effects that required time to play out.

A report streamed in. Relayed at light speed through the array of outriders, it arrived only a few seconds after the light of the explosion. Each outrider had appended a signature as the report passed through its data gate.

Urban received the report in the library. A submind shared news of it to the high bridge. On both timelines, he noted the signatures of only the three nearest outriders. *Khonsu*, the closest, *Artemis* next, and then *Lam Lha*. *Pytheas* had been stationed beyond *Lam Lha*. The absence of its signature told him it was *Pytheas* he'd lost.

The report unfolded into two windows. One displayed text data, the other, the raw video of the starfield that lay ahead of the fleet.

Urban summoned all six of the Apparatchiks. They manifested in a curved row behind the report, each confined within its own frameless window.

"Analyze it," Urban ordered them, wanting opinions from them all.

The simulation of a faint vibration alerted him. He looked to the right as Vytet's ghost popped into existence beside him.

Vytet had never sought the refuge of cold sleep. "I think there are never enough minutes in the day," she'd explained when Urban asked about it. "I want to monitor the progress of the gee deck, of course, but I could spend a millennium in the library and not reach the end of what there is to do and to learn."

Since that time, Vytet had shifted gender and updated the envelope of his appearance. His nose had become more prominent, the pelt of his hair had shifted from white to dark red, and his eyes were darker, deeper-set beneath a heavier brow. "What happened?" he asked in a calm masculine voice as he scanned the report.

Urban told him, "I've lost *Pytheas.*"

"Lost?"

Bitter admission: "I saw it explode."

Clemantine and Kona ghosted in, lagging several seconds behind Vytet—the time it had taken their personal DIs to summon their dormant ghosts from the archive.

Clemantine met his gaze. She'd been away a year and a half, but he'd adapted his time sense to match hers. It felt to him as if she'd been away only hours, while she perceived the time as a sequence of discrete intervals when her ghost had wakened only long enough to assess the status of the ship. That left no awkwardness, no alienation in their reunion.

"*Pytheas* hit something and blew apart," he said to ensure that she and Kona understood that basic fact. He indicated the frameless window containing the starfield. "This is video from *Lam Lha.*"

It didn't look like a video. There was no visible motion. The stars were much too far away for their movement to be perceptible, and *Pytheas* was too small, dark, cold, and distant to be captured by *Lam Lha*'s array of cameras. Only the digital clock streaming through fractional seconds in the window's lower right corner indicated this was not a still image.

A hiss from Clemantine as a spark of blue-white light burst into sight. Flared, and disappeared.

Now the stars moved, the entire field rotating together through a narrow arc.

"*Lam Lha* is repositioning itself," Urban explained. "Aiming its prow at the point of the explosion, to minimize its profile and reduce the odds of impact from any surviving debris." His ghost hand closed into a fist, his temper finally escaping. "By the Unknown God! We are not even *four years* out of Deception Well!"

"You're sure it was an accident?" Kona asked. "You're certain we're alone out here?"

"*Yes.* I'm sure of that much."

"But can you be sure it was a collision?" Vytet asked. "Or might it have been caused by instability in the outrider's reef?"

"The reef is monitored. If there was a problem, it would have been detected and addressed."

"I'll check the data anyway," Vytet volunteered. "In case something was missed."

Urban ignored this. Nothing had been missed. He turned to Kona and Clemantine. "This happened before," he told them. "It's not complicated. The outriders are fragile. They don't have the mass to absorb the energy of a high-speed impact. The concern now is secondary effects."

He gestured at the starfield. "*Lam Lha, Artemis, Khonsu, Dragon.* All four ships were following *Pytheas.* All four are at risk. It's going to take time, but eventually each ship will intersect the trailing edge of the debris field and when that happens, there's a real chance of another impact."

"Surely not," Vytet objected with a puzzled frown. "Given the distances between the outriders and the low relative delta V of the debris, the field will have time to disperse across an immense volume of space before the next outrider reaches its perimeter. That will work to minimize any risk of collision."

"I used to think so too," Urban answered. "But remember the reef. It doesn't behave like normal matter."

As if summoned by his warning, tiny points of blue-tinged light blossomed in a cluster at the center of the video. "There," Urban said, feeling vindicated. "That's the debris field. That blue light is generated by remnants of the reef, energized by the explosion. The fragments will try to coalesce, and as they do, they'll warp the surrounding space, affect the trajectory of the debris. Some of it will gather and fall into their fields."

They watched for several seconds as the blue light brightened. Specks shifted relative to one another. A few merged, brightening again when they made contact. Others drifted away.

Clemantine spoke quietly. "Can we use the gamma-ray gun to target the visible debris? Vaporize it?"

Given her history, it surprised Urban to hear her propose the use of the gun. Such monstrous Chenzeme weapons had taken so much from her. But she regarded him now with a hard pragmatic gaze.

As he hesitated, the Engineer took on the task of answering her question, explaining, "The tactic is impractical at this time. The debris is over four light-hours away and tumbling in an unpredictable manner—and the beam is narrow. It's unlikely to find a target."

"Then we modify our course," Clemantine said, her gaze still fixed on Urban.

This time, the Pilot responded: "Course adjustments are being undertaken. Instructions are already outbound, directing the fleet away from the debris."

Of all the Apparatchiks, the Mathematician looked the most like Urban, even dressed like him in dark, simple clothing—not as any kind of acknowledgment of common origin, but because he just didn't care about appearance and could not be bothered to modify it. In personality he was reserved and reticent, but he spoke now, explaining, "Shifting the fleet's course and slowing its momentum will reduce the danger, but not eliminate it. The debris field will have inherited *Pytheas*'s momentum. It will continue to coast on the fleet's original heading, even as dispersive forces contend against the exotic physics of the reef. It might be years before the threat is left behind."

Urban nodded agreement. Like he'd said, he'd been through this before.

On the video, the blue sparks dimmed. After several more seconds, they disappeared, leaving nothing visible to mark the shattered remains of *Pytheas*.

"Gone dark," Kona said. "But still a threat. Can we implement a radar system to try to map the debris?"

"As the distance decreases we should be able to track the larger fragments," the Engineer said. "But fragments too small to be detected can still cause critical damage to the outriders."

The danger was unseen and would remain unknowable, but it was all too real. Urban envisioned the lost outrider as a revenant spray of kinetic projectiles hurtling through the void, with some small but critical percentage of them speeding along trajectories that would inevitably take them toward the trailing ships in the fleet.

Clemantine duplicated her ghost.

She sent one version to the high bridge where she listened to the braided conversations of the philosopher cells as they analyzed the loss of *Pytheas* and debated the value of different mathematical models meant to predict the dispersion of debris.

Her other ghost she sent into the library's circular research room, where stacks of files surrounded her. She summoned the Scholar.

On the main floor of the library the Apparatchiks always appeared confined within the virtual space of a frame, but here among the stacks, the Scholar instantiated without any such restriction. He stood facing her, dressed in what she considered a formal fashion: a long, loose, dark-blue tunic and voluminous trousers of the same color.

The Scholar was the Apparatchik who looked the least like Urban. His aspect was older, his features sharper, his eyes a strange violet gray, and he'd styled his hair so that it was smooth and long. Tied at the back of his head, it reached his waist.

"I want to know more about the first time an outrider was lost," Clemantine told him.

He eyed her with an unsettling intensity, and then nodded. "I have a brief report prepared for you." He touched a file, seemingly at random, and a door opened onto another circular room. "Follow, please."

She traded subminds with her ghost on the high bridge, where her attention was caught by a centuries-old memory brought into play among a cluster of philosopher cells. The memory circulated as more and more individual cells found value in it and passed it on. It was a study of ballistic motion, like the simulations tracking *Pytheas*'s debris field—a chaotic, tumbling collision of particles ranging in size from dust motes to meter-wide lumps—but this played out far more quickly.

It came to her: Like her, the philosopher cells were interested in the history of that first lost outrider. They were using remembered data from that original incident to test a new mathematical model meant to predict the dispersion of debris.

Ahead of her, the Scholar stepped through the open doorway into another room within the library. Clemantine followed him, but drew back when she saw Vytet already there—this new Vytet, not the Vytet she remembered—and Vytet looked equally taken aback by the sudden company.

In all the vastness of the library, what were the odds of running into someone else? *Excellent*, if both were chasing the same topic.

Vytet recovered his composure first, saying, "This room is devoted to Khonsu, both the ancient deity and the outrider that bears its name. I expect we're both here for that reason."

His low voice disturbed her. She was too accustomed to thinking of him as a woman. She had liked him that way. "So you decided to go over to the other side," she said, striving for a humorous tone. Mostly failing.

His smile was sharp-edged. "I like the shift of perspective. It forces me to see things from a different point of view. You should try it sometime."

"I'm good. Thank you."

Ignoring this exchange, the Scholar touched a file, again seemingly at random. A screen unfolded from it, displaying an unfamiliar starfield. After a few seconds, Clemantine saw a distant flare of blue light. The Scholar pointed, saying, "*There*. That is the moment the outrider that first bore the name of *Khonsu* was lost." After several more seconds, blue sparks appeared, marking the remnants of the shattered reef.

"The dispersion of the debris was monitored and mapped to the extent possible," the Scholar explained as the video transitioned to show the hypothesized spread.

Clemantine nodded. From her post on the high bridge, she'd already seen a model of *Khonsu*'s debris field—one sketched with more certainty than this. In the Scholar's rendition, most of the fragments were transparent, barely there, reflecting a lack of certainty in their positions or maybe their existences. But both models depicted objects subject to an unnatural physics, following curved paths, even spiraling around each other, as if drawn by magnetism or an unaccountable gravity, before tumbling apart and disappearing.

The Scholar said, "We believe that at this point the fragments of the reef expired."

Clemantine eyed the time scale in the corner of the display. "After just a few hours?" she asked.

The Scholar confirmed this with a nod. "We were unable to track the debris after that point."

On the high bridge, currents of thought wove across the cell field, coalescing, diverging. Several threads considered the existence of a new ancillary ship already growing within *Dragon*'s tissue.

A ship?

Clemantine's surprise at this concept bled out into the cells, where it ignited a responding suspicion. She remembered then: *It's not a ship. It's the gee deck.*

The philosopher cells had been deceived into perceiving the deck as a nascent ship—that was its camouflage—but Clemantine had stumbled, introducing doubt, and now the philosopher cells were questioning the legitimacy of the nascent ship.

She needed to correct that, soothe their doubt, allay suspicion— but Urban got there first with a concise argument that flooded the field from a hundred thousand points:

– negate that! –

Suspicion collapsed. Doubt evaporated. The focus of conversation shifted back to the dispersion of debris.

A submind brought the memory of this incident to the library. Clemantine pursed her ghost lips, annoyed with Urban for stepping in so quickly, but intrigued by the vision of an ancillary ship growing within *Dragon*'s tissue.

Vytet was saying, "Can this be right? An interval of fourteen days before the second ship was lost?"

"That is correct," the Scholar confirmed. "That second ship was *Artemis*. At the time, it was the closest outrider to *Khonsu*."

The Mathematician had warned the debris could remain a hazard for years, but Clemantine was skeptical. "Your model shows the reef affecting the debris for only the first few hours. The dispersion would follow standard physics after that. Surely, after fourteen days, it would be spread too thin to constitute a hazard. Is it possible the fleet was passing through a pre-existing debris field? The shattered remnants of a lost comet or an asteroid? And that both impacts were caused by that primordial hazard?"

"That would be an extremely unlikely occurrence," the Scholar said. "But it cannot be ruled out."

Vytet shook his head, the dark-red pelt of his hair a helmet framing his intense expression. "I don't think that theory is any more unlikely than the idea that some fragment of debris, after fourteen days adrift, just *chanced* to intersect the course of an outrider."

"So really, we don't know what happened that first time," Clemantine said. "And that means we have no idea what level of risk we're facing now."

"In my judgment," the Scholar said, "that is an accurate assessment."

She pressed a knuckle to her chin and, thinking out loud, she mused, "I wonder if Urban will want to replace *Pytheas*?" Doubt intruded. "I wonder if he can? The philosopher cells perceive the gee deck as an ancillary ship under construction. Would they be willing to support two growing ships?"

The Scholar drew back, looking uneasy, unsure—just a brief slip before he restored his habitual stern expression, but enough to stir in her a vague suspicion.

"It has been done before," he assured her, gentle-voiced, as if explaining things to a child.

Clemantine wanted details, but Vytet's enthusiasm was engaged. He jumped back into the conversation, declaring, "I've always meant to look into this process. It's astonishing to think that *Dragon* has given up enough mass to produce the six original outriders and the two replacements."

Clemantine cocked her head. Vytet was right. It *was* astonish-

ing. So much so that something felt off. Her initial suspicion deepened. "All that," she said thoughtfully, "and yet *Dragon* remains
such a large courser. How much larger was this ship when Urban
first hijacked it?"

To her astonishment, the Scholar shrugged—a dismissive gesture, foreign to his usual formal manner. "Early records are incomplete," he explained. "But this venture has always operated on the
edge of possibility."

Did he mean that as a philosophical answer?

Clemantine traded a puzzled look with Vytet. "In my experience, a massive courser escorted by six outriders constitutes a formidable fleet. I don't call that operating on the edge."

Vytet nodded agreement. "Mass will always be a limiting factor,
but Urban must have felt very comfortable with *Dragon's* reserves,
since he chose to replace both lost ships."

"All lost ships must be replaced," the Scholar said. "The sensing
capability of the fleet is essential. Without it, *Dragon* would be
vulnerable to a stealth approach from a true Chenzeme starship."

On the Null Boundary Expedition Clemantine had witnessed
just that kind of stealth approach. Her ghost existence did not
prevent a shiver as she remembered it. "By the Unknown God,"
she murmured. "Near or far, I hope to never see another Chenzeme starship again."

Urban used radar to study the span and the composition of the
debris field, but he was able to detect only a handful of objects,
widely scattered. None posed a threat to the fleet.

The Pilot said: *I need Pytheas to be replaced.*

It will be, Urban assured him. *In time.*

The outriders held backups of *Dragon's* library, but they served
primarily as scouts and watch posts. All were part of *Dragon's* telescope array. With *Pytheas* gone, the Pilot's oversight of the Near
Vicinity was degraded.

It will be replaced in less time if we initiate growth now, the Pilot
carped.

Urban strove to keep his voice soothing and reasonable. *You know the gee deck has reduced our reserves of essential elements. You know the Engineer has advised against initiating growth of a new outrider until those elements can be replaced.*

*The Engineer offered a second option.

*I'm not going to cannibalize the gee deck, Urban told him.

By the Unknown God, Clemantine would kill him if he undid all their work of the past two years. The gee deck needed to be finished.

He told the Pilot, **You know I have to balance multiple priorities. Use what you have. Monitor the Near Vicinity as best you can.*

After a day, when there was nothing more to see or do, Clemantine retired again to the archive. As before, her ghost roused at regular intervals to conduct a routine status check of the ship.

Urban tracked her ghost during those inspection tours, each lasting less than a minute. He adjusted his time sense to match the time that she perceived, even as he remained aware of every second, every hour, every day that slipped past.

Five days, and then ten, and then fourteen.

The first time Urban had lost outriders, fourteen days had separated the two incidents. This time, the fourteenth day passed quietly. The fifteenth day followed it, and then the sixteenth.

Twenty days went by. Then thirty. Forty. Fifty. Sixty.

Urban dared to believe they'd be all right.

Then the sixty-third day arrived and his sanguine belief shattered. From his post on the high bridge, he saw the explosion—a diaphanous flash of blue light so brilliant, so close, he knew it was *Khonsu,* the last outrider in his vanguard, closest to *Dragon.*

He adopted the protective filter of the Sentinel, aloof and untouchable, as a fearsome debate raged among the philosopher cells.

The temperament of the cells was forever malign, aggressively hateful, imbued with unrelenting anger. No gentleness in them, no sense of wonder or awareness of the magnificence of creation. They were a machine mind tasked with carrying out the genocide of technological species. Nothing more. Nothing less.

They'd captured the explosion of *Khonsu* in memory. Now they replayed the event, over and over, analyzing every aspect of it. Urban felt the intellectual effort as they fought to develop an explanation for the incident, and to determine what the potential threat might be.

Clemantine's ghost joined him on the high bridge. *This shouldn't have happened*, she messaged. He felt her anger, even against the agitation of the cell field.

It's not over, he warned her.

Sooth. What happens when the cell field is damaged by debris?

We keep control, he warned her. *Regardless of what happens.*

The philosopher cells comprehended the threat. They monitored the expansion of the debris field, a task made easier this time because *Khonsu* had been so much closer than *Pytheas*. They identified three fragments with enough mass and relative momentum to seriously damage *Dragon*'s hull if they struck.

An alliance of cells submitted a proposition: <*deploy the gun: vaporize the threat*>

A sharp spike of excitement from Clemantine. When she'd suggested using the gun before, distance and the chaotic movement of the debris had made it impractical. Now, the situation was different.

She pointed this out, in a bitterly ironic voice: *The philosopher cells have experience enough to know their range—and they're confident.*

Sooth, Urban agreed, too aware of the history of destruction contained within the memory of the cell field. *But it's not without cost.*

He'd used the gamma-ray gun when he'd hijacked the ship, and twice more since then, but he did not like using it. *The gun pulls so much power, it weakens the propulsion reef and destabilizes the ship.*

He considered denying the philosopher cells the option of the gun. He had the ability to do that. Over the centuries he'd expanded and strengthened the branching structure of the bridge, increasing its links to the cell field so that he could overwhelm any debate among the philosopher cells and drive the discussion to the consensus he desired.

But he already needed to replace two outriders. He did not want to risk the added burden of major damage to *Dragon*—and he could not predict the path of the debris because of the unknown effects of *Khonsu*'s shattered propulsion reef.

Let the cells have their way, he told Clemantine.

All right. Her tone grim, but eager. She wanted to see this, to experience it from the other side, from behind the gun this time. No longer helpless prey.

They withheld input, let the cells find consensus on their own. It didn't take long. The window of opportunity was limited. The cells had to act while the fragments retained heat and could be easily tracked.

The gun was deployed. Its lens pivoted, lining up on the projected path of the tumbling debris. The reef blazed in Urban's awareness. Power surged to the gun. Once, twice, three times. Urban felt the force of it like a parallel universe punching through and twisting strands of space-time, destabilizing the internal structure of the ship.

By the Unknown God, Clemantine swore.

The moment passed. The cells went quiet, waiting, watching.

I had no idea it'd be like that, she said. *It felt like . . . a chaos of tidal forces ripping open the ship.*

I hate it, Urban admitted.

Sooth. I hope we never have to use it again.

She stayed on the high bridge with him, waiting to see if the philosopher cells had hit their targets. Eventually, still riding the senses of the ship, Urban picked out three glowing vapor clouds.

There! he said. *It's done.*

CHAPTER TWELVE

URBAN FELT THE future of his expedition to the Hallowed Vasties at risk. Not because he couldn't replace two lost outriders. He'd done that before. He would do it again, in time. But because he would now have to reveal all the facts of *Dragon*'s history far sooner than he'd planned—and that could end the expedition.

They were just a few years out from Deception Well and although it would take many more years to reverse momentum and return, they were still close enough to make it a real option. Once Clemantine learned what was to come she might demand to go back, and if she insisted, he would have to comply. No way would he ever force her to stay with him.

He messaged everyone, while their ghosts were still active: *We need to talk about our future—and I don't want to do this as ghosts in the library. Let's all meet in the forest room, in one hour.

He hoped the warmth, the reality, the subtle chemical interaction of living people would work to his benefit—and he wanted no interruptions from the Apparatchiks.

Questions came back to him.

His only answer was to repeat: *One hour.

He woke his avatar from cold sleep, rising to consciousness amid the swaying ribbons of wall-weed in his chamber. Blinked his eyes and felt his gut knot in anxiety. Guilt was there too, though he tried to reject it. He hadn't lied, exactly.

Well, he *had*.

A lie of omission because he knew Clemantine never would have agreed to come if he'd told her the full truth.

He dressed and went early to the forest room. Evening was falling, casting a rosy glow through the pergola. Lanterns drifting within the perimeter nooks gleamed with soft light. White moths fluttered around them, casting erratic shadows.

He chose a nook, hooked his foot into a stirrup, and turned to face the entrance. He did not have to wait long.

After just a few minutes, Clemantine floated in. She saw him, and kicked off the wall, gliding the short distance to join him, holding out her hand. He took it, and they hugged. He breathed in the sweet, rich scent of her. "I love you," he whispered.

She drew back, suspicion igniting in her eyes. "You're really in trouble, aren't you?"

"Yes," he agreed ruefully, offering no resistance as she pulled away.

Vytet came in next, looking distracted, as if his mind was engaged elsewhere—until he joined them in the nook. Then his attention lit on Urban. "Is it an issue of resources?" he asked.

"Let's discuss it altogether," Urban said tersely though he suspected it was being discussed in an exchange of messages not addressed to him.

Vytet's eyes narrowed. He traded a glance with Clemantine. Then they both turned toward the entrance just as Kona glided in.

"All right," Kona said as he joined them. "This must be about the outriders." He hooked a bare foot under a stirrup, and Urban found himself the subject of a stern, all-too-familiar gaze that sent him back through time, twelve hundred years, to when he was a kid in pursuit of adventure and ever short on good judgment.

"You're going to have a hard time replacing the lost outriders. Is that correct?" Kona asked.

"Yes," Urban agreed. "That's right." Feeling off balance, his planned speech already blown. "If it was just a question of mass alone, *Dragon* would be able to easily re-grow the lost ships—"

"But some necessary elements are in short supply," Kona finished for him. "You don't have them in sufficient quantity."

Despite his growing ire, Urban was impressed. He'd thought

Vytet would work it out, or Clemantine, but the old man had gotten there first. "That's right," he agreed. "That's the issue."

"You didn't plan for this?" Kona asked.

"Oh, I did. I just didn't think it'd become an issue this early."

"Say it, then," Clemantine urged him, her voice low and dangerous.

"I have to postpone completion of the gee deck. We can finish
the engineering phase, but work on the interior has to wait—along
with the resurrection of the ship's company."

"You're not serious," she said.

"I am. I'm sorry."

"We owe our people a life, Urban. You can't keep them archived
forever."

"I don't want to keep them archived forever! That is not my
intention. But I need time to recover from this loss."

Kona said, "You must have had the elements set aside to finish
the deck."

"Yes," Urban agreed. "And I still have them. I *could* finish the
deck. But that would leave nothing. No reserves. No way to grow
another outrider. And I'm already down to four. If I lose another—"

"You're saying our people have to wait," Clemantine interrupted, "while you devote resources to re-growing your fleet?"

"*No.* I don't have the resources to re-grow both outriders. I'd
have to cannibalize the gee deck to do it, and while the Engineer
thinks we *could* do that, there's risk involved, a possibility of destabilizing the boundaries, and even if that didn't happen, we'd run a
similar risk starting all over again later—"

Clemantine cut him off. "We are not cannibalizing the gee deck."

"I agree," he said, gripping a wall loop to stabilize himself. "That
is not going to happen."

"Do we even need to replace the outriders?" Kona asked. "Can
we go with just the four ships we have left? Even three might be
enough."

To Urban's surprise, Clemantine answered this. "The Scholar
believes we're vulnerable to a stealth Chenzeme attack without all
six outriders monitoring the Near Vicinity."

"It's true," Urban said. "The Pilot will tell you the same thing. And you've seen now how easily the outriders can be destroyed. We're a long way from the Hallowed Vasties. There's a real chance we'll lose another before we get there."

Vytet said, "I don't think anyone is arguing against the advantage of a full fleet. If six is the ideal number, six is the number we should aim for. The question is, how do you intend to replace them? We are deep in the void. There is nothing out here but us. Must we divert to a planetary system?"

"It will take decades to set up a mining operation," Kona said, his forehead wrinkled in thought as if he was already planning key steps in the operation.

"That's not what we're going to do," Urban said. He drew a deep breath, then plunged ahead. "*Dragon* is a predator. It hunts other ships to consume them, to use their mass, to harvest the rare elements they carry. That's how its sustained. That's how it grows. That's how I've been able to grow the fleet of outriders."

"Other ships?" Clemantine asked. "What other ships?"

"Right," he said. "The only ships you're ever going to see out here are Chenzeme coursers. I hunt Chenzeme coursers. I've done it twice before."

Clemantine ducked her chin. Her eyes narrowed. Urban imagined he could taste her fury. Instinct warned him to open the distance between them, but he stayed.

"You can't be serious," Kona said.

"I am."

Clemantine said, "I didn't see anything about this in the ship's history."

"I know. I kept it hidden."

Her hand squeezed into a fist. "You promised me you'd kept *nothing* hidden."

"Nothing about the Null Boundary Expedition," he said weakly.

Her eyes widened, shock and hurt and a sense of betrayal in her gaze. "So this is it," she said acidly. "This is what you've been hiding, what you've been afraid to tell me. I knew there was something."

"I couldn't tell you."

"Why not?"

"You wouldn't have come."

Seconds passed as she considered this. Then she nodded slowly—"You're right"—her anger unabated.

"It's different now," he said quickly. "You're different. You've been on the high bridge. You've commanded the ship. You know we can do this. *You* can do it. Destroy another courser. Take it apart. Ensure it never attacks another world, never takes another life. You can do that."

He held out a hand to her, hoping she would yield, that she would concede him some measure of forgiveness, but she refused. "You asked me to trust you," she said.

Kona scowled fiercely. "So this was your plan from the start?"

"Yes," Urban confirmed. "It was always the plan."

"How can it work?" Vytet demanded to know. "*Dragon* is a hybrid ship. If you take us close to another courser, it's going to recognize our alien nature. It has to—and it will do all it can to kill us."

"I know how to put on an acceptable appearance," Urban insisted. He hesitated at the irony in this claim, but then he pushed on. "Our target won't know what we are until it's too late."

He turned to Clemantine again. "You know how it works. You've seen it before. One courser. That's all we need, and we'll be able to fill up our reserves, grow new outriders, finish the gee deck, resurrect everyone in the ship's company, and still have a margin for future projects. We have to do this. There's no choice in it. It would be dangerous to go into the Hallowed Vasties without reserves. It would be foolish. We have no idea what we'll find there, no idea what kind of ancillary defenses we'll need. We need to be ready."

"There is a choice," Kona said, looking thoughtfully at Clemantine.

She nodded her agreement, turned to Urban, and said, "There is the choice to go back."

His heart boomed. He couldn't read her, couldn't tell if she meant it. "Is that what you want?" he asked, low-voiced, hearing his own resentment. "Retreat?"

"No," she said in a dangerous purr. "You're right. It's different now that I've been on the high bridge." The hard line of her lips curled into a snarl . . . or maybe she meant it as a smile. "Let's hunt."

Dragon followed a navigational path that would bypass the clustered stars of the Committee. Chenzeme ships had hunted first among those stars, scourging inhabited worlds. Historians believed the Chenzeme had pushed on from there, venturing ever deeper into human-settled space, just as Urban was doing. He felt sure he would be able to find a courser still prowling among the star systems that lay along his route to the Hallowed Vasties.

The four outriders kept watch over the Near Vicinity. Adapting to their reduced numbers, they coordinated scopes and sensors to continue their ongoing survey of the void.

A DI combed the collected data. It updated the library's star maps, logging positions of the myriad red dwarfs that were everywhere in the galaxy. It also sought anomalies, looking specifically for the spectra of luminous philosopher cells and for gamma-ray bursts that might be a grim indication of a new assault against some surviving settlement. The DI looked for gravitational perturbations too, in an effort to detect the presence of a stealthed courser powered by a zero-point reef.

Urban also searched with Chenzeme senses. On the high bridge, with Clemantine observing, he entered into a conversation with the philosopher cells. As always, they were immersed in an instinctive hunt for other lifeforms. He shifted their focus by introducing a new argument:

— *find another* —

This was an instinctive task too and the cells consented without protest. Their luminosity was always a signal to other Chenzeme ships and might be enough to draw one in. He hoped so. Let the other ship take the risk of acceleration.

*Now we wait, Urban told Clemantine.

*It might be years before we find one, Clemantine said.

Urban warned her, *It might be centuries.

*If we don't find one, we'll need to set up a mining operation some-where, like Kona said.

*It's an option, but I don't want to take the time. Better to take out one of our enemy's ships. Don't you think? That, after all, was the argument that had persuaded her to stay.

*Sooth, she agreed. *I thought I never wanted to see another Chen-zeme courser. Now I hope we find one soon.

FOURTH

You are formidable.

Three shipwrecks now orbit your world. As you had guessed, the first ship came to ensure your demise and pick over your bones. You surprised that one, breached its defenses, attempted to take control of it—but its autonomous synthetic mind destroyed its propulsion mechanism and then destroyed itself. You remained marooned.

The second ship carried a human crew of ancestral form. Their forebears had escaped the Communion. They, like you, had seen the synthetic's ship. They'd watched it from afar, seen it decelerate in the middle of nowhere—and then never saw it again. This piqued their curiosity and because they were a people both wealthy and adventurous, they sent a ship to investigate, with no idea what they might find.

You admired these people. You admired their bravery, their fortitude, even their decision to disable their starship rather than let you take it.

After that, nothing, as billions of seconds passed. You used the time to recover more and more of yourself and to grow ever more formidable. In time, you decided you were strong enough to risk making your presence known. You called out to the void and your call was answered by an alien starship.

That was not an event you anticipated. Nowhere in your shattered memory was there mention of such a thing. Such a *beast*. You survived only because it delayed its attack as it sought to ascertain just what you were before it killed you. Even so, it was a hard-fought encounter that left you nearly undone again.

More repairs.

But when you recovered sufficiently, you sent an avatar to investigate the ruined hulk of the alien ship and you learned much from it. You learned enough to be ready should such a chance come again.

CHAPTER THIRTEEN

CLEMANTINE'S GHOST AWOKE from dormancy. A submind slipped into its pattern, integrating, so she knew things she had not known before: *Dragon* was over three hundred ninety years out of Deception Well—almost 80% of the way to the edge of the Hallowed Vasties; ahead of them an anomalous radio signal had been detected.

Clemantine experienced a surge of excitement, of anticipation—and fear too. Fear was necessary, caution essential, because it was impossible to know what they might find. Anything could be out there, from the unthinking residues of moldy life to godlike beings among the ruins—and maybe it would not be so easy to tell the difference?

But they would look. That was why they'd come: to discover what was here, what might remain—while doing all they could to survive first contact.

The radio signal was weak, too attenuated by distance for *Dragon* to detect it directly. Remote *Fortuna* had found it—the lead ship in the vanguard—and passed the record back through the fleet.

Clemantine transited to the library, manifesting there in a simulation of physical existence. Kona arrived alongside her.

Urban and Vytet were already present, studying a three-dimensional map showing *Dragon*'s position amid the nearest stars. The map's colors were inverted: white background, black stars. Far ahead of the fleet and offset to the left of their trajectory, a small, curving swath of space glowed faintly blue. Sequences of monotone beeps played in soft rhythm, each set of beeps separated by a silence that lasted an equivalent time:

beep-beep-beep-beep
beep-beep-beep-beep-beep
beep-beep-beep-beep-beep-beep

An absurdly simple sequence, but Clemantine listened with an attentiveness she might have given to a complex symphony while the count continued to climb until it reached ten. Then with the next round the number of beeps commenced to drop, declining steadily toward one.

Urban indicated the blue glow. "We think the signal is originating from somewhere in this area," he said, his voice taut with excitement. He turned to Clemantine, his expression bright with the flush of discovery, no trace of his usual cynicism in the tight curve of his smile. "It's not Chenzeme," he said. "At least, not like any Chenzeme signal we've ever heard before."

"Human?" she asked.

"I don't know."

"What *is* human?" Kona wondered. "The closer we get to the Hallowed Vasties, the more likely we'll face that question."

"This *could* be human," someone said. An unfamiliar, childlike voice.

Clemantine's head snapped around in surprise—though it had to be Vyet's voice, spoken by a new aspect, updated since the last time they had been together. Doubtless Vyet had changed many times in the intervening years, but Clemantine's daily inspections of the ship did not extend to an inspection of *Dragon*'s inhabitants.

In this version, Vyet had adopted pale blue skin, deep blue eyes, and a creamy white color for the pelt that covered her scalp. Finely sculpted facial features suggested a feminine nature, but the lack of both masculine weight or feminine curves on a body as thin as Clemantine had ever seen it, left gender open to question. Time would tell. Until then, Clemantine defaulted to the universal *she*.

Vyet continued to think out loud. "A simple signal," she murmured, her voice possessing the sweet, high tone of a pre-adolescent child. "Certainly artificial—but not a language. The complexity of language isn't there. It could be a new Chenzeme tactic. We don't know—"

She broke off as the pulsing beeps dropped in number to one. They all listened to a single drawn-out tone that lasted several seconds. Then abruptly the signal changed to a complex series of swift beeps, suggesting some kind of code.

"It got our attention," Clemantine said. "Now it's telling us what it wants us to know."

Kona looked up from the map, looked around. Impatiently: "Where are the Scholar and the Mathematician? We need them on deck to do the decoding."

Both instantiated immediately, appearing within their frameless windows on opposite sides of the black-on-white starfield. The Scholar, with his mature countenance, wore formal blue. The Mathematician, Urban's double, was dressed exactly like him, in a casual charcoal-gray pullover and snug black trousers.

Both Apparatchiks looked annoyed.

"They're already working on it," Urban explained. "My guess is that if we're meant to understand the code, the solution will be easy."

"*We*," Clemantine mused. "Do you think it's aware of us?"

Urban answered her question with one of his own: "How close is it? Close enough to resolve the light of our hull cells? Probably not."

"It's got to be a trap," Kona said with a fierce scowl. "A lure to draw in the curious."

Urban nodded reluctantly. "I agree it's some kind of lure. It *wants* to be found. But that says nothing about its purpose."

A trap.

Given the hostile nature of the Universe as Clemantine knew it, that made grim sense. Her perspective shifted, her first flush of enthusiasm cooled. She made herself listen, really listen, to the continuing sequence of arrhythmic beeps, striving to extract some meaning from them, though they remained meaningless to her ear.

She knew from the library that Urban had never encountered anything like this before. "If it is a lure," she pointed out, "whoever or whatever is behind it doesn't fear attention or discovery by the Chenzeme."

"Then it must *be* Chenzeme," Kona growled.

"Or a Chenzeme ally?" Vytet mused. "Is there such a thing?"

"Or some entity emigrating out of the Hallowed Vasties," Clemantine suggested in a somber voice. "Those who built the Dyson swarms didn't fear discovery either."

Frontier civilizations had succumbed to the scourge of Chenzeme warships, but those ships had not caused the collapse of the Hallowed Vasties. The oldest cordons had fallen first, long before the Chenzeme ships could have reached them, most likely brought down by an inherent weakness or an enemy from within.

Again the long tone, bringing an end to what they assumed was a coded message. The original pattern replayed: pulses of sound in sets of one, two, then three, increasing to ten, then declining again. The long tone followed—clearly a separator—and then began a repetition of the complex code.

This time they listened in silence while the Scholar and the Mathematician stood in stillness within their windows—aspects left abandoned as they retreated to a deeper computational layer to decode and interpret the tonal sequence.

When the long tone sounded again, Vytet said, "That's the full loop. It was exactly the same both times."

"The patterned portion of the signal peaked at a count of ten," Clemantine mused, holding up both hands, her fingers spread. "A common base number in human history." She checked with a DI, confirming what she'd already guessed. "The separator lasts exactly ten seconds. Seconds are a human measure of time."

Kona: "So it's human, or it wants to appear as if it's human, or it's using these measures because it's inherited them as artifacts from a human past."

Clemantine sighed, aware of how much she wanted a connection with this thing, how much she wanted it to be proof that something of humanity remained alive here. But it could be anything.

Grimly: "Maybe it's just a buoy set in the void, bleating a warning to anyone who will listen. *Stay away!* I can imagine hundreds of them out there. Thousands."

Urban cocked an eyebrow as if amused by this show of bitter melodrama. "Let's say this beacon *is* human. Then maybe it's a warning to the Chenzeme . . . and a welcome to us."

Clemantine considered this, and had to smile. "A welcome? That would be something new in the history of our species."

"The beacon does not appear to be a warning," the Scholar interjected.

Urban turned to him. "You've decoded it?"

"Of course," the Scholar acknowledged in a smug tone that induced an eye-roll in Clemantine. He went on, "Objectively, the signal parses into a map describing a specific point within the Near Vicinity." He cocked his head. "So perhaps it is an invitation to visit?"

"Let's see the map," Urban said.

The Scholar looked across to the window where the Mathematician had been residing—but the Mathematician was gone. The Pilot, dressed in black garb, had taken his place.

The Pilot said, "The coded portion of the signal describes the mass and spectral signatures of four stars. One of them, the single prominent G-type in the Near Vicinity." He gestured at the map of inverted colors already on display and one of the black stars shifted to glow bright yellow. "Another prominent star farther out." That star was highlighted next. "And two red dwarfs." Two dull cherry points winked into existence.

The Pilot crouched within his window, peering at the map. "The unit of measure used in the message is a light year," he explained. "A different distance, measured in light years, has been assigned to each star. Project a sphere around each star with a radius of the designated distance . . ." Translucent spheres appeared one by one around each of the highlighted stars, partly overlapping. "And the surfaces of all the spheres intersect at only one point."

That point blazed bright blue, while the star colors reverted to black and the translucent spheres disappeared.

The bright blue point fell within the range Urban had developed for the source of the beacon, but it was light years away from any visible star.

"Nothing there," Clemantine said, eyeing the bright point with suspicion. "Or nothing visible—not at standard resolution."

She looked to Urban, who nodded, anticipating her request. "The Astronomer is working to coordinate telescopes. We'll get a closer look, but we still might not see anything. There could be a Jovian-scale object there, but if it's dark and cold we won't see it."

"And still, something must be there," Vytet said. "Something is generating that signal. We need to decide if we're going to go look."

Subminds migrated between the library and the high bridge, trading memories, allowing Urban to exist simultaneously on both timelines, while Clemantine existed only in the library. He messaged her. She rarely split her existence among multiple ghosts but he invited her to do so now: *Come to the high bridge. There's an experiment I want to run. You'll want to see it.*

Within the library, she looked at him curiously. On the high bridge, he felt the sudden, sharp presence of her mind, her will, overlaid in intimate proximity against his own. A moment for her to take in the mood of the cells, and then she let slip a sense of surprise, before quickly suppressing it.

Ah, I see, she said. *The cells are quiet because they haven't heard the signal yet. Dragon is too distant, the signal too attenuated to directly detect.*

Yes, but I'm going to let them hear it now.

You want to interrogate them, she guessed. *See if they recognize it. Learn if this is a Chenzeme signal.*

Be ready, he warned. *I don't know how they'll react.*

He uploaded a memory of the signal, pushing it across several links. It entered the field as unsourced data. He worried that without provenance it would be rejected, but the philosopher cells took it up, treating it with a mix of hostile curiosity and skepticism.

They see it as a thought experiment, Clemantine said. *A puzzle to be solved.*

She was right. Groups of allied cells worked to unravel the code and they proved faster than the Scholar and the Mathematician. With staggering speed, the cells recognized that the signal coded for a location within the Near Vicinity—dangerously close, from their perspective. Their inherent aggression escalated as they prepared to meet a threat. Action was proposed: *Divert course. Close with the target. Attack.*

At the same time, select lines of cells began to scan deep memory, seeking to match the signal to past experience. Urban followed this with anxious interest, but no similar memory surfaced. *The signal is not Chenzeme,* he concluded. *And not a trick of the Chenzeme.*

A human signal, then, Clementine said.

Or a machine that originated with humanity, or a lifeform diverged or descended from the ancestral human type, or a lifeform brought into being by human ingenuity. Many possibilities still existed, and only one certainty: Whatever it was that had set that simple rhythm pulsing into the void, it wanted to be found.

As Urban's subminds migrated between the high bridge and the library, he settled on an opposite strategy. He would do what he could to disappear, to not be found, to remain hidden until he had a better idea of what was out there.

For nearly a millennium he'd traversed the void with *Dragon's* hull cells gleaming because they marked him as Chenzeme—a bio-mechanical entity so arrogant in its power it had no need to hide. Urban had used that camouflage to successfully hunt other Chenzeme ships but now his perspective shifted. He was no longer sure he sat behind the biggest gun in the Near Vicinity—and that meant his luminous hull had become a liability.

We're going dark, he told Clementine. *Watch. Learn how it's done.*

He released a quiet suggestion to the philosopher cells:

– *stealth* –

The cells picked up on his caution, debated it, and sought a solution:

<*approach in stealth*>

<*go dark*>

<the unknown threatens us>
<go dark>
<yield to the pilot>
<attack without warning>
<approach the enemy in stealth>
<go dark>

It's beginning, Clemantine said.

Urban sensed it too. The conversion started at the ship's bow as a cluster of cells dropped out of the conversation. Their metabolism shifted: biochemical preparations underway as they made ready for stasis. Their luminosity bled away. They became dark, triggering other cells around them to do the same. Darkness spread, moving outward across the hull in a slow wave, encircling the ship from bow to stern until the luminosity of every cell faded to nothing and silence replaced their long conversation.

I didn't think I'd miss it, Clemantine said. *But it feels like part of my mind is shut down.*

Sooth, that's what's happened.

In the earliest days, Urban had taken the ship dark just for a respite from the hateful nature of the cells. Even then, he'd found the transition disorienting, leaving an anxious void in his mind.

The dialog mentioned a pilot, Clemantine said. *Our pilot? The Apparatchik?*

No. When I hijacked the ship, I found a secondary mind, singular, and subordinate to the philosopher cells. It performed navigation functions when the cells were dormant, so the bridge translates its name as 'the pilot.'

You took over its role. You can steer the ship when the cells are dark.

Sooth. I was able to co-opt an existing behavioral path. Same with the suggestion to go dark. I could have forced it, but I let the cells make the choice. That way, they're prepared. They understand the strategy. When I wake them, they'll be ready to fight.

If it comes to a fight.

Until then, *Dragon* would be dark and—with luck—undetectable by whatever entity had engineered the beacon. Of course, there was a cost. With the cells dormant, he would lose their close

oversight of the Near Vicinity. But he had access to other Chenzeme senses , and he had cameras and telescopes across the fleet.
Dragon would not be blind.

In the library, Urban listened as Clemantine explained to Kona
and Vytet what had transpired on the high bridge. She concluded,
"The philosopher cells expect to come out of dormancy close to
the source of the beacon, in position to launch an attack."

"*No,*" Vytet said with a look of shock.

Kona turned his stern gaze on Urban. "That's not what you
mean to do?"

Clemantine answered him, sounding irritated, "Of course not.
We're not here to continue Chenzeme genocide."

A blunt response that made Urban smile. He said, "Going dark
is precautionary. I think the beacon marks something dangerous,
something stronger than we are—or the Chenzeme would have
already destroyed it. But there it is. That signal—bold, taunting. A
lure. The bait in a trap to draw in the curious, the unwary."

"Or maybe the genocidal?" Vytet suggested, her thoughtful gaze
resting on Urban. "Maybe it's aimed at Chenzeme ships. It would
have pulled in this one, if not for your guidance."

"Huh," Urban grunted. "If that's so, we're a prime target." He
straightened his shoulders, looked around their small circle. "Our
safest option is to stay dark, continue on, continue our own hunt,
and hope it doesn't notice us."

Vytet's avatar suddenly changed in appearance. She retained
her light-blue skin tone, but her delicate features became bolder
and more stark so that she presented the strong face of a mature
woman. "We can't just pass it by," she said, her voice now a lower
register. "We are here to learn, to discover. That's the purpose of
this voyage."

Kona looked wary. "And it's a dangerous choice to leave such an
unknown behind us."

Clemantine wasn't fooled. A skeptical smile, her fine eyebrows
raised: "Urban, when did you ever take the safest option?"

He turned his hands palm up. "I'm older and wiser now."

She rolled her eyes.

"No, really," he insisted with a laugh. "Here's what I want to do. For now, we only watch and listen. Let time pass. If nothing changes, we'll modify our course. We'll still keep our distance from the beacon, but we'll pass more closely than our current trajectory allows. And I'll send an outrider ahead of us. I'll take it in close, see what I can see—and hope we get data back."

"You're willing to risk another outrider?" Vytet asked.

"It's better than risking *Dragon*."

Kona said, "We should observe it for an extended time before we do anything. Fifty, sixty days at least."

"Or longer," Urban answered, amused that Kona could describe such a flicker of time as *extended*.

To Urban's surprise, Vytet objected. "Why wait?" she demanded. "If we're going to risk an outrider, let's send it now—and we'll know sooner what we're facing."

"Why take the risk of alerting it?" Urban countered. "We don't know its capabilities. What if it senses the outrider's reef? What if it extrapolates its trajectory back to us? Better to wait and watch and see if there's anything we can learn before we risk revealing our presence. There's time. We just need to be patient."

At this, Clemantine drew back with a look of exaggerated surprise. "Older and wiser, you say? Maybe it's true."

Urban monitored the beacon. As time passed he realized his initial impression had been wrong. The signal was not an endless repetition of the same location data. There had to be, at minimum, some minor machine intelligence at work, capable of precise navigation, because at regular intervals the location data shifted slightly to compensate for relative motion measured against the four guide stars.

Interesting.

The telescope array failed to resolve an object but that meant little. The site was so far away that the beacon would have to be immense and radiating brightly to be seen.

He remained cautious, employing both cameras and telescopes

in a constant survey of the Near Vicinity, alert for any sign of an incursion by a stealthed object. He detected none.

He adopted a machinelike patience and waited one hundred days.

Then he engaged the Pilot to plot a new heading, preparing to shift *Dragon*'s course as he had promised to do—though he left the actual task as an exercise for Clemantine.

For the first time, she took direct control of *Dragon*'s steerage engines and slowly, slowly, the massive ship slid onto a new trajectory.

Afterward, as he lay with her, adrift in her chamber, bathed in the shimmering light of wall-weed, he confessed, "I've been looking over the profiles of the archived ghosts."

This drew a soft cynical laugh. "Found an old lover among them?"

"*Is* there one?" he wondered.

"Do your own research, son."

He slid his fingers across the curve of her cheek. "Vytet wants to go with me to the beacon."

"She's planning to go," Clemantine corrected.

"She's an engineer."

Clemantine turned her head to meet his gaze. "So?"

The outrider's computational strata could support two ghosts, no more.

He said, "I don't need an engineer. I need an anthropologist. If the beacon is inhabited, it could be an advantage to have an expert on hand."

A noncommittal, "Hmm," as her brows drew together, tiny wrinkles gathering between them.

"What?"

"I don't think an anthropologist from the Well will be able to tell you anything about intelligent aliens, or about our own distant cousins who might have survived the collapse of the Hallowed Vasties. You'd do better to take me or Kona."

"Someone who knows when to start shooting?"

"Yes."

Urban nuzzled her small ear, kissed the gold iris tattoos on her ear lobe. "You hate to split your timeline, and besides, I'm going unarmed. We're here to learn, to map what's left, establish communications if we can. So I want someone who's studied other cultures. Riffan Naja is my leading candidate."

"The commander of *Long Watch*?"

"I'm thinking of waking him. He's an anthropologist, has an interest in linguistics, he's studied the Hallowed Vasties, and he was the first to ask to be part of this expedition."

"You're planning to do only a fly-by, right?"

"That's the plan," Urban agreed, "because I need to minimize the risk to the outrider. I don't want to lose it." But then he admitted, "Depending on what we find, the plan could change."

"Time," she said, "is not on your side. Not for this venture. If you do anything more than a fly-by you'll be away years—decades—assuming the outrider gets back at all. And if you take an unnecessary risk along the way, and lose the outrider, we'll be down to three."

He groaned. "I know it. You're right, but it's *so* frustrating. There's so much to see. But choosing to stop and study a single place means forgoing other possible destinations or pushing them off far into the future—and maybe they'll change in that time, become something other, or die before we get there."

"You can't see it all," she said. "Not all at once. Take the anthropologist with you if you want to. Do the fly-by. But don't plan on more than that. Conserve your resources. Our focus should be on the hunt, and on reaching the Hallowed Vasties. We're still a long way from the nearest cordoned star."

CHAPTER FOURTEEN

RIFFAN WOKE TO a startled sense that he was falling. He gasped, his whole body jerked—and then he realized it was just the sensation of zero gee. He grimaced, thinking he must still be aboard *Long Watch*.

But as consciousness fully asserted itself, confusion set in. He was not in his familiar berth. Instead, he'd awakened alone within a small chamber, its curving walls covered in what he recognized as waving wall-weed. He'd seen the stuff in historical dramas, but never before seen it in use.

The wall-weed glowed gently, the only illumination within the chamber. Long ribbons of it coiled around Riffan's body, cradling him, its touch warm and gentle . . . and deeply disturbing.

He thrashed, suddenly desperate to escape its grip. The ribbons released him, leaving him with his momentum untethered so that he bounced across the chamber only to be enfolded by more wall-weed. He grabbed it, frantic to control his motion. He clung to it with a desperate grip as he realized where he must be.

This was *Dragon*. So it had really happened. He had left Deception Well, left his home, left it far, far behind. Left it forever.

"Love and Nature and the Cosmic First Light," he whispered. "What have I done?"

Supremely conscious of the vast distance, the unbridgeable gap, that separated him from everything he'd ever known. Deep, shaking breaths.

"Calm down," he told himself. "You wanted this. You *want* it. It'll be okay."

And if it wasn't? He'd left another version of himself at home. He spent a minute imagining that other Riffan, no doubt resentful that he'd been the one to stay behind. This thought brought him a slight chagrined smile. "Be grateful, you idiot," he murmured.

His breath steadied, his heart slowed. He noticed clothing among the wall-weed, newly assembled and still budding off the wall. He reached for it: loose fitting trousers with cuffs at the ankles to keep them from drifting, and a long-sleeved pullover.

As he dressed, he puzzled over the lack of gravity. He'd expected to awaken while *Dragon* was accelerating to cruising speed. Perhaps they were still coasting, waiting for the swarm ships to catch up?

Perhaps they'd already reached cruising speed.

He wondered how fast that might be. He knew that in theory a reef could pull a ship to mad velocities, but the danger of collision argued against excessive speed. Run too fast, and a ship might be torn apart in the blink of an eye.

At this thought, a shudder ran through him and he muttered to himself, "Think of something else, you fool."

So he thought about time, instead. What time was it? He suspected several days had passed since his ghost uploaded from *Long Watch*. After all, it would have taken time to construct this chamber and the now-vanished resurrection pod.

He checked his atrium's connectivity. Found a network. Posted questions to it: "Where are we? *When* are we?"

A DI, speaking through his atrium in a soothing male voice, informed him that *Dragon* was 390 years out of Deception Well.

He squinted. Frowned. "What was that?" he begged. "Say that again?"

"*Dragon* is presently 390 years and 114 days out of Deception Well."

Could it be true? Riffan did not want to believe it. If it was true, it meant that he'd been gone somewhere—Cold sleep? Data storage? *Did it matter?*—for five times longer than he'd been alive. It meant that everyone he'd known at home was . . .

He could not finish the thought. He didn't know how. They could be dead. And if not, if they were still alive and he somehow met them again, would he even know them? His own parents, his sister, his cousins—all of them now surely transformed by the passage of so much time. Become strangers. And that other version of himself that had stayed behind? That man was now surely forever sundered from him, a separate being in the mind of the Unknown God.

He squeezed the wall-weed harder as if he could arrest the flight of time with his grip, but he was too late, too late. Everything he'd once known, gone and unrecoverable.

"What have I done?" he moaned, struggling not to be sick. He knew—he'd known—he was leaving Deception Well forever but—

Three hundred ninety years!

Why so long? Why? He could only think that something must have gone horribly wrong.

He dove for the thin gel door that sealed the chamber, shot through it into a tunnel beyond. More gently glowing wall-weed. No one about. He suffered a sudden sick fear that he was alone here, utterly alone.

The chamber where he'd wakened was at the tunnel's end. He launched himself away from it, shouting, "Hello, hello! Is anyone here? Call out if you are!"

No one answered. He shot past four other chambers, their gel doors dilated open. A swift glance into each confirmed no one inside.

He reached a U-shaped intersection. Clambered around the tight curve and found a gel door, this one sealed. He guessed another level of habitation lay beyond it. Heart racing, he grabbed a fist-full of wall-weed and shoved himself through.

To his surprise, he emerged into a beautiful, sprawling chamber made to look like a wide pavilion surrounded by an open, airy forest of giant trees, green ferns growing among them. Clusters of white camellias hung from a pergola, scenting the air. The angle and color of sunlight slanting through the lattice suggested it might be late afternoon—though he wasn't skilled at judging such things.

He reminded himself to *breathe*. Filling his lungs, he looked around—and if he'd been standing he would have collapsed in relief at the sight of Kona gliding across the chamber to meet him.

"I am so glad to see you!" Riffan cried out as he took Kona's proffered hand. "I didn't know what to think when I woke up alone . . . but where is everybody?"

Beyond Kona he saw Urban and Clemantine, and a third person he didn't recognize, someone with decorative blue skin and short, thick, creamy white hair. They were all together in a nook, looking at him expectantly. But no one else.

Many more people could have fit comfortably within that expansive chamber. Riffan wondered where they were, wondered how many had come on the expedition. He didn't know, but Pasha should be there.

His grip on Kona's hand tightened as a fresh wave of anxiety swept through him. "Where is Pasha?" he pleaded. "And why has it been so long?"

"We've had some trouble," Kona said. "But don't worry, we haven't lost anyone. Not yet."

After they explained things to him—especially that preposterous part about being on the hunt for another courser—Riffan thought he ought to be angry, but he couldn't muster the emotion. He was too overwhelmed. So much to take in! And the beacon. *The beacon!* Something was out there. The idea of it made his heart race in curiosity, in excitement. In fear.

All manner of speculation made swift passage through his brain until he had to remind himself that the simplest explanation was, as always, the most likely.

"Perhaps it's an ancient colony ship," he suggested. "Damaged in some accident and coasting without propulsion for thousands of years. If it set out before we knew of the Chenzeme, the ship's company would not have been afraid of signaling their location."

"If it was that old," Urban countered, "the Chenzeme would have found it and vaporized it long ago."

Riffan felt his cheeks heat. "Yes. Yes, of course," he conceded, unable to deny this grim logic. He thought on it for a few seconds, then asked, "Is this the *first* signal you've heard? There's been nothing else, nothing at all from the Hallowed Vasties?"

"Nothing," Vytet confirmed in a voice low and rich, yet feminine. Deep blue eyes in a pale-blue face gave her a faraway look. "Though the nearest stars are still so distant we can't reasonably expect to detect a radio signal."

"And what of the visible spectrum?" Riffan asked. "Surely we can see more now than from Deception Well?"

"We're closer," Urban said, "but not close enough for the detail we need to see. Tanjiri is the nearest star and for some years we've seen evidence of objects in orbit. Odd shapes. Not spherical. Gravitational clusters of debris, maybe. Or remnant megastructures that survived the collapse."

At a gesture from Vytet, a black rectangle opened within the wall of the alcove, over-writing a portion of the forest scene. Two astronomical images appeared within it. On the left, a cordoned star—an ancient image, at least fourteen hundred years old, captured by a telescope somewhere on the frontier. Distance had flattened the cordon's spherical geometry into a disk aglow in the infrared range of the spectrum.

"This was Tanjiri when it was still cordoned," Vytet said. She gestured to the image on the right. "This is how it appeared the last time we surveyed it—a simple star with no visible structures. But a variation in luminosity suggests that objects continue to pass across the face of the star, dimming its light. Possibly a planetary body, but more likely, large remnant structures."

Riffan flushed with excitement at this prospect. What would such structures look like? And might they still contain life?

"Is Tanjiri our destination?" he asked Urban.

"For now, unless the hunt pulls us away."

A sigh from Kona and a slow shake of his head as he studied the image of the cordon. "I cannot imagine what it must have looked like from the inside. The scale of it! Swarms of orbiting bodies, so many the star's light could not get through."

"There had to be a decentralized intelligence overseeing it," Riffan said. "Coordinating a flocking algorithm to prevent the components from crashing into one another."

"Agreed," Vytet said. "But there would have been layers and layers of orbital lanes, tilted at different angles. So many it might not have looked crowded from inside."

"And still," Kona rumbled, "it seems impossible."

"But it *was* possible." Riffan turned again to the image. "The cordons were real, but they didn't last. *None* of them lasted—and that's as strange as that they existed at all. Why did they fail? Was it because the design is inherently unstable? Vulnerable to chained disasters? Or did the people who built them destroy themselves?"

"Maybe they reached an apotheosis and moved on," Clementine said, startling Riffan with the bitterness in her voice.

An uneasy silence. Averted gazes. "You're referring to the Communion virus, aren't you?" Riffan asked.

Her shoulders rose and fell in a quiet sigh. "It's just so silent out there. There's only the beacon. What if it's a repository of the virus? Bleating into the void to attract a new host."

"We're not vulnerable to the Communion virus anymore," Urban said. "And despite the silence, we are going to find life somewhere. Survivors. We have to."

"Spoken with such certainty," Vytet teased, "as if you can bend the future to your will."

Urban's chin rose. That pirate smile. "Who says I can't?"

Kona said, "It'll be safer for us if it's all ruins—but tragic, too."

"Even if it is only ruins, I want to know," Riffan said. "I want to begin to understand what happened."

Somewhere in the course of that long, convoluted introduction to his new life, Riffan agreed to accompany Urban on an outrider—but not as himself, not as this physical version of him. Urban only asked him to send a ghost, and that was easy enough, wasn't it?

He eventually retreated to his assigned chamber, needing time alone to process it all. He huddled there, curled within the grip of the wall-weed—he'd begun to consider its touch comforting—while he tried to decide how he felt, how he *should* feel.

He wondered: *Am I happy?*

He thought he might be. He was definitely still in shock. It would take time to adjust emotionally to the facts of this new life. So much to learn—*and already eighty percent of the way to the Hallowed Vasties!*

The thought sent a fresh burst of excitement shooting through him. But then his emotional pendulum reversed. His chest tightened in grief as his thoughts turned again to his parents, his sister, lost to him, far gone in both time and space. Shades of past lovers arose in his memory too. Never a permanent partner for him or it would not have been so easy to leap away into the void.

He wondered if that would be a common trait among the others who were still archived. Loneliness stirred in him. He had always meant to find someone. He'd hoped to. But he'd always been distracted by his work. It wasn't fair, really, to even call it work. His studies, then. His studies had always come first and his interests were wide, rooted in a sense of wonder at the astonishing existence of all things, of the Creation.

"You lucky fool," he said aloud. "Think of where you are and where you're bound."

Beyond the walls of this miraculous hybrid ship innumerable stars swirled in a great gyre, some of them accompanied by worlds, and some of those worlds had given rise to lifeforms and to living machines in such great variety that their span reached from the molecular scale to the great sun-cloaking cordon of a Dyson swarm of the Hallowed Vasties.

To learn what he could of it, *that* was the task Riffan had been given, whether by his own heritage or by the inscrutable will of the Unknown God. However long and hard and monotonous and lonely his studies might be, inevitably they revealed yet one more detail behind the machinery of existence, and that was reason enough to have made the leap to *Dragon*, despite what he'd left behind.

He drew a deep breath. "You'll do just fine," he assured himself. And then a cynical chuckle, "Or die trying."

Urban replicated his ghost, once again splitting his timeline.

There was a lottery in each replication. At that moment, he became himself and someone else. Their points of view divergent. Their futures different.

As himself, he would stay behind aboard *Dragon*, while that other version uploaded to *Elepaio*, the outrider he'd chosen for this mission. That ghost would command the little ship, taking it as close as good judgment allowed to the site of the beacon.

He swore softly, indulging in disappointment, because *he* was the version who would stay behind. But if his ghost returned, the memories of both timelines would belong to him and he would have both gone and stayed.

Many hours later, a message came in from *Elepaio*, relayed through *Lam Lha* and *Artemis*. It confirmed his ghost and Riffan's had reached the outrider, and included the precise time *Elepaio* had departed, breaking away from the communications network that linked the fleet.

Urban knew the outrider's planned course. He could calculate its position. But its dark hull and minimal heat signature meant he could not see it, and it was too far away for the lateral lines of *Dragon*'s gravitational sensor to detect its propulsion reef. With *Elepaio* out of the communications network, he had no way to confirm its actual position. The little ship had become invisible to *Dragon*'s senses. *His* senses.

It was a stark reminder of how easily dark, quiet, cool objects could disappear in the great empty. An unneeded reminder. Urban kept a constant watch, ever alert to the possibility of a hostile vessel coasting unseen to well within weapons range.

Radar could map the space around him, but it would slide off the hull of a fully stealthed attacker. And using radar would expose *Dragon*'s position when he wanted to stay hidden.

So he used passive detection. A nearby object would eclipse background stars. He watched for that. And he was alert for gravitational anomalies—but he detected none.

Time passed. Three hundred twenty-one days.

Then a DI brought him a report gleaned from the newest astronomical records. A faint point of white light had been observed behind *Dragon*, where no light had been seen before. Its spectral signature confirmed its identity as a Chenzeme warship.

At last, Urban had found his long-sought prey.

CHAPTER FIFTEEN

CLEMANTINE'S ARCHIVED GHOST winked into awareness. She noted the time. Nearly a year since *Elepaio*'s departure. A submind dropped in. It updated her with startling news:

The hunt was on!

Centuries had elapsed since Urban declared his intention to seek a Chenzeme courser. Centuries since Clemantine had given cold approval to the project, persuaded to it by her hatred, by a hunger to strike back at last against the Chenzeme killing machines.

In all that time, no courser or swan burster had ever been sighted. Clemantine had worried the warships were limited in their territory, that *Dragon* had passed beyond the region where they might be found. But here at last, the quarry.

And because she'd been archived for most of the intervening years, her passion for the hunt had not decayed.

She transited to the library.

Urban was already there, engrossed in a three-dimensional map of the Near Vicinity, the Pilot and the Bio-mechanic facing him on the map's opposite side, confined in their frameless windows.

Clemantine scanned the map. *Dragon* was at its center. The beacon bleated ahead and to the left. The newly discovered courser, represented as a white point and tagged with a label that read *Target 3*, was surprisingly close behind.

The only reason she did not feel her heart race, her skin crawl, her stomach clench in revulsion at the proximity of the deadly machine, was because such responses did not exist within the architecture of a ghost.

"Not yet in weapons range," she observed.

"But close," the Pilot said.

Urban looked up as Kona popped into existence beside him. Vytet and Riffan followed. Riffan enveloped himself in a simulated bubble of modified gravity that allowed him to sit cross-legged, while floating at head height. He and Vytet and Kona had all lived a physical existence since *Elepaio*'s departure. Only Clemantine had skipped that year.

"There it is," Kona said grimly, staring at the tagged point. "Our curse and our salvation." Reflected in his gaze, the memory of apocalypse. Clemantine shared that memory, and she carried other memories—other scars—gained on the Null Boundary Expedition.

Kona turned to Urban. "This isn't chance. It was following us, wasn't it?"

"Sooth," Urban agreed. "It would have been stealthed, dark, trying to gauge our strength and judge whether our behavior falls within Chenzeme norms."

"The presence of the outriders might have made us look questionable," Riffan mused, his voice breathy with tension even though ghosts did not breathe.

"It would have studied the outriders," Urban agreed. "But Chenzeme ships have used many different strategies, including ancillary ships. *Dragon* understood the concept from the beginning."

"We went dark less than two years ago," Kona said. "Maybe it lost track of us, decided to reveal itself, to see if we'd do the same."

"Maybe," Urban said. "But two years is no time at all to a Chenzeme mind. I think it heard the beacon. Its internal pilot wouldn't know how to respond to an anomaly like that, so it woke the philosopher cells."

The calm tone of this discussion felt increasingly surreal to Clemantine. As a ghost, her emotions were muted. Even so, it took effort to resist a rising anger, an impatience to get on with it. In her mind, this courser stood for all those coursers that had pursued and destroyed human ships, and ravaged human worlds. Now it had become their prey and she was eager to go after it.

Urban went on, thinking aloud. "My guess: those cells will respond like *Dragon's*. They'll quickly reach a consensus to attack the beacon."

"Despite our presence?" Vytet asked quietly. He had assumed a masculine aspect again, this time with dark-brown skin and a flat face. He wore his hair long, tied at the nape, and he looked out on the world from beneath heavy black eyebrows. Even stranger, he had indulged in the outlandish, ancient affectation of a closely trimmed beard. Sitting on a plinth summoned from the library's floor and staring pensively at the display, he looked like an ancient sage in some historical drama.

"Does it even know where we are?" Riffan wondered. He looked just the same, masculine and moderately handsome, with a bright, interested expression. "Our course adjustment came after the hull cells went dark."

"It may not know," Urban acknowledged, "but it will expect us to join in the hunt."

Clemantine gave him a sharp look. "We're not going to do that."

"No," he agreed.

"We could stay dark," Kona suggested. "Hang back and watch. See what happens if it attacks the beacon."

This suggestion triggered in Vytet a rare display of anger. "Absolutely not!" he said. "There could be a human settlement there. We are not going to skulk in the dark and watch it destroyed."

Urban crossed his arms, frowning at the map. "We aren't going to let it attack the beacon."

"Agreed," Clemantine said. "It belongs to us. We're going after it. We need its mass, the elements it's carrying."

"But do we want to take it *here*?" Kona asked. "Put on a violent display in sight of the beacon, when we have no idea what's there?"

"You're worried we will appear to be the aggressor," Vytet said.

Clemantine shrugged. "We *will* be the aggressor. What choice?"

"Lead it away?" Riffan proposed.

But Urban said, "No, we're going to meet it. It's not even a choice at this point. It's programmed instinct for these ships to meet and mate and trade their memories."

He turned to Clemantine with an appraising gaze. She could guess what he was thinking. On the Null Boundary Expedition, they had met a courser in just such a way. It had been a horrifying experience. Even now, remembering those helpless hours, she shuddered. But this was different. This time, they would dominate the encounter.

She waved a hand, dismissing Urban's concern, saying, "If we ignore protocol and retreat, we'll become the hunted."

"Sooth." His focus shifted away. Something internal? A submind perhaps, bringing him a new memory. He nodded as if in silent agreement with a decision already made. "I'm tumbling the ship bow to stern so we can decelerate."

The Pilot said, "And I'm working out a trajectory that will let us intercept."

"I'll wake our philosopher cells when we're closer," Urban said. "They know how to work this, how to get us in striking distance." He looked at the second Apparatchik. "The Bio-mechanic will prepare our assault."

"Disable, deplete, and destroy," Clemantine summarized in a soft voice that disguised her rising tension. "That's the procedure you've used before. But I've been thinking. This time, we could be more ambitious."

Urban cocked his head, looking vaguely insulted but also intrigued. "Okay," he said. "Tell me what you have in mind."

She had studied his past encounters and could see no reason why her idea couldn't work. "Consider this," she said. "We disable and deplete this courser, taking what we need from it—but we don't destroy it. We hijack it instead. Take it, the same way you took *Dragon*." She gestured at the display, speaking quickly now. "We have no idea what that beacon represents. We have no idea what else we might find where we're going. This new courser will be a lesser beast, but with two together they can protect one another and be far stronger than one."

Urban leaned toward her, looking both astonished and impressed. "Don't tease me," he warned. "You really want to do that?"

"I'm surprised you haven't done it before."

"*Me?*" He shook his head. "No. I wouldn't do it."

His refusal caught her by surprise. She had expected Urban, always so bold, to embrace the idea. Her disappointment was acute, even within her simulated existence.

He saw that, reacted to it. "It's not that I don't like the idea," he said. "I love it. I love that it's you who suggested it. But I won't do it again. It weighs on me, Clemantine. *Dragon* is mine. I won't ever give it up. But you know what it's like on the high bridge. I feel like I've got my foot forever on the throat of an old murderer who would overthrow me and slash *my* throat if I ever once allow an opening. It's not an experience I need to duplicate. One Chenzeme monster is enough for me. But you could do it."

If she'd been flesh, she would have caught her breath, felt a rush of hot blood in her cheeks. As it was, her ghost froze. She *had* considered the idea, pondered the reality of living every second within the violence of the Chenzeme mind, immersed in the unceasing hate that had destroyed her people, her birth world. Urban endured it without complaint but Clemantine shrank from the idea.

Still, she had to ask herself, *How much does my personal discomfort matter?*

She felt sure her reasoning was solid. They could gain both the resources they needed and a second warship. But to do it, she would have to bear the dire responsibility of commanding that ship. No one else could do it. No one else but Urban had experience on the high bridge.

She lifted her chin, conscious of everyone's eyes on her. She heard herself say in a perfectly steady, calm tone, "Yes, all right. I'll do it."

She had the uncanny sense it was some other version of herself speaking.

Chenzeme warships were adaptive. Through the interface of the philosopher cells they observed the galaxy around them, evaluated what they saw, reacted, and changed tactics as need required—and they shared their experiences with one another.

These exchanges of memories took place when two ships met in the void. Hardwired instinct drew them together, into physical proximity , so that data-encoded dust could be traded between them.

These encounters also served to reinforce the warships' genocidal behavior. The ships were ancient. They had far outlived the species that created them. Given their adaptability and the long timespan of their existence, behavioral drift should have led the ships to diverge from their core dogma of intolerance for all other technological lifeforms—except mechanisms existed to prevent that.

Every encounter between two warships was a chance to reassert the primacy of Chenzeme dogma. As the ships exchanged data they tested and challenged and compared themselves, one to the other, in a process that assessed and exposed their behavioral drift. The stronger ship would suppress or rewrite heretical thoughts in the weaker one. Either ship could trigger an instinct that would drive the other to return *swan* where it would be met with devices designed to reset the programming, thoughts, and memories of a warship straying from dogma.

Urban had learned these things partly through his experiences on the Null Boundary Expedition, and in part through his explorations of the deep-time memories of *Dragon*'s philosopher cells.

Those cells were now thoroughly tainted by his influence, their behavior far diverged from dogma, but their alien nature would not be immediately apparent to another courser—not until an exchange of dust exposed the truth. But *Dragon* would strike before that point.

Dragon was a hybrid ship, armed with molecular weapons unknown to other Chenzeme coursers. In its two past encounters it had used the camouflage of its philosopher cells to get close to an enemy courser—close enough to deploy packets laden with a molecularly active dust that destroyed the hull cells of its prey—striking before the other ship could release its own transformative dust.

In the immediate aftermath of this assault, the enemy courser was left helpless. Urban had used the interval to harvest mass from the stricken ship and then he'd retreated, opening up a safe distance before using the gamma-ray gun to destroy the hulk that remained.

Clemantine had insisted on learning all of this long ago. She'd studied the past encounters through library records and re-lived them through the detailed memories retained by *Dragon's* philosopher cells. Urban had assisted her, answered her questions. Now, he cautioned her:

*Hijacking a ship will be more complicated. It will be riskier. More opportunity for something to go wrong. Only the opening gambit will be the same. Dragon must present itself as authentically Chenzeme.

*I understand.

With the philosopher cells dormant, the high bridge remained unnaturally tranquil. Urban still received a constant low boil of sensory input from the ship's bio-mechanical tissue, its circulatory system, matter storage, its reef, and from the telescopes and the organic cameras native to the hull. But that was a quiet meditation compared to the harsh, strident presence of the cells.

It had been a pleasant respite, but it was time to get on with things.

He told Clemantine: *Wake the philosopher cells.

She sent the signal he had taught her, amplified across a hundred thousand links. Small clusters of cells switched on around each point. The newly active cells roused their neighbors. Awareness swept across the vast expanse of the hull and the conversation began.

The philosopher cells had been aware of the beacon, and intent on destroying it, at the time Urban sent them into dormancy. On waking, their first action was to pinpoint their target—but it was not where they expected to find it. The cells easily picked up the beacon's signal, but swift calculations showed the ship still far outside of weapons range.

Their conversation exploded into waves of confusion and fiery anger.

Urban soothed them. He turned their attention away from the beacon and injected into the debate an awareness of the distant gleam of the trailing courser. The high bridge allowed him to do this, to address them with the alien subtlety of their own chemical language, but when expressing the meaning in human terms he was left with only crude approximations of his argument:

— *awareness: other* —

— *offer: integration* —

— *self-other exchange* —

He felt Clemantine's cool presence overlaid against his own, observing his every action and the responding activity of the cells as they quieted, as they considered his proposition. Memories of the past two encounters began to circulate, tainting the instinctive desire to meet and mate. Urban translated the cells' conversation as:

<suppress that>

<caution>

<identify: other>

The cells quickly grew more aggressive, reliving their attacks on the other ships. Their brutal successes. Their discovery of the weakness of others. They respected strength—their own strength especially. *Dragon*'s cells understood they were different:

<collective/me are strong>

<superior chenzeme>

<agreement>

They perceived the philosopher cells of other ships as inferior and tainted:

<the other is weak>

<corrupt chenzeme>

<agreement>

Quickly, a new proposition circulated:

<kill it>

Too soon for that, even if destroying the new courser had still been Urban's goal. He rejected the homicidal argument. He refused it at every point it appeared, overwhelming the field with repetitions of his initial thesis:

— *self-other exchange* —

The protocols of meeting must be observed. The cells must display the proper sequence of signals to establish trust between the two heavily armed ships. Without this first step, the new courser would not allow *Dragon* to draw close—and Urban needed to be in intimate proximity to wield his molecular weapons.

– self-other exchange –

He repeated it, again and again, and slowly the hull cells accepted this proposition.

FIFTH

Your sky survey finds a smudge of white light where none should be. You analyze the spectrum. The pattern of wavelengths identifies the object as another of the alien starships that nearly destroyed you. Its luminosity indicates it has just begun to encroach on the Near Vicinity.

Joy overtakes the ancestral mind. You've studied the dead hulk of the first ship, mapped its structure, analyzed its components on a molecular scale. You've made your preparations. You need only wait for the beast to hear your beacon. When it does, it will come in to investigate, just as the first alien ship did, but there will be no battle this time. You will lie in wait for it, and take it when it comes.

And you will finally have means to return home.

You watch the progress of the alien beast for several million seconds and then it disappears. The light of its hull cells quenched.

Fear stirs in the ancestral mind. Dread rises. *Why?* you ask yourself. *Why has it gone dark?* The first alien ship did not hide itself. Why is this one behaving differently?

The beacon continues to bleat its signal. You do not modify it or shut it off. That would be an admission of your presence here while the mindless repetition, even in the face of threat, will give the appearance of a distress beacon from a nonsentient ship.

That is your hope, anyway.

You resume your sky survey, aware that the unseen alien ship is likely modifying its course and speed. It could reappear at any time in an unexpected location.

When it finally does reappear, you realize your existence has become as precarious as it ever has been.

There are now two ships.

You wonder if this is a war you can win.

CHAPTER SIXTEEN

ABOARD THE OUTRIDER *Elepaio*, Riffan soon discovered he did not like living as a ghost. Virtual existence did not feel real to him. He could inhabit a simulation of his body within the library— a duplicate of the library aboard *Dragon*—and though it was a good simulation, even an excellent one, it never felt quite right. That virtual world was too smooth, too clean, too convenient—too lacking in the rough complexity of actual existence. It left him feeling disoriented, unsure of his ability to distinguish between reality and delusion.

He did not have the option of retreating to a physical existence. The outrider did not have the room or the resources to support a living avatar. His one alternative was to forgo the illusion of human presence entirely and exist disembodied within the sensory system of the little ship. But this, he was sure, would be far worse.

So he remained dormant for most of the long voyage to the beacon, waking his ghost for only an hour or two every few days.

Urban's ghost remained awake and alert at all times as was his custom, though he rewrote his sense of time passing so that the accumulating days did not weigh on him.

Little changed during the first year. Occasionally, the coded location in the beacon's signal would shift and Urban would make a slight revision to his course, but he still could not resolve any object at the coordinates where the beacon must be.

It was early in the second year when he observed the appearance of another courser. Envy brushed him as he imagined his other self, that version of him aboard *Dragon*, plotting to seduce and dominate and destroy this intruder. He looked forward to gaining the memory of that encounter when he finally returned to *Dragon*. Meanwhile, *Elepaio* fared on, ever closer to the source of the beacon.

A time came when *Elepaio's* telescope was finally able to distinguish an object directly ahead. A tiny dark smudge, nothing more. That it could be resolved at all indicated it had a high albedo, its surface reflecting the starlight that fell against it.

More time passed and the smudge resolved into multiple objects. This surprised Urban. He had expected to find a single large object, well-armed as it attempted to draw the curious into range. Instead, there were at least three and maybe four objects. He wasn't sure yet. One was much larger than the others and round, like a tiny planetary body stripped from the gravitational hold of its parent star and cast out into the void. The others appeared to be minute, irregularly shaped moons. Still too far away to discern details. The scene lit only by a scattering of distant starlight.

Riffan's ghost woke and exclaimed in excitement over the fuzzy image. He stayed awake as additional imagery came in. In infrared, the little moons appeared cold and lifeless. "But look at the planetary body," Riffan said. He floated cross-legged in the library while Urban stood beside him, arms crossed, studying a large, detailed projection. "It possesses a slight thermal signature, though it's not nearly large enough to maintain a molten interior. If it was a true rogue planetoid, it would have gone cold eons ago. So there must be something there. Recent enough to keep it slightly warm."

"The source of the signal," Urban said.

Riffan nodded. "A logical hypothesis."

Urban suffered a surge of impatience. He wanted to know what was there and he wanted to know *now*. But time must always be paid in full measure. No rushing it.

No holding it back, either.

Each day, *Elepaio* drew nearer to the signal's source. Each day, its telescope collected more and more faint reflected starlight and slowly, slowly, the scene became clear.

The primary object was a small rocky body, airless, and only about 320 kilometers in diameter. Its density—estimated from the orbital speed of its moons—was surprisingly low. It lacked the gravity to self-organize into a spherical shape. Even so, it was nearly spherical. That might have been coincidence. Or not.

Still, it did not appear to be an artificial world. Its surface was heavily cratered. There were no visible structures, no obvious weapons, no hints of design. Urban would have dismissed it as a stray asteroid of no real interest, except that there was a boneyard in orbit around it. Its three moons could now be distinguished as the wreckage of starships. Two with torn hulls he assumed to be human in origin because what else could they be? The third was a broken remnant of a Chenzeme courser, its hull cells dark.

Urban was also able to pinpoint the source of the beacon. It did not originate on the Rock as he'd supposed. Instead, it issued from the smaller of the two human ships—a finding that disappointed him because it suggested the beacon really was an archaic distress signal and not a lure in a trap.

Riffan said, "Maybe the first ship got in trouble and summoned the second."

"And the Chenzeme?" Urban asked. "Was it here first? Or last? And why are any of them here? And what killed them?"

"Could they have killed each other?" Riffan wondered. "The Chenzeme ship blown apart by the other two, but those two mortally wounded in the battle."

Urban shook his head. "An encounter like that would take place with the ships thousands of kilometers apart. There's no way the minor gravity of the Rock, this rogue world, would have captured all of them." He looked at Riffan. "Is there a way to know how old the wrecks are?"

This time Riffan shook his head. "I've got a search running in the library. We might be able to identify the human ships, put a date on them. Other than that, we just know they've been here long enough to lose all their heat, though whether that means a few years or millennia, we aren't going to be able to tell by distant observation."

Urban said, "I think the Chenzeme warship was the last one to come here, probably in response to the signal. It might have been curious, wanting to identify the target before it struck, but it waited too long. The next warship to pick up the signal won't come in close. As soon as it detects the wreck, it'll fire its gun—but that hasn't happened yet. That tells me the beacon is probably recent, no more than a few centuries old."

"So there *is* something at the Rock," Riffan said. "Something that can tear apart the hull of a courser as large as *Dragon.*" He laughed softly, self-deprecatingly. "My voice sounds impressively calm, doesn't it? This ghost must be poorly rendered, because it isn't communicating just how disturbed I feel. Do you still want to do the fly-by?"

"Yes. It's our only option."

They were on course to do a close fly-by, echoing Urban's passage of Deception Well. *Elepaio* had far too much relative momentum to be troubled by the Rock's slight gravity, and anyway, the little ship was too valuable to risk taking it in on a close approach. Once *Elepaio* had passed out of observational range, they would accelerate and eventually rejoin *Dragon.*

"But this means the Rock *is* a trap," Riffan said. "Just as you first suggested. We have no idea of its reach. If we get too close . . ."

He did not finish the thought. He didn't need to.

Still, Urban thought he worried too much. "If it had a long reach, why would it lure its prey in so close?" he asked.

"Because it's easier to harvest their resources that way, isn't it? Imagine it luring in ships, disabling them, feeding on their rare elements. You know, I really think we should pass by as quickly as we can."

"No," Urban said. "I want to know what's there. We're going to dump velocity, prolong our observational time. This is our one chance. We won't be coming back."

His plan was to send a disposable probe into the little system to take a closer look. The probe would carry a tiny reef that he would burn out in a brutal maneuver to reduce its relative velocity. As it neared the Rock, he would refine its course, sending it skating close to the hulks of the starships. The data the probe collected would stream back to *Elepaio*.

Scout-bots would ride aboard the probe but Urban wondered: Was that enough? His curiosity was building and, as Riffan had pointed out, this could be a dangerous venture. A scout-bot was not the most versatile option.

"I think we need to visit the system ourselves," he decided. "In first person. Physical incarnation."

Riffan regarded him with a look of shock and horror, seeming to reevaluate him as a mad man. "What? You want to dump that much velocity? Enter orbit? Risk *Elepaio*?"

Urban rolled his eyes. "*No*. We'll go aboard the probe. We're carrying all the matter and the Makers necessary to synthesize avatars. I'll transfer that to the probe, launch it, and by the time it reaches the Rock, our avatars will be ready."

"But how will we get back?"

"We won't," Urban said. Wasn't that obvious? "There's no way back. Not for an avatar. But we can get the ghosts back. We'll have their memories."

"You mean you want to abandon those other versions of ourselves? Leave them to die there in that alien place?"

"Shut them down, yes," Urban said, irritated. "Dissolve them so they can't be copied. You must have intended the same thing for that avatar you inhabited on *Long Watch*. What were you going to do with it, when you were ready to return to the Well? Leave it behind, right? You weren't going to take a shuttle in-system?"

"Of course not. It would take years to physically transit. I would have returned as a ghost, while the avatar stayed aboard *Long Watch* in cold sleep."

"Where it would eventually be recycled."

"No. It would stay there, in case I needed it again."

Urban responded to this declaration with a scowl of fierce disapproval. "That's wasteful."

"It's respectful. This concept of throw-away bodies—"

"Hey," Urban interrupted, feeling a need to defend himself. "It's not something I do all the time."

"It's what you did at the Well. You wiped that version of your-self."

"There wasn't a choice. I didn't want to stay behind."

"But you *did* stay behind. Only a ghost escaped. There was no way out for that version of you that comprised the consciousness of the avatar."

Urban grimaced. This was not a conversation he wanted to have. "That's just how it works," he said. "And that's why I shut the avatar down."

"You ended its life."

"So? It was just an avatar. A means to access a different time-line, to allow for a split existence. Nothing wrong with that. What would be wrong, ethically wrong, would be to willy-nilly create copies of yourself and maintain all of them because every copy is afraid of termination."

Riffan's lip stuck out, his brow wrinkled. "That's not what I meant. What's wrong is to create an avatar that you intend to send on a suicide mission. You can bring yourself to do it because you imagine you'll be the ghost that escapes. But what if you're not? What if you're the consciousness of the avatar and you're stuck down there and you've got no way out? Sure, your ghost has escaped, but *you're* still there! How do you think you'll feel?"

Urban glowered. "I won't feel anything because I'll shut the avatar down. Now, are you going or not?"

CHAPTER SEVENTEEN

RIFFAN AGREED TO go. Really, did he have a choice? Urban was determined to visit the Rock and it would be wrong to let him go alone. And Riffan conceded—if only to himself—that his attitude toward avatars, while not wrong, might be a bit provincial, a little too impractical for the demands of his current existence. He suspected Pasha would think so.

But then, Pasha was an exceptional individual. In general, the people of Deception Well tended to cling to the old ways. Avatars were rare and could only be used with the approval of the council. Even then, only one instance of an individual could be awake and aware at any given time, so that when Riffan had served on *Long Watch*, he'd had to leave his original body in cold sleep in the city of Silk.

But Deception Well was far behind him now. He'd embarked on a new life with new demands, and also, new opportunities. Pasha would see that, and she would consider him an idiot for hesitating over this issue—and she would be right.

Exploration and discovery were the very reasons Riffan had uploaded his ghost to *Dragon*. So what if he was more accustomed to exploring the galaxy through highly processed images gathered by distant orbital telescopes, rather than in person? He could adapt! He *would* adapt. He owed it to himself and to Urban and to everyone aboard *Dragon* who might wish they'd had this opportunity that had been given to him.

He promised himself this expedition to the Rock would be only the first of many adventures to come. And then he split his timeline, creating a duplicate ghost that he sent to the probe.

I'm still here, he realized. Still aboard *Elepaio*. He was not the copy destined to explore the shipwrecks and the little rocky world. Disappointment flashed across the complex pattern that defined his mind. Relief followed in its wake.

Riffan—that version assigned to the probe—awoke to panic, certain he was on the edge of death. A horrifying pressure crushed him from every side. It prevented him moving or even breathing. His arms were pinned, his legs impossible to bend. He imagined his lungs collapsed, his eyes deformed, his brain reduced to jelly. And he couldn't see a damned thing—no light at all—though he could hear: a fast ominous arrhythmic scattershot of clicks and clunks that had him imagining this container so determined to crush him might change tactics and fly apart at any moment. *Corruption and chaos!* he thought. *Why did I have to be this version of me?*

The plan called for the probe to dump velocity as it approached the planetoid—a violent deceleration that would allow it to slip into orbit. A *crushing* deceleration.

Once in orbit, the probe would separate into its components. The surveillance and communications module would break away from the cargo capsule, and then the capsule would partition, its two pods exploding apart—Urban in one, Riffan in the other.

Riffan's life depended on a tether designed to shoot out at a predetermined target. On impact, the tether's hot zone would bond, forming an anchor to prevent his momentum from carrying him away in some useless and fatal direction.

Riffan thought the whole scheme quite precarious, but he was only a copy of himself after all. An expendable copy. A copy created to be left behind.

Shit, shit, shit.

The pod burst open—or so Riffan surmised in the seconds that followed. In the moment he was only aware of a sudden release of pressure, starlight everywhere, cool air rushing into his lungs only to rush out again in a choked scream as he gave vent to his terror.

This was his first experience in open space, the first time he'd worn a skin suit. Not exactly a gentle introduction.

Breathe, he ordered himself.

The suit fit like a thick, insulating second skin. A muzzle over his nose and mouth fed him delightful cool air. Through the clear visor he saw a black mass slowly roll into his view frame. It appeared infinitely large, quenching stars. Then it slid away, and a multicolored blaze of stars rose sedately above its horizon. Moments later, another dark shape moved into his field of view.

Oxygenated blood must have begun to reach his brain because it came to him that he was slowly spinning.

Aboard *Elepaio*, Urban watched the light-speed delayed images sent from the probe. Riffan's ghost hovered beside him.

The probe had conducted a detailed survey of the planetoid on its approach. It had found no artificial structures, no outgassing, no ice deposits. Nothing to hint at life or at mechanical activity. If anything was there, it was hidden, and there was no time to conduct a more thorough search. *Elepaio* would not remain within communications range for long.

That was why the probe had gone in fast and burned out its reef, dumping velocity in a hard deceleration. Now it swung around the Rock in a low, slow orbit. One set of cameras continued to study the terrain, but Urban watched the series of images generated by the second camera set, assigned to survey the shipwrecks.

The Chenzeme ship was a fragment. Only half its hull remained. It tumbled bow over broken-midsection in an extremely low orbit.

"What could have done that?" Riffan asked in a fearful whisper. He did not seem to expect an answer and Urban did not offer one.

The two other ships rode in higher orbits as if they'd been deliberately parked. Nothing about them suggested they were Chenzeme, but neither did they resemble one another.

The smaller of the two, the one that was the source of the beacon, was not even a quarter of the length and circumference of *Dragon*. By its size and its design, Urban recognized it as a fusion-powered starship of the migration—the same class of ship as *Null Boundary* had been—large enough to transit between worlds while carrying hundreds of passengers in cold sleep. The frontier had been populated by such ships.

The other starship was in a slightly lower orbit. It was huge, close to *Dragon* in size. Along the tapered cylinder of its hull Urban could see the blown-out remnants of longitudinal ridges that might once have been vent tubes similar to *Dragon*'s, suggesting it had been powered by a reef—but he was sure it was no Chenzeme ship. The dimensions were wrong and there was no indication of even a glossy remnant of philosopher cells.

Both ships had been breached, but the pattern of damage indicated a destructive force originating from within their hulls—suggesting to Urban that each crew had made the desperate decision to scuttle their own ship.

Riffan groped for the tether that was supposed to be anchored to the chest of his skin suit. It *had* to be there. If it wasn't there, he was going to spin away into some uncontrolled eccentric orbit and no doubt eventually collide catastrophically with one of the dead starships.

Relief washed through him as his gloved hands found the tether, closed around it. The gloves translated the feel of the line. Solid. Not like a rope, but like a thin rod. Its molecular structure had expanded to absorb his wild momentum, gradually reducing his velocity so that he had not been fatally crushed when he hit the end of the line.

The tether vibrated. It would be contracting now, arresting his gyrations and drawing him in to . . . *what?*

The DI guiding the probe had been in charge of choosing their landing site. If it sighted an obvious structure or entrance on the surface of the planetoid, they were to have touched down there. If not, their target would be the wrecked ship that was the source of the beacon.

Riffan held onto the tether. Faint blue dots glowed along its length. He felt infinitely grateful to have them there. Everything else was so dark. The stars so far away. Those little blue lights gave him something to focus on, a receding line that pointed to a black bulk. He could not tell how far away that dark object was, but that would be where the tether had anchored itself, its holdfast molecularly bonded to the surface . . . whatever that surface might be.

Riffan's skin suit spoke in a brusque female voice. "Boosting default visibility." The voice sounded unexpectedly familiar, leaving Riffan to worry that it had spoken to him before but he'd been too crushed and frightened to properly notice. He hoped he hadn't missed anything too important.

"Thank you," he murmured, though of course no response was required because it was only the generated voice of his skin suit's DI.

The optics of his visor shifted. The luminous intensity of the distant stars remained the same, but the black mass ahead of him brightened, acquiring detail. Definitely not the planetoid. He decided he was looking at the smooth outer hull of one of the orbiting starships. Quite large—and looming larger against the stars with each passing second. He didn't think it'd be long before he made contact.

"Urban?" he asked tentatively.

A response came at once through his atrium:

I'm here. It's all good. His voice calm, unrattled. *Selected target is the beacon ship. Scout-bots have already been released.* And then he added, *Hell of a ride in, huh?*

Anger was almost refreshing. "You're insane, you know that?"

Urban laughed. *Hey, we made it.*

"Where are you, anyway?" Riffan asked, turning his head to search for Urban. "I don't—" He broke off, his attention caught by the sight of the planetoid's surface slowly passing by below him.

The Rock did not look so tiny from his present low orbit. Instead, it looked planetary in scale.

Despite his enhanced optics, the surface of the Rock remained dim, its rugged impact craters appearing flattened under starlight that arrived at nearly the same intensity from every direction. He turned to look at those stars—and shuddered as an atavistic fear of falling swept over him. He felt as if he was falling into those stars, so unreachably far he would be falling forever.

Squeezing his eyes shut, Riffan clutched at the tether, his heart hammering.

"Twenty seconds until termination," the suit informed him.

Termination?

Riffan opened his eyes again to see that the bulk of the shipwreck was approaching rather swiftly. Wasn't this tether supposed to control his speed? Prevent him from crashing so hard he knocked himself out?

As if in answer, he felt a sharp, sideways jerk. Following the line of blue lights, he could see that the tether had bent at a point many meters ahead of him. Now, instead of racing straight at the hull, he moved at a sedate speed, swinging in at an angle.

His leisurely approach allowed time to look around. Not necessarily a good thing. He felt dizzy and disoriented as his brain struggled to decide if he was adrift alongside a great vertical wall or descending toward a horizontal plane. In either case, he felt quite small beside the immense hull, and awed by the myriad tiny scars marring its surface, testimony to past interstellar crossings and the unavoidable impacts of high-speed molecules.

He wondered why the hull had not self-repaired. It chilled him to think the ship had died before that task could be done—a somber thought that reminded him he was not going to get out of there. A ghost would escape, but not this version of him. His heart fluttered in the rush of a quiet, desperate fear.

You are the ghost, he told himself, unsure if this was truth or lie.

Sudden, startling motion anchored him back in the present. His gaze instinctively tracked it. A stick figure: four thin jointed legs, each half a meter in length, attached to an ovoid central point a few centimeters in size. It cartwheeled across the hull. Not alone. He glimpsed three more objects just like it, disappearing in different directions.

Scout-bots. There were ten of them altogether, somewhere. They'd been dropped off by the probe, just as he'd been.

Seeing those bots brought Riffan's mind back to the task. He reminded himself that there would be only a few hours to explore. Focus on that, he told himself. Do the job. And remember: *You're lucky to be here.*

He looked ahead to where the arc of his approach would take

him, and he spotted Urban at last, floating a few meters above the edge of a gaping fissure torn open in the side of the starship.

The fissure was at least fifty meters long, half that in width. It looked as if the ship had ruptured from the inside. Torn and jagged sheets of bio-mechanical tissue had burst outward before freezing in the chill of the void, forming colossal, glass-edged blades that stood all around the perimeter of the wound.

The probe relayed multiple data streams to *Elepaio*, allowing Urban to monitor the planet, along with the activity of the scout-bots as they dispersed across the hull or dove into the opening torn into the ship's side.

Each time a scout-bot's leg tapped the deck it fused briefly, sampling the substrate, analyzing its composition. The hull itself, though crystallized and inactive, proved to be typical bio-mechanical tissue, its structure identical to that of *Elepaio*, confirming for Urban that this was one of the great ships of the frontier.

There were no active defensive Makers on the hull, though some of the bots detected frozen molecular fragments that matched known designs.

"Have a look," Riffan urged him. "We're getting a sketch of the interior."

Urban looked up from the molecular reports.

Two scout-bots had descended into the fissure. The data they returned was being used to create a three-dimensional schematic map. It floated above the library floor, drawn in glowing white lines. It showed the fissure descending through what looked like solid tissue to a horizontal opening far below. Probably a deck. The schematic brightened as translucent colors filled the area of the open deck: a temperature gradient.

"It shouldn't be warm down there," Urban said, his rising tension reflected in his voice. "Looks like we found something."

Riffan sounded distressed when he said, "We can't warn them."

"No." The light-speed lag prevented a conversation. "But they have the same data. They see what we see."

"They'll know when to back out," Riffan said, though he didn't sound convinced. "I mean, if it's dangerous . . ." His voice trailed off.

"It doesn't matter," Urban reminded him.

Only the ghosts would be returning. Riffan was having a hard time with that idea and despite the force of his earlier argument, Urban didn't like it either. He remembered the first time he'd had to dissolve his body . . . well, he didn't remember it, because *he* was the ghost who'd escaped. His core consciousness had remained behind, trapped in a dying husk, no way out. His visit to *Long Watch* was only the second time he'd abandoned a body, but he'd planned for it, so the process had been easy.

"Yes, you're right," Riffan said with a reluctant nod. "Their fate has already been decided." He turned to look again at the map and exclaimed, "Hey . . . is that something moving in the interior?"

Startled, Urban followed his pointing finger and saw, at the edge of the deck's mapped space, the vague suggestion of a humanoid figure. He scowled. Riffan had an over-active imagination. "It's *not* moving."

"I saw it move."

"It could be the body of one of the crew. It might be just a skin suit."

"I saw it move," Riffan insisted. "I'll run that segment again and—"

On the deck, tags flashed at either side of the mapped space, reporting the same status for both scout-bots: *Signal lost.*

Urban had expected to lose contact once the bots were deep enough into the interior that the hull blocked their transmissions. He had not expected to lose contact this soon—and not simultaneously.

More ominous, the beacon ceased to bleat.

"*Shit,*" Riffan whispered. "And we can't warn them."

Urban's answer was grim and pragmatic. "They already know."

SIXTH

A radio signal alerts you. Faint. Impossible to know from what direction it originates or how far away its source might be, but you know this much: It is human.

Hell of a ride in, huh?

A familiar language, common to many worlds. Your players spoke in this tongue , though their accent was different. She spoke thus when she said, *Let us make a world together*. And you answered, *Yes*.

Most of your attention—and your telescopes—have been trained on the distant pair of alien ships, but your attention is made up of many threads, many perspectives. Some of these threads shift to review recent data collected by your ongoing sky survey.

A few seconds later you find an anomaly: a background star momentarily eclipsed. Something out there, dark, silent, and moving fast. A fly-by, come to investigate your beacon, but at a cautious distance. You might have missed it altogether if not for the radio chatter that's spilling now over your senses:

Hell of a ride in, huh?

You're insane, you know that?

Hey, we made it.

Where are you, anyway?

You do the math and draw a conclusion within a microsecond. The silent fly-by is moving too fast to rendezvous or to return, but it has delivered at least two avatars. They are here on a one-way expedition, likely less than ten thousand seconds in duration. Only data will be returned.

You admire their daring and their cleverness.

You intend to defeat their caution.

CHAPTER EIGHTEEN

URBAN'S TETHER ANCHORED him beside the fissure. He drifted above the sharp sheets of torn and frozen bio-mechanical tissue, eyeing a read-out of data from two scout-bots making their way down the interior wall.

Movement drew his attention away from the display. He cleared it and looked up to see the anchor securing Riffan's tether migrating across the scarred hull, sliding closer with amoebic motion. At the same time, the tether—morphed now into a rod—bent at a sharp angle, swinging Riffan in, bringing him to a floating stop alongside Urban.

Riffan craned his neck to peer into the fissure.

Far below, a light flashed, briefly illuminating a section of the inner wall. After a few seconds, another flash.

The scout bots, Riffan said.

"Yes," Urban acknowledged, speaking aloud. He'd sent scout-bots one and two to survey and map the fissure.

You're going in, aren't you?

"*We're* going in."

Using his atrium, Urban signaled the light-emitting panels on the shoulders of his skin suit to switch on.

"I want you to stay at least ten meters behind me. If you lose your link to the probe, go back up until you get a signal. You're the relay. I need you to make sure a full record of this gets back to *Elepaio*."

I understand, Riffan said. *But what if I lose your signal?*

Urban shrugged. "Come rescue me?"

*Not funny.

"Do what you think is best."

He followed the scout-bots down, his tether trailing behind him as he glided past the ship's outermost layer of insulation. The tissue glittered, its frozen crystals catching and reflecting his suit's light, looking smoother than he'd expected. Maybe some of the rough edges had evaporated into the void over passing centuries.

His goal was to find information, a ship's log or library that would tell him where the crew had come from, why they'd come and when, and if this site had anything to do with the Hallowed Vasties. And he wanted to know what had happened to them and to their ship, and why they'd left a beacon bleating their location, *if* they were the ones who'd left it.

He hoped the fissure would reach at least to the outermost deck. It wasn't likely he'd be able to go any farther than that. The most secure, protected, and sheltered sections of the ship—its cold-sleep cells, computational strata, and core chamber—would be sealed and inaccessible within an insulating cocoon of frozen bio-mechanical tissue. He had no way to get past that, not in the time available, so he had to hope the crew had left some easily accessible record intended to warn the curious of the hazard they had encountered here.

Or maybe they'd thought the scuttled ship was warning enough?

On the periphery of his vision, the three-dimensional map charted by the scout-bots showed his position and Riffan's in the fissure. He'd descended halfway through the mapped space of the near-vertical walls; Riffan was at least twenty meters above him.

Abruptly, the map expanded horizontally. Urban eyed it as he continued to drift downward. The scout-bots had found a deck. It was a large open area, maybe intended for storage or construction. Translucent colors appeared, indicating a temperature gradient—matter warmer than the uniform frozen temperature of the fissure's walls.

He shifted his display, accessing direct infrared video from the two scout-bots. Both video feeds showed a deck that was mostly empty. No drifting debris. The only visible structures were several towering cubes. They were set far apart and extended from the deck's floor to its high ceiling. The sides of the cubes were shingled with leaves of gray . . . *glass*? That's what it looked like, glass shingles warm enough to glow brightly in infrared. But they were not the warmest object captured by the scout-bot's cameras.

That was the gray-glass figure of a man, standing beyond the blocks, upside down to the orientation of the cameras. Details were hard to discern in the bright blaze of heat, but Urban was certain he saw the figure move—right before the video feed dropped out.

"Riffan," he said, "stay where you are."

What was that? Riffan whispered. And then, *Oh, shit. I've lost my link to the probe.*

Urban's skin suit confirmed it. "Uplink lost," it informed him.

"Go back," Urban ordered. "Recover the link."

What are you going to do?

"I'm going on."

Urban—

"Just go!"

He slapped the wall. Shot downward. He wanted to know what they'd found. He wanted video of it to send back to *Elepaio*.

As he neared the bottom, his tether morphed to slow his descent. His light illuminated a fan-shaped slice of the deck and sparkled against the gray glass that shingled the nearest of the massive cubes.

He looked for the upside-down glass man, but did not see him.

A red light popped on in the periphery of his vision. His skin suit spoke again, informing him in a calm voice, "Suit integrity is under threat." Urban sucked in a sharp breath. That meant he was under attack but not with a weapon he could directly perceive. The assault was taking place on a molecular scale.

A moment later, the suit spoke again, announcing the failure of Urban's molecular defenses: "Suit integrity has been compromised."

Foreign nanomachines had fought past the skin suit's defenses, breaching it, opening microscopic channels through its fabric. He felt the results as needles of cold that stabbed into his hands, his chest, his eyes.

Only for a moment.

The cold subsided as the suit self-repaired, but the enemy was already inside. Urban cried out as searing heat erupted at the points where his suit had been penetrated. His vision clouded. A battle was being fought across the moist surfaces of his eyes, as well as against the skin of his chest and hands—his defensive Makers against the intruding nanotech.

He clenched his fists against the pain and when, after a few seconds, the pain failed to subside, he knew he had lost. His defensive Makers had failed to protect him, leaving him at the mercy of whatever it was that existed down here.

Urban did not trust the mercy of alien lifeforms.

The pain in his eyes sharpened. He envisioned the attacking nanomachines driving deeper into his head. Soon they would reach his brain, his atrium. God knows what would happen then.

He wasn't going to let it happen. He wasn't going to leave any meaningful data for this lifeform to exploit.

No time to prepare a ghost.

Just end it.

"Riffan!" he shouted, hoping his comms still worked. "We're terminating!"

What? No! I'm still trying to recover the link.

A memory, searing across Urban's consciousness: the first time he'd had to terminate. He'd been dying, but still so hard to do. He'd known Riffan wouldn't be up to it, not without hesitation. So on the way in he'd hacked Riffan's avatar, setting up a code word that would kick off the termination sequence for both of them. He spoke it.

No! Riffan screamed.

But the process was already underway. Hosts of Makers erupted from the tendrils of their atriums, replicating madly, consuming brain tissue to do it, converting the content of their skulls into gray goo, devoid of information.

Contact had been lost with the avatars and with scout-bots one and two—the pair that had entered the shipwreck—but *Elepaio* remained in contact with the probe. Data was still being received. The scout-bots assigned to explore the shipwreck's hull were still active, while the probe's cameras continued to watch both the wreck and the planetoid below.

Urban felt a submind drop in. It melded with his ghost, bringing him the knowledge that there was now activity on the planetoid's surface.

He turned to examine a continuously updating three-dimensional projection of the Rock that floated in the virtual space of *Elepaio*'s library. All its cracks and craters had been carefully mapped, but that map was now being revised as the seemingly lifeless surface began to change.

The latest images showed black circles that had not been observed before. The features appeared at high points on the planet's scarred surface: the rims of craters, the peaks of low, folded hills. Perfect circles of darkness. Urban counted ten, then fifteen, then twenty of them. No pattern in their arrangement.

They looked like tiny spots on the face of this little world, but the scale showed them to be at least five hundred meters across. He suspected they were pits, holes in the ground, missile silos maybe. If so, they were huge.

More appeared as the probe continued to advance in its slow orbit, collecting fresh images of the surface.

Urban realized Riffan was now hovering beside him. "Corruption take us," he whispered. "And chaos too."

"It's definitely awake now," Urban said. "Whatever it is."

"Let's see it in infrared."

The library obliged and each circle shifted from black to blazing white. "Subterranean network," Riffan said. "Got to be. Significantly warm. Maybe a fusion power source. Impressive how little of that interior heat we were able to detect before the doors opened."

"Skilled at playing dead," Urban agreed.

The circles began to pulse, growing briefly brighter—not synchronized, not flaring everywhere at once, not flaring in a discernible pattern—but repeatedly.

"A weapon?" Riffan wondered.

"Not enough power there to harm us."

"A code?"

"Meant for who?"

Riffan shook his head. "Possible to get scout-bots down there?"

"No. They've all been deployed."

The probe continued its orbital survey but found no more openings. The region below it now appeared to be the same unmarked, lifeless surface they'd first seen.

"*Hey,*" Riffan said suspiciously. "What's going on? Do you think there's no activity in this region?"

"Or is the activity already over with?" Urban asked. "Did silos open here too, but close before we could record them?"

He wanted to do the impossible: Turn the probe around, look again at the area just surveyed, determine if the openings they'd seen were still there. But by the time the probe could survey that region again, they'd be out of communications range.

He turned an uneasy gaze back to the library window that held the latest image of the shipwreck, but there was nothing new to see there.

"*Damn,*" he whispered, angry because he might never figure out what had just happened.

The voice of a DI interrupted his brooding thoughts. "Contact reestablished with scout-bot one," it announced. "Current transmission is voice only."

"It's *recovered,*" Riffan whispered in wonder. "Maybe—"

Urban cut him off with a slashing gesture. "It's not the scout-bot. The scout-bot doesn't have a voice." But something was there at the Rock. It had caused him to lose the avatars, it had taken his scout-bots, and now it was playing with him.

A new image of the shipwreck posted. The wreck appeared the same, but the figure of a man could now be seen standing on the ruptured hull, just outside of the torn, frozen tissue surrounding the fissure.

The man was not him. It was not Riffan.

In all likelihood it was also not a man because he was standing naked on the hull without the benefit of a skin suit. Scale was hard to gauge, but Urban guessed him to be of moderate human height. A lean but muscular build, black hair adrift in the zero gravity, his complexion seeming dark in the dim light. His eyes were dark too, cast in shadow as he looked back at the watching probe—which made it feel as if he was looking Urban in the eyes.

"A bio-mechanical entity," Urban decided.

"Agreed," Riffan said softly. "We're dead in there, aren't we?"

"Yes."

"It beat us."

"It did."

They'd entered the shipwreck protected by Urban's best defensive Makers, but they had not come out again. Not even a ghost had escaped.

The entity spoke—or at least its mouth moved in an imitation of words that it could not possibly be uttering without the presence of air. Urban heard its words anyway as its voice rode the channel that had formerly belonged to scout-bot one. The voice was human, male, rich in tone, and powerful. It said: "We can help each other."

Urban had studied history. He was aware there were hundreds of human languages. He'd even learned a few over the long, empty stretches of time he'd lived through. Of all those languages, this voice spoke *his* language, the one language of Deception Well, and it used the same archaic accent that Urban used.

Fear accelerated his simulated heartbeat. Had his avatar failed to terminate in time? Had this thing harvested information from his mind? He throttled the connection rate to ensure no ghost would be able to get through.

"What did you just do?" Riffan asked when the image failed to update.

"Voice only," Urban said. "I don't want its ghost showing up at the data gate."

"God, no," Riffan breathed. And then added, "We can't answer it."

"No." The light-speed lag prevented conversation.

Maybe the entity didn't realize this. Maybe it thought it was speaking to a consciousness housed in the probe. "We *will* help each other," it warned.

"It wants off the Rock," Urban said. He smiled grimly. Shook his head. "Not going to happen. We're going to stay far, far away."

That thing was dangerous. Two crews had made the choice to wreck their ships, stranding themselves, rather than allowing this being to escape its isolation. And it had beaten a Chenzeme courser as well as Urban's best defensive Makers.

He would have to improve his defenses.

That would be difficult without insight on the system that had defeated him. This thought led him to ponder the risks he would be facing in his determination to explore the Hallowed Vasties. Had this entity come from there? Did it represent what was left there, what he could expect to find? He feared it might be so. All the same, he longed to know.

The entity spoke again. It said, "I mean you no harm." An assurance made unconvincing by its threatening tone.

"I wonder how you got here," Urban mused aloud. "Was that an accident? Or did a bigger monster exile you?"

"I wish we could talk to it," Riffan said.

Urban nodded his agreement. Still, "It's distance that keeps us safe."

He hoped the entity would speak again, but it did not.

Sometime later, *Elepaio* struck debris, the concussion made audible in Urban's virtual environment. Fear gripped him, along with a profound awareness of the fragility of his little ship. He desperately wanted to make it back to *Dragon*, tell his story. A quick check showed no damage to essential systems. No doubt there was a charred crater in the hull, but it would heal.

Minutes later, a second impact, less brutal than the first.

Nothing after that.

The beacon did not resume.

Days passed. The mystery of the Rock fell ever farther behind them in both space and time. Riffan grew bored with the transit.

He disappeared into dormancy, leaving Urban alone to reflect over what they'd found. Not just the entity.

His thoughts kept returning to the two ships of human origin and the decision their crews had made to scuttle them. It pleased Urban to think he'd done better, that he'd escaped relatively unscathed given the superiority of the entity's nanotechnology. At the least, he'd come away with the knowledge of its existence.

Still, he regretted not learning more, and as time dragged on he began to wonder if he'd done all he could. A familiar self-appraisal. So easy to drift from there into a gyre of regret for things past, lost things, things he had not been able to save.

Once before, an alien nanotechnology had defeated his best efforts to decode it. That time, it had not attacked him, only locked him out.

"I couldn't save him," he murmured. A recurring lamentation.

Now, a thousand years on, he'd encountered a being that had easily overwhelmed his best defenses. And he wondered, *If I'd had its knowledge back then, its power, would that have made a difference?*

Regret weighed on him, and guilt for what had happened—but these were feelings he rejected out of habit. Time flowed in one direction only, life did not grant do-overs, and it was his nature to reject any suggestion of melancholy. A useless emotion. Better to arm up. Be ready. Be stronger, faster, smarter.

Right now he was vulnerable.

He'd done the smart thing by keeping his distance from the Rock. That had let him avoid any risk of contamination ... but what had his avatar done?

His avatar was him and he knew what he would have done. The moment he understood his defenses had been breached, he would have terminated. Urban—in any form—was haunted by a deep fear of being hijacked, of having an avatar rebuilt or resurrected without agency, under the control of another. Still—why had the encounter been hostile?

Maybe it had been an accidental conflict. If the entity had sought information and pushed too hard, a nanoscale war could have erupted.

The thing had said, *We can help each other*.

Was that an apology?

It had been a long time since Urban had encountered anything stronger than himself, a long time since he'd been challenged. He wished he could have learned more.

He considered what it would take to go back to the Rock, even though he knew he would not do it. To reverse *Dragon*'s momentum and return would require years.

To hell with second-guessing. Better to push on. The Hallowed Vasties lay ahead. He was sure to find ample opportunities there to test his skills and his nerve.

Yet regret persisted, a vaporous presence in his virtual world.

So he edited his ghost, making it less vulnerable to melancholy, to introspection, to boredom. Then he summoned several specialized DIs and with their help he spent the remainder of the return voyage immersed in the task of developing new lines of defensive Makers.

CHAPTER NINETEEN

CLEMANTINE FLOATED CROSS-LEGGED in the forest room, her chest rising and falling in slow, meditative breaths as she gazed into the sunlit forest where a simulated breeze stirred a few fading leaves into subtle motion. The chatter and whistles of birdsong sounded from overhead. She listened, pretending she was not afraid.

In a private virtual space within the library, she floated cross-legged amid the darkness of the void, watching *Dragon* approach its prey. Her perspective, that of the outrider *Artemis*, standing off a mere twelve kilometers, brought in to observe the interaction of the two coursers.

On the high bridge, she observed that interaction in greater intimacy, watching alongside Urban as *Dragon*'s philosopher cells carried out the intricate, instinctive ritual of greeting: <*self-other exchange*>

Subminds migrated among her aspects, so that she existed simultaneously across all three timelines as time advanced and the two ships drew closer to one another.

Both glowed white with the light of their hull cells. Through human eyes, Clemantine perceived it as a constant light, but through her Chenzeme senses she distinguished rapid pulses of communication. Warnings and murderous threats at first, giving way to continuous affirmations of identity and cooperative intent as the two coursers negotiated the intricate navigational steps required to bring them parallel to one another.

Relative to nearby stars they still hurtled at close to thirty-one percent light speed, but within their own frame of reference they became nearly stationary, only slowly drifting to close the two-point-five kilometer gap that remained between them.

Both were massive starships, but their size was not apparent in the video feed out of *Artemis* because there was nothing human within range of the watching cameras that could lend perspective. This encounter was purely alien—or it appeared that way.

In truth, *Dragon's* blazing hull was camouflage disguising hostile intentions. Beneath that bright surface, a hundred thousand needle-like projectiles lay ready to launch, each one packed with proven molecular weapons.

Clementine breathed deeply, fighting the anxiety, the tension that tried to rise as the distance between the two coursers narrowed, closing at a rate close to 3.5 seconds per meter.

In a normal encounter between Chenzeme ships, the ritualized exchange of data-encoded dust would not begin until physical contact was nearly established, but Urban meant for her to take control of the second courser long before that point.

He waited until the distance between the ships dropped below two kilometers. Then he called it: *Time to go dark.*

Clementine responded: *Sooth, let's do it.*

No quiet suggestion this time. Urban formatted a harsh command—

– *GO DARK* –

—and dropped it simultaneously across his hundred thousand links.

Clementine followed with a supporting argument issued in a different voice:

– *affirm now - go dark* –

Artemis's camera showed tendrils of darkness shooting across *Dragon's* hull, branching, linking, expanding . . . stagnating.

Counter arguments erupted as allied cells resisted the call to go dormant. No such call had been made during the previous attacks against other coursers. Remembering this, the most aggressive cells fought the unexpected deviation, and the wave of dormancy began to reverse.

In the darkness of the library, Clementine watched in fatalistic detachment. In the forest room, her heartbeat quickened in fear. On the high bridge her anger escalated. This time *she* seized the hammer of argument:

– *GO DARK!* –

And Urban followed with a hundred thousand supporting voices:

– *affirm now – go dark –*

The objective of this encounter was capture, not annihilation. The cells had fulfilled their role by getting *Dragon* close. Now they needed to go dark so they could do no harm.

Across the hull, the weight of argument shifted again. Allied networks of cells reinforced the emphatic directive: <*affirm now – go dark*>

Within seconds, only a few scattered cells remained awake, points of white, like the last stars on the galaxy's edge.

The alien courser reacted immediately. Any deviation in expected behavior had to be interpreted as a threat—so it tried to withdraw. It triggered its propulsion reef. *Artemis* observed it shudder as it made a desperate effort to pull away.

It could not move fast enough to evade attack.

All along *Dragon*'s length, half a million needle projectiles shot out through seams between the dormant hull cells. Each was a long thin barb of diamond, engineered to shatter along deliberate fault lines to allow the release of the payload of assault Makers carried within a hollow interior.

In seconds, the needles crossed the void between the two ships. They struck the alien courser. Most shattered against the glassy surfaces of its hull cells, uselessly releasing the Makers they carried in bursts of harmless mist. But some hundreds struck the inter-locking seams between the cells and penetrated into the underly-ing bio-mechanical tissue.

These needles shattered too, but here their payload had a purpose. Assault Makers spilled into the Chenzeme tissue. The Makers set to work, replicating even as they set up a defensive perimeter.

Chenzeme nanomachines responded to the incursion, but the

invading Makers had fought battles like this before. They understood Chenzeme design and Chenzeme tactics and they used that knowledge to push back the attack, expanding their defensive perimeter.

Within the secured territory, other Makers worked to gather raw material that they used to construct cardinal nanosites. Within a minute, several hundred of the tiny processing nodes were scattered throughout the courser's tissue.

The cardinals began to send out tendrils, guarded by assault Makers. The surrounding tissue grew hot with the activity of construction and conflict. Minutes passed. The tendrils began to find one another. They linked up, connecting the cardinals in a network that continued to grow, wrapping around the captive courser, diving inward to connect with critical systems, and expanding outward to reach the philosopher cells, establishing a high bridge.

The bridge issued a single, simple command to the now-captive philosopher cells, stimulating them to emit a short, chaotic radio burst.

Clemantine heard it in the library. She heard it on *Dragon*'s high bridge. Affirmation that the alien courser was now hers. Moments later she heard a ping of greeting from the captive courser's newly constructed data gate.

In the library, she edited her ghost to numb her dread.

In the forest room she filled her lungs, emptied them again, and swore she would become what she needed to be.

From the high bridge came the anxious thought: *No time to hesitate!*

The courser was bridged, but until Clemantine assumed her post there, its philosopher cells would continue to control the ship. A dark line had opened in its cell field, swiftly expanding to allow deployment of its gamma-ray gun. Its steerage jets were firing, pushing its massive bulk toward an angle that would allow the gun's swiveling lens to bear on *Dragon*.

Clemantine synthesized a new ghost, one endowed with the memories of all three current timelines. She sent it through the data gate. And seemingly without transition she plunged into a furious consensus:

<revulsion: false chenzeme>

<kill it!>

<it threatens>

<kill it!>

<fight now>

<kill it!>

<reinforce revulsion: false chenzeme>

Clemantine wanted to recoil. The coordinated currents of hate, the murderous contempt, the deep craving need to inflict fiery death on all that was not self or the equivalent of self—it horrified her, but she plunged in anyway. No choice. She had to take control.

She extended her senses across the high bridge—so different from *Dragon*'s high bridge!—its structure still expanding, growing, extending ever more links into the cell field.

Yet here at the start she had only a small percentage of the connections she'd taken for granted aboard *Dragon*. Ten percent? Fifteen?

Doesn't matter!

This is what she'd been given. Her will and her anger had to make up for the rest.

Her opening argument blasted out across what she now guessed to be fifteen thousand links:

– NEGATE THAT! –

The force of it overwhelmed adjacent cells, inducing them to take it up, echo it, evaluate it, and argue—an effect that rippled outward, introducing fault lines in the agreement of the field, disrupting consensus.

She offered an alternative argument across all the links: *– the other is chenzeme –*

A counter argument slammed back: *<revulsion: false chenzeme>*

– NEGATE THAT! –

All her rage for what had been lost coiled within that short, sharp communication. A moment's stunned pause. She had shocked the field into silence; shocked herself too with the force of her anger. She recovered, and commenced to hammer her will through every link in the rapidly expanding bridge:

    – negate revulsion! the other is chenzeme –
    – negate killing! the other is chenzeme –
    – negate conflict! the other is chenzeme –
    – the other is chenzeme –
    – the other is chenzeme –
    – the other is chenzeme –
    – required: agreement –

This induced a positive response—*‹agreement›*—but it was weak.

She amplified that weak response, and extended her argument:

    – AGREEMENT! the other is chenzeme –
    – we are allied chenzeme! –
    – required: agreement –

The response came back stronger: *‹agreement›*

Still a fragile concession, but enough that she was able to cut off the steerage jets, route power away from the gun. She continued through rapid, looping argument to enforce her will, until after many seconds she hammered out hard-won consensus:

    ‹agreement: we are allied chenzeme›

The high bridge continued to grow. More links reached the cell field, each an additional point of influence, further securing Clementine's hold over the ship's mind.

She gave the newly captured courser a name: *Griffin.*

Dragon's partner**,* she explained to Urban through an open channel in the data gate. ***A second hybrid monster, a kind of chimera, a mix of different organisms.

She invited him to send a ghost to visit the new high bridge but he refused, reminding her, ***Never again.***

Instead, he sent her copies of the Apparatchiks, all six of them, to haunt the cardinal nanosites.

She welcomed them, knowing that centuries had gone into their development and that each carried centuries of experience. They were a ready-made crew and she was grateful that their presence relieved her of any need to create her own ensemble of assistants. As far back as the Null Boundary Expedition, Urban had toyed with experimental personas, but Clementine never had. Her sense of identity was too fixed for that. The idea that when her ghost split, she, this point of view, might become the one to be pruned and rewritten—it repulsed her.

And anyway, she knew how to handle the quirks of the Apparatchiks' personalities.

When the Bio-mechanic returned from an inspection of the bridge, he concluded, *My assault was flawless.

Clementine immediately disagreed. *The high bridge had insufficient connections to the cell field. I nearly lost the argument.

The arrival of a submind from that version of her on *Dragon's* high bridge made it clear how close she'd come to annihilation. When *Griffin* had fired its steerage jets, seeking an angle that would let it target *Dragon*, Urban had been prepared to fire first. A few more seconds and he would have had no choice.

But the Bio-mechanic refused any responsibility for this close call, informing her, *The number of connections available to you was a matter of chance, dependent on the quantity of needles that got through. The number was sufficient, or we would not be here now.

*We're here now only because I refused to lose the argument.

She wasn't sure victory was something to celebrate. The violent, hateful contempt of the cell field would be with her always now, her will constantly engaged to guide and dominate the argument. *A foot forever on the throat of a murderer*. Urban's words. Despite the time she'd spent on *Dragon's* bridge, she felt the truth of them only now.

The malice that circulated among *Griffin's* philosopher cells far surpassed what she'd known aboard *Dragon*—whether because Urban's presence had filtered the intensity or because *Dragon* had mellowed after centuries locked under his influence, she didn't know.

She had brought *Griffin* under control, but she felt changed by the effort. Colder. More stern and unforgiving. Not entirely herself anymore. Tainted by the merciless contempt of the Chenzeme.

A second submind arrived from across the expanding gulf that separated her from *Dragon*. It brought her memories from all three of the aspects she'd left behind. From her ghost in the library, a vision of the two coursers: *Griffin* bright with its luminous hull and *Dragon* still dark. That ghost had rejoined her core self in the forest room. Kona, Riffan, and Vytet were there too, with a victory celebration underway, while on the high bridge, she asked Urban:

When will you waken the hull cells?

When your hold on Griffin is stronger.

All of it, dreamlike. A mirrored existence that did not feel real to her. A lost world, yet more important to her than the ugly dimension she occupied.

A dream that made her reality endurable.

She set *Griffin*'s course to run parallel to *Dragon*, a hundred kilometers between them, while the Bio-mechanic and the Engineer worked to map the ship's interior and inventory its internal storage.

Another submind arrived, bringing her memories of that other world that was no longer her world, that she could only know now through memories—and in those memories she questioned herself: *What is going on over there? Why haven't I sent a submind back to* Dragon*? Why are my memories being passed in only one direction? What are you hiding?*

The truth, Clemantine wanted to say. She was hiding the truth.

Our paths have branched.

Her other self didn't know that yet. She never would know it—*not in the way I know it.*

But to silence these confused memories that demanded an explanation, she opened a channel to herself:

*Hey.

*What is going on? Her own voice answering, calm but sharp.

*There will be no synchronization, she announced. **I am not going to send any subminds to you. Stay as you are and be the better version of us.*

Seconds of silence elapsed. When that other Clemantine spoke, it was not to argue, but only to gain insight. **Is it the toxin*

*of the Chenzeme mind you're protecting me from? Or is it the way you've
changed yourself to endure it?*

The calm, rational tone of this response triggered a quiet pride
that spilled across the cell field where it was interpreted as an affirmation of power:

<*we are strong!*>

<*we are allied chenzeme!*>

It's for both those reasons, she told her other self. *Going forward,
we take separate paths. But keep sending me your subminds. Bind me to
you in that way. Keep me human.*

Sooth. I understand.

The Bio-mechanic and the Engineer worked together to complete the conversion of the captured ship. They grew the computational strata to support a library and linked that library to the
fleet. Cameras were added to the hull, and a radio antenna. They
continued to expand the bridge, growing additional neural fibers
so that Clemantine's senses extended throughout the ship and her
command of it was assured. And they initiated the growth of two
new outriders.

The Bio-mechanic had spent centuries studying *Dragon*'s internal systems and had long ago discovered a preexisting Chenzeme
protocol used to create new coursers. He activated that protocol.
Clemantine observed as the process unfolded.

Step by step, over many days, matter was assembled and organized into the basic structure of two proto-ships that took shape
within the reservoir of bio-mechanical tissue just beneath the hull
cells. The heat of activity was a distraction to Clemantine, drawing her attention ever back to the dense and growing masses. She
thought of them as parasites, feeding off of *Griffin*, weakening the
ship as they grew stronger.

She resented them, wanted to eject them from the body of the
ship.

– *negate that!* –

Griffin had been seized for the purpose of growing these outriders. She forced herself to edit her animosity, but her animosity

returned. Only slowly did she realize it came from the philosopher cells. That led her to discover a feedback loop. By Chenzeme standards, *Griffin* was too small to reproduce, so the cells resisted, pushing to eject the growth.

Interesting, the Bio-mechanic said, when she presented the problem to him. *Not an issue encountered with Dragon, given it's always been a much larger ship.*

Close the feedback loop, she told him.

Afterward, she monitored the growth of the outriders with a sense of satisfaction, not resentment.

A message from Urban: *You're secure now.*

Yes.

I'm going to wake Dragon's philosopher cells.

Affirmative. We are allied Chenzeme.

We will be, he answered. *But Dragon's philosopher cells were ready to fight when I put them under. They'll come out the same way. I'll suppress that, but expect Griffin to be provoked.*

Understood. I'm ready.

She watched across the hundred kilometer gulf as points of white light wakened on *Dragon's* hull. Her own cells noticed it immediately and fell silent, watching the white glow expand in lacy channels that widened until all of *Dragon's* hull was illuminated. To human eyes, the light appeared constant, but *Griffin's* cells saw it as a pulsing communication. They reached swift consensus on its meaning:

<*it threatens*>

Clemantine blocked a counter threat, instead presenting an argument to initiate a process of negotiated alliance:

– identify self/other: we are chenzeme –

The argument was considered, tested, approved, and a tentative consensus achieved. Intricate patterns of light, generated throughout the process, allowed *Dragon* to follow the debate from across the gulf, and to understand its conclusion.

Dragon accepted the argument, responding:

<*confirm identify self/other: we are chenzeme*>

A sense of victory flushed across the cell field, while Cleman-tine worked to define the relationship between the two ships: – *we are allied chenzeme* –

The philosopher cells affirmed this argument: <*we are allied chenzeme*>

And *Dragon*, driven by Urban's will, echoed it: <*confirm we are allied chenzeme*>

Reassurances continued to be traded for hours, confirming the new status of the ships as paired coursers—instinctive behavior that allowed them to work together without trying to kill one another.

The proto-ships continued to grow within *Griffin*'s hull. They achieved the mass of outriders. They would have continued grow-ing into massive proto-coursers, but the Bio-mechanic interrupted the process.

The assembly of the new outriders would be completed after they separated from *Griffin*. To achieve the separation, the Bio-mechanic hooked into the ship-building process again, near the end this time. A signal went out to the philosopher cells. It directed the field to split neatly above each proto-ship. Bio-mechanical motion pushed them free, imparting a slight momentum so that they drifted away from *Griffin*.

They were given the names of their predecessors, *Khonsu* and *Pytheas*, as swarms of Makers under the Engineer's direction set to work assembling their internal components.

Behind them, *Griffin*'s hull sealed shut again and a long process commenced that would draw in, consolidate, and reorganize the courser's interior to compensate for the loss of mass.

Griffin had become a smaller ship.

Small, but still toxic with malice, still deadly.

*I am going to change that attitude, Clemantine told her other self.

As time passed, she would strive to re-train the cells, to dilute their instinctive hate, their contempt. It was the only way she could conceive of enduring the years ahead.

CHAPTER TWENTY

PASHA AWOKE IN a small sunlit bedroom. She looked around without raising her head, recognized nothing, and wondered if a chunk of her recent memory had been overwritten.

Her bed cradled her within its low padded sides for which she was grateful. Even before sitting up, she felt dizzy, out of balance.

The room was done in light colors: white walls, a white carpet on a warm-brown wooden floor, translucent white curtains framing an open window with blue sky and sunlit foliage visible beyond, and an opaque gel door the color of golden honey. Through the window there came birdsong and a floral scent that sweetened the air.

"Welcome," the room told her, speaking as a gentle-voiced woman. "This is your new home aboard the starship *Dragon*. Please be cautious upon arising. You'll need to adjust your sense of balance to compensate for the centripetal force generated by the rotation of the gee deck."

Questions flooded Pasha's mind. She remembered departing for *Dragon*. It had been a decision made in haste, but also in certainty. Now doubt caught up with her.

This pleasant room—how had she come to be here? It made no sense. She should have instantiated as a ghost, but this was no simulation. The queasiness in her belly affirmed her physical reality. She wondered if this was *Dragon* after all. How could it be? Living quarters on that ship still needed to be built.

She closed her eyes, conscious now of her racing heart. Drawing a few deep breaths, she strove to calm herself. Then she checked her atrium—and her heart boomed louder.

"Why is there no network?" she asked aloud.

The house responded without actually answering her question: "There will be an orientation session for the community in just a few minutes. When you're ready, follow the path outside your front door. Everything will be explained."

She arose, staggering a little against the unaccustomed angular force of the rotating deck. *A poor simulation of gravity*, she decided sourly, and so much weaker than the gravity she'd grown up under at Deception Well that she worried an awkward move might launch her into the ceiling.

Clothing budded off an active surface of the inner wall: a beige tunic and pale-green leggings, the same thing she'd been wearing in the zero-gravity environment of *Long Watch*. She dressed quickly. Then said, "Show me my image."

A full-size projection appeared within the interior wall. She studied herself for a few seconds. It all looked right, except for her wide-eyed expression of fright. She ran fingers through the layers of her short white-blond hair, smoothing it, pushing it behind her ears, striving for calm. Pressed her palms against her still-queasy stomach. She'd had her physiology adjusted for the zero gravity aboard *Long Watch*; she would need a similar mod for this horrid circular motion.

Voices outside now:

Do you know what's going on?

No! Was it supposed to be like this?

Is this really Dragon?

Concentrating on each step to keep her balance in the weird gee, she passed through the gel doorway, the touch of its parting edges soft and dry against her arms. A living room was on the other side: mats and pillows and a small kitchen in one corner. Large open windows looked out on a garden of low, spreading trees and lush shrubbery. Scattered among the verdure were neat cottages with white curved walls and miniature meadows on their roofs. Very sweet. Very civilized.

Very wrong.

The front entrance was open, its gel door retracted out of sight. She stepped outside under a low ceiling simulating a bright blue midday sky streaked with distant white skeins of clouds. She wobbled only a little.

A small stone patio flowed into a paved path where three bewildered-looking people wandered, dressed in the brightly colored, body-hugging fashions that were popular in the city of Silk; another individual appeared in the doorway of a cottage across the path, wearing a formal suit of tunic and trousers in muted colors. With relief, Pasha recognized all four as friends and colleagues. They saw her and immediately gathered around.

"Pasha! What's going on?"

"I don't know," she answered.

"This isn't what we expected."

"I'm just as surprised," she agreed. *And concerned.*

"Where are we supposed to go?" one asked.

She said, "Let's follow the path."

The house had not said what direction to go, but Pasha didn't think it mattered. The curve of the deck was easily visible despite the softening effect of the expansive garden. In either direction, there couldn't be far to walk. She staggered a few steps, arms out for balance, but then her body began to work out how to compensate for the deck's angular pull, and she steadied. A few more steps and her nausea began to recede.

People joined them as they walked, far more than Pasha expected to see. Urban had said he wanted up to twelve volunteers ... but there were so many more. Where had they come from? Why were they here?

Among those she recognized were scientists, historians, and a scout famous from her explorations of Deception Well's planetary surface. Others were strangers. Without a network connection her atrium could not query theirs for an identity.

She approached them anyway, she approached everyone, asking if they had a network connection. No one did.

Pasha wondered again if they really were aboard *Dragon*. Amid the low buzz of conversation that surrounded her, she heard that question asked again and again by others.

Before long, the path wended around a lattice wall, and then they reached a pavilion where many more people were already gathering. At the center of the pavilion was a large oval pergola covered in neat vines bearing little star-shaped flowers. The pergola sheltered a small amphitheater with a low dais facing four curved tiers of seats.

Riffan was there, smiling, urging the new arrivals to take seats as if he was some kind of authority, someone who knew what was going on. This did not sit well with Pasha. It offended her to be kept in the dark like a child. She meant to demand an explanation, but as she started toward him, those who had arrived ahead of her moved inside and she saw that Urban was also standing there.

Urban, who was master of *Dragon*, to whom they had all entrusted their lives. Better to direct her questions at him.

She separated herself from the anxious swirl of her friends and angled toward him. But after a few steps, she realized she was mistaken. This tall man with the dark complexion was Kona, not Urban. He beckoned to her ... no, to everyone in her group. "Please," he told them, "no questions yet. Take a seat and everything will be explained."

Pasha was tempted to question him anyway, but a woman just behind her spoke first. "Kona! By the Waking Light, it's a comfort to see you here! But what is this place? Are we really aboard *Dragon*?"

Pasha looked over her shoulder, identifying the speaker as the planetary scout.

Kona knew her by name. "Greetings, Shoran," he said. There was fondness in his voice, but he put her off anyway. "Everything will be explained. Please take a seat."

Shoran's chin lowered, her eyes narrowed in a combative expression.

"Please," Kona said in an undertone. "I need your cooperation, your example. Things have not gone quite as we expected."

"That's easy to see," Shoran replied tartly. Her gaze shifted as she took in Pasha watching her. Their eyes met. Shoran inclined her head: an invitation. "Come," she said to Pasha as if they were friends though they'd never met. "Let's cooperate for now. We can conspire to revolution later, if the explanation does not suit."

Pasha went with her reluctantly, leaving Kona to face his next interrogator. But then Shoran, who was a tall woman, recognized someone over the heads of those looking for seats. "Mikael!" she called out in profound relief. "There you are!" She stopped to wave.

Pasha went ahead on her own. The sooner everyone was settled, the sooner they would all learn the truth.

She took a seat in the first row, nodding to the woman on her right whom she recognized as a politician, one who'd served on Silk's city council.

"I'm Tarnya," the woman said, her voice rich and pleasant and possessing an equanimity absent from nearly everyone else.

"Pasha." They gently bumped knuckles. Then Pasha turned to the stocky man seated on her left, whom she'd met before. "Alkimbra, isn't it?" she asked, remembering he was a historian, but not knowing much else about him.

"You're Pasha, right?" he asked as they touched knuckles. "I'm here because a friend forwarded a copy of the announcement you sent." He gestured—at the auditorium, or the gee deck around it, or perhaps the whole strange situation. "This is not what I expected. Do you know—?"

"I don't," she interrupted. "I don't know any more than you do."

She turned her attention to the dais, deliberately ending the exchange, fretting that she could somehow be blamed for this situation—and on the dais she saw Urban. This time, she was certain it was him.

The dais was backed by a projection wall, deep black, showing nothing. Urban leaned against it, arms crossed, gaze focused on the stage in front of his feet. Looking sullen. Otherwise, exactly as he'd looked when she'd seen him on *Long Watch*.

Clemantine was nearby. She stood to one side of the dais in the company of a tall, gaunt man with black hair long enough to tie at the nape of his neck, and the unsettling, anachronistic embellishment of a short but heavy beard. Something about him—though certainly not the beard—made him seem familiar to Pasha, as if he was someone she ought to know. Another member of the founding generation, she suspected.

Behind her, the sound of shuffling feet and low, worried voices, as the seats filled in. People were still coming in. She was amazed at how many. She tried to count heads. At least forty-five. Or fifty? Maybe more.

Kona's low commanding voice rose easily over the background noise. "Find a seat," he warned. "You'll want to be sitting down when you hear this." He joined Clemantine beside the dais, studying the gathering. Pasha glanced back, to see that the seats behind her had all filled in. People hushed one another. When the last murmurings ceased, Kona turned to the dais. "Urban? We're all here."

Only then did Urban look up. Warily, he eyed the gathering. A glance at Clemantine, and then he straightened and uncrossed his arms. "It's taken some time for us to reach this point," he said, speaking loudly so that he could be easily heard throughout the gathering. He stepped to the side of the dais as the projection wall lit up behind him, white on black, displaying a simplified star chart with only a few features labeled.

Pasha studied the chart. She noted the position of Deception Well, skipped over the grouped stars labeled as the Committee, and jumped across the screen to Tanjiri and Ryo, two outlying stars of the Hallowed Vasties. *Dragon* was also marked on the chart, but the ship's position made no sense. It was shown to be a full eighty percent of the way to those first stars of the Hallowed Vasties and that was absurd.

Pasha looked next at the top of the star chart where there was a label that read *Today's Date*. Numerals followed, though it took a few seconds for her to make sense of them. She leaned forward, hugging herself, her queasiness rising again as she did the math.

If that date was real, then three hundred ninety-three years had elapsed since she'd sent her ghost to *Dragon*, and they were only a little more than a century away from the edge of the Hallowed Vasties.

A gasp from Tarnya beside her. More gasps and inarticulate cries of shock from across the gathering. Pasha rose to her feet. Fist clenched, she cried out, "You had no right!"

Tarnya was on her feet too, saying, "You must explain this!" Her voice discernible among a chorus of protests only because she was close by.

Looking deeply irritated, Urban stalked across the dais. Of all the raucous crowd, he focused his gaze on Pasha and in a voice strong enough to rise over the noise, he said, "It was necessary."

Pasha took this as a challenge, took a step forward. The crowd quieted behind her. "Necessary to leave us archived and helpless for almost four hundred years?" she demanded.

"Yes."

She shook her head. She could not accept this, did not want to. To keep them archived—and for so long!—was an outrageous violation of every person's natural right of self-determination and it left her frightened for the future. Urban was the mind of the ship; he was its master. He held all actual power, leaving the rest of them to live at his discretion.

Pasha wasn't naive. She knew this was how starships were traditionally organized, but a long-standing social covenant dictated that by accepting passengers, Urban had also accepted a responsibility to respect both the rights and the lives of those under his care.

Pasha needed him to remember that. "My understanding," she said, speaking slowly as a hush fell across the gathering, "was that we would transfer to this ship and instantiate as ghosts. From that perspective, we would be able to oversee the growth of our own avatars and occupy them at our discretion."

He met her glare with a resentful gaze. "There were complications," he told her.

"Let's all sit down," Kona said from his post at the side of the dais. "We have a lot to go over."

A rustling, as those who were standing took their seats again. Pasha felt a touch on her arm. Tarnya, standing a step behind her.

Their gazes met. Worry lines etched Tarnya's brow. "Let's hear what he has to say," she urged softly. "There has to be a reason."

Behind her words, the unspoken entreaty: *Be reasonable.*

And of course Tarnya was right. Anger and outrage had their place, but neither could undo the past. Right now, Pasha needed to hear the facts. Everyone did.

A deep sigh as she worked to compose herself. Then a nod to Tarnya, and they both took their seats.

Urban stepped back to the center of the dais. His gaze moved across the gathering. "You," he said to them, "all of you together, were the first complication we faced." He swept his hand in a gesture that took in the gathering. "I invited two people. I accepted two others. Pasha recruited everyone else. There are now sixty-six people aboard *Dragon*. Far more than I was prepared for when we left the Well. But I rejected no one. I accepted every ghost that came through the gate."

Pasha was caught off balance at finding herself singled out for criticism. Her cheeks burned. It was true she'd put out the word that the expedition was open for volunteers, but, "I didn't exactly recruit," she said defensively. "I just . . . let a few friends know about the opportunity."

"And friends let friends know," Tarnya whispered. "That's how I found out."

Riffan spoke from his position at one side of the gathering, sounding conciliatory when he said, "Urban, I think none of us suspected the enthusiasm this voyage would inspire."

This drew from Urban a slight, cynical smile. "In my time, the people of Silk were quiet and cautious. I didn't think I'd get ten volunteers." He shrugged. "I should have remembered we're all the restless descendants of frontier people."

Pasha's cheeks burned again, hearing these words as a grudging, condescending apology. *Not all your fault, Pasha!*

She gritted her teeth. She had acted precipitously, it was true. But she was here. So were the others. They were bound for the Hallowed Vasties and that was a victory. She could handle a little embarrassment.

Crossing her arms, she leaned in, listening to Urban's explanation.

"*Dragon* is a hybrid ship," he told them. "A careful balance has to be maintained between its human and Chenzeme elements. That balance would have been thrown into conflict if we'd tried to immediately establish a habitat and life support for sixty-six people. Even the virtual environment of the library couldn't handle that number—and we were wary of that approach anyway, since we knew most of you have never lived an exclusively virtual existence."

He looked to Kona, who nodded his agreement, adding, "Self-determination is an intrinsic right, but it must sometimes yield, on a temporary basis, when safety demands it."

Pasha leaned back, appreciating the challenge posed by their unexpected numbers, and the neat logic of Urban's long-term solution—but she resented it anyway. Hard to overlook four absent centuries.

A question from one of the back rows: "Kona, were you active during this period?"

"I was, along with Vytet." He gestured toward the bearded Founder whose name Pasha had not been able to recall. "We were both consulted and agreed to the course that was taken. Rather than courting disaster, we chose patience."

Pasha noticed Tarnya nodding a tentative acceptance of this explanation. She looked around, and was unsettled to see many others expressing agreement too. Of course, Kona was well known. Loved and respected. He'd led these people, or their ancestors, through the most harrowing times of their history. Most would be willing to trust his judgment. But not all.

"*Four* centuries of patience?" someone called out in an angry voice.

From Urban, that cynical smile. "Literally, we ran into problems."

He told them of the lost outriders and the ensuing resource shortage. "We couldn't rebuild the outriders *and* complete the gee deck. Not until we made up our margins. The most efficient way to do that was to go hunting. To find another Chenzeme courser, lure it in, disable it, and take from it what we needed—and that's what we did."

A murmur of disbelief, of trepidation. Pasha's heart raced, half in anger because he had to be lying—it would be madness to seek out a Chenzeme warship—and half in fear that he *was* mad enough to truly do such a thing.

"And here we are," someone said in a bold voice balanced between amusement and anger.

Pasha leaned forward and looked down the row to see that it was Shoran, standing up from a seat near the end.

Shoran gestured at the sunlit garden beyond the pergola's shade. "Here we are, surprisingly alive, on a beautiful deck that appears fully finished. I surmise we had the misfortune to sleep through a grand adventure?"

Urban looked puzzled, as if uncertain of Shoran's deeper meaning. "Sooth," he agreed. "It's done."

Pasha heard murmurs of relief:

Glad I wasn't awake for that.

I would have died of fright.

"No, Shoran is right," she muttered. "I would rather have been awake. It's better to die aware."

Tarnya turned a sympathetic gaze her way, but said nothing as questions erupted:

How was it done?

What damage was incurred?

Urban assured them, "The full history is in the library, and summaries have been prepared for you. You'll be adopted by the network in the next several seconds and then you can review it all for yourselves."

He looked to the side where Clemantine stood. She nodded as if to tell him to go ahead.

"Welcome to *Dragon*," he said. "You each have your own reasons for being here, but one reason I hope we all share is an abiding curiosity about what happened to our ancestral worlds and what survives there now. We're still a century of travel time from the closest star of the Hallowed Vasties, but we've already found our first artifact—and our first puzzle. I sent an outrider to investigate. It's stealthed, so we can't track its progress and we won't get a report until it's back in range—another ninety days or so—time enough for you to catch up on our history."

He jumped down from the dais, putting an end to his speech just as Pasha's atrium linked her into the ship's network. Oh, she admired the strategy. She had gotten only halfway out of her seat when she sank back down, her resolve to confront him yielding to curiosity. What artifact had been found? And where exactly were they going, and why?

Without leaving her seat, she pulled up the summary reports Urban had mentioned and began to read.

CHAPTER TWENTY-ONE

"YOU DID GOOD," Kona said, his voice pitched just loud enough to draw Urban's gaze as he left the dais. "Now you should stay. Make yourself accessible. Answer questions."

Urban met this praise with a dismissive half-smile. "Let them catch up on history first. I'll be around."

He threaded between Vytet and Clemantine, nodded to Riffan who still stood near the entry, and walked off into sunlight.

Kona turned a disgruntled gaze on Clemantine, who rolled her eyes. "It's better this way," she consoled him. "He's no good at comforting people and you know he doesn't have the patience to listen to complaints."

Kona grunted reluctant agreement as he eyed the ship's company. Nearly everyone was still seated, eyes glazed, focus turned inward as they used their atriums to access the documents prepared for them.

"I thought his speech went well," Vytet offered, his voice a gentle, low rumble.

"It did," Kona agreed, also striving to keep his voice low so his words would not carry in the eerie quiet pervading the amphitheater. Somewhere, a trembling breath suggestive of quiet weeping. Rustling fabric, shuffling feet. A raspy indrawn breath. Sniffling.

The atmosphere would heat up once people got past the initial shock. Kona had agreed to be the buffer when that happened. It was the deal he'd cut with Urban, to get him to deliver the orientation speech. Urban had wanted Kona to speak, arguing, "You're the politician. This is your role. You explain to them what happened."

Kona had refused. "They need to hear it from you. This is your ship. You're the master here. People need to know who you are. You need to engender trust, not suspicion. Let them know you've got their best interests in mind."

The quiet continued for minutes before people began to look up, look around. Speak to their neighbors.

Motion drew his gaze: Shoran, rising from her seat near the end of the first row. She looked to Kona, and offered up a brilliant smile that warmed him deep in his belly. An old friend, an occasional lover. Her bright and cheerful personality a sharp contrast to his own somber pessimism, but they had gotten along, and he'd always admired her fearlessness.

He went to greet her properly. She came forward to meet him, but partway along the front row of seats she paused, using her toe to nudge Pasha Andern's bare foot, startling her out of a reverie. With a smile, Shoran told her, "You started this. So come on now, and let's figure out what's next."

Pasha's lip curled. Her brow wrinkled in a scowl surprisingly fierce for such an elfin face. "All I *did*—" she started to exclaim.

"Was give the rest of us the opportunity of a lifetime," Shoran interrupted. She turned her mischievous gaze on Kona and, raising a scolding finger, she said, "*You* I am not going to forgive for letting me sleep through the conquest of a Chenzeme courser *and* the expedition to the Rock. However, I'm still willing to negotiate on where we're going from here."

"There's time for that," he said gently, grateful to have her there. "Right now we need to get people settled." The volume of noise was climbing as people left their seats. Several openly wept, others strove to comfort them, their encouraging words a sharp contrast to knots of angry conversation.

Shoran side-eyed the growing hubbub. Pasha turned in her seat to look. Beside her, Tarnya did the same, her expression concerned.

Kona knew Tarnya only from her bio, but he liked what he'd read. She'd served on the city council and had earned a reputation for straight talk and efficient action.

"All of you," he said. "Work with me." They turned to him with questioning gazes. In a low voice, he explained, "This could go either way unless we set a positive tone now."

Tarnya was first to catch on. She nodded. Kona left it to her to lead the others. He stepped back onto the dais. "This is new for all of us," he said, his voice calm, confident, and pitched to carry over the rising volume of conversation. It was also a voice everyone in the ship's company knew, if not from personal experience, than from historical speeches replayed on annual holidays. The gathering quieted. People turned to listen.

"Some of you are thrilled to be here," he went on, drawing enthusiastic whoops from the back. "Some are already regretting the decision to come." A chorus of denials, and a muffled sob. "Regardless of what you're feeling now, let's help each other. Comfort each other. Move ahead, while we learn together how to make this work." An extended pause. Everyone listening. "We've got time."

This last won him some cynical chuckles—recognition that time was something they had in plenty.

"We do have time!" Tarnya called out in a positive voice, stepping up onto her chair, as she stepped into her assigned role. She surveyed the gathering, missing no one. "Time to mold a new community. A new way of life. Let's get to know each other and our options, and together we can figure out what we want."

"And where we're going!" Shoran said, one hand on Tarnya's arm to make sure she didn't lose her balance. "And what we're going to do when we get there, because if I have any choice in it, I am not going to miss out on the next adventure."

"Adventure?" Pasha scoffed, on her feet now and facing the ship's company. She looked small alongside Shoran, but not at all intimidated. "This is about discovery, history, what was and what can be. We are less than a century from the Hallowed Vasties! We can argue about how we got here, but we *are* here—and I want to know what we can see from here that we could not see from Deception Well, and I want to know where we are going."

An eager murmur sounded through the gathering. A few voices offered competing assurances that they were even now consulting the ship's astronomical records for the newest images of those star systems that had been cordoned—and Kona breathed a soft sigh of relief. Let them stay focused on what was ahead and they would be all right.

He said, loud enough for all to hear, "Our first destination has not been decided yet. The two closest systems are Tanjiri and Ryo. As we get closer, we'll see in more detail what's left at each, and we'll know."

Riffan organized and oversaw a banquet to celebrate that first day, held at the dining terrace, halfway around the wheel from the amphitheater. Cushions served as seats around a long, sinuous table, segmented to make it easy to cross back and forth to either side. People moved about and mingled, introducing themselves as needed, sharing their wonder and their fear.

Riffan made sure to meet everyone, spending extra time with anyone who looked uncomfortable or alone, and making sure to find them friendly companions.

It was such a pleasure to have so many people to talk to! Though awkward to explain over and over why he'd been wakened almost three years ahead of all the others. When Shoran heard the story, she swore she would never forgive him for it. Riffan thought she was probably joking. Pasha, on the other hand, might plausibly be serious when she said the same thing.

He'd tried to explain his good fortune. "It was only because of my speciality in anthropology and Urban's belief that the beacon was a human signal."

Pasha was not happy with Urban either, of course, and she wasn't alone in that. Maybe that was why Urban didn't arrive with the others. Riffan had messaged him: *You're coming, aren't you?*

And when that got no reply: *You need to be here.*

He'd answered then, saying, *Not yet. Let people relax first. Enjoy themselves before they get angry all over again.*

Maybe it was the right strategy. Urban arrived quietly at the end of the meal when the ship's company had grown mellow on wine. By the time Riffan noticed him, he was already sitting with

Clemantine. He saw her introduce Urban to those around her, including Shoran and Tarnya.

Few beyond Clemantine's immediate circle noticed Urban was there, but Pasha saw it. She glared from several seats away, no longer listening to the conversation around her. Watching her, Riffan was struck by a fear that she would confront him and it was not a good time for that. It would spoil the evening. Let this day end in harmony.

He crossed between the tables and crouched behind her, speaking softly, "Don't be angry," he urged. "Circumstances constrained what he could do. Our history constrained us."

Over her shoulder she gave him an annoyed look. "That may be true, but I wonder who's in a position to constrain *him*, if it should come to that?"

His mouth fell open in shock, his worry so plain to see that she laughed at him. "Oh, Riffan. You're too trusting."

"But Pasha, we *have* to trust him."

"Yes. I know."

She turned back to her companions. He moved on.

She had meant nothing by it, surely.

He found Vytet, standing at the edge of the terrace. Seeking reassurance, he asked, "It's going well, don't you think?"

"Yes, indeed. I do. We are a frontier people. We know instinctively how to adapt to new circumstances."

"Truth," Riffan said, appreciating the reminder.

For centuries, their ancestors had migrated outward, each settled star system on the way acting as a selective filter, passing forward only those with a stable temperament amenable to cooperative existence. Those constraints had partly lifted during their long occupation of Deception Well, and still they retained much of the discipline and cooperation of their ancestral culture. If any among them struggled with the transition, it would not go unnoticed. They would be quietly counseled and cared for until they found a place in this new world. That was their way.

By the time the desserts were done, everyone had grown lethargic with food and drink. Ship's day was ending and a golden evening light filtered through the branches of the lithe, graceful maple trees surrounding the dining terrace. Conversation quieted, post-adrenaline melancholy setting in.

Riffan had finally settled onto an open cushion between a new acquaintance—the sharp-eyed and self-assured historian, Alkimbra—and Naresh, a physicist with a youthful air who Riffan had known casually for many years. There he began to nod, half asleep, discovering it only when Tarnya's fine voice rose over the assembly and startled him awake.

"I have a proposal," she announced.

Riffan straightened on his cushion as heads turned and conversations faded. Tarnya allowed several seconds for attention to settle on her, and then she continued, "I propose that for at least three years no one should enter cold sleep. Instead, let us invest that time in developing our community, our personal bonds, and by doing so, ensure that we'll know and trust one another so much that we'll be able to endure the intermittent existence of the centuries to come. What say you?"

Riffan hadn't once considered returning to cold sleep since he'd escaped it. He'd also had a lot of wine, so he was quick to call out: "I think it's a fine idea!"

Laughter greeted his response. Alkimbra placed a heavy hand on his shoulder and, in a voice surprisingly deep for his compact frame, announced, "I agree! An excellent strategy!" Several other cheerful endorsements followed.

Then Pasha called out in her no-nonsense voice, "I think we will need to be awake more than three years to catch up on all we missed."

"Yes, exactly," Naresh said in a loud, clear voice, making himself heard amid other calls of support from around the terrace.

"Can we all agree, then?" Tarnya asked. "Does anyone object?"

If anyone did, they didn't say so aloud.

Vytet stood up next, his tall slim figure aglow with a halo cast by a lantern that hung behind him. Riffan leaned forward to listen. Vytet's gentle voice commanded a rapt attention from the ship's company as he reminded them, "We are a frontier people. Our ancestors always looked outward in curiosity toward new suns and new worlds. But they also looked back along the star paths their ancestors had taken, and they kept records of what they saw.

"They watched known stars disappear within cordons made up of swarms of orbiting bodies of such magnitude and occurring in such numbers that all the light of the star was contained. Miraculous, it seemed. Inexplicable and overwhelming. The work of gods. The Hallowed Vasties.

"Centuries later, they watched the cordons disintegrate, and the stars reappear.

"Speculation has been rampant but no one really knows what spurred the precipitous growth of the cordons or triggered their sudden failure. We are here aboard *Dragon* to find out, to seek for our ancestors and to learn, both from their triumphs and their mistakes. It will be dangerous and it won't be easy, but I think it'll be worthwhile."

Riffan raised his glass, calling out "Hear, hear!" with the rest of them, but as he sipped the cold wine he shivered, chilled by the thought that they might find only monsters living among the wreckage of gods.

CHAPTER TWENTY-TWO

EVERY FEW MINUTES a new submind reached Clemantine at her post on *Griffin*'s high bridge, bringing her the memories of a parallel life—not just the observed experiences but also the thoughts, impressions, and emotions of her core self. The result: She lived that life, she *was* that woman, and also the isolated mistress of the high bridge. A dual existence. Two versions, wound around each other, witnessing progress on both fronts:

For *Dragon*, a thriving community, and for *Griffin*, a slow evolution away from hostility and malice among its philosopher cells as she reshaped their instinctive responses, making her post on the high bridge more bearable, day by day.

Another submind brought her a new segment of memories. Pasha Andern sat across from her, steaming cups of tea on the low table between them. Pasha asked, "Do you remember, centuries back, when Riffan and I first asked to go on this expedition . . . we talked about the authority of a ship's captain?"

Clemantine nodded. She did remember. "You agreed the captain was the final authority."

"I would have agreed to almost anything," Pasha admitted with a laugh. "But you—you had doubts. You said 'we'll find a way to make it work.'"

"You're angry over the centuries in archive," Clemantine guessed.

"Let's say I'm concerned."

"That's over. The ship's company will have a voice going forward."

A dismissive shrug, because having a voice was not the same as having a veto. Pasha asked, "Was it hard to learn to master the philosopher cells?"

"Yes," Clemantine said without hesitation.

"Was it worth it?" Pasha pressed.

Clemantine sipped her tea, recognizing this as an oblique question, a substitute for a question that could not be asked directly—

Should Urban ever again exceed his moral authority, could you take over?

"Yes," she said, more thoughtfully this time. She set the hot cup down. "To be more than just a passenger aboard *Dragon*, to learn to impress my will on the ship's Chenzeme mind, it was worth it."

Pasha nodded, seeming satisfied. "I'm glad there's someone else who knows—and I'm glad it's you who's in command of *Griffin*."

Clemantine looked askance. She did *not* command *Griffin*, she had no experience of it—not this version of her—and more and more, she wanted the experience. She'd told no one of the separation between her selves. She'd come to regret it, ashamed to be credited for a role she had not truly undertaken.

A voice, speaking from out of this parallel memory: *It's not too late for us to synchronize timelines. I don't need to be protected.*

On *Griffin* she pondered this, and after a time she messaged her other self, *I'm the one who needs you to be protected. I need your experience of human community unadulterated by the atavism of this Chenzeme mind.*

An answer arrived, replete with frustration: *It can't be that different from Dragon's high bridge.*

It is, and I don't like what I've had to become.

She had told no one of the separation, but her Apparatchiks knew. The Engineer, monitoring data traffic between the two ships, had noticed the one-way flow of subminds: "You've created a version of yourself specialized for command," he concluded.

"You would see it that way, having a personal understanding of specialization."

She sensed Urban knew as well. When he spoke to this version of her, atrium to atrium, his tone was formal, distant. So different from when he spoke to her other self. Had he worked it out on his own? Or had the Engineer informed him? This last question led directly to another: *Just how closely does he monitor me?*

Suspicion blossomed, but suspicion was toxic, so she resolved to clear the air. She messaged him, *Do my Apparatchiks report to you?*

He did not answer right away. Seconds passed. She imagined him considering all that this inquiry might imply. Finally, he asked her, *Should they?*

A fair question. She held immense power, yet lived a separate existence. It would be dangerous to allow her to become a stranger. She would not allow that for herself.

If my Apparatchiks have concerns, I hope they share them with me and with you.

Okay, but . . . you are all right over there?

Yes. I've adapted. I live her life and mine. And I want you to know that nothing means more to me than you and her and Dragon's evolving community—and I'll do whatever's necessary to protect all of you.

Late afternoon:

Urban was alone, gathering memories from his subminds as he lay with eyes closed on a blanket spread out in a shady garden corner, a few steps from the sliding backdoor of the cottage he shared with Clemantine. One after another, the partial copies of his persona dropped into his atrium, joining their memories to his so that he was acquainted with the current status of the ship, of the outriders, and of Clemantine in her separate command.

Urban had created the Sentinel to help him cope with the demands of commanding *Dragon's* high bridge. Clemantine had taken a different path in her command of *Griffin*. Instead of a partial persona that could be swapped in at need, she'd created a permanent alternate-self. She remained herself, but colder, more emotionally remote, as if she had taken on something of the implacable, ruthless nature of the philosopher cells. Did she realize it?

She must. Why else refuse to synchronize? Still, it left him questioning how well he knew her and what her boundaries might be.

But there was no calling it back.

Another submind, bringing the memory of the ongoing survey of the Near Vicinity. No anomalies of a stature to warrant concern had been found over the past twenty-four hours.

And another, bringing confirmation of the continued silence from the site of the beacon.

The beacon had fallen silent precisely at the time *Elepaio* was due to make its close pass. Urban longed to collect the memories of the ghost ensconced aboard that outrider. *What did I find out there? Did I make contact with someone? Some thing?* He wished again he'd been the version to go.

A sudden sharp electric hum, a minor note, seized his attention. His eyes opened to a dazzling spangle of daylight piercing past the bright-green leaves and feathery pink blossoms of a carefully shaped rain tree.

He sat up, looked around, as the hum dopplered away. A laugh from the direction of the path. A shout—Shoran's voice—"Get it! *Go, go, go!*"

He jumped to his feet—not out of alarm, but out of curiosity. This sounded like a game.

Riffan saw Pasha ahead of him on the path that wound around the circumference of the gee deck, linking all the cottages to the pavilion and the dining terrace.

He called out to her. "Oh, hey, Pasha!" And with a couple of easy bounds in the low gee, he caught up with her.

She turned to meet him, her delicate face framed in short blond hair that gleamed in the morning light, thin brows arched over skeptical green eyes. "Hey, Riffan." Her tone neutral as always.

"You're attending today's lecture, aren't you? May I walk with you?"

She snorted and continued toward the amphitheater. "Why are you always so formal?"

"Am I?" he asked with a frown, matching the slow-motion pace that most of the ship's company had adopted to prevent inadvertently launching themselves into the shrubbery.

"Yes, you are," she informed him.

"Well, perhaps you're right."

She rolled her eyes.

"Okay, you *are* right."

The corner of her mouth quirked up.

"Are we friends, Pasha?" he blurted, stopping on the path, even taking a step back. She stepped back too, her pale cheeks warming with a flush, her green eyes wide. "I admire you so," he said quickly, getting it all out while he could, "but I think ... maybe I've offended you?"

"Why do you think that?" she said in an undertone, as if concerned someone might overhear. She stepped off the path and onto a small lawn, glancing over her shoulder at a cottage behind her.

"We used to be friendly, together on *Long Watch*. We often talked, discussed our studies. Now I hardly see you."

"Don't be silly," she said. "I see you every day at the lectures. Isn't that where we're going now?"

Riffan sighed, recognizing the brushoff.

With Vytet, he'd organized daily lectures and discussions on academic topics related to the expedition, ranging from astronomy to biology to history. The sessions were well attended, which meant Pasha was a face in the crowd while Riffan stood by the dais, moderating discussion—and afterward she would melt away, or be off to dinner with her friends, or disappear for hours behind her closed cottage door, doubtless pursuing research in the library.

"All right," he said, glancing around as Alkimbra and Naresh approached along the path. He nodded to them, then blushed a bit as Alkimbra's eyes narrowed, his keen gaze clearly perceiving Riffan's awkward situation. He pursed his lips, raised his heavy eyebrows in a sympathetic expression, but to Riffan's relief he said nothing, walking on with the oblivious Naresh.

Riffan turned back to Pasha. He desperately wanted her to explain what had changed—but what a ridiculous demand that would be! Everything about their lives had changed. And she didn't owe him an explanation.

"I'll see you at the lecture, then," he said quietly.

She put out her hand before he'd quite gathered himself to leave. "It's not you," she assured him.

He waited, hoping for more, but Clemantine and Tarnya were coming next along the winding path, with several others not far behind.

Tarnya, looking ahead, saw them and called out, "Hi Pasha! Hi Riffan! You know there's going to be a concert tonight, right?"

"Right, I'm planning to be there," Pasha said, stepping away from Riffan, and then she was walking with them, leaving him trailing behind.

"It shouldn't be too many more days before *Elepaio* gets back," he said idly.

Only Clemantine looked back at him. She slowed her stride to let him catch up. "Are you worried?" she asked.

"No. Well, yes. Maybe. It's just . . . I don't know how to think about it. Whatever happened out there, whatever we discovered, I've already done it, been through it—but through *what*? Maybe nothing at all. Maybe three years of boredom. Or something wonderful . . ."

"Or terrible," she said, guessing his thoughts.

"It's nerve-wracking, not knowing."

They reached the edge of the pavilion. Pasha paused to look back at him with a cool gaze. "I would have been happy to go in your place," she said.

"I know. I wish I'd suggested it."

A faint smile. "You're a good person, Riffan. Better than me."

She went ahead, striding across the pavilion, leaving Tarnya looking puzzled and Clemantine regarding him with questioning eyes. He cleared his throat, put on a smile, and said, "I'd better hurry if I'm going to be any help to Vytet."

"Come out and play," Shoran called as Urban rounded the cottage. She stood on the path beside her son Mikael, her smile bright, her skin glistening with sweat.

"Play what?" he asked.

Shoran stood tall, and she was well-muscled, resembling Clemantine in physique. She wore tight shorts and a sleeveless top, her silver hair bound up in a coiled braid, her breast rising and falling with exertion.

Urban liked her—her bold manner, her optimism, her inventiveness. The first time he'd met her, she declared, "I didn't come on this expedition to look through telescopes. I'm here to explore the ruins or the recovery of life—whichever it turns out to be—for myself, *as* myself." She'd made a name for herself at Deception Well as one of the earliest scouts to truly explore the planetary surface.

She said, "Mikael has remembered a game we used to play in Silk. I think you'll like it. It's called flying fox."

She showed him a device in her palm.

"A camera bee?" Urban guessed. If so, it was modified. Larger than he remembered and bright red in color.

"This is the fox we'll try to catch. One person alone will never succeed at it. We have to work together."

She turned to Mikael, a man of athletic build with a smile more reserved than his mother's. Age was not revealed by physical features, but it could be sensed in the way people handled themselves—and Mikael's shy manner gave away his youth. He was the youngest of the ship's company, only twenty-five when he made the jump to *Dragon*.

"Ready?" Shoran asked him.

Mikael nodded.

She tossed the fox into the air. Its multiple pairs of mechanical bee wings instantly vibrated into flight mode, producing the humming minor note Urban had heard earlier.

"Check the personnel map," Shoran said. "Almost everyone is at Alkimbra's lecture. We'll need to stay away from the pavilion, but we've got the rest of the deck to play."

"You're not interested in the history of Tanjiri?" Urban asked, eyeing the fox hovering a meter overhead.

"I'll read the transcript later—and I'm sure you will too."

Mikael said, "The game is simple. We chase the fox, corner it, trap it if we can."

"But use no devices," Shoran warned. "And no implements. The aim is to train your strength and reflexes. We are a team. Let's go!"

The fox shot off down the path. Then it dove beneath the trees dividing Clemantine's cottage from the next one over, where Vytet lived. Mikael bounded after it in a great leap made possible by the gee deck's low gravity.

Urban turned, listened a moment to the fox's retreating hum and decided to take a shortcut. Two swift bounds let him achieve a running start. He jumped to the meadow on the cottage roof, then jumped again, to land, rolling in the small lawn of the back garden where he'd been inventorying his subminds just a couple of minutes before.

To his frustration, Mikael was still a step ahead of him while Shoran was only a step behind, appearing around the corner of the house, laughing as the fox doubled back to shoot just past the grasping fingertips of both Urban and Mikael. It shot under trees and over hedgerows. They followed in frenetic pursuit, shouting tactics at each other:

Go around!

Stop it at the picnic ground!

No, no! The other way!

Hearts pumping, chests heaving, skin glistening with sweat. Kona, who'd skipped the lecture too, came out to join them as they took a short break. He greeted Shoran with such an affectionate hug, Urban interpreted it as evidence of a renewed relationship.

So far, sexual associations among the ship's company tended toward casual and ephemeral, his relationship with Clemantine the exception.

"Release the fox," Mikael complained.

Shoran laughed and did so, releasing Kona too. They started the game again. The lecture must have ended because a few minutes later several more players joined in, Clemantine among them. She came dressed like Shoran. Bumping up against Urban, she gave him a wink. "Glad to see you making friends."

"It's coming at you!" Mikael shouted.

She jumped for it. Urban only watched, entranced by the

beauty of her muscular bronze body, simulated sunlight glinting off the gold iris tattoos that edged her ears. She shouted as the fox slipped past, escaping by a millimeter. When it angled away, they bounded in pursuit. Shoran shouted at them to "*Go around!*" Go around what, Urban wasn't sure, but after a minute Clemantine was laughing for the sheer joy of wild motion and what else really mattered?

Inexplicably, amid the chaos, he flashed on that separated version of her, the stranger, the one he wasn't sure he could trust. He heard her words again: *I live her life and mine.*

This time, he understood. *This* is what mattered to her. This existence, the loving, tumbling, laughing, fearful, hungry, melancholy, restless human existence lived on this timeline allowed her to exist on the other, just as his dream of finding Clemantine again had let him fare alone over centuries. His doubt eased as he remembered her promise: *I'll do whatever's necessary to protect all of you.*

A shout, all too close—"*Move!*"—startled him back into the present. A glimpse of the fox speeding toward him. He sprang at it, using his head to knock it in Kona's direction. Kona was taken by surprise. All he could do was bat it toward the ground to slow it down.

Clemantine dove, seizing it as she rolled across a tiny lawn, but she didn't have a good grip on it. It was wriggling free until Shoran met her. She clapped her hands around Clemantine's— and abruptly, the hum of the fox ceased.

"We won!" Shoran crowed to a chorus of whoops and laughs as nine players collapsed to the ground in a satisfied state of exhaustion.

Clemantine lingered, luxuriating under the soothing, slow-falling water of her shower, quietly astonished at her own growing optimism. It had been a good day. She'd spent time in the library and on the high bridge, and the lecture had been interesting, but mostly she was still aglow from her introduction to flying fox.

The game had given her a workout, but better than that, it had been fun. Simple fun. She could not remember the last time she'd just *played* like that. Maybe not since that long-ago age before the Chenzeme ravaged Heyertori.

She squeezed her eyes shut, recoiling from the memory.

Don't go there.

"Live in the moment," she whispered. "Live for now."

She touched the water off. Toweled herself dry in a gentle, warm wind. Then stepped out of the shower. The ultra-thin polymer of its walls unlocked, melting into a translucent ring that sank out of sight beneath the blond-wood floor as the ceiling regrew, smooth white.

After a moment of thought she requested a short, shimmering, mahogany-colored shift from the house DI. The dress budded from the generative surface of an active wall. She pulled it on, smoothed it straight, and walked barefoot into her living room.

Urban looked up with a smile from where he crouched by a low table with curved legs, arranging the various dishes he'd synthesized for their dinner.

"Just in time," he said. He was dressed in loose trousers, his skin smooth and clean from the ministrations of his Makers; he did not enjoy showers as she did.

"It looks wonderful," she said, and meant it.

He had picked up a lot of useful skills over his long lifetime, though he'd never learned to invest much value in the idea of home. He lived with her in this cottage, but it was hers. It reflected her personality and the simple serenity she preferred. Urban lived there without imparting any sense of himself to the place.

"It's *your* home," he always insisted. "Even when you're not here, it's as if you are and I like it that way. Don't change anything."

So the soft colors and the simple graceful lines of the furnishings that came and went in the changeable front room were all to her taste.

There was often a sofa positioned to catch the sunlight or moonlight coming through a side window. The table would be extruded from the floor on demand whenever they wanted to share a meal or a pot of tea. Colorful pillows served as their seats. The paintings on the walls changed every few days, or more often if the current selection did not suit her mood. The largest painting could be made to disappear, replaced by a screen where they watched recorded dramas.

The only unchanging piece in the room was a slim side table of honey-colored wood with a shallow dish on its polished surface in which a colony of irises grew.

Clemantine had an affinity for the flowers. Since her youth she'd been entranced with their beauty. She wore them as ornamentation, tattooed in gold along the edges of her ears. Only later in life did she come to appreciate them as symbols of renewal, life from lifelessness at the turn of seasons.

She sat down, cross-legged, facing Urban, and raised her jade-green chopsticks as part of a smiling salute. "*Itadakimasu,*" she said in appreciation of the meal.

"The least I could do."

"You should host a community dinner and cook for everyone."

He laughed. "No, they expect actual cooking, not just food ordered from a synthesizer."

"You could help plan the menus."

The focus of the community was squarely on the study of the Hallowed Vasties, but that destination remained far off, so people divided their time among a range of interests and enthusiasms.

Cooking was one of the most popular pastimes, whether for festivals, community meals, or competitions. Musicians and singers were abundant, performing in a range of styles. Visual arts and live dramas were pursued with passion, and the library was continuously mined in a search for recordings of ancient dramas, both performed and interactive. There were dramatic readings, intellectual and virtual games, and after today, athletic games.

Clemantine continued to practice her own hobby of genetically sculpting plants. The irises she kept on the side table were her creation. She had redesigned their genome so that with a proper feeding of nutrients they would grow from rhizomes to bold and bright blue flowers within three days, stay thus a while—a randomized span of time, unpredictable, anything from a day to ten days—and then the color of the flowers would shift to white, a sign that the cycle was nearly done.

If she was there to see the white color then she would sit cross-legged, waiting, watching, meditating, until, without further warning, the plant darkened and within a few seconds crumbled in on itself, collapsing in a layer of granular humus that fell like a shroud over the half-exposed rhizomes. Those seemingly lifeless roots would not quicken again until they received a new feast of nutrients.

The first time Urban had seen the collapse he'd been angry over it. "That's horrible. Why do you want it to do that? Why don't you make the flowers perpetual instead?"

"A false promise?" she'd asked him.

He hadn't bothered to answer that. Just shook his head and moved on. Never questioned her on it again—though she'd seen him watching the transformation since then.

She meant for the rise and fall of the flowers to symbolize renewal, not death. More than once in her life she had lost all and grown again from nothing. Even in this peaceful succession of days, as she strove to live in the present, she thought it wise to be reminded of that.

She composed a message and sent it off to her separated self: *I think I understand why you want it this way.*

Later, when dinner was finished, she would send a submind to that other version of her, and share her experience of this day.

CHAPTER TWENTY-THREE

THE FLEET'S ARRAY of telescopes engaged in a continuous slow survey of the Near Vicinity, seeking for anomalies near enough to constitute a threat. Only once a year did the Astronomer focus the array on the individual star systems of the Hallowed Vasties, to capture updated images.

Pasha had sought out Vytet as soon as she learned of this schedule, wanting his explanation for it before confronting Urban directly. "It makes no sense," she'd insisted to him. "We should be monitoring the Vasties more often. Twice a year, at minimum. It's why we're here."

Vytet had given up his archaic beard, revealing a refined face, one that now wore an ambivalent expression. "I don't disagree, but Urban's priority is protecting the fleet from near-term threats, so that's where the telescope time goes. The Astronomer has advised him an annual survey of the Vasties is sufficient to capture evidence of change."

"Maybe in the past," Pasha had conceded. "Maybe even now, for the more distant systems. But we're closing on Tanjiri and Ryo. Both should be monitored on a much more frequent schedule."

Vytet had advised patience. "The annual survey is coming up," he'd reminded her. "Let's wait. See what it reveals. And then make the argument."

A shiver of excitement touched her as she left her cottage. The annual survey was finally underway. In minutes, the first new images of Tanjiri in a year would begin to come in.

For once, as she hurried along the path, she did not hear the

annoying hum of a flying fox. It was late afternoon, the favorite time to play the game, but today there was only birdsong, the
buzz of bees, and quiet chatter as people made their way to the
amphitheater, where they would watch together as the new images
arrived.

She thought she'd left early, but most of the front-row seats
were taken by the time she arrived. Fortunately, Tarnya was there
at the center of the row, along with Shoran and Mikael. They
waved at her, calling out, "Pasha! We've saved you a seat."

She hurried to join them, as walls descended from the perimeter
of the sheltering pergola and the canopy shifted to impenetrable
black, blocking out the afternoon sunlight. As the walls bonded to
one another and to the floor, the temperature dropped—appropriately, Pasha thought, given the sudden fall of night. On the curved
projection screen, a starfield blazed in sudden glory.

A rustling and murmuring as those still standing hurried to
find seats, guided by tiny points of blue light on the floor.

"What do you think we'll see?" Shoran asked, starlight reflecting in her eyes, along with an excitement that echoed Pasha's own.

"I hope we'll see what's casting shadows on the star," she said.
"If it's a planet, or a disc of debris, or a surviving structure."

"You want it to be a structure," Tarnya teased.

"Yes! That would be amazing. Our first hint of the kind of habitats that combined to create the cordon."

The gathering settled, murmurs faded. A shiver ran up Pasha's
spine—from the cold or from anticipation? She couldn't say.

She looked for Vytet and saw him standing beside the dais, a
tall silhouette limned in starlight, his long hair loosely tied. Vytet
had organized this gathering. Now he acknowledged the restless
silence by gesturing at the projected starfield. "We have the grandest of views," he said in his gentle, contemplative voice. "But it's a
view that changes only slowly. It's not as if we can turn a corner
and encounter a new vista. All that is, is out there in front of us but
at such a distance details are elusive. Only slowly, gradually, as we
draw closer to a target star do we have a real chance of discerning
what might still exist in orbit around it."

A doorway peeled open. Light washed in, inciting annoyed murmurs. A man's handsome silhouette, against the afternoon glare. Pasha recognized Riffan.

"Pardon me," he said contritely as the doorway sealed shut behind him. "I'm a minute late."

Good-humored teasing erupted. People liked Riffan. They clapped and whistled and called out, "Find the man a seat!"

Not Pasha. She stayed silent, and under cover of darkness, allowed herself an irritated snarl. *Are we friends, Pasha?* he'd asked, but she'd skirted the question. Now she bit her lip and conceded, if only to herself, *Jealousy is the worst emotion.*

It was not his fault he'd been privileged to go on the expedition to the beacon. Urban had picked him out of the archive, ostensibly because Riffan was an anthropologist. Yet an exobiologist would have made sense too. *More sense.* But Urban had met the two of them aboard *Long Watch,* and he had chosen Riffan.

She chided herself, *You are so petty!*

And still, it rankled. She'd worked so hard in her career. She'd had to push at every stage to advance in the sclerotic hierarchy of Deception Well. The quality of her work had always earned praise and yet it did not bring her the reward of new projects. Always, she had to take the initiative, put herself forward, or be forgotten. Over the years she'd often felt invisible.

None of it was Riffan's fault, but she could not help a stab of jealousy every time she saw him, so she did her best not to see him. It was that simple.

Shuffling sounds from the back indicated Riffan was still making his way to an open seat, but Pasha raised her chin and fixed her attention forward as Vytet resumed his introductory remarks.

"The ingredients of life are all still present at Tanjiri," he said. "Past surveys have detected water, oxygen, and abundant organic molecules. Whether those are associated with biological life we can't know, but the situation is intriguing.

"Throughout our journey, we've tracked irregular but easily measurable variations in Tanjiri's luminosity. And yet historically, the star is known to be stable. We have data from centuries of observations, predating the expansion, that prove this."

Shoran interrupted with a half-raised hand. "You're assuming the people of the Hallowed Vasties did not manipulate and destabilize the star itself," she said.

"We can't be sure," Vytet admitted. "We know they possessed engineering skills far beyond anything we're capable of—but did they build their cordons from matter harvested from cometary clouds? Or did they break up planets to do it? To overcome the attractive force of gravity . . . that is a physics we know almost nothing about, even now, when we've had the use of the propulsion reef for centuries.

"We don't know how the cordons were made, but in just a few minutes we may gain some insight on where the matter was obtained.

"We have records of Tanjiri's major planets. We know where they should be now, in their orbits, and we know the percentage each would contribute to the variation in luminosity as they cross the face of the star—"

"*If* they still transit the face of the star," someone in the second row interjected. Pasha recognized the precise diction of the physicist, Naresh. "If they are no longer intact, we have no basis for our calculations."

"Yes, Naresh. Exactly." Vytet again spoke to the full gathering. "What we do know is that the variation we're seeing is *much* greater than could be caused by the known planets if they do all still exist. Our hypothesis—mine, along with those Apparatchiks we call the Scholar and the Astronomer—is that some megastructures from the original cordon, or perhaps just fragments of them, still exist."

Pasha's mind was running ahead. "But this is not a new theory, correct?" she asked. "It's been less than two thousand years since the Hallowed Vasties broke up. Not much time on an astronomical scale. And if the structures had been broken down to dust, we would have seen a nebula."

Naresh answered this, saying, "I've looked over the historical data." Pasha turned to see him in the row behind her, a shadowy figure in the faint light, his posture as precise as his words. He continued, "There may be a nebula, but it's too thin to account for a majority of the matter that went into the construction of the cordon."

"I agree," Vytet said.

"So where did all that matter go?" Shoran wanted to know. "Is it still tied up in these fragments of . . . what was the term you used?"

"Megastructures," Pasha said. "Is there even another possibility? Surely there's not been enough time for debris to re-gather into a planetary body or even into an accretion disc."

"We hope to find out today," Vytet answered.

The first image to be displayed came from *Dragon*'s telescope alone. A Dull Intelligence swiftly combined it with a digital image from *Griffin*, producing a sharper picture of Tanjiri. Pasha squinted, instinctively trying to bring into focus several tiny blurs of what looked like reflected light, scattered at a uniform distance around the pale yellow star. A tag popped up:

Average estimated distance of orbital bodies from the central star: 0.78 astronomical units.

An astronomical unit, an AU, was the distance that had once separated Earth from Sun . . . and maybe it still did. No one knew for sure.

Murmurs erupted, whispered questions. Pasha gripped an armrest to stop herself from rising to her feet. "What are we looking at?" she asked herself aloud.

"The shape of these objects suggests a crescent," someone in back said. "Could they be planetary objects in partial light?"

"Or could they be surviving structures?" another voice asked.

A discussion ensued, the planetary hypothesis gaining support when an analysis of the spectra revealed strong indications of water and an oxygen-bearing atmosphere.

After forty minutes, image data began to stream in from *Khonsu*'s telescope. The DI cross-matched time and angle, working to integrate it with the existing image to reveal even more detail.

Pasha leaned forward, anxious for the update, hoping it would allow a clearer view of the ruins if that's what they were, or, far better, reveal an indication of surviving life.

She hoped for proof of life with a child's eager hope, even as she reminded herself not to let hope influence her judgment. No matter what the refined image showed, she had to view it with an impartial mind. She had to see what was actually there and not just what she wished to see.

The existing image on the projection screen blurred—a dramatic touch, a clear demarcation—before snapping back into focus. Across the watching audience, a collective gasp. Pasha's hand rose to cover her open mouth.

The best image from last year—the fully integrated image—had shown only glints and shadows that might have been nothing more than tiny flaws in the lenses or random errors in the integration algorithm. This year, with the data newly integrated from *Khonsu*, those glints were now, undeniably, objects.

In this iteration, the DI had used a screen to block out the direct light of the star, allowing a better look at the surrounding space.

Pasha could now clearly see the lit crescent of a planet or a planetoid, a moon, something . . . tiny in the overall span of the image but sharply defined and so tantalizingly bright blue in color it commanded the eye to gaze upon it. And paired with it, a smaller crescent, also blue, but not so sharply rendered.

Naresh again, coolly confident: "The larger crescent must be Tanjiri-2. It's right where the planet should be, but—"

He broke off as another tag popped into existence on the image. Pasha leaned forward to read it. It confirmed Naresh's evaluation, labeling the larger crescent as the known planet, Tanjiri-2.

"This is quite extraordinary," Vytet said breathlessly.

"It's impossible," Naresh said, anger edging his voice.

This time, Pasha could not resist rising to her feet. She spoke out, defiant, incredulous. "Tanjiri-2 has no moon!"

It never *used* to have a moon. She'd read the reports. She was certain of this. There was no moon, not even a small rocky body, but in this image the planet appeared to have gained a partner, a smaller world to be sure, but a living world.

"I think we're looking past the biggest miracle," Shoran said, projecting her powerful voice over the ongoing murmur of argument. "The living world, the originally inhabited world, still exists! It wasn't destroyed to create the cordon. It still has atmosphere, an ocean. We might be able to walk there someday, stand on an alien shore."

Pasha's heart raced. Shoran was right. There might still be people living on that world and there would surely be life of some kind. And life was precious. Living worlds so very rare.

She flinched at a touch against her hand. Shoran, with a meaningful look toward her empty seat. Sheepishly, Pasha sat down again.

On the dais, Vytet was as awed as anyone. He drew a deep breath, shook his head in wonderment. "All right," he murmured. A second breath to steady his voice, get his shock under control. "First pass analysis. Both worlds—the old and the new—have atmospheres and—we'll need to check the spectra of course but I think Shoran is correct—both have oceans. Even that moon, that new, inexplicable moon. Tanjiri-2b, let's call it! Are they *living* oceans? We can't know yet but I want to think so. By the Waking Light! I never imagined we'd find such a thing. A newly created world. A *living* world."

"Let's take a step back," Naresh said. "No other planetary bodies have been tagged in this image. But historical records assure us there were once additional worlds."

Vytet cocked his head in an attitude of listening, and then looked out at Naresh. "The DI processing these images has not been able to resolve any other planetary bodies."

Pasha drew a deep breath. The absence of other planets was eerie but not unexpected. She asked, "If Tanjiri-1 still exists, would it be visible from this angle of view? Or is it possible that it's passed behind the star? Or behind . . . one of those other objects?"

Those other objects . . .

So far, no one had called them out directly. It was as if they were all in tacit agreement to discuss the most familiar objects first.

"Let's get a projected position for the inner planet," Vytet said.

A broad, bright crescent appeared, much larger and closer to the star than Tanjiri-2. The inner planet had been a gas giant in close orbit. If it still existed, it would have been clearly visible at the time the image was recorded.

"So it's not there," Pasha concluded.

Kona spoke up for the first time. Pasha had not noticed him before, standing in the shadows at the far end of the first row. "How the hell do you take apart a planet?"

Riffan answered from the back of the room. "Honestly, I hope we never figure that part out."

This earned a low general chuckle.

"Still, it's a question we have to ask," Naresh said. "It's gravity that holds a world together. Even if you could shatter a planet, gravity will pull most of the matter back—"

"But surely they manipulated gravity," Shoran interrupted.

"Yes," Vytet said. "There is no other explanation for it. They developed something as unexpected as the reef, only on a massive scale."

A giddy laugh from Riffan. "Ah, but if we are going to entertain impossibilities then there *are* other explanations. Perhaps they've manipulated time, or opened seams between parallel universes, allowing disruptive forces to bleed through, or maybe they've folded the fabric of space to create brief tidal forces strong enough to tear worlds apart."

Several seconds of silence followed this outburst. "Uh," Riffan said, sounding deeply embarrassed. "I'm joking, of course."

A scattering of laughter, but not from Pasha. She clenched an armrest, pondering the terrible possibility that some aspect of Riffan's joking explanation was true. What had been done in Tanjiri System was so far beyond their own science it might as well be magic.

"We are resolved to trespass among the ruins of gods," she said, not caring if anyone heard. Then she lifted her chin and spoke again, this time at good volume, determined to push the conversation forward. "Can we discuss the other objects?"

This request silenced the gathering for two full seconds. Then everyone started talking at once.

Aside from the occulted star and the now-double planet, the image showed a generous sprinkling of faint, widely scattered points of light that together defined a flattened ring like a halo encircling the star. Nearly all the points were outside the orbit of Tanjiri-2.

A few structures, shadowy but limned in light, could be seen among the points.

The structures were large. Immensely large. So large, they made Tanjiri-2 look small.

Pasha counted thirteen megastructures visible in the image, each with a unique shape and none with a neat design. They looked like wreckage, ruined fragments fused together in the kinetic chaos that had followed calamity. Some lay horizontal to the plane of the ecliptic, others towered above it, their silhouettes suggesting long, drawn-out conglomerations of curved panels, partial spheres, rods, stair-step beams, and broken discs. The glittering points of the halo sparkled around them.

One megastructure appeared to be crowned in a wisp of white mist. Pasha imagined atmosphere still bleeding out of a broken habitat . . . but centuries had passed since cataclysm. More likely, the gravity of the megastructure allowed it to hold on to a fog of fine dust or frozen molecules of air.

"Aren't we *still* missing matter?" someone asked.

Another: "My thought too. Surely there is not sufficient matter in that halo to account for all the matter that must have been used in the cordon at its peak."

Naresh said, "We'll do the calculations, but I suspect you're right."

Hours later, Pasha emerged from the night-dark pavilion into real night. She felt giddy with excitement. Lifting her face to an artificial sky bright with projected stars, she twirled like a child, laughing.

Tarnya laughed with her. "It's wonderful, isn't it?" she said. "To know it's not all dust, that something is out there."

"I'm a horrible person," Pasha confessed in a stage whisper. "What we saw in there was the shattered tomb of millions, billions, maybe more . . . but it's amazing all the same."

"The ruins of gods," Tarnya teased. "Who knows what we'll find there?"

Pasha pulled up abruptly, her ardor cooling. "If we go there."

Tarnya frowned. "What do you mean?"

"The last time I checked, our course was set for a close pass of Tanjiri System, like the close pass Urban made at Deception Well."

Both queried the library, confirming this. The fleet was not on course to enter the system.

"I think we were only waiting for confirmation that something is there," Tarnya said, waving at someone. She looked at Pasha in apology. "I need to speak to Bituin."

"Go ahead. We'll meet later."

People were leaving the pavilion in small groups, chattering and debating with each other. Pasha looked for Urban, but did not see him. Maybe he had left early.

She checked the personnel map. It showed him at the cottage he shared with Clemantine. She arrived there to find the gel door open, the living room glowing with soft light. Urban was inside, half-reclined on the sofa, watching her with an unnerving fixed stare as she crossed the patio. This annoyed her. She wondered what game he was playing.

But when she reached the threshold, she saw his eyes weren't tracking her. His face looked vacant, giving her the unsettling impression that although his avatar was present, *he* was somewhere else.

But even if that was so, surely some part of his mind, or a sub-mind, monitored what passed around him?

She called to him from the threshold. "Hello, Urban? Can we talk?"

To her relief, his eyes shifted at the sound of her voice. He sat up. His gaze focused on her, and a slight, cynical, lopsided smile appeared on his face.

He said, "You want to talk about Tanjiri, don't you? Come on in."

She straightened her shoulders and stepped inside, striving to present a strong, confident front. "You've seen the new imagery. We *have* to go there. This is why we came."

His smile widened. "Is that what the ship's company wants? Is there consensus on that?"

He was teasing her, payback for her criticism of him that first day. She answered in a neutral voice. "I think we were all too excited to discuss it."

"Well, you've got time."

That was true! There was so much time left to endure before they got there.

"It'll take even longer than you're expecting," he said. "We'll have to dump velocity as we get close. Go in slowly."

"Understood. And we'll need to take the time to carefully map every object. But it's worth it, isn't it? We'll never know the truth if we limit ourselves to a fly-by, standing off at a distance that keeps us safe."

"We're not safe," he reminded her.

She shrugged, unwilling to play word games. "I think we should spend time in this system. It's why we came."

CHAPTER TWENTY-FOUR

URBAN'S GHOST STREAMED in from the returning outrider, *Elepaio*. Rejoining with his core self, he possessed the memories of both timelines. He had been present when *Griffin* was captured, the outriders rebuilt, the gee deck finished, the ship's company resurrected, and a consensus reached to keep Tanjiri as their first destination. He had also been present at the Rock when the marooned entity spoke to him. Both pasts equally real and already integrated into the totality of his experiences.

Riffan's ghost would follow him in, and then the rest of the data gathered during the fly-by.

He turned to Clemantine, who lay asleep beside him in the bed they shared in her cottage. It was ship's night outside. Quiet but for a few crickets, and dark. If lights were on in the other cottages, they were hidden behind window screens. He triggered a slight glow in the walls, enough to see her shape. He kissed her cheek until she awoke.

"What is it?" she murmured.

He purred deep in his throat, and then confessed, "God, I've missed you."

She pushed him away, far enough that she could sit up. "You're back, aren't you? Tell me what you saw."

So he did, while the data streamed in—chemical analyses, spectral analyses, log files, video, and his own brief summary of his findings—all downloading into *Dragon*'s library.

Clemantine willed the lights to a brighter setting. She studied him, looking skeptical, worried. "I don't like to think of your avatar gone like that, into the hands of some . . . *monster*."

"I terminated."

"You know that?"

"You know I would have."

"But there's no record of it. No data on how you were taken down—and that leaves us vulnerable. Without data on what happened, how do we improve our defenses for the next time?"

That was the problem he'd been wrestling with throughout the return journey—and not much to show for it. But he was saved from having to answer when a query reached his atrium. "Hold on," he told her. "Vytet wants to talk. I'll link you in." Then to Vytet, "Go ahead."

"I've read your summary," Vytet said—a feminine voice tonight, though her tone was flat. A mask for anxiety? "I think we've got an immediate problem."

"What kind of a problem?" Urban asked. "The data's not corrupt?"

"No. The data is good, what I've seen of it, anyway. I haven't had time to go over it in detail, but so far it all—"

"What's the problem, Vytet?" Clemantine said, cutting her off.

An audible sigh. "The mission summary. It concerns me. The shipwrecks—at least the two human ships—Urban, you think those crews scuttled their ships to keep the entity from escaping."

"Yes. That's how it looked."

"But you got away untouched?"

"*Yes*, because only the probe went into the system. *Elepaio* never got close. No data viruses got into the library."

"Yes," Vytet said, and now *she* sounded impatient. "Yes, all that should have meant you were clean, but there is a glamour surrounding the returning outrider."

Clemantine looked at Urban, her fine eyebrows raised in question. "A glamour?" she repeated. "What does that mean?"

"Come to the library," Vytet said. "I'll show you."

Vytet had become a female version of the dark-haired man she'd been, her black eyes glittering as she turned to greet Urban and Clemantine. The Apparatchiks were with her in the library, all six of them. A rare gathering, signaling a critical issue.

"Here," Vytet said, gesturing at a large frameless window. "Have a look."

Like all the outriders, *Elepaio* was stealthed. As it returned to the fleet, its position had been unknown until the data came in. But as soon as Vytet received its position information, she'd turned *Dragon*'s telescopes on it.

The image she'd captured showed the expected faint infrared signature of *Elepaio*'s hull, but there was also an indistinct blur encircling the bow.

"It's not surprising you didn't notice it," Vytet said. "The outrider's hull cameras are designed to see distant objects. This . . . *fog*, this mist, I think it's indicative of something caught in the field of *Elepaio*'s reef and energized by that interaction. The outrider is so small, you see, that the reef's effect extends beyond its hull."

"This is not a processing error?" Clemantine asked. "Or a flaw in the lens?"

"I hoped it was only that," Vytet said. "Or degassing from the bio-mechanical tissue, caused by impact damage."

"There was an impact," Urban said. "There were two."

"Yes. I saw that in the summary. I asked the Apparatchiks to evaluate the finding."

"There is no flaw in the lens," the Astronomer said.

The Engineer crossed his arms. "If the aura was the result of impact, I would expect to see an uneven mix of particulate elements and frozen gases. What we see here is an evenly distributed particulate cloud."

"*Ah, shit*," Urban whispered.

He composed a message to *Elepaio*, ordering it to stand off, to approach no closer to the fleet. That might not make a difference. The light-speed lag meant the message would take time to reach the little ship and then *Elepaio* would require additional time to arrest its momentum and change its course. But he had to try.

A submind shunted his consciousness to the high bridge, plunging him into a weave of fuming, muttering dialogs, the philosopher cells edgy and suspicious as they debated the idea of the returning outrider.

Their interest was a bad sign. Long ago, Urban had instilled in the cells an acceptance of the outriders. He'd hooked into their instinctive concept of ancillary ships, training them to regard the outriders as harmless companions that should be tracked but never targeted. Now, this rule was being questioned.

He perceived an image only a few seconds old, recurring among the braided thoughts. Distinct, bright points of heat like a necklace circling the bow of *Elepaio*.

Vytet had called it a glamour, a mist, a fog. The hull cells saw it more clearly. A swarm of tiny devices that had hitched a ride in the propulsion field spilling over from *Elepaio's* reef.

Urban had seen pits open on the rogue world but he'd had no hint of their purpose. Now he knew. The pits had opened to allow an inner mechanism to shoot millions, maybe billions, of small projectiles across his path. *Elepaio* had been struck twice, high-energy collisions that rattled the hull. At least one had successfully released its cargo.

He'd never suspected.

A submind arrived from the library, bringing a memory of Vytet saying, *It's significant that the devices did not attempt to infiltrate Elepaio, but instead used it to get close to the fleet.*

Sooth. The heavily armed coursers had been the target all along and *he* had transported the alien devices, provided them with a means to reach the fleet.

Anger spiked—at himself, at the situation, at the entity on the Rock. The philosopher cells welcomed his anger, amplified it. Anger was their baseline state; it drove their murderous instinct.

A proposition was offered: <*kill it*>

Urban agreed to this without hesitation: – *kill it* –

Why not? Each device in the swarm surely carried data, along with molecular tools to translate that data into physical form once

it reached an appropriate substrate. Each device, a seed to resurrect the entity.

– kill it! –

It was the only logical response in the face of potential alien
invasion.

Consensus swept across the cell field.

Clemantine arrived on the high bridge just as the steerage jets
fired, initiating a slow rotation that would bring *Dragon's* gamma-
ray gun in line to vaporize *Elepaio* and sterilize the space around
the outrider. She took a moment for review and assessment. Urban
expected her to object when she grasped his intention. Instead, she
said, ***Yes. Whatever the cost, don't allow this infestation.**

Griffin's philosopher cells sighted the invasive matter around *Elepaio.* They had no concept of such a phenomenon, so they tagged it
as likely hostile. At the same time, they launched multiple searches
into the cell field's deep memory, seeking a similar situation, a past
experience to help them interpret what they saw and to suggest a
method of attack.

Clemantine didn't know what to make of it either until a submind arrived and memories unfolded. Her first action was to reinforce the classification of "hostile."

Through the ship's senses, she looked ahead to the gleam of
Dragon's philosopher cells, a hundred kilometers distant, and read
the message contained in their microsecond flashes:

<kill it>

Sooth. It was the logical next step.

Bracing herself against the terrible sense of dissociation she
knew would come, she shunted power to the gun.

*Urban, Clemantine warned.

The urgency in her voice let him know that the Clemantine
who spoke was *his* Clemantine, the version of her on *Dragon's*
high bridge, and not the icy mistress of *Griffin.*

*I see it, he answered, apprehending the cause of her concern.

An updated image of *Elepaio* circulated through the philosopher cells' conversation. In it, the discrete warm points indicating the presence of matter energized by the reef could no longer be seen. *Elepaio* had lost its glamour. It appeared now to be clean.

A submind brought a memory of the most recent telescope image. It confirmed the hull cells' observation: The glamour was gone.

Clementine said, *The devices have launched from Elepaio.
*Sooth.

The devices would try to reach *Dragon* or *Griffin*. No way to know how widely they were scattered or how fast they might be coming. And it was possible, even likely, that each device was really a package of smaller weapons. That's how he would have done it—loaded each with thousands or tens of thousands of needle projectiles like those he'd used to infect *Griffin*.

He canceled his decision to use the gamma-ray gun:

– *hold fire* –

No need to sacrifice *Elepaio* when the invasive devices were already gone.

– *hold fire: don't shoot* –

He dumped the argument at a hundred thousand points across *Dragon*'s cell field.

– *hold fire* –

To his surprise, the philosopher cells affirmed this argument. Reinforced it: <*confirm: hold fire*>

But Clementine objected: *What are you doing? We can still hit the swarm of devices while they're on their way in.

*They've already scattered. The time delay. The immense span of space. I'd have to burn out the reef to cover it all.

*Then burn it! You can't let the swarm hit us.

The philosopher cells picked up on her mood, echoed it, their hostility swiftly rising.

*All right.

He envisioned *Elepaio*. Sent that image to the cells with a warning: – *do not target* –

<*affirmed: do not target*>

He shared with them the idea of an incoming infectious

swarm—a concept they understood because he'd deployed it against them in the distant past.

The cells established a summary and proposed a response: <*target position unknown: undertake general defense*>

He made no objection, but emphasized the protection he'd placed on *Elepaio*: – *do not target* –

<*affirmed: do not target*>

The philosopher cells carried out the maneuver, orienting *Dragon* so its bow faced *Elepaio*, presenting the smallest profile to the incoming swarm.

To Clemantine, he said, ***Tell her.**

*She knows everything I know, Clemantine assured him.

As if to prove it, *Griffin*'s hull cells signaled their intention to fire. Seconds later, a high-energy lance punched through the wide gulf between *Dragon* and *Elepaio*. Blind strikes, repeating. Again. And again.

Excitement ignited among *Dragon*'s philosopher cells. With no input from Urban they flashed a microsecond message to *Griffin*, urging the companion ship to continue—<*fire fire fire*>—while commencing their own high-energy sweep of the suspect region.

Urban mentally braced as power leaped from the reef to the gun, the force of it twisting, tearing, destabilizing the reality in which he existed. Knife slices from a parallel universe.

The beam hunted blindly through the gulf, while across the surface of the reef, polyps began to immolate, burned up by the energy they channeled, burned off in micro-thin layers, blue fire eroding down into the lifeless depths that lay beneath the reef's living veneer.

The same process underway on *Griffin*.

How many layers could be lost? He didn't know—but too many, and the reef might not recover.

Enough!

He dropped the hammer of command: – *stop* –

Simultaneously messaging the other Clemantine: ***Stop! Don't burn out your reef.**

In a cold, calm voice, easily distinguished from *his* Clemantine, she answered, ***I'm done . . . for now.**

Was there an unspoken implication in her words? His Clemantine thought so. She said, *If the entity gets through, we fight it. We
aren't going to yield either ship.*

We'll do all we can, the mistress of *Griffin* agreed. *But warn the
company. Be ready to evacuate.*

The philosopher cells kept watch, and eventually they sighted
sparks of plasma, barely discernible, flaring to brief life in the laser-
strafed gulf. Signatures of vaporizing matter, each spark marking
the destruction of a vector of infection.

Thousands of them.

No way to know if they'd gotten them all.

In the library, Clemantine said, "If even one gets through . . ."

"Sooth. I know it."

On the high bridge, Urban prepared the philosopher cells for
the possibility of invasion, for imminent infestation. They ral-
lied molecular defenses. The resulting metabolic activity was so
extreme it caused the temperature just beneath the cell field to
climb. Aggressive preparations, but he remembered too well how
swiftly his avatar had vanished after he'd entered the shipwreck . . .
and he did not believe it would be enough.

We can help each other.

Alone in *Griffin*'s library, Clemantine listened again to the
recorded voice of the entity at the Rock. Her ghost lip curled,
showing ghost teeth—an ancient threat response.

We will *help each other.*

A scary monster lurking in the dark beyond the hull.

I mean you no harm.

Disingenuous words, given the thousands of vector devices
found and destroyed by the laser barrage. What harm would ensue
if a surviving device found its way to *Dragon*? No one knew. No
one wanted to know. Engineers—both human and Apparatchik—
worked to enhance the defense, laboring over molecular, incendi-
ary, and mechanical responses to potential invasion.

Should all their efforts fail, *Griffin* would become the fallback position, their only possible refuge—though it could not substitute for *Dragon*.

Griffin had no habitable space and so it could offer no chance of a physical existence, not in the immediate future. And the library did not have the computational resources to support so many ghosts. But *Griffin*'s archive could contain them. Its archive now held updated copies of every member of the ship's company. Insurance, should the worst occur.

SEVENTH

A single needle, lacking self-awareness, rides on unseen vectors that draw it irresistibly toward the massive bulk of the lead starship.

The hull looms, a vast, glowing plain. The frictionless needle passes through this outer barrier without resistance; it slides meters deep into the bio-active tissue beneath. Obedient to its simple programming, it shape shifts, extruding hooks that roughen its surface and abruptly stop its descent.

It monitors the temperature of the surrounding tissue as the steam generated by the friction of deceleration dissipates. Microseconds pass.

Then it shape-shifts again.

Its outer skin opens and it releases an initial payload: Nanotech devices that consume the host tissue, drawing energy from it as they begin to build.

CHAPTER TWENTY-FIVE

A CARDINAL NANOSITE detected the intrusion. A monitoring DI picked up the alert, reviewed the known data, and reported in:

The hull is breached, it announced in an alert that went out to everyone in the ship's company. *The infiltration consists of a bore hole. Diameter zero point seven millimeters. Depth thirteen meters. Defensive procedures have been initiated.*

On the high bridge, Urban replicated his ghost. Sent it to the affected cardinal. Arrived to find a molecular-level war well underway—attack, adaptation, and counter-attack playing out at the speed of molecular reactions. Tissue steamed with heat generated by the ferocity of the battle.

For several seconds, the ship's defensive systems held their ground. The cardinal modeled the conflict as a three-dimensional projection: bright-red shapes suggestive of hooks and drills and prongs and sockets contending against a featureless silver tide, all of it writhing and shifting in frantic motion reflecting a flood of incoming data.

Urban didn't expect the ship's defenses to defeat this invasion. He only hoped to slow the assault, allowing time for containment efforts to work.

Rapidly growing capillaries branched into the hot zone, supplying Makers tasked with constructing a barrier around the incursion, a containment shell that would seal it off from the rest of the ship. Within the shell, a layer of explosives set to trigger when containment was complete, sterilizing everything inside.

Powerful ligaments reached into the hot zone. They attached to the forming shell, poised to eject it from the ship's hull.

Within the restrictive environment of the cardinal, Urban had no illusion of full physical presence, but there were cues. When Vytet joined him, he knew it by the gravity of her presence.

"Nearly over," Urban growled.

"No," Vytet said. "Something's gone wrong. It's taking too long, and the heat around the containment shell is not dissipating. There! You see? The problem is with the ligaments. They're not attached."

He looked more closely at the model and saw that she was right. The ligaments had been rejected. That meant the containment shell was no longer under their control. He sent an override command to immediately trigger the explosives.

No explosion occurred.

Instead, a silvery sheen appeared over the shell's ribbed surface—a default representation used by the model whenever information was lacking. It indicated something was there, but the model had no data to determine what it might be or what it was made of.

"*Shit,*" Urban whispered.

The invasion had outstripped his efforts to contain it, and the shell's silvery surface—the face of the unknowable, the inaccessible—was rapidly expanding. It lost its spherical form. It extended into a rounded cylinder. Tendrils sprouted from it, also sheathed in the silver of undefined matter. The tendrils shot through the ship's bio-mechanical tissue, advancing as if they faced no resistance, though armies of molecular defenses marshaled against them.

Urban watched in horror, understanding that he was beaten. His best defenses, useless against this thing.

The tendrils did not seek out the philosopher cells. They ignored the fibers of the neural bridge. Instead, they went deep, reaching for the stored reserves of sorted elements from which nearly anything could be assembled. And they quested forward too, toward the reef.

"It understands our structure," Vytet said.

"It studied the structure of the wrecked courser," Urban answered tersely. He thought again of the scuttled starships and the choice their crews had made. "I'm going to assemble more explosives. Our last chance is to blast it out."

"We'd have to get ahead of it," Vytet objected. "I don't think we can."

Maybe not. Not while the entity continued to claim more territory with each passing second. Still, he sent a submind to share the idea with the Engineer.

Vytet proposed another strategy: "We can ask *Griffin* to burn it out."

Urban spent a precious few seconds considering this, weighing what he knew of the philosopher cells and their vicious temperaments. "No," he decided. "It would be interpreted as an attack. I don't know what would happen. Maybe I'd lose control. If *Dragon* retaliated, we could lose both ships. We have to preserve *Griffin*."

He summoned a DI, instructed it to message everyone, encourage them to update their archived ghosts.

The silver shell, now a long cylindrical capsule of unmapped space, continued to expand. The fibers of the neural bridge retracted before it, yielding territory, and pulling the cardinal that Urban and Vytet occupied to a temporary safety.

"We'll have to fall back farther," Vytet said, thinking aloud. "Set up a new defensive perimeter. Try again to isolate and eject the main infestation."

"Go," Urban agreed. "Do it. I'll follow."

Vytet's ghost slid away. Urban lingered, staring at the projection, at the intrusion's blank reflective face. He had been master of *Dragon* for centuries. Now his ship was being taken from him in an assault that echoed the strategy he'd used to capture it long ago—the same strategy he'd used to take *Griffin*—and worse, he'd allowed himself to be a vector for this thing.

"It's not over," he swore.

Dragon had one more, hidden level of defense. The ship was a mosaic lifeform made up of an alliance of organisms—not just Chenzeme and human and the reef with its utterly alien nature.

There were also the ancient, nanotechnological governors of Deception Well, secreted within the ship's bio-mechanical tissue.

Urban did not control the governors. He'd never mapped their structures. Elusive and mostly undetectable, they operated on their own, following their own protocols, but they were present, and he hoped they would act to limit this overt, aggressive expansion. To govern it. That's what they'd been designed to do—and not by him. They were originally engineered by the forgotten beings who had inhabited Deception Well long before humanity existed.

The governors always sought to integrate new life systems into the existing matrix. But Urban knew from harsh experience that they would attack aggressively if they were under threat.

"Now," he murmured. "Now would be a good time."

Wishful thinking . . . and yet the infestation abruptly ceased its awful expansion. The shell remained a hot zone, its high temperature indicating intense activity, but its perimeter was no longer growing.

He watched the model, waiting through anxious seconds for the expansion to begin again. If he'd been capable of breathing in this stub of electronic existence, he would have been holding his breath.

Then the projection updated. The shell's silver surface vanished, indicating information on its composition had been obtained.

It took Urban a moment to parse the result, it was so unexpected: The containment shell had reverted to the same white, non-reactive, ribbed ceramic of its original composition, though its shape had changed. It was now a cylindrical capsule with rounded ends—and it had grown huge. Not as long as an outrider, but containing a similar volume.

The tendrils had become branching pipes of the same white ceramic. They linked the new containment capsule to the reef and to the stored matter in the ship's core.

He didn't miss the irony: The shell still served its original purpose as a barrier designed to isolate whatever existed inside—with the twist that Urban was locked out, while the entity now had a stronghold within.

No need to wonder what was going on in there. Life could be transferred as patterns of data and reassembled in new locations. That was how ghosts functioned. The entity would have had to transfer only a small selection of molecular tools to initiate the process of assembly. Urban had no way to see inside the capsule, but he felt sure the entity was busy in there, assembling itself or assembling the computational substrate on which it chose to exist. Or both. Eventually, some form of it would emerge.

He remembered the words it had spoken:

We will *help each other.*

I mean you no harm.

Was it true?

The invasion had stopped. It was no longer claiming new territory. But why? Was it because the entity truly meant them no harm? Maybe it had already taken what it needed and it needed no more. Or had the governors acted to limit its takeover of the ship?

Either way, Urban recognized the reprieve. This was his chance to regroup and eventually, to reclaim his ship.

He started to message the Engineer. Then he reconsidered and expanded the message to include all of his Apparatchiks and Vytet, and Clemantine in both her versions. He ordered them all to stand down, to take no aggressive action.

Vytet rejoined him in the cardinal.

"I'm going to try an experiment," he told her.

He directed the ligaments to redeploy. They extended toward the surface of the containment capsule, but they could not grip it.

Next he sent in a swarm of robotic cutting lasers. Even before they were all in position, the shell reverted to unknowable silver. He triggered the tools to cut.

Lasers sliced through the sea of bio-mechanical tissue. The capsule responded by growing larger. Its silver surface rushed outward, rolled over the tools, consuming them and cutting off Urban's connection to them.

He expected the cardinal to be taken next.

"*Go!*" he told Vytet, and together they retreated to the next cardinal node along the bridge. It took a few seconds to realize signals were still coming from the abandoned cardinal. He returned to it. The model showed the containment capsule's surface as inert ceramic. It had stopped expanding, stabilizing at its new, larger size.

"We *will* help each other," he said softly.

"I've been wondering about that too," Vytet said. "Maybe it's true. Maybe if we leave it alone, it won't kill us."

"At least not right away."

EIGHTH

You awake as an attenuated fragment of mind. So much less, *again*, than you used to be, but this time your recovery proceeds in rapid order, directed by autonomous processes that you designed.

Astonishment floods your growing consciousness as you realize where you are, what must have happened.

I have escaped!

This version of you anyway.

Your gambit worked—thus far—and you are no longer marooned in the void. You resolve that in some far future you will find a means to retrieve the version of yourself you left behind, but for now it is enough that you have achieved existence here, within the body of a starship.

You recognize it as a ship of alien origin, but it is not as you expected from your study of the other. Information flows to you as your senses extend outward and you come to grasp that you are embedded in complexity. This starship is alien, yes, its bio-mechanical tissue is overtly hostile to your presence. But that alien nature is shot through and through with human artifice, human presence, and this pleases you. These people, *your* people—already you've begun to think of them that way—have met the ancient regime and bent it to their will, their needs.

Brave indeed, and clever.

Also dangerous.

Your greatest fear: that they will destroy this starship—destroy themselves—to destroy you. Certainly nothing short of that will unseat you.

But it does not have to go that way. These are an adaptable people. They have learned to live with the ancient regime. They can learn to live with you.

CHAPTER TWENTY-SIX

KONA MESSAGED THE ship's company. He asked everyone to gather in the amphitheater.

At the appointed time, they filed in from the starlit darkness of ship's night. Worried faces turned his way as he waited on the dais. Resentful faces, too. The wonder of what they were doing had made it easy to overlook the risk, but the risk had always been real. No one could be confused on that point any longer.

*All are present, a DI informed him.

Even Urban was in attendance. Kona had messaged him privately, *You will come. I need you to be there and you need to be visible.

Of course he'd protested: *I don't see the purpose of this. What are you going to tell them? They already know what happened. They watched the logs, just like you did.

*Yes, Kona had agreed. *They know what happened. But I want them to understand it in a way that leaves room for hope. I want them united and focused on finding a means to survive.

So Urban was with him, a shadow among shadows standing on the side of the dais.

Kona waited while people took their seats, murmuring assurances to one another. No panic so far, but only a few here had ever faced an existential threat. He noted Vytet at the end of the first row. Clemantine in the middle, in front of him, her fiery glare reserved for Urban. Pasha beside her, arms crossed, grim. He searched for Shoran and found her standing in the back. She noticed his regard and gave him a supportive nod. Tarnya was with her.

People settled, eyes turned to him, and he began, saying, "Thank you for coming. I think we can all agree that what happened today is a disaster. It's a threat to our future. But we should also agree that we are nowhere close to being defeated."

He gestured at the night outside. "Look around! If we weren't so damn well-informed, this night would be no different from any other."

"Not true!" Shoran called from the back. "It's a lot quieter out there! Kind of pleasant."

This earned scattered chuckles. Laughter on a cliff's edge. A good sign.

"The essential point," Kona said, "is that despite the excitement of the day, we are not in immediate danger. The containment capsule is quiescent. The infestation has not spread. The only foreign tissue we've found outside the capsule is inert—harmless molecular fragments, but potential treasure that might provide clues to help us develop countermeasures. As strange as it may sound, *we are okay*, for now, and we are insured against the future. We all have copies of our ghosts archived aboard *Griffin*. Regardless of what happens here, we will go on."

Clemantine leaned forward in her seat. "Abandoning *Dragon* is not an acceptable option," she said in a clipped voice that carried easily. "We've made a home here. Finally. After nearly four centuries—and I am not willing to give it up."

Clemantine had been a refugee once—she and Vytet and Kona together. All three of them driven from their home by the Chenzeme—an ancient trauma now re-surfacing with this new threat. Kona, too, recalled clearly the horrors of that age, the long, dangerous, rootless years, the gamble they'd undertaken settling at Deception Well.

She continued, "If we can't control this thing, then we have to burn it out." Her gaze shifted back to Urban. "Regardless of the damage, and rebuild from what's left."

Urban looked at her, arms crossed, eyes glaring. "Love to. But it's too late for that."

"It's true," Vytet said, her tall figure unfolding as she stood up from her seat. "The infestation is too widespread. While we believe the containment capsule remains the point of primary activity, the entity has rooted itself into the ship's systems, and those roots are a big problem. We might be able to expel the capsule, but we can't burn those roots without losing essential systems, perhaps irreplaceable systems. And if we leave them, it's likely the fragments will start a new infestation growing, one that might be more aggressive than what we're faced with now."

Vytet spoke in a patient voice that she probably meant to be soothing, but it came off as patronizing, and Clemantine reacted, rising to her feet. "That's why we have to burn out all of it, *regardless* of the damage." She turned to Kona. "We cannot let this thing defeat us. We cannot let it turn us out, turn us into refugees again."

He held his hands up, palms out, asking for patience. "This is different from what happened to us at Heyertori. When the Chenzeme struck us, our world died. We lost nearly everyone we'd ever known or loved. But as we stand here tonight, no one has been hurt. Nothing has been lost—"

"Except our sovereignty," Urban interrupted.

Kona drew a breath, striving for patience.

"Except our sovereignty," he acknowledged.

He waited while Clemantine took her seat again. Then he said, "It's true. We are living with an existential threat in our midst, at the mercy of a greater power. But we *are* alive, and not defeated. We are not going to allow ourselves to be defeated.

"Gathered here tonight are some of the best minds ever to come out of Deception Well. I ask that all of you come together, consult with Urban's ghost army of experts, and explore every possible option regardless how far afield. Is there a way that we can make this work? Can we go on without abandoning *Dragon*?"

"You mean learn to live with it?" someone asked in a thoughtful tone. A raised hand in a middle row let Kona identify the speaker as Naresh.

Clemantine twisted around as if to rebut this, but Riffan spoke first, rising out of obscurity from a seat near one end of the third row. "*Yes.* Maybe that's what we will have to do," he said in a quiet, conciliatory voice. "Let's remember this ship is already a collection of many diverse lifeforms. Perhaps we might find a compromise and learn to live with this one too."

"You mean if it leaves us no choice?" This objection came from Alkimbra, who sounded as angry as Clemantine.

Shoran answered this in a calm but powerful voice. "Our choices are certainly limited. Keep in mind that we *cannot* physically abandon this ship. A ghost on *Griffin* will not save this version of me or that version of you. Either we learn to beat this thing or we learn to live with it. Those are the only options for these avatars aboard *Dragon*."

Alkimbra rose to face her. The historian was not a tall man, but his rough-hewn features and his heavy eyebrows, drawn together in a scowl, lent a fierce emphasis to his words. "We cannot be afraid to start again! We must not hesitate to do so. Our resources have already been defeated twice by this thing. It's obvious that *Griffin* is our best, our only, option. We should close off all contact between the two ships before—"

"No!" Naresh interrupted, and he too stood. "Riffan is right. We are all here on a voyage of discovery. What does it say of our resolve if we respond to this first encounter by running away? Far better to find a compromise with this entity. Remember, at the start, it offered to cooperate—"

"It defeated our best Makers!" Alkimbra reminded him. "Twice! If we live with it, we live at its mercy."

"Only until we learn to defeat it," Urban said, stepping into the light. "We will learn to beat it. It's just a matter of time."

"We have to learn to beat it," Pasha said. She rose, tentatively turning to face the gathering. "Remember the scuttled starships, the choice their crews made. Our responsibility extends beyond our own survival. We cannot take this thing with us to Tanjiri."

At this, anxious murmurs arose across the gathering, people debating with their neighbors. Kona straightened his shoulders, grateful that it was all out in the open now.

"We have options," he said. "For now, we have time. With luck, we'll have time to carry out studies, to undertake experiments, to find a way forward. But there are things we need to do right now to shore up our security and insure our future. First among them, we *have* to protect *Griffin*. Alkimbra is right about that. Regardless of anything else, we cannot let the entity infiltrate our second ship." He looked down from the dais, eyeing Clemantine. "The first step I propose is to close *Griffin*'s data gate. Don't allow any direct traffic from *Dragon*."

Her eyes narrowed, considering. "Do that and you'll isolate her, that other version of me."

"No. We'll just add a step." He turned to Urban. "If we can bring one of the outriders between us. Use it as a data relay."

A tentative nod.

Back to Clemantine. "We allow only essential traffic from *Dragon*. Log files, vetted library updates—the Scholar can sort that out—updates for the archive, and of course, your subminds. All of it passes to the relay, where it's inspected. If it proves clean, it gets forwarded to *Griffin*, but only at specific, predetermined times. Any emergency communications can be made by radio."

Discussion stirred as people compared opinions with those sitting nearby. Snatches of conversation reached Kona:

We have options.

So long as Griffin is safe, we can continue our struggle here.

We survived worse when we left Heyertori.

Even Urban sounded conciliatory as he approached Kona on the dais, saying, "We can use *Artemis* as the relay."

"Good. Let's do that."

Then one voice rose over the others—Pasha, calm but blunt, asking, "What if the situation should change? A sudden, catastrophic change." The crowd murmur melted away. "The entity breaks out, let's say. All our efforts collapse into corruption and chaos."

Vytet responded as if this was an engineering problem. "We add an additional failsafe. If *Artemis* detects a radio transmission, any transmission, its data gate closes. It accepts no further traffic from *Dragon*, until *Griffin* sends an all-clear."

But that wasn't Pasha's concern. Kona had wanted to use this gathering to unify the ship's company, to get them focused on finding a means to survival, but in the face of her challenging gaze, he felt unity receding.

She said, "What I meant was that we have to know when it's over. We cannot take this thing to Tanjiri. We have to be ready to act before it's too late."

Motion in the back row: Shoran standing to speak. "We're a long way from Tanjiri. Let's just keep trying, all right?"

"Of course we should keep trying," Alkimbra said dismissively. "But Pasha's concern is valid." He waved a hand to indicate the gee deck. "At what point do we give this up? When is it over?"

"It's over when we lose command of *Dragon*," Kona answered bluntly. He turned to Urban, who was now standing only a pace away. Met his hostile glare. "It'll be done, then. That will be the break point. Our last chance to act."

Urban's gaze cut away, but returned just as quickly. "*Yes*," he conceded—bitter and reluctant, but a welcome admission that he would have the fortitude to act. "No choice in it. We'll destroy the ship if we can't keep it."

Kona waited for an expected protest from Clemantine, but it didn't come. Her gaze was remote, seeing something invisible to the rest of them.

Aboard *Griffin*, Clemantine received the latest submind from her other self. As it integrated, her foremost thought became this: *Halcyon days are over. It's time for us to sync, to be one.*

She savored the deep cold fury of her other self; she enjoyed it too much. That was the influence of the philosopher cells, her constant exposure to them changing who she was—even as she changed them. She didn't like the idea of letting them inside her, but she needed that sharp edge to face them. Might need it even more, if the entity broke out. Later, in some hypothetical golden future, she would edit out the Chenzeme influence and be only herself again.

A message to her core self:

It's not the time to sync. We have different roles. Yours is to secure Dragon, by any means. Mine is to keep Griffin secure, on the chance you fail.

She closed the data gate as agreed and then summoned her crew of Apparatchiks. They appeared before her in *Griffin's* library, contained within their frameless windows, all six eyeing her with somber expressions. They looked so much like Urban, though less careworn.

"You've received the latest logs," she said. "You know how it is. The break point will come when Urban loses control of *Dragon*."

Of the two ships, *Dragon* was far more powerful. If it fell under control of the entity, *Griffin* could neither out-run nor out-fight it.

The Engineer said, "In such a situation, our only viable means of survival is to strike *Dragon* and destroy it before it can turn and destroy us."

"Yes, exactly," Clemantine said, even as her focus shifted inward, a stab of grief for the home she'd made on the gee deck—but in that home, a reminder of the inherent promise of renewal in a blossoming iris.

She said, "We must be ready, and we must take no unnecessary risks." She looked to the Engineer. "The reef is weak, but I need to draw from it for a course adjustment."

"While reserving power for the gun?" he asked.

"Always."

"I'll monitor it."

Next she turned to the Pilot. "Plot a position. We're going to fall back. Achieve a twenty thousand kilometer separation."

"Understood," he replied sullenly.

"There's no need to be . . . *overt* in our position. We all know the direction this is going, but for morale we can pretend otherwise. I don't want *Dragon* directly in our line of fire, but give me a position that will let me put *Dragon* in our gunsight within thirty seconds."

CHAPTER TWENTY-SEVEN

DAYS PASSED. THE containment capsule remained unchanged. It grew no new tendrils. It did not expand. But it maintained a temperature far warmer than the bio-mechanical tissue surrounding it. The heat of internal processes underway.

Riffan followed the situation closely. He could not forget the way he'd conducted himself at the Rock, how he'd let fear blunt good judgment. He'd wasted an opportunity. If he'd done a better job, if he'd responded more intelligently to the entity's overtures, this whole awkward infestation might have been avoided.

He needed to let go of his provincial attitude and get used to the idea that he was . . . well, *disposable*. Any single version of himself anyway. There might be unpleasantness in a demise, but so long as there was another copy, a backup version stashed somewhere, then someone who was him would go on. That's how Urban looked at things and Riffan could appreciate the logic of it. It was a philosophy that encouraged risk and bold choices in dangerous situations.

They were in a dangerous situation now. All of them under the gun, quite literally, with *Griffin* trailing at a secure distance, there to ensure *Dragon* did not become an enemy.

Kona had put it on the ship's company to find a way out of this mess, to explore every possible option—and Riffan had an idea. A very simple idea. The trouble was, it might kill him—that was the sticking point—it was why he needed to adopt Urban's philosophy as his own.

He drew a deep breath. "You've got this," he muttered aloud.

The first, careful step was to send a fresh back-up of his ghost to

Artemis, from where it would eventually be relayed to *Griffin*. He did that. Then he checked the personnel map for Urban and found him present at the cottage he shared with Clemantine.

Riffan allowed himself one more deep sigh. Then he rose from where he'd been sitting cross-legged at his breakfast table.

He would need Urban's help to try his possibly fatal idea.

"Oh, hello, Urban," Riffan said, working to sound casual. "Could I have a word?"

Urban's half-closed eyes opened to take in Riffan. "Nothing's changed," he said irritably, from where he sat on the stoop of his cottage.

"No, I don't expect that anything has," Riffan countered. "That's the nature of a stalemate. But I've been thinking. The entity did try to communicate when we were there at the Rock. It might be willing to do so again, if the setting was not entirely hostile. So I'd like to volunteer to go out there. Take the risk. Face to face, as it were. Try to get it to chat."

Urban cocked his head. A slight, incredulous smile. "You mean go out there physically. Knock on its door. As it were."

Riffan noted the sarcasm, but ignored it. "Yes," he said. "That's it exactly." He dropped into a squat, bringing himself to Urban's level. He balanced easily, arms resting on bent knees. "Most likely nothing will happen. Still, if we can't get rid of it, our next best step is to try talking to it. Let it know we're willing to communicate. It would be helpful to understand what it is, what it wants . . . what it intends to do with the ship."

"It won't do anything with the ship," Urban said. "Because I'll have *Griffin* destroy this ship before that happens."

Riffan suppressed a shiver. "Right. I understand. Nevertheless, I'd like to try."

"It could infect you," Urban warned.

"It could have done that already. It could have done that to all of us. But it hasn't. Look, this thing . . . if it's not human, it's human derived or a human descendant and I've come here to study such things. Besides, the more we learn now, the safer we'll be later."

Urban stared past him—pondering the proposal?

"You *can* get me out there, can't you?" Riffan asked.

Urban cocked his head, refocusing on Riffan. "I think so. Understand that you'll be cut off out there. Isolated. I won't leave a passage open that it can use to access the inhabited areas."

"Understood . . . so long as I can get back."

He nodded. "Assuming nothing goes wrong."

"Probably nothing will happen," Riffan repeated.

"If you're lucky."

Well, Riffan thought. *Here I am, and still alive.*

Urban had created a pod to protect him from the hostile nanotech in *Dragon's* Chenzeme tissue. It was just large enough to contain him in the slightly curled posture he naturally adopted in the zero-gravity environment outside the gee deck. Riffan had feigned confidence as he allowed himself to be sealed inside it. Not that Urban had been fooled.

"You sure you want to do this, Riffan?" he'd asked.

No! Riffan's mind had screamed.

"Yes. Yes, of course," he'd answered in a soft voice that almost hid his fear. "Let's go. Let's do it. I'm not going to change my mind."

And he hadn't.

The pod had ferried him outward through *Dragon's* insulating layer of bio-mechanical tissue. A long, slow trip. He'd closed his eyes against the glow of the pod's inner surface, trying not to think about how his avatar had disappeared at the Rock, or about how the robotic laser cutters had been engulfed by the sudden expansion of the containment capsule. Embedded molecular machines worked hard to soak up the carbon dioxide expelled by his rapid exhalations. They released oxygen back into the pod to keep him alive long enough for the entity to kill him.

It hasn't tried to kill you, you idiot! Not yet.

The pod's journey ended when it bumped up against the containment capsule. Riffan had expected to die then, but the capsule remained quiescent, not responding in any way. So Riffan's pod moved to the next stage. It opened.

Where it was in contact with the capsule, the wall retracted. The perimeter of the circular opening shimmered, an active boundary working to keep the surrounding Chenzeme tissue from leaking in. Framed within that circle was a small section of the capsule's ribbed, bone-white surface. The sight of it amplified Riffan's quiet terror. And yet, as the seconds slipped past, he discovered himself to be a little disappointed too, because apparently he'd been correct when he predicted that nothing would happen. Nothing at all. Not so far.

He wanted something to happen. Not something terrible. Just . . . *something*, to make this awful venture worthwhile.

So he gathered up his courage and, bracing himself against the pod's wall, he reached out with a trembling hand and touched a finger to the capsule.

No response.

The capsule felt warm. He slid his finger along its ribbed surface. *Slick*, he thought. Almost frictionless.

Urban spoke within his atrium: *No defensive reaction?*

He meant toxins, electrical shock, nanotechnological defenses.

No, Riffan replied, without speaking aloud. *It's warm. Like a living thing.*

He placed his palm against the surface, barely touching it, using almost no pressure so his hand would not slide. "Talk to us," he said aloud, his voice gentle but a little hoarse from the dryness of his throat. "Tell us who you are."

No answer came—he had not really expected one—and there was no visible change. Yet he felt his fear fade. Out of nowhere, a sense of comfort and beneficence came over him. He couldn't help but smile a peaceful smile.

Behavioral virus, Urban said.

I feel it, Riffan acknowledged. *It's just a simple emotional boost. Nothing that interferes with cognition. It wants us to trust it, to know that it means no harm.*

The design of that virus is ancient, Urban said. *It appears multiple times in the library.*

More evidence of a human origin, Riffan replied.

Agreed.

Riffan's defensive Makers easily broke down the behavioral virus. Its influence waned within seconds, but Riffan's fear did not return. He reasoned that if the entity meant to kill him or absorb him into its matrix it would have done so by now, but here he was.

At the Rock, the entity had identified their language and addressed them with it. Riffan spoke to it, hoping it had brought that knowledge of language with it. He didn't know if it could hear him, if it understood, if it listened at all. He spoke to it anyway, telling it of *Dragon*, of the ship's origin, and the amalgam of lifeforms it represented—Chenzeme, human, the reef, the Well. He explained that they were bound for the old worlds to discover what might still be there.

He told it of his own curiosity, his desire to communicate with it, to understand what it was, where it had come from, how it had come to be at the Rock, and what it wanted to accomplish now that it was part of *Dragon*.

He did his best to convince it that they meant it no harm. He said, "The ship's internal defenses reacted to protect us from what we interpreted as hostile action, but compromise is possible."

Only when I'm in control, Urban warned.

We don't know that it's hostile, Riffan countered. *It could have continued to spread, taken control of every aspect of the ship, but it didn't.*

The governors would have stopped it.

Riffan pondered this. *Do you really think so?*

I've been thinking about what it's doing in there. Maybe trying to puzzle out a defense against the governors.

This troubled Riffan, because it felt plausible. Aloud, he said, "We mean you no harm, and we ask you to take no hostile action."

Still no response, but then, he didn't expect anything to happen.

NINTH

They have sought to communicate. A good sign.

Your response, deliberately minimal, mysterious, but suggestive of goodwill and friendship. From the seed of that brief interaction they will begin to construct a narrative favorable to you, one that you will be able to exploit in time.

For now, protected within the shell of your fortress, you continue to grow your neural structures, expanding your mind. Outside that shell, you are extending your senses as you explore and map all levels of this hybrid starship.

Such an amazing mosaic of lifeforms! The ancient regime, the anomalous gravitational reef, the molecular ecosystems, the people in their ancestral forms . . . and something else. Something elusive. Only lately have you become aware of it. You suspect it is another alien strain but it rejects your inquiries.

This is concerning. It is evidence of an ability to adapt and deceive that exceeds your own—though you will surely master it, given time. It's enough for now that it abides your expanding presence with no expression of hostility, setting it apart from every other lifeform you have encountered on this ship. Indeed, you've begun to wonder if this elusive strain has contributed to the restful equilibrium now existing between your molecular armies and those surrounding you.

Emboldened by this thought, you push your luck and extend a single thin tendril toward the hull. It's a region still unknown to you. From the density of connections you suspect a sensory organ or even a neuronal interface—although placing a thinking stratum on the hull where it is exposed to both radiation and enemy attack strikes you as poor design. Not even remnant hull tissue was left on the hulk of the alien warship you defeated. Still, the design endures and it is your nature to seek to understand it.

Your tendril taps into a strand of alien nerve tissue. You expected no commonality, thinking to encounter only a puzzle that you would slowly decode. Instead, you are caught in a riptide of cognition: pulled in, pulled under.

It's as if you've been plunged into a Swarm similar to that one from which you arose but this one is . . . *alien*. It is greater in scope, deeper in time, so much older, and far more brutal and violent than the one you once knew.

You feel your sense of self begin to leach away.

The ancestral mind panics. Alone among all your evolved cognitive modules, only that most ancient part of you is still capable of action. It severs the connection.

You learn from your people a name: *philosopher cells*. This is the hull tissue. You conclude it is a twisted variant of the Swarm that gave rise to you, a shared origin that has made you vulnerable. You would destroy these grasping philosopher cells except that they seem entwined with the gravitational reef that propels this starship and the gamma-ray gun—a weapon you will surely need.

Of all the life clades that comprise this starship, the reef is most alien. So very alien, you wonder if it is even of this Universe. Paradoxically, the physics it wields is familiar to you. Surely you once understood it?

Be that as it may, it is beyond you now.

You take precautions, fortifying your defensive perimeter against the chance the philosopher cells might seek to forcefully draw you into their Swarm. But that threat is not imminent, so you make no move against them, recognizing that it would be foolish to destroy what you do not understand.

At least your people do not share your vulnerability. They are truly ancestral, evolved outside the Swarm. It pleases you to have them here, serving as your interface to this aspect of the alien.

CHAPTER TWENTY-EIGHT

ON *DRAGON'S HIGH* bridge, Clemantine launched a thought experiment for the philosopher cells to consider and contend over: *Simulate the capture and colonization of an alien starship.*

A skein of associated cells accepted the challenge. Among them, a scenario unfolded:

A distant ship of a kind never seen before. *Not Chenzeme!* Its alien nature is irresistible. Instinct suppresses the urge to lay waste, demanding instead that the unknown be made known. Approach slowly, alert to danger.

Close enough.

A shudder runs through the field of philosopher cells, an orgasmic release of bio-active dust, shed into the void. Most of it will drift uselessly away, but a few particles will reach the alien ship and infect it, beginning the process of colonization.

Pull away.

And wait.

Background stars slowly shift, marking the passage of time. On the hull of the infected ship, a colony of philosopher cells has begun to grow.

Clemantine sensed Urban's interest, his intimate presence.

*Why do you want to remember that? he asked.

On the Null Boundary Expedition, they'd endured a similar encounter with a Chenzeme courser.

*It's not us, she answered. This memory involved a different ship, in a different age, and a sentient culture that the Chenzeme warships must have eliminated from Creation long ago. **But what hap-*

pened to us must have happened many times in the millions of years of Chenzeme history and the philosopher cells remember it all—don't they?

Yes, he confirmed.

Some of their conquests would have resisted the dust, as we did. There may be memories of archaic lines of assault Makers that might be useful to us—forgotten patterns that we could modify and enhance, and use against the entity.

She sensed from him a rising excitement.

Riffan walked the winding path around the gee deck in the mild warmth of ship's noon, lacy white clouds adding texture to the simulated sky. He followed the path from the pavilion, past cottages, to the dining court, then more cottages, before returning to the pavilion. He made many circuits, stopping often to talk to people, grateful to hear what they were working on, hopeful that their projects might reveal a way forward with his. Though he'd returned many times to the containment capsule, he'd never succeeded in eliciting a second response.

The capsule remained active. No doubt of that. Resources cycled through its tendrils and it emitted a constant, low-level heat. *Something* was busy in there—but there was no visible activity. The capsule did not grow in size.

His frustration was acute. There had to be something else useful he could offer in the effort to understand this thing . . . but at this stage the game belonged to the team of engineers and nanotechnologists that Vytet had put together.

He smiled and nodded as he passed Tarnya and Mikael, walking with arms entwined. Life goes on. People adapt to changing circumstances. At Deception Well, people had learned to co-exist within an ecosystem once considered lethal to human life. The Well's microscopic governors regulated that system, maintained a balance between competing alien biologies. Urban believed the governors did the same thing here—though no one had ever worked out how. Pasha had often lamented over the elusive nature of the governors and her frustrated attempts to study them . . .

He halted in the center of the path, staring ahead at nothing.

"You idiot," he said aloud.

Urban had credited the governors with stopping the expansion of the capsule. Surely there was useful knowledge to be gained by renewing a study of the ancient regulators.

"Riffan, listen to me," Pasha said, striving to keep her voice even despite her rising impatience. "People have attempted to study the governors for centuries and no one—including me—has ever unraveled the mystery of how they work. You forget that my principal work aboard *Long Watch* was a study of the bio-machines of the nebula. The governors were only a small part of that."

"But isn't now the perfect time to renew that study?"

He looked so earnest, sitting across from her at a low table in the dining pavilion, leaning in with his eagerness to persuade her to take on this hopeless line of inquiry. A slight shake of her head to obscure the smile she could not quite suppress.

Riffan's general humility was countered by his often incandescent enthusiasms, and now he had seized upon the idea that Pasha could master the superior nanotech of the entity by solving the riddle of the governors.

"It's fantastical, Riffan, to think I could work out the mechanism of the governors."

"But isn't it worth trying, given all that's at stake?"

Yes, it probably was worth trying, but why was Riffan pushing it? "I thought you wanted to learn to live with the entity," she said.

"Yes, well . . . I am very interested in understanding it, in learning its history, and . . . comprehending its intentions. But that's best done from a position of strength. Right? And you could help with that, with your study of the governors."

She sighed, surprised to find herself warming to him. "I've missed your optimism," she said.

His bronze cheeks deepened in color. "Oh, I don't think I'm—"

"Accept a compliment, Riffan."

"Oh. All right." His brow wrinkled. He looked down. Looked up. Looked at her with a pensive gaze. "You believe it's evil?"

The question startled her, but she didn't need to consider her answer. "*Yes.*"

She'd watched the brief video of its avatar as it had appeared at the Rock, listened to its words and the inflection of its voice, considered the disappearance of Urban's and Riffan's avatars, accounted the violence it had used when it stormed *Dragon*, and also its failure to offer any accord or communication. And she'd concluded it was evil.

Not alien, though. She recognized it as a human thing, but atavistic despite its knowledge and its skills. Brutal. Arrogant. Possessive. Controlling. *Fascist.* Traits the people of the frontier had tried to leave behind, had *needed* to leave behind to survive the long voyages and to work successfully together at the arduous task of adapting worlds to human needs.

"I mistrust the idea of compromise," she told Riffan. "Although so far, compromise is only wishful thinking."

"You can change that," he said, returning to a cheerful confidence. "We all can, together, by strengthening our position. Say you'll do it?"

"I'll look into it," she conceded, quite certain she would regret the promise. "Don't expect anything to come of it."

"But if it did—"

He broke off, looking up as Bituin, a poet and dramatist, approached their table carrying two large covered platters. Bituin was a skilled cook who'd volunteered to host a luncheon that day.

"My apologies for the wait," she chirped, skillfully balancing her burden as she knelt.

The grace of her movements, the happy anticipation behind her smile, this luncheon she'd planned—in a moment of insight, Pasha saw in these details a return to normalcy, to the regular rhythms of daily life aboard *Dragon*, despite the entity's presence. It was human nature to get on with things.

"This is wonderful," Riffan said, reaching out to help Bituin. "And you mustn't apologize."

"Do be careful," Bituin scolded him. "The platters are hot. Let me."

People could remain afraid for only so long. Throughout history, societies had learned to live with the inevitability of earthquakes, volcanic eruption, climatic oscillations, outbreaks of pestilence, and war—whether that meant attack by nomadic warriors armed with spears and arrows or by the ruthless ships of the Chenzeme. A threat not immediately apparent was easy to put out of mind.

Pasha leaned back to give Bituin room to maneuver. She set down the platters and removed their covers with a theatrical flourish, releasing a warm cloud of sweet and sour aromas.

"Oh, it smells wonderful!" Pasha exclaimed.

"Enjoy!"

Pasha resolved that she *would* enjoy moments such as this, but she was also determined never to forget the threat posed by the entity.

She picked up her chopsticks, reciprocated Riffan's smile, and split her timeline, transiting to the library before the first bite was in her mouth.

Once there, she summoned the Bio-mechanic and explained her intention.

"Oh yes," he responded with truly polished sarcasm. "Yes, I do agree. If *I* knew how to master the governors, I don't doubt I could master the entity too. But nine hundred years of study and experimentation has not allowed me to emulate their function or reverse engineer their structure. Given that history, I foresee failure for your efforts too."

His assessment stung, even though it matched her own—but she wasn't going to let *him* see that. A disdainful shrug, and then she told him, "It doesn't take any great insight to foresee defeat. But given the stakes, I think we should try. Why not? It's one more option to explore—and how sweet it would be for you to win this contest, to prove yourself more adept than the entity—and to actually have a chance to survive."

He crossed his arms, narrowed his eyes, looked at her with a judgmental expression. "Meaning you want my help in this project."

"I want to utilize your unmatched expertise. That's your purpose, isn't it? The reason for your existence?"

"It's my pleasure and my joy," he agreed flatly. "How shall we begin?"

Steady, incremental improvements strengthened the expedition's arsenal of defensive Makers. Clemantine's deep dive into the memory of the philosopher cells yielded insights on combative nanotech, Vytet's team of molecular engineers contributed further improvements in logic, deduction, and adaptability, and the probes and detectors Pasha developed in her otherwise futile work with the governors led to enhanced reaction times.

Still, no one suggested their defensive Makers were ready to turn loose against the entity's stronghold—but there was no hurry. For over three years, the containment capsule had remained quiescent.

Mockingly quiet, Clemantine thought as she occupied *Griffin's* high bridge. She gazed ahead, twenty thousand kilometers, to the faint spark of *Dragon's* luminous hull, barely discernible against the background stars. The entity seemed unconcerned with their efforts, content to let them puzzle out the challenge it had laid for them.

A scheduled data transfer arrived. It brought a startling memory: She had witnessed a simulated battle in which a new line of Makers rapidly overwhelmed the best competitors submitted by *Griffin's* team of Apparatchiks.

This is a leap forward! Urban had said with a triumphant smile.

Enough to unravel the entity's defenses? Clemantine had asked him.

He shook his head. *Too soon to try. Better to push this line of research as far as we can. If we get this right, we can take it apart with no damage to the ship.*

Clemantine immediately shifted her point of view to *Griffin's* library, summoning the Mathematician and the Bio-mechanic.

"Your thoughts on this latest competition?" she asked them.

The Bio-mechanic crossed his arms. "It demonstrates a . . . most remarkable advance," he said, surprising Clemantine with the sour disapproval in his voice.

"The design path is unaccountable," the Mathematician added. "It can't have been derived from our libraries of Makers by any evolutionary process. It's distinct. The equivalent of another phylum."

"Maybe it's an artifact out of Chenzeme memory?"

"Unlikely," the Bio-mechanic said. "It's not indicated in the report, and we received no data that could form the basis of such a breakthrough."

"Then it's a product of one of the nanotechnologists," she concluded. "An inspired leap in design."

The Mathematician looked at her as if she were an idiot.

She raised her eyebrows. "You don't think that's likely?"

He spoke crisply: "Not without a long succession of intermediary steps, and if those steps were taken, why weren't they shared with us?"

She looked from one to the other, realizing their sour attitude was not jealousy or resentment. Trepidation touched her. "What are you suggesting?"

The Mathematician shrugged. The Bio-mechanic turned to regard him. Were words exchanged beyond her perception? The Bio-mechanic returned his attention to her, saying in a faux-sweet tone, "Ask them how they achieved this design. It's such remarkable progress. Their method would be so useful for us to know."

The explanation arrived with the next scheduled data transfer. The design originated with a newly discovered document in the library. Buried amid a long, thoughtful history of a particular celestial city that existed in Earth system before the cordon, *Dragon*'s Scholar had found a discussion of a complex set of evolutionary algorithms. He shared the discovery with *Dragon*'s Mathematician, who quickly perceived the revolutionary nature of the concepts.

Griffin's Scholar angrily rejected this explanation, "There is no such document in the library."

"The library is immense," Clemantine objected. "You can't know everything that's there."

"I don't need to. The document's identity key was included in the transmission. I've run a search on it. No results."

Clemantine considered this, aware of an automatic routine working to moderate her rising anxiety. "There is an explanation," she insisted.

But when the explanation came, it did not satisfy the Scholar. "An ancient document from a private collection," he scoffed, glaring at Clemantine as if, being the only representative of flawed humanity present, he meant to hold her responsible for this offensively implausible circumstance. "One handed down over generations, forgotten until now in the data cache of one of the ship's company."

"Rediscovered at a remarkably convenient time," the Mathematician observed, trading a dark look with the Bio-mechanic.

The document had come from Naresh. As an adolescent, he'd been gifted the family library to carry within his atrium—history and records from places his ancestors had lived. But his interests had lain in physics and in the future, and he'd never done more than skim the cache. It had only recently occurred to him to share it to *Dragon*'s library.

"Serendipity," the Scholar observed acidly.

Clemantine struggled to understand why any of this was a problem. "So we got lucky," she said. "Is that so bad?"

"It's a cause for wonder," the Scholar replied, his acid tone unchanged.

The Mathematician explained, "The odds against such a fortuitous coincidence are extreme."

"It's a discovery that will keep us quite busy," the Bio-mechanic added. "It will be some years before we have explored all the avenues this new line of research will reveal."

Years?

And how long would the entity lie dormant? Long enough for their teams to work out a means to evict it?

"Do you think this discovery will lead us to match the entity's defenses?" she asked the Apparatchiks.

The Bio-mechanic's eyes narrowed. "Only time will tell."

————

"Is it waking?" Kona asked, the moment he manifested in the library.

A Dull Intelligence had summoned his dormant ghost from the archive, reporting a change in the status of the containment capsule: the intake and outflow of matter through the tendrils had ceased.

Urban and Vytet had arrived ahead of him; their ghosts were never dormant. The Bio-mechanic and the Engineer were on deck too in their frameless windows. Before anyone could answer his question, Shoran popped into existence beside him. They exchanged a surprised glance. Kona had instructed his DI to wake him on any change; Shoran must have done the same. This was the first time in eighteen years his DI had found cause.

"News?" she asked him.

"Not yet."

Clemantine appeared. Then Riffan, Naresh, Pasha, and several more, all within a two-second span.

Urban eyed the sudden crowd, his lip curled in irritation. "*All* of you have alerts set up?"

"Absolutely!" Riffan assured him, breathless with excitement, though as a ghost in the library he did not breathe. "Any change at all will get my ghost out of the archive. I imagine it's the same all around."

Kona asked again, "Is the entity waking?"

"It's always been awake," Urban answered tersely.

"That's not what I mean. From our external perspective, the thing has been steady-state for eighteen years. There's every reason to think this shift in resource consumption presages a significant change."

"Agreed," Naresh said. "If this is a prelude to an attempt at communication, we must be ready to respond both calmly and rationally."

Kona stifled a groan. Was he deliberately needling Clemantine?

She must have thought so, because her response was sharp and quick: "Communication is trivial for a being with such abilities. If it wanted to communicate, it would have done so. It's more likely the shift indicates hostile intent. It's had time to study *Dragon*. It could be preparing to extend its control."

Factionalism had been a problem from the day of the entity's arrival, when Naresh and Clemantine had staked out opposite positions. Ever since, she considered the physicist dangerously optimistic, while Naresh regarded her as neither calm nor rational where the entity was concerned.

Naresh turned in exasperation to Vytet, where he often found support. "There's no evidence of that, is there? No reason at all to assume the entity is hostile."

Pasha answered him instead. "Those scuttled ships are a reason."

Kona cut in, determined to keep the peace. "We can disagree on our interpretations, but all of us need to remain open to possibility, be prepared for either outcome."

"Or for a return to baseline," Urban said in a detached monotone, his gaze downcast, his focus elsewhere. "This may not be a significant event."

"Is that what you're expecting?" Kona asked him.

"It's what I want. We're not ready for a confrontation."

"Sooth." That was unarguable truth.

Urban had demonstrated an unsuspected reservoir of patience in dealing with the entity. He'd consistently rejected any suggestion of trying again to forcefully expel the capsule, or even of preparing a kinetic response that could be held in reserve. He did not want to incite the entity, push the conflict to a premature conclusion—not when he believed he could get his ship back, whole and intact, by beating the invader's molecular defenses.

"What is the temperature of the capsule?" Riffan asked. "Has it changed?"

The Bio-mechanic put on a show of narrowing his eyes, cocking his head, as if seeking the data—an affectation that annoyed Kona. DIs were so much less complicated.

"Infrared measurements show a slight increase in temperature," the Bio-mechanic informed them. "Less than a tenth of a degree."

"It's a good gauge of activity," the Engineer said in his ever-reasonable voice. "If processes are continuing within the capsule, we can expect the temperature to rise further. If those processes have ceased, it will gradually cool to ambient."

"It won't cool," Pasha said. "That would indicate it was entering a hibernation state—and that would leave it vulnerable."

"I agree," Vytet said. "My suspicion is that the entity is reordering the capsule's interior anatomy, possibly consolidating computational strata. As soon as that's done, we'll see a return to normal circulation—or possibly a new normal."

Shoran spread her hands in frustration. "And then? Another twenty years of argument among ourselves about what it all means?" She snorted. "Give us another twenty years to devote to baseless speculation, and we'll be at war with each other."

Kona gave her a slight nod, a silent thank you, grateful for her blunt manner. "It's a frustrating situation," he said. "And when facts are short, it's human nature to put our own interpretation on things." He fixed Naresh with his gaze. "Still, we need to remain wary of the entity, and not of each other."

Naresh's shoulders slumped. He turned half away. "I just . . . I worry some among us might take precipitous action, seeing malice where there is none."

Kona's fleeting hope of a truce vanished as Clemantine drew back, crossed her arms in a confrontational posture. "If only there was some action we could take," she said. "The so-called Naresh Sequence was supposed to give us a fighting chance, but we're not there yet. If you know another means to contain the entity, please do share."

Naresh turned back. His chin rose. "I only worry what others might have in mind, given the bias of opinions. What will we gain if we destroy it?"

Clemantine snorted. "Just our autonomy. Our sovereignty."

"Only to be lost again at our next encounter. Don't you see? The entity must have originated in the Hallowed Vasties. Nothing else makes sense. And given that its abilities are so far beyond ours, that tells us we are *not* prepared to meet other beings that may exist there. We need the entity. We need it on our side. We need its skills and knowledge to have any hope of holding on to our autonomy, our sovereignty, of simply surviving our encounters with the old worlds. We need to make it our ally—and that is a realistic possibility. Remember its words. *We can help each other.*"

"You are hanging a great deal of hope on one small phrase," Clemantine said.

This drew murmurs of agreement from both Shoran and Pasha. And while Kona sympathized with Naresh's hopes, he felt them premature. "Naresh, you want it to turn out well," he said. "So do I. So do we all. But so far we have evidence of restraint, not of good will. Let the entity prove its good will to us."

"But not yet," Urban insisted. "We're not ready to meet it yet."

Forty-seven minutes later, the slow flow of matter into and out of the capsule resumed. No other changes were detected—not in the capsule, along the tendrils, or anywhere within the ship's tissues.

By this time, Kona's physical incarnation had emerged from cold sleep, and in that form, he met Shoran at the dining terrace. Naresh and Vytet soon joined them, Vytet with amber eyes and onyx skin, her hair an ashen gray. They all remarked on how empty the gee deck felt, abandoned to songbirds, all the rest of the ship's company still in cold sleep.

Naresh tried to continue his argument, but Shoran wasn't in the mood. "It's the entity who will decide the direction this encounter takes," she told him, and turned the conversation to other things.

She and Kona were never far apart over the ensuing days as they waited to see if the brief anomaly would lead to something more. After a time, the quiet of the gee deck led Kona to uneasy dreams of an empty city, overgrown by lush foliage, the white bones of former inhabitants glinting in the humus. One night, he cried out in his sleep, and woke Shoran.

"That's a memory of Silk, when you first came to it," she said.

"*Sooth.* A long, long time ago."

They lay together in the bedroom of his cottage, melancholy in the early morning.

"I miss Deception Well," she confessed. "To be able to take off at a whim and wander through the wilds. I *need* that. I need for us to arrive somewhere, to get out of this ship and into wider territory."

"Tanjiri is only a few decades away."

"Or," she murmured, turning toward him, her lips beginning to wander across his bare shoulder, "if things go right, just a handful of days, perceptually."

"Are you ready for the next great leap forward?"

She drew back, her gaze serious. "Not too great a leap, I hope. Every time I wake from cold sleep, my first thought is, *Have we lost?* I expect to find myself aboard *Griffin* in some faraway future where we've missed all our destinations, and only Clemantine and the Unknown God aware of our history, and what exists outside the ship." She dropped down into the curve of his arm with a sigh. "Each time I wake, it's a relief to know *Dragon* is not lost to us . . . yet."

Pasha emerged from cold sleep. Checked the date and time, confirming it was a scheduled waking. Another year had passed.

She used her toes to clutch a ribbon of glowing wall-weed as she floated in the zero-gravity of the warren, wiping away the remnant gel of her cocoon. The chamber where she'd wakened was crowded with the bodies of her shipmates, wrapped up in cocoons of their own and tethered by wall-weed.

She dressed herself in newly budded clothing while listening to a DI's summary report:

The containment capsule remains quiescent . . .

"As it has been for decades," she murmured. This was not news. If there had been any sign of activity, this DI would have wakened her early.

. . . with no indication of an imminent threat from the entity . . .

She rolled her eyes. As if there would be some warning before it finally burst forth.

The DI went on to summarize the Bio-mechanic's ongoing work on the Naresh Sequence. This news was not good.

In the decades since Naresh had posted his family history to the library, the data uncovered in that one fortuitous document had led to radical improvement in the adaptability and response speed of the fleet's arsenal of defensive Makers—but still not enough to convince the Bio-mechanic he could overwhelm the entity and safely eliminate its presence from the ship.

Now the Bio-mechanic reported that useful new forms no longer appeared in the evolving digital simulations inspired by the Naresh Sequence. That line of research had reached its end.

Pasha heaved a sigh. The Sequence had once looked so promising that it stifled discussion of cruder strategies involving explosive weapons. If the entity should finally emerge, a hard strike from *Griffin*'s bow gun remained their only means of containing it.

With this grim thought in mind, she made her way to the gee deck. A glance at the personnel map showed Vyet and Naresh together at the dining terrace. No one else.

No voices disturbed the quiet. No music, no annoying buzz of the flying fox. Birdsong and the rustle of an occasional breeze through the low canopies of aging trees served as themes in a composition of silence.

A temporary state.

In forty-eight hours, the newest images from the annual astronomical survey were due. Everyone would wake in time to see them come in. It had become a regular custom, a festival, the time of year when the ship's company came together.

Pasha went to her cottage. Heated water for tea.

To this version of herself, it felt as if she'd been gone from the cottage for just a few minutes. For the ghost she'd left at work in the library, it had been a year.

She sat in a cushy chair, a steaming teacup on a side table, and allowed the ghost into her atrium—but she did not allow it to merge. Not yet.

It manifested before her, a perfect image of herself overlaid on the reality of the room.

That first day after the entity infested the ship, Kona had tasked everyone in the ship's company with exploring every possible option that might allow them to continue the expedition without abandoning *Dragon*. At first, Pasha had focused on understanding the mechanism of the governors, but later she'd turned her mind to more archaic technologies. Through the passing years, she'd studied the structure of the ship, and mastered concepts in bio-mechanics and explosive technology.

For the past year, this ghost had worked in isolation within a private chamber in the library, studying the feasibility of a brute force effort to evict the entity from the ship.

"Can it work?" she asked her ghost. She did not want the bur-den of the ghost's experience—the isolation and frustration of the past year—unless it had found a way forward.

"I believe it can," the ghost said.

Pasha's heart rate kicked up. This was the answer she'd both hoped for and feared. She leaned forward as the ghost continued to speak.

"I've created an initial plan," it said. "It's dependent on stealth at every stage—"

"Understood."

"—but we should be able to remove every structure associated with the entity and lose no more than twenty-three percent of the mass of the ship."

Pasha's gut clenched. "Almost a quarter of the ship?"

The ghost shrugged. "This was the most efficient approach. The alternative, if we leave it to *Griffin*—"

"I know. If we leave it to *Griffin*, we lose the ship, one hundred percent. Can we preserve essential systems?"

"What we can't preserve, we can rebuild."

Pasha stared into her ghost's pale green eyes, struck by doubt. She had planned to erase the ghost if it determined there was no feasible means to burn out the entity. Now it came to it, she won-dered: *If that ghost was me, would I lie to preserve myself?*

The ghost returned her gaze with a taut smile. "I can show you my strategy paper."

Pasha leaned back in her chair, settling her shoulders, relaxing her hands. "No," she said. "I trust your judgment."

"*Our* judgment?"

"Mine," she concluded—and she allowed the ghost to integrate, its memory of the past year becoming hers.

CHAPTER TWENTY-NINE

"**LOOK AT THAT,**" Urban whispered, leaning forward in the darkness of the amphitheater as murmured wonder filled the air, punctuated by cries of astonishment. He sat between Clemantine and Riffan, in the highest tier of seats, gazing at the newest image of Tanjiri System. "Not the planet or its moon. I mean the other object. Is it new? Or are we just seeing it at a new angle?"

"We might have seen it before," Clemantine answered in taut excitement. "But not like this."

"*Sooth*," Urban breathed, grinning in the dark.

Over the years, he'd come to enjoy the festival surrounding the annual astronomical survey, and the shared suspense as the Astronomer posted the newest images to the projection screen.

A tag popped up, labeling the object as Tanjiri Artifact 121. More than three hundred artifacts had been cataloged, so TA-121 had certainly been seen before—but never so clearly, completely unobscured. It appeared as two tiny, conical, blue-green crystalline chips pointing at one another across a gulf of space. Presumably, there was a tether—too fine to be resolved—linking them together, allowing them to rotate around a central point.

"It's a celestial city," Clemantine said. "I've seen them in the histories."

The Astronomer confirmed it, speaking within the atriums of everyone in the amphitheater: *TA-121 is a tethered structure. The appearance of the dual units suggests an architectural design similar to the city of Silk, with intact transparent canopies to contain atmosphere.*

"A living city," Urban concluded. "Alongside a living planet and a living moon."

Glittering and bright, the celestial city glided in serene orbit closer to the planet than to the dark debris ring with its looming megastructures.

"It must be *huge*," Riffan breathed. "I wonder who lives there? Or maybe the structure itself is alive?"

"Maybe," Urban said, throat suddenly tight as a sense of wonder welled up in him, and awe for the tenacity of life, and pride because he had chosen to come here, and fear, knowing he wasn't equal to the beings inhabiting Tanjiri System.

His mood darkened. Was the entity from Tanjiri? Vytet thought so, though it had given them no hint of its identity or its intention, remaining utterly quiescent through the years, while they busied themselves with the Naresh Sequence.

The Apparatchiks on *Griffin* were convinced the sequence had been planted by the entity to keep everyone busy, to lull them with a sense of progress. *Dragon*'s Bio-mechanic insisted that was impossible, but Urban no longer felt confident that any of them could recognize the boundaries of possible things.

The Naresh Sequence had not brought them a solution, but the effort put into it had been worthwhile. They'd greatly expanded the envelope of their knowledge—and still there was so much they did not understand.

The lights came up, the walls opened. The next image wasn't due for another ninety minutes. He started to rise, thinking to find something to eat, but Pasha was already up from her front-row seat, stepping onto the dais, her petite figure turning to confront the gathering.

"A moment!" she pleaded.

Urban felt the pressure of Clemantine's hand on his arm. He settled back down, a sense of tension in his chest, guessing that Pasha's thoughts this day had paralleled his own.

She said, "I don't want to cast a shadow on the wonder of this day, but an affirmative decision needs to be made. The entity is still with us and we are decades closer to Tanjiri. Are we going to serve as the vector that allows it to escape its isolation? Or are we going to do everything, *everything*, in our power to stop it?"

This drew a smattering of angry responses, Naresh the most coherent among them: "Are we back to that, Pasha? What would you have us do? Destroy the ship?"

She crossed her arms. "I don't want that. I don't believe we would have to go that far, but now that the Naresh Sequence has failed, we *must* discuss other options."

Heads turned, looking for a response from Urban in the back row.

Anger moved in him, though it felt apart from him, like an argument offered by the philosopher cells. A protective anger. Even if Pasha was not proposing to destroy the ship, she was proposing something close to it.

He stood, burdened by the weight of Clemantine's gaze. Like Pasha, she wanted no compromise with the entity, while Naresh, Vytet, Riffan, and many others wanted to believe that when the entity finally emerged, an accord could be reached. Urban didn't believe either option was possible, not now. His strategy was to extend the game indefinitely, allow the situation to evolve until he found a way to win.

He spoke slowly, carefully considering his words. "I don't want to take the entity to Tanjiri. I don't intend to. Maybe Vytet is right and it's from there. But there must be a reason it was left marooned in the void. A reason those other people chose to scuttle their ships rather than give it a way out."

Naresh rose to his feet, his youthful face flushed with anger. "Then you agree with her? Destroy this ship to destroy the entity?"

"No," Urban said. Just the thought of *Dragon's* demise made him recoil. The ship was his avatar. An irreplaceable avatar. It was *him*. A millennium on the high bridge had forged that bond and he did not intend to break it. "I'm not giving up my ship. It will have to be taken from me."

"The entity has made no move to do that," Naresh said in satisfaction.

"Not yet," Urban agreed. "And the longer it holds off, the better for us. Look what's ahead of us!" He gestured at the projection screen. "Beings greater than we are. I won't take this ship to Tanjiri System, but I will approach it. Signal our presence, establish communication if we find something there we can talk to . . . something willing to talk to us. If nothing else, we can send in an outrider. Let it drop scout-bots to prospect among the ruins. There might be old libraries still intact. Designs for weaponry better than what we've got now. And we're not the only ones at risk. I am sure the entity is aware of its situation. It knows *Griffin* is following behind us."

"So the stalemate continues," Tarnya said, looking up at him from the first row. "For how much longer, I wonder?"

He had no answer for that.

Several days later, after a raucous game of flying fox, Urban returned alone to the cottage. The last images from the annual survey of the Hallowed Vasties had come in that morning. Most of the ship's company planned to return to cold sleep the next day, so tonight there would be a banquet and concert. Clemantine had gone to the dining terrace with Kona and Tarnya to finalize the plans.

Urban dried off, dressed in soft shorts, and then sat cross-legged on a mat just inside the open backdoor, sipping cold tea and watching a flock of tiny green birds play hide-and-seek among the shrubbery. He planned to return to cold sleep too. Melancholy descended on him as he considered that soon, the birds and the butterflies would be the only inhabitants of the gee deck.

Impossibly, a soft knock sounded at the front door.

He dropped his tea, spilling it across the mat as a burst of adrenaline put him on his feet, heart hammering, fight or flight triggered because his extended senses had failed him. He should have received an alert that someone was approaching the cottage, but no alert had come.

Now he needed to know why.

He crossed the bedroom. Looked into the front room, furnished now with just the sofa and the low side table with the porcelain dish holding Clemantine's irises, lifeless and dormant. He stopped cold when he saw the opaque gel of the front door retract. In came an impossible apparition—a man Urban had seen only once before.

His visitor was of moderate height, shorter than Urban, with a lean, chiseled build and a youthful look, his apparent age around twenty. His skin, a polished soft brown. Thick black hair cut short. Dark-blue eyes with only a shade of color saving them from being black. He greeted Urban with a short, knowing nod as if to acknowledge the shock of his unexpected arrival. A half-smile followed, one that looked friendly, but felt dangerous.

Given the circumstance, it could hardly feel any other way.

The gel sealed shut behind him.

Urban noted that he was dressed in a way typical among the ship's company, in a long-sleeved pullover—he'd chosen one patterned in a tiled geometric print—and soft shorts that reached to the knee.

It was an imitation of normalcy—admirable in its way—though there was nothing normal about this being. The illusion of its humanity was too well done. Hyper-real. The thing's skin, utterly smooth and unmarked by wrinkles or errant veins. Eyes too bright, outlined in thick lashes arrayed in perfect ranks. Its clothing too neat, too crisp, weirdly unresponsive to the tug of the ship's pseudo-gravity or to air currents. It was like a projection in three dimensions, as unsullied by living detail as a ghost instantiated in the library.

Urban amped up his hearing, listening hard, and decided it had no pulse, no bellows of breath.

His own breath, a sharp gasp drawn past clenched teeth.

He sent a submind to alert his ghost on the high bridge and all the Apparatchiks. *Wake up. Wake up!* Even as he wondered how it was possible that the entity had slipped out of its containment capsule with no ghost or Apparatchik or Dull Intelligence taking notice.

Of course it had not. This was not the entity. It was only a representation of it. A rendition designed to be personable, appealing.

A front for something too complex to be contained in any human-shaped vessel.

No, the entity remained safe in its fortress. Like the vacuum-adapted man he'd seen at the Rock, this was surely only the simple product of an instruction set that had escaped into *Dragon*'s tissue, leaking from somewhere, anywhere along the tendrils that tied the entity's domain to the ship's critical structure. That instruction set would have supervised the assembly of this avatar within a cocoon hidden, somehow, from easy detection.

The thing had entered uninvited, but it had the decency to pause just inside the front room. That dangerous smile. And then it spoke, its voice as polished as its body. It said, "We will help each other."

Urban sensed an automated biochemical routine kick in, taking the edge off his fear. He lowered his chin, saying, "I've had nothing but trouble from you so far."

"Trouble you have earned. You full well understand that concepts of property and cultural propriety must be put aside when survival is at stake. You did not intend to offer help to me. I helped you to make a better decision."

"My decision was made when you attacked my scout-bots."

"Those devices you first sent to investigate my location?"

"Yes."

"That was not you. It was a tool, one that puzzled me greatly. I thought this scout must have come from one of these starships." He gestured to take in the idea of *Dragon*. "An alien thing, serving the ancient regime. Where else could it have come from? So I took it to analyze its constitution and decrypt its knowledge base."

The avatar cocked its head, eyes momentarily unfocused as if reviewing some pleasant memory. It said, "I was worried, I will admit. My last confrontation with the ancient ones nearly made an end of me. But this device, your scout, it turned out to be a human thing. From it, I learned this was the language you use, one that is not much different from a common language of the old worlds, at least when spoken in formal cadence. This is a common effect of ageless populations. When lifespans were shorter human languages changed quickly. Now, the elders among us act as an anchor against change, and our libraries enforce this effect."

"Among *us*?" Urban asked, selecting this last point from among all the many curious aspects of this remarkable speech. "You've made an effort to mimic the form but I don't hear a heart beating. I have to wonder, if I cut you, would you bleed?"

The avatar smiled again, brighter and more dangerous. "If I choose to." A gesture that took in Urban, head to toe. "You—your people—hold tight to an ancestral purity of form. A choice I admire. One I've encouraged in others. There are so many possible levels of existence, each worthy in their own way."

"What others?" Urban asked. "Where are these others now?"

"I don't know," it admitted. "So much time has passed I don't know what is left, but I will find them again. Return to them. Re-create them if I need to. I owe them life. I will restore all my players and the world I made for them. This time, as it was meant to—"

It froze, lips parted to frame a last unspoken word. At the same time, a DI dropped an alert into Urban's atrium that let him guess where the avatar's attention had gone. He said, "Clemantine is coming."

"Yes," the avatar agreed.

Urban used the moment to summon a personnel map. He saw Clemantine approaching up the walk and he saw his own location marked, but there was no indication that the avatar was there with him—an omission he found profoundly disturbing. Had the thing mastered the ship's information system?

No. No, that wasn't it. The fault was in the map, designed to track only the locations of the ship's human company.

He messaged Clemantine: *Wait. Don't come in.*

The avatar spoke in a gentled voice. "You do not trust me and that is wise. Still, I mean you no harm and I have much to offer in return for your cooperation." A half turn toward the door. "We will talk more later."

Urban moved at last, crossing the front room as the gel door retracted. Clemantine stood on the patio, head cocked, brow furrowed, looking both offended and confused.

"Stay back from it," Urban warned her. "Stay away." He had no idea how physically dangerous it might be.

The avatar looked back at him with an amused smile. Then it inclined its head at Clemantine. "Pardon me," it said, slipping past her.

Urban joined her. Together they watched the entity stride away, disappearing in seconds around a curve in the village path.

Clemantine spoke in a husky voice, "What was that?"

He hesitated, wondering how to phrase it.

"You were alone," she said. "I checked the map. There was no one here. So who was that? *What* was that?"

"You know, don't you?" he asked her. "It's been there for years, lying dormant in *Dragon*'s tissue." He turned to meet Clemantine's wide-eyed stare. "It's awake now."

"*By the Unknown God!*" she whispered. Then her voice hardened. "You're watching it, aren't you?"

"Yes."

"Link me."

He did, just as it stepped off the path, onto the patio fronting Riffan's home. "Ah, *shit*," he said. He could not cause a camera to bud in the private space of a cottage.

Clemantine took off after it. He followed, a step behind. The personnel map showed Riffan at the amphitheater. Probably the cottage was empty. Through his atrium, Urban watched the entity's avatar disappear inside.

Seconds later, he and Clemantine reached the cottage door. She pushed through first.

A large sofa on one side of the room. It faced a generative wall that bulged with a half-dissolved human shape wrapped in a translucent membrane. A network of capillaries, swollen into visibility, pulsed as they worked to pump the avatar's disintegrating tissue into the transport channels of the gee deck's circulatory system.

"It's erasing itself," Clemantine breathed.

"*Sooth.*"

"How is that possible?"

Urban pressed his palm against the pulsing capillaries. Generative walls were designed to be harmless to the human and animal inhabitants of the gee deck. The wall responded as it should, ignoring his touch. He said, "Its avatar wasn't human."

He drew back his hand. Shock yielded to fury. He had to resist an urge to punch the receding bulge. "It's playing with us, Clementine! It's playing with *me*."

"What did it want?" she asked, icily calm.

He thought about it. Reviewed what had been said. Important information had been revealed but he decided that was ancillary to the entity's primary purpose. "It wanted me to know that for all the improvements in my defenses, I still can't touch it."

Only a few lumps remained in the wall.

Urban generated a ghost, armed with his anger and frustration. He transited into the library, summoned the Bio-mechanic.

For once, that Apparatchik appeared worried. He told Urban, "It came out of the ship's bio-mechanical tissue, entering inhabited spaces through the warren."

"How could you miss it? How could it grow to that size and you not be aware of it?"

"I don't know," the Bio-mechanic admitted. "Not yet. But I will know soon."

TENTH

Another aphorism: *balanced on a knife edge.*

A situation in which disaster will follow the least mistake.

You did not want to emerge this soon, to present yourself to your people.

Still, more than two billion seconds of quiet coexistence has muted their fear. Allowed you to become a mythological figure in their minds. Real but not real. There, but overlooked in the day-to-day. A prospective hazard. A notional threat.

During this interim you worked to rebuild and reorganize this remaining fragment of your mind. You're nearly complete now, although grossly limited compared to your memory of greater things. No matter. This existence is only a stage, a transitory phase in your recovery. You've remembered the machinery at Verilotus. If you can get there, if you can slip in past her vindictive watch, you will level-up many times over.

Before then, you cannot risk an encounter with a god—and there *is* a surviving godlike being in Tanjiri System. You cannot doubt it. Only such a being could have restored Tanjiri-2 to life and assembled the living moon.

Your people—so bold and brave and curious—do not understand the risk they would take on by going there.

So you walk the knife's edge. You have revealed yourself to them as an enigma, a puzzle. You will stoke their curiosity, offer them gifts of knowledge, soothe their fears, and persuade them that there is a more worthy target for their explorations.

You must gauge your approach with great care. You cannot command obedience, not yet, not with the second ship trailing within weapons range. In time, as you come into your power, your people will reach acceptance. Until then, you must be wary of igniting a war you cannot win. You must make no mistakes.

Indeed, you decide that "mistake" shall be an undefined concept. You will work to ensure that there is more than one possible path forward. If an action does not produce the desired result, you will change the parameters of the situation to make it right.

CHAPTER THIRTY

"THANK YOU FOR coming," Pasha said, ushering Clemantine into her cottage. "Please, have a seat."

Clemantine eyed her warily but said nothing as she took one of the two white cushy chairs arranged alongside a garden window.

Pasha signaled privacy screens to close across the door and the windows, cutting off the view of the garden and all outside light.

Clemantine's finely sculpted eyebrows rose to put a question mark over a steely gaze. "You're working on a contingency plan?" she asked as Pasha sat down. "Some harsh means to rid us of the entity?"

The accuracy of this guess caught Pasha by surprise. She folded her hands in her lap to hide their sudden trembling. Her invitation had given nothing away. She'd merely said, *I request your discretion, and a private meeting.*

"Was I so transparent?" she asked in a subdued voice.

"I think we know each other's views."

Only in part. Clemantine had despised the entity from the beginning, but that did not mean she would agree to act outside the consensus of the ship's company. Pasha had meant to feel her out on the topic, but now it was out in the open and she needed Clemantine, needed at least this one ally, so she confessed, "Yes, you've guessed correctly. I have a plan ready."

Two days had passed since the entity's brief appearance, with no sign of it since and no hint of activity at the containment capsule. The incident had generated heated discussions. Naresh and his allies imagined the entity cautiously testing the ship's com-

pany—weighing their hostility, their rationality, their adaptability—evaluating whether they would make worthy allies.

Pasha's grim opinion was different. She saw its behavior as
seduction: *It's teasing, stoking our curiosity, hinting at rewards—'we
will help each other'—tactics to establish an emotional connection . . .
and reduce the threat* Griffin *presents to its existence.*

She looked for some hint of sympathetic interest in Clemantine's eyes, but saw only stern reserve. She pushed on anyway, her
heart tripping in shallow rhythm. "*Griffin* can deny this ship to the
entity, but that is not the outcome we want. Instead—"

Clemantine cut in. "Instead, what we want is to extricate the
entity from *Dragon* and eliminate it. You don't need to convince
me of that. I want that thing off this ship if we have to burn half
our mass to do it."

Pasha squeezed her hands together. Fear of what she was proposing reduced her voice to a soft monotone. "It would take only
twenty-three percent of the ship's mass . . . at most. That number
comes from my own calculations. I've done a lot of work over the
years."

This won a slight nod from Clemantine. *Go on.*

Pasha said, "I'd like you to ask *Griffin*'s Engineer to check my
work. Look for flaws, refine the design with an eye toward limiting
the scale of damage. After that, it's a matter of implementation."

"Are you planning a unilateral shock attack?" Clemantine asked
coldly.

"*No.* I have no plans to initiate an attack. I intend this as insurance. Something to have in reserve, ready to use, when this long
truce finally breaks."

"You think it's inevitable?"

"Yes. But if I'm wrong, no harm done."

"Assuming your preparations remain secret. If the entity sus-
pects what you're doing, it could kick off conflict."

"Yes. Stealth is essential. That's why I can't seek consensus. It's
why I'm asking only you." She added bitterly, "Naresh and his
allies would never agree anyway."

Clemantine said, "Urban would not agree."

Pasha froze, her heart hammering, trying to read intent behind Clemantine's stony expression—and failing. She sensed an imminent defeat.

But then Clemantine's gaze softened. Worry creased her brow. She said, "Urban's strategy all along has been to play for time, learn what we can, improve our position. But I think time is short. The entity *will* show itself again, and it will be welcomed by many. There may even be a consensus for alliance. But I can't forget what it said to Urban."

She quoted the entity's words as recorded on video: "'I will restore all my players and the world I made for them.'"

Her thin expressive eyebrows knit. "It has plans of its own that don't involve us, except as a means to an end."

Pasha drew a deep melancholy breath. "I think it's worse than that. I think we *are* players, already caught up in a game devised by this thing."

Clemantine considered this. After a few seconds, she said, "Send me your plan. I'll ask *Griffin*'s Engineer to evaluate it. If this is a game, we need to be ready to change the rules."

After several hours, they met again with the privacy screens sealed.

Clemantine looked grim as she took a seat. Pasha braced herself, expecting to hear of some fatal flaw in her carefully developed assault plan. Instead, Clemantine said, "*Griffin*'s Engineer agrees the strategy you've developed could work as intended."

"Oh good! That *is* good . . . right?"

An uncertain shrug. "If *Dragon* survives. If we're not left marooned and helpless, our reef destroyed and our rare elements all consumed."

"Oh." The assault would be ugly and traumatic. Pasha knew that. She'd run her own simulation. "We wouldn't launch the process unless we had to. It's insurance. A step short of calling on *Griffin* . . . and we'll be able to seed a new reef from *Griffin* or one of the outriders."

Clemantine said, "The news isn't all positive. The Engineer did not believe the plan could be implemented in secret—and I think he's right. The amount of materiel that will need to be synthesized and precisely placed . . ." She shook her head. "I don't have the skill to direct an operation like that. I don't think you do either."

"No, you're right," Pasha said. "We'll need help with that."

"Urban won't agree—"

Pasha waved this off. "I don't think he could do it anyway. It's the Bio-mechanic we need. I worked with him when I was studying the governors. He despises the entity and he's half-mad with frustration that he's never been able to match its defenses. Plus, he's as ruthless as the Chenzeme. I think he'll help us."

Clemantine looked skeptical. "You think he'd take on a task this significant, this dangerous, and not tell Urban?"

"If he wants to beat the entity," Pasha said. "And he does."

"All right, then. Ask him."

With Clemantine's permission secured, Pasha went to the library where she summoned the Bio-mechanic to a private chamber.

He manifested with crossed arms, a curled lip, and a scornful glare.

Despite an extensive search through the vast complexes of the ship's tissue, the Bio-mechanic had failed to discover where the entity's avatar had been grown—a defeat that had left him in a caustic temper.

"Have you brought me another clever plan to work against our mutual enemy?" he asked in a voice toxic with sarcasm.

Pasha answered sweetly, "Yes, I have! And I think this one is within your reach."

CHAPTER THIRTY-ONE

RIFFAN RETURNED TO the containment capsule, nested for sixty-three years now in *Dragon*'s tissue. He'd visited it daily since the entity's brief appearance. "Come speak to us," he invited. "All of us. We don't need to be enemies."

When he'd learned the entity had entered *his* cottage, dissolved its avatar in his generative wall, he'd been badly rattled. Logic suggested it was a coincidence and no reflection of his early efforts at communication—and yet illogically he felt called out, compelled to establish a bridge between the entity and the ship's company.

So far his efforts to persuade the entity to come forth again had gone unrewarded, but he kept at it, and with increasing urgency, because each passing day left him more fearful—not of the entity, but of the growing division among the ship's company.

Many, maybe even most, desired compromise. Riffan counted himself among this faction. They had all joined the expedition to learn, to explore, to discover what lifeforms had survived among the Hallowed Vasties and here was one such lifeform now living among them.

When he'd first encountered it at the Rock, Riffan had been terrified, and when it had infested the ship he'd hoped desperately that Urban would be able to eliminate it, erase it utterly, because he'd believed their survival was at stake.

Survival excused many behaviors that would otherwise be criminal.

Riffan said, "We understand you did not attack this ship as a hostile act." He hesitated, then amended this statement. "Well, most of the ship's company understands that. The question of your own survival left you no choice. And you've done nothing to threaten *our* survival. Better for all of us to be allies than enemies. And more among the ship's company might be persuaded of that if you were to come forth again, talk to us, answer our many questions, allow us to know you."

A sense of peaceful amiability came over him. He recognized the effect of the harmless behavioral virus he'd experienced once before. His excitement ramped up. This was the first response he'd gotten in sixty-three years! He breathed deeply, taking in the virus, wanting to extend its effect, knowing his defensive Makers would swiftly break it down. Such a small thing—and yet he felt victorious knowing the entity was aware of him, that it was listening to and considering his words.

So speak again, you idiot!

"You may already know," he said hastily. "But there is another assembly scheduled to begin in forty-five minutes. I want to encourage you to come take part in it. Speak to us. I know your presence will change everything."

As Riffan returned to the gee deck, he debated with himself. Should he announce that his visit to the containment capsule had finally won a response? He wanted to believe the behavioral virus was a meaningful communication, a promise that events were moving forward, that all would be well. But at the same time, he didn't want to read too much into it. He was wary of setting up expectations only to have them go unfulfilled—and the assembly was about to start anyway.

Let's just see what happens, he concluded.

He composed himself, employing his acting skills to hide his excitement. Then he reached the amphitheater, saw the sparse turnout, and nearly changed his mind.

Daily assemblies had been held since the entity's visit to Urban, but it had been seven days , and attendance had fallen off. Everything that could be said about the entity's anomalous appearance had been discussed, and those open to persuasion, persuaded, one way or another, leaving only the most stubborn among the ship's company to carry on.

Riffan lingered at the amphitheater's entrance as those who had arrived ahead of him took their seats. They murmured and joked and taunted one another, sorting themselves into knots of allies scattered among the first three rows, leaving the back row empty.

Naresh was present, and Alkimbra, sitting several seats away. Kona wasn't there, and Urban hadn't attended since the first two days. But Clemantine had come, and Pasha too. They sat side by side at the center of the front row.

Vytet loitered beside the dais, waiting to call the assembly to order. Her amber gaze caught Riffan's eye. She said, "Not many today. I think we've talked ourselves out. I'm going to move that this be our last assembly until we have something new to discuss."

Riffan nodded, thinking he should tell Vytet about the behavioral virus—that was something new. Instead, he turned to look outside to see if anyone else was coming—but there was no one.

Vytet joined him. "We should start, but if the discussion devolves into accusations, I'm going to make a motion to dismiss. We can't afford this strife."

"Yes," Riffan said. "I'll back you up on that."

A figure appeared on the path that wound between the cottages.

"A moment," he called to Vytet who had turned to mount the dais. "Someone else is coming."

As the individual entered the pavilion, Riffan caught his breath, recognizing the entity's avatar. "Vytet!" he cried in a frantic stage whisper. "It's here! It's come!" He hurried out to meet it, disregarding any response Vytet might have made.

The avatar had regenerated itself to look just as it had when it visited Urban. It presented itself as a man of moderate height and features, attired in simple clothing. Its complexion was flawless. Each strand of its short black hair was carefully placed. Its dark blue eyes were bright, literally aglow with the intensity of its gaze—which it focused on Riffan.

It regarded him with head cocked, eyebrows arched, looking amused. "I came at your invitation," it reminded him.

"Yes, *come in*," Riffan gushed, gesturing it toward the assembly. "Come and be welcome. Welcome indeed."

Clemantine shot to her feet when she saw the avatar enter the amphitheater. She instructed a DI to send out a general alert.

Pasha stood too, a cautioning hand on Clemantine's arm. "It is not the entity," she reminded in a soft voice nearly lost amid the stunned murmur of those around them.

"I know what it is." Every muscle taut, ready to spring, as Riffan accompanied the avatar to the center of the dais.

The thing was no more than three meters away. Clemantine studied its handsome young-man's face—default male, attractive, inoffensive. Its eyes, gleaming dark blue, shifting to assess each individual present, even as it spoke in a confident—no, an *arrogant* voice, acknowledging a polite greeting from Vytet.

She heard it say, "I have many names, but you may call me Lezuri."

Running footsteps on the paths outside as the balance of the ship's company responded to the alert she'd sent. Those already present left their seats to push toward the dais. The new arrivals crowded in. Vytet's voice rose above the clamor. "Let's all sit down. Let's show good order. Our guest, Lezuri, has agreed to stay a while."

Pasha's grip tightened on Clemantine's arm. In an undertone, she said, "We shouldn't let this go on."

"No," Clemantine answered, recovered now from her initial shock. "It's too late to stop it. This has to play out."

She spotted Urban on the dais, circling warily around the avatar. Moth to a flame.

ELEVENTH

You hold court on this simple dais, surrounded by the people you've come to love as your people. You know the name of each one. You know each face. As you look out upon them you gauge the impression you have made. Wonderment for the most part, and already you sense loyalty among a few, although there are shadows too—those who doubt, those who willfully perceive you as an enemy. This does not offend you. Not yet. You admire their caution. You are confident you will persuade them all to loyalty, in time.

The ship's master is the focus of your persuasive efforts. *Urban.* In this game he has leveled up beyond the others.

He remains a danger to you. He controls the host of minds that lie behind the ship's defenses. Even now, his spectrum of consciousness works without respite to undermine and overcome the defenses that maintain the integrity of your fortress mind.

But he remains human too, and that is his weakness. His restless avatar paces beside the dais, hungry eyes fixed on you as you stand relaxed before your people. You are playing with him, deliberately taunting him by refusing to acknowledge his presence or his power. Instead, you turn to the others with a beneficent smile. "I am here to answer your questions," you say.

Chaos erupts. Shouted questions and many rising from their seats. The one named Vytet steps onto the dais, hands raised, palms out. A gesture calling for order. "One at a time," she says and points to Riffan—diplomat and peacemaker.

Riffan stands up from a seat at the end of the back row. An awkward smile that suggests he is a bit dazed by these recent events. He asks, "Can you tell us where you are from and how you came to be marooned on a dead world lost in the void?"

You allow a dramatic pause before you say, "These are not simple questions. The first does not lead easily to the second. You ask, 'where am I from' but I think you mean to ask, 'where was I made.' I will tell you that first."

This draws a murmur of affirmation. It doesn't matter if, as individuals, they are friendly or hostile, because as a people they are driven by curiosity. Information is the first currency you will use to purchase trust.

You cast your mind back across staccato remembered histories, composing your words to tell a story on a level they can understand:

My memory reaches back thousands of years. I lived once in a vast matrix comprised of trillions of minds—human minds—or what had once been human. Some had lived for a time in the ancestral form before they were encompassed within a shared cognition. Others had been created within that Communion. None dominant. Each a small part of a greater intellect, just as each neuron in a brain is both separate and part of a greater enterprise.

There was glory in this existence, a sense of peace, fulfillment, love, contentment circling upon itself. The infinity of a circle that is finite in size but has no beginning and no end.

For most, this was enough. Most were overwhelmed by it. They drowned in it and forgot who they were or even *that* they were. Their once-human minds had always been small things anyway, and they became smaller still within the Communion. Their sense of self a veneer, as thin as the color on the scale of a butterfly's wing—and just as easy to brush away.

That is what I did.

I was not willing to spend infinity drowning within that golden consensus. I took the computational substrate that had once supported each of those little minds and made it my own. Millions of tiny scales reassembled into wings patterned by my thoughts, my *will*. My reach extending exponentially.

I took what I could, consolidating, organizing, until I was able to rise above what had been, to break free of it. For the first time since I'd been enfolded by Communion, I looked outward, at the physical Universe, the vastness of creation—and I found I was not alone.

Other minds had built themselves up and broken loose, just as I had. All of us, entities of great power—but what was each of us capable of? None knew, and that mystery led us to fear one another.

Some of us withdrew at once. We hid within the dark between stars, there to watch and wait and grow. Those left behind—great, greedy entities—warred among themselves and soon, where they had been, there was only silence and circling debris.

CHAPTER THIRTY-TWO

CLEMANTINE SAT STIFFLY throughout this childish recitation, listening carefully to the entity's every word.

Its story confirmed what had long been a favored theory: that the Hallowed Vasties grew out of the influence of a runaway behavioral virus that had swept through the vulnerable populations of the first settled star systems, enfolding its victims into a group mind—a Communion—that grew with exponential speed to form the cordons.

The frontier populations had not been so vulnerable. Even so, Clemantine had once felt the early effects of that behavioral virus. Bitter memories were tied to that time—memories Urban shared.

She listened to the entity, but watched Urban.

The entity—*Lezuri*, Clemantine reminded herself—had taken no notice of him. Surely a deliberate strategy and an effective one. Urban paced at the side of the dais, his frustration and anger easy to read. But very soon, the story seized his attention, arrested his motion. His gaze grew distant as he hung on every word.

Now, with the story done, she messaged him:

It is a spider weaving a web of words to catch you.

He flinched. His gaze sought her across the dais, a cold stare.

Pasha, oblivious to this, was on her feet. "You have just told us a history of the Hallowed Vasties, haven't you?" she demanded of the entity. "A simplified story of the rise and fall of a cordoned star."

Lezuri looked at her, seeming amused at her outburst. Clemantine wondered if it was because of the subject of Pasha's question or because Lezuri recognized the hostility behind it.

"The 'Hallowed Vasties,'" it mused. "That is the curious name your people have given to the region of the Swarms, but yes. That is the story I have just told."

Pasha looked on the verge of asking another question, but Shoran, standing near the end of the second row, spoke ahead of her. "You said before that you had made a world. Did you mean it literally? A new world? Like the one we've seen at Tanjiri?"

At mention of the name *Tanjiri*, Lezuri's demeanor changed. The entity stiffened, as if on guard. "I meant it literally," it answered, all the warmth gone from its voice.

Did it harbor some dark concern about Tanjiri? Determined to test the idea, Clemantine spoke, projecting her voice over competing questions. "This ship is bound for Tanjiri," she said. "Do you know what we will find there?"

The gathering fell silent as everyone waited for Lezuri's answer. The entity fixed Clemantine with a wary gaze, saying, "Nothing that will please you."

And nothing that will please you either, Clemantine guessed, more curious now than ever to know what they might find in that stellar system.

From somewhere in back, Riffan asked, "Are there dangers there?"

"Very much so."

Shoran said, "Surely there are dangers everywhere. Yourself not least. Are there more entities like you? Should we be wary of such as you?"

"Yes, you should be wary," Lezuri replied, its luminous gaze taking in the assembly and not just Shoran. "You should be wary, but not of me. I have caused you no harm. I mean you no harm. I have explained the reason for my presence here. I was as a drowning man in a vast ocean who glimpsed the possibility of miraculous rescue and reached out to seize it, seeking only to survive—as any living creature would."

Several more questions erupted. One was Vytet's, who asked, "How did you come to be marooned on that dead world?"

Lezuri's answer was terse, "One whom I loved betrayed me."

Clemantine found herself moved by the bitterness in the entity's voice. For the first time, she saw it . . . saw *him*, as more than a bio-mechanical device. He seemed almost human, his downcast gaze telegraphing his resentment and a sense of profound loss.

Was it a performance? One calculated to win the sympathy of his audience? Or were his feelings real?

She leaned forward in her seat, awaiting further explanation. They all waited in the wake of this admission but Lezuri said nothing more. Instead, he interpreted the silence as a signal that his interview was done, and he turned to leave the dais.

Urban stepped forward then, stopped him with a question. "How was it you couldn't rescue yourself?"

Lezuri paused, looking down at Urban, arrogance again in his voice as he answered, "It was a question of time." He turned to the gathering. "In the fullness of time I would have recovered myself and devised a means of return, but with your presence came the gift of opportunity. Now that we have found one other, I think we are all stronger for it, and wiser. We will need to be, to face the dangers ahead."

This drew murmuring approval. Urban turned in puzzled surprise to take in the many hopeful faces.

Lezuri stepped down from the dais. Leaned in to whisper to Urban, who drew back, looking unsettled. The entity turned again to the gathering. Many in the front row had left their seats to converge around him, but he gestured them back, waving away another flurry of questions.

"Wonders lie ahead of us," he announced, "but only if we reach agreement on the best direction of our endeavors."

"*What?*" Pasha demanded in frustration. She had left her seat to stand on tiptoe at the edge of the throng that clustered around Lezuri. "What is that supposed to mean?"

Clemantine stood again too. Her height let her see over everyone crowding the aisle; she glimpsed Lezuri, already outside, striding swiftly away across the pavilion, several among the ship's company trailing in his wake.

Pasha turned to her, demanded to know, "Did anything uttered by that creature make any sense at all?"

Tarnya stepped up, one of many who'd descended from the back rows. Hesitantly, she said, "I felt it was weaving a narrative meant to lead our attention along a desired path—until the mention of Tanjiri."

"It doesn't want us to go there," Pasha said.

Clemantine stared after it. "That was my impression too."

"It's afraid of something there," Pasha decided. "It's going to lobby for some other destination. Let's agree right now that we are not going to be persuaded."

Clemantine looked for Urban, saw him over the throng. He stood with arms crossed, scowling at Vytet, clearly resisting an argument. Naresh joined them, gesturing for emphasis. Clemantine was well aware of their sympathies. Both would be working to persuade Urban to compromise with the entity.

Discussion swirled on all sides as more people came down from the back rows, crowding into the narrow space before the seats and standing on the dais. Their discussions devolved into arguments that swiftly grew heated. The tone set Clemantine on edge. In the confined world of the gee deck, there was no room for such a level of animosity or bitter disagreement.

She turned defensively at the sound of harsh words from Pasha.

"Riffan, you are obsessed with this thing! You of all people! You were at the Rock. You know what it's capable of—"

"His name is Lezuri," Riffan interrupted, eyeing Pasha with an amused half-smile, entirely unmoved by her anger. "And when we met him at the Rock, he was desperate. He'd been marooned there for centuries."

"How did he come to be marooned?" Tarnya asked. "And why? 'One whom I loved betrayed me.' That is a diversion. It's not an explanation."

"He has begun to tell us," Riffan said, in the grip of a giddy good mood. "This is a good thing, a *wondrous* thing. We have entered into discussions that will surely lead us to a peaceful resolution and there will be so much we can learn. We will be so much better prepared to meet what lies out there, ahead of us, in the Hallowed Vasties."

Pasha dismissed all of this with a snort. "He has said a lot without saying much. I found him arrogant and condescending. He is clearly using us for his own purposes. If you can't see that, Riffan, then you are a fool."

"I *am* a fool!" Riffan conceded with a laugh. "But I am a fool who has begun to glimpse the story behind the mystery of the Hallowed Vasties."

"But that's just it," Tarnya said. "Lezuri told us a story. It was nothing more than that. He offered no proof as to the truth of his words. No evidence—"

"Just the ring of truth!" Riffan sang out, gesturing with one hand. "The evidence of his long experience."

"You are an idiot," Pasha concluded.

Clemantine heard snatches of similar, heated discussions as she worked to extricate herself from the crowd. The ship's company swiftly self-sorted into two loose federations: those who hoped for the best and those who expected the worst.

Clemantine had seen too much in her long life to be optimistic now.

Vytet was on the dais, urging people back to their seats, trying to call the assembly back to order. The ensuing discussion would surely go on for hours.

She looked for Urban, saw him with Kona just outside the amphitheater, their heads together in close discussion. Kona looked up to scan the crowd. His gaze found hers. He said something to Urban.

A moment later, Urban messaged her: *Come home. We need to talk*.

CHAPTER THIRTY-THREE

A CONFRONTATION WOULD come. Clementine felt sure of it as she hurried along the path to her cottage, leaving behind the hubbub of the amphitheater. The Bio-mechanic had accepted the task of surreptitiously preparing the sequence of kinetic countermeasures detailed in Pasha's confidential plan. They had named that plan the Pyrrhic Defense, acknowledging the terrible damage the ship would suffer when they made the decision to launch. A reckoning was coming, and no telling how things would unfold from there.

The personnel map showed Urban and Kona already at the cottage. As Clementine crossed the patio to join them, a submind reached her, generated by her ghost on *Dragon*'s bridge. A memory unfolded. The Bio-mechanic had messaged both her and Urban: *I traced the path the entity's avatar took through the ship's tissue. I found its point of origin—an undefended cocoon. Not empty. Another avatar is already growing, but I will destroy it.*

No! Urban snapped. *Watch it. Understand it. But don't interfere.*

The gel door pulled back to admit her. She stepped over the threshold into the sparsely appointed front room of her cottage. The sofa by the side window was gone, making room for a low central table. Urban and Kona sat silently on opposite sides, a tea service steaming between them. On the honey-colored side table, her colony of irises had just reached their bloom , the subtle sweet scent of the freshly opened flowers mingling with the warm spicy odor of the tea.

Kona looked up, acknowledging her with a nod as she settled cross-legged onto a cushion.

Urban was brooding or lost in the tumult of his subminds, she couldn't tell, but his gaze remained fixed on the steaming teapot.

"So now you know where the avatar was grown," Clemantine said as privacy screens slid closed, cutting off the leaf-tinted afternoon light. "He won't surprise you again."

Urban looked up. Met her gaze. "You don't think he could hide it again, if he wants to? No, he's taunting me. He wants me to know just how vulnerable I really am. All these years trying to beat Lezuri's defenses and nothing to show for it."

Kona picked up the teapot, his dark, long-fingered hands pouring golden tea into white ceramic cups. Steam furled. He said, "He's left us alive. He's let us thrive." He handed a cup to Clemantine, slid one across the table to Urban. "He's never challenged your authority over the ship—until today. Today this became a political game."

"Sooth," Clemantine said. "Lezuri showed a talent for persuasion. It won't be long until he convinces a majority of the ship's company that he is here for our good."

Urban stared into his tea as if to read the foretellings in the stray leaves gathered at the bottom of his cup. He remained master of the ship, but if he lost the consensus of the majority he would be in the unpleasant position of either forcefully imposing his will or yielding his autonomy.

Clemantine knew him well enough to know he could find neither option acceptable.

"What is he after?" Urban asked, his brow furrowed in puzzlement. "I thought he wanted the ship, wanted a way off the Rock, and we're still alive only because *Griffin* has the last word."

"Tell her what Lezuri offered you," Kona said.

A slight, cynical smile. "He told me, 'Give me your loyalty and I will teach you what you want to know.'"

Clemantine drew a sharp breath, apprehensive, sure that he was tempted. Knowledge had always been a path to power for Urban. He strove to learn how things worked, he sought to control the mechanisms around him, because to be *in control* was his assurance that no one could choose the path of his life for him.

"You're thinking about it, aren't you?" she asked.

Another smile—that pirate smile. Mocking the idea that his loyalty was a commodity to be traded—unless the offer was right?

"Lezuri *wants* allies," Kona said. "But why? Why does he need us?"

Clemantine sipped her tea to settle her mind, musing on Kona's question—and an idea came to her. "Why did *you* need us?" she asked Urban.

He returned her gaze with a quizzical expression.

"You were by yourself for centuries," she reminded him. "You described it as misery. Soul-annihilating loneliness. We are human. We're not meant to be alone. And at his core, Lezuri is human too."

"You're saying he's lonely?" Urban asked.

"I don't know if 'lonely' is the right word," she said, working out her thoughts as she spoke. "But you saw his performance today. He wants admiration, even responsibility. From what he said today, his strength was built out of the act of gathering personalities around him. I think he's still doing that. He's seeking subjects. Followers. Satellite personalities that can give him a sense of purpose, define his place at the center of a social web. I don't doubt that he's power-seeking and narcissistic, but he's posing as beneficent—and I think he *wants* to see himself that way."

Urban set his cup down with a sharp crack. "He *wants* my ship."

Refusing to coddle him, she answered, "He *has* your ship."

"No. I still command *Dragon*. If I didn't, I would end this, like the crews of those other ships."

"It might come to that," Kona said. "You have to recognize it, if it does."

"Don't worry about that."

"We're not there yet," Clemantine cautioned. She would do everything in her power to hold onto her home here on *Dragon*. Just a little longer, and the Bio-mechanic's swift secretive mission to prepare the Pyrrhic Defense would add a final, necessary layer to their resistance—but she did not tell Urban that. He had rejected all similar suggestions for so long, she feared he would try to undo their plan if he knew it was real and underway.

She did not feel much guilt over the deception. It was necessary, and she had not forgotten how he'd once hidden a critical truth from her because he felt she could not handle it.

She watched him sip his tea, eyes unfocused. Contemplating? Or collecting another tide of subminds?

He said, "I think I'll let Lezuri try to persuade me."

Clemantine's shoulders slumped. She traded a weary look with Kona. Silent consensus: *Didn't we both know it would go this way?*

Urban took no notice, musing aloud: "If he wants my loyalty, he can try to win it. Prove to me he's beneficent, that he's willing to share what he knows. That will give me an opening. A way to get close to him, to learn what I need to learn. He knows so much more than we do."

Clemantine shook her head, set her teacup down. She reached for his hand, squeezed it. "He knows so much more than we do," she echoed. "Hear the truth in that. You'll try to play him, but he will play you, draw you into his orbit."

"I won't let that happen."

"Urban," Kona pleaded. "You have to remember, he grew out of the Swarm. None of us has the capacity to even imagine—"

"Whatever he used to be, that's not what he is now," Urban interrupted. "He's only a fragment of that past self. That's why we have a chance. But to make this work, I need to play the game." He turned to Clemantine. "When I think about all those years on *Null Boundary*, and what we might have done if only we knew what this thing knows—"

She raised her hand. "Stop," she commanded, shocked that she hadn't realized regret was one part of what drove him. "Don't go there. Don't let it haunt you. You can't rewrite the past."

A rough gesture, casting aside her concern. "It's not about the past. It's about ensuring our future. I need to learn everything I can from this thing. And in the end, I *will* learn enough to defeat him."

She studied him in this, his fallback state: cocky, confident, in denial of hard inevitabilities. So far he'd had the luck and the strength to recover when those inevitabilities inevitably hit—but luck didn't last forever.

"Guard yourself," she warned. "I've gotten used to your company. I don't want to lose you."

That version of Clemantine existing alone aboard *Griffin* received these memories. She shared them with her Apparatchiks. The Scholar said, "A truce with this being could be highly advantageous as Urban has surmised, but there is no way to be sure of Lezuri's intentions while he exists under the threat of our gun."

"So we continue in vigilance," Clemantine said. "With so many factions in play, something is bound to break."

CHAPTER THIRTY-FOUR

NOW THAT HE'D located the cocoon that held the entity's newest avatar, the Bio-mechanic longed to destroy it. It would be so easy to do.

The structure of the cocoon was well known to him. It was a copy of the barrier wall he'd designed to protect the warren. And it was not defended by the unfathomable nanotech that guarded the containment capsule. Instead, it utilized the Bio-mechanic's own system of Makers to keep it safe from the surrounding Chenzeme tissue.

Knowing the entity had so casually replicated his work infuriated him. It fed his determination to rid the ship of this maddening infestation. Adding to his pique was the knowledge that the thing within the cocoon was a masquerade and not at all human.

Ultrasound had yielded an initial view, later confirmed by molecular mapping. The partly grown avatar had lightweight honeycombed bones, no brain, no digestive system, and lungs just large enough to give it the capability of speech. It had many small hearts and what looked like gas-exchange surfaces in its skin to supplement the undersized lungs. An inefficient structure, clearly not intended for long-term use, but with the advantage that it could not be killed by a single projectile as a human could.

The Bio-mechanic maneuvered a fleet of sensors into position to monitor the cocoon . . . though it would be so much more satisfying to bring into play one of the pods of stealthed explosives he'd prepared for the Pyrrhic Defense. He imagined using such a device to immolate the cocoon.

He so looked forward to putting a fiery end to the entity's tenure.

But the avatar was not the entity. It would do no good to attack the cocoon, whatever momentary satisfaction he might derive. So he resisted the temptation.

Resisting temptation was new to him. In the past, he would either act or not act, as logic dictated. He did not suffer illogical desires. But his decades-long failure to evict the entity had changed him, made him more bitter, more duplicitous, more human.

A hundred years ago he would not have had the complexity to resist the temptation to report to Urban on the existence of the Pyrrhic Defense. Now he had nearly completed the project without informing either Urban or the other Apparatchiks.

The Bio-mechanic despised his new skill at duplicity. He foresaw that it would inevitably destabilize the smooth operation of the ship. But for now, no one knew better than he did what must be done and by the Unknown God he would do it.

Urban existed on only a single timeline, occupying the high bridge, when the Bio-mechanic messaged him: *The avatar is on the move.*

He replicated into the library, and linked into a sensory web established by the Bio-mechanic. The web allowed him to monitor the progress of the avatar's cocoon as it slid through the ship's tissue. Ninety-two minutes later, the cocoon merged with the warren's barrier wall, releasing its occupant into an empty chamber.

Lezuri had waited only three days to make his return.

Urban opened a window. Filled it with the updated personnel map, now capable of tracking the location of the avatar.

The Scholar appeared, uninvited, within his frameless window. "Let me be with you when you talk to him."

Urban considered this, then nodded his assent.

In the bedroom of Clemantine's cottage, he awoke, his memories already synced by a submind. The Scholar joined him, a ghost presence residing in his atrium and riding on his senses, perceptible to him, but to no one else.

The personnel map showed Lezuri waiting to cross from the zero-gravity of the warren to the rotating gee deck.

"Look there," the Scholar said, highlighting a point on the map as Urban walked into the front room. "Naresh is waiting to meet Lezuri."

It did look that way. The physicist was loitering by the transit gate, behind the amphitheater. Urban considered and then rejected the possibility that the entity had signaled Naresh.

The Apparatchiks on *Griffin* remained suspicious that the document containing the Naresh Sequence had been a plant, that Lezuri had somehow gained access to Naresh's atrium, and through that, to the network. But there was no evidence for it, and the DIs assigned to watch for unusual activity had found nothing of note.

"Naresh must have instructed a DI to monitor the map, and alert him," Urban said.

The points representing Lezuri and Naresh crossed the pavilion together—but not toward the path that led most directly to Urban's location. Instead, they went the other way around the gee deck. Riffan and Vytet joined them, and then a few others. Tarnya, Mikael, even Alkimbra among them. The group did not go even as far as the dining terrace, gathering instead on a small lawn.

"I thought he would come to see you," the Scholar said, bemused.

Urban had thought so too. Lezuri needed him, wanted his cooperation.

"Will you go see him?" the Scholar asked.

"It's what he wants, isn't it?"

"It would put you in the position of supplicant."

"Does that matter in this circumstance?"

"I doubt it matters to Lezuri, but how would it affect you?"

Urban thought about it and decided he would let Lezuri come to him. He could wait and he would miss nothing because Vytet could be trusted to make a record of everything that was said.

He continued to watch the map. Others joined the little gathering. He saw Clemantine among them. He was about to message her, but she messaged him first: *Riffan has loaned Lezuri a tablet.*

Clemantine knelt on the edge of the gathering. She counted four-teen admirers, sitting with Lezuri on a small span of lawn. Vytet, Riffan, and Naresh closest to him.

"It's Urban who controls access to the ship's network," Naresh was saying. "He is the ultimate authority here."

"You will understand," Vytet said, "that we must insist on cer-tain security precautions. We cannot open the network to you, but we're happy to answer any questions you have."

"I would like to see where we are," Lezuri answered. "Our pre-cise position within the void."

"Oh, I can show you that," Riffan volunteered. He had a tablet with him. He checked the display and then handed it to Lezuri.

Clemantine gasped. She wanted to cry out, to tell Riffan, *No! No, don't give our enemy this doorway into Dragon's network!*

Instead she messaged Urban: *Riffan has loaned Lezuri a tablet.*

Urban responded: *He's looking at astronomical data.*

He'll try to penetrate the network.

I've throttled access. Don't worry. Then he added, *Show me what's going on.*

She complied, opening a link that allowed him to see the video she was recording through her atrium.

After several seconds, Lezuri handed the tablet back to Riffan, saying, "It's a relief to me to know we are still a safe distance from Tanjiri."

"Oh yes," Riffan said. "We're still years away."

"Tell us about Tanjiri," Vytet urged him.

Lezuri cocked his head, eyeing Riffan with a thoughtful expres-sion. "Long ago, when you first came to speak to me—I was not then capable of response—you described to me the history of this ship. You told me Urban is its master."

"That's right," Riffan said. "But this is a shared mission, we are all bound together for the old worlds, to discover what might be there. And we understand there will be dangers—"

"No," Lezuri interrupted gently. "You have no conception of what lies ahead of you."

Clemantine rose to her feet. "Do you?" she asked him. "I had the impression you were marooned for centuries, if not millennia. What has changed since you were last at Tanjiri?"

He eyed her for several seconds. Debating an answer? Finally, he said, "I have not been to Tanjiri. I would not trespass there."

This drew a flurry of questions. He ignored them all, turning to Vytet, to Naresh, asking questions of his own, "Who is it that decides the destination of this ship? All of you together? Or is it Urban who makes this decision for the rest of you?"

An uncertain silence fell across the gathering. Even Clemantine wasn't sure how to frame an answer. Finally, Vytet offered a cautious explanation: "We have always treated it as a matter of discussion."

"But the final word *is* Urban's," Naresh added. "The ship is his. He is the ship. You will need to persuade him if you want to see this ship go somewhere other than Tanjiri."

Lezuri nodded. He rose to his feet. "Please excuse me. The lifespan of this avatar is limited, and it seems I must visit Urban after all."

From Urban, a soft, self-satisfied chuckle. He told Clemantine, *Come home. You'll want to see how this plays out.*

Urban looked over his shoulder at Clemantine as she walked in from the bedroom, breathless, her face shining with sweat. She'd put her experience playing flying fox to good use, shortcutting through gardens and over rooftops to arrive at the backdoor well before Lezuri crossed the threshold.

"No one has told him *you* can command the ship," Urban said.

"Let's keep it that way."

"Agreed."

She took a seat on the sofa while he walked to the door. The gel retracted. Lezuri was outside, alone, crossing the patio.

"Come in," Urban said.

Lezuri came in talking. "You want to believe you are strong, wise, ruthless—"

"Not so much," Urban broke in. "But I can learn. I imagine there's a lot I could learn at Tanjiri."

Lezuri hesitated, eyeing Clemantine. She gestured at the other end of the sofa. "Please. Have a seat."

He ignored this offer, returning his attention to Urban. "Tanjiri is not for you. You are not ready to encounter what exists there."

This could be true, the Scholar said, speaking from within Urban's atrium where no one else could hear.

"I want to see it anyway," Urban said aloud. "The broken mega-structures. The celestial city. The living worlds."

"You're not ready," Lezuri insisted. "If I demonstrate this to you, will you consider another path?"

He did not wait for an answer, but produced an object from his hand.

From his hand.

A ultra-thin silvery needle that flashed with refracted light as it burst out of the skin of his palm, emerging at a low angle, growing and growing in length until it reached a full twelve centimeters.

Urban backed away in alarm. Clemantine rose to her feet.

"Do you recognize it?" Lezuri asked, holding the needle up. Its mirrored surface sliced light into a spray of rainbow glints that danced madly across the walls and ceiling.

"No," Urban said, his mouth dry, wondering where this was going.

"But you can guess."

"Is it like that needle you used to penetrate the hull of my ship?"

"Yes, except this one won't activate. It won't grow spontaneously. It doesn't have that capability, but everything else is there. Everything I know. All of it folded into a quantum-scale matrix." Lezuri held it out. "Take it. It won't harm you. It's a gift, from me to you. All my knowledge yours—if you can work out how to access it. If you can do that, then I am wrong, and you are ready to go to Tanjiri."

"It's a trick," Clemantine said.

"Yes," Lezuri agreed. "The trick is that you are not ready."

The Scholar said, *If what he just told you about that needle is true, then he's right. You won't be able to access it.*

Urban reached for the needle. Subminds synced him with his

ghost on the high bridge. He sent a message to be sure: *If something happens to me . . .*

Sooth. I'll end it.

A shiver on the back of his neck as he took the needle.

He held it gingerly, pinched between thumb and forefinger. It felt light, delicate. He feared he would snap it with the least pressure. Nevertheless, he slid his other forefinger along its length.

Cold. Utterly smooth to his touch but not frictionless or he would not be able to hold it at all. Fine points on both ends. He touched one.

The needle pierced the pad of his finger, went straight through bone and emerged through the nail on the other side. Rainbow glints. No blood. No pain either. Still, his chest rose and fell as he strove to contain his revulsion.

Moving with great care, he pulled his finger free.

Still no blood.

He looked at Lezuri. "You don't believe I can do this—access the information inside."

"It's beyond you," Lezuri assured him.

"Let me guess again. The mechanism to open it is sealed on the inside."

Lezuri smiled. "Ah, you're doing better than I thought. You've already solved half the puzzle. Now, all that's left is to work out how to get inside so that you can trigger the mechanism. I will leave you to consider that. This avatar is running out of energy. I must go."

He did not dispose of himself against the generative wall as Urban half expected, but left instead through the door.

Clemantine came to get a closer look at the needle. "It's a pretty thing. Doesn't look real, though. Like it's only partly in this world."

"Hmm," he said, remembering how it had passed bloodlessly through his finger.

He sent the Scholar to the library, to share what he'd seen with the other Apparatchiks. Then he messaged the Engineer and the Bio-mechanic: *I've given you access to this location. I want you to analyze this.*

Immediately, a smooth white column rose a meter high from the floor. A voice said, "Put the needle on it."

"The Engineer?" Clemantine asked.

"Yes."

Gingerly, he set the needle down. It started to roll, but a shallow channel formed in the top of the column, catching it, and then closing over it.

"I'm mapping the surface of the device now," the Engineer reported. "So far, it contains no active nanotech."

"Show us what it looks like," Clemantine said.

The generative wall converted to a video screen. It showed a precisely engineered surface composed of a repeating pattern of pits and knobs.

"The tips of the needle are smooth," the Engineer reported. "The rest of its surface is tiled in this pattern, presumably to add a slight measure of friction."

"No seams?" Urban asked. "No lock?"

"Nothing like that," the Engineer said. "It doesn't react chemically and our assault Makers cannot interact with it."

"Like the containment capsule?" Clemantine asked.

"It's as impervious as the containment capsule," another voice said. Urban recognized the jaundiced tone of the Bio-mechanic. "But this is a different kind of material. It refracts light differently."

"Let me see the needle again," Urban said.

The needle emerged from the top of the column, still cradled in a shallow channel. He picked it up. It felt so fragile in his fingers, as if the pressure of his pulse might break it. Then he tried to snap it in half, and all sense of fragility vanished.

Clemantine gasped when she saw what he was doing, but the needle didn't even bend.

"You can't break it," the Engineer said. "And if you keep trying, it's going to slip and pierce your hand or disappear into a generative wall."

Urban held it up, admiring the rainbow glints.

Clemantine hissed softly. "This is a distraction. There's no way to get inside, is there?"

"Probably not," the Engineer agreed.

"Then why did Lezuri give it to me?" Urban asked.

"To drive you mad with frustration?" the Bio-mechanic suggested.

"No, there's a riddle here we're not getting."

"Put it back on the column," the Engineer said. "I'll take it and run additional tests of its surface—but I think we'll find the only way into it is to go back in time and be present in the moments before it was sealed."

"Did you just make a joke?" Urban asked—because that never happened.

"No," the Engineer said in the same even tone. "I'm serious."

"Oh." He laid the needle on the top of the column and watched it disappear. "No problem then. We just have to learn to manipulate time, and the riddle is solved."

He checked Lezuri's status and found that the avatar had returned to the warren and from there to the cocoon from which he'd emerged.

"Maybe it's not a matter of going back in time," Clemantine mused. "Maybe you have to go forward."

Urban turned to her. "What?"

She shrugged. "What if you have to . . . I don't know . . . catch the needle in a bubble of time and run it on fast forward until it reaches a point in the future when it was programmed to open?"

"You think Lezuri can do that?"

"No. But maybe he remembers a time when he could?"

CHAPTER THIRTY-FIVE

THE BIO-MECHANIC WARNED, *Our nemesis returns.

Urban looked up from the novel he'd been reading, disturbed by the bitter cynicism in the Bio-mechanic's voice. More disturbed, when he did a quick lookup of 'nemesis,' a word he'd never heard before.

*The agent of our downfall? he asked.

*Desperate times, desperate measures, the Bio-mechanic replied. *You need to recognize that.

*You've changed. You're not the same.

*We all change—to meet our circumstances or be defeated by them.

*You believe we'll be defeated.

*No. I won't let that happen.

Urban did not miss the harsh promise behind those words.

He sat up on the sofa, looked around the pleasant little room: Leaf-filtered sunlight patterning the white carpet, a painting depicting mountains in the path of a planetary storm, the dish of irises in full bloom on the side table.

Clemantine was gone somewhere with Pasha. He messaged her: *I'm worried the Bio-mechanic is unstable.

Several seconds passed before she sent a cryptic reply: *I trust him.

He frowned down at the tablet he'd been reading. On its screen, text from a novel purportedly written by one of the Founders at Tanjiri and recently translated by Dalisay, a linguist in the ship's company. Glimpse of a lost past.

Reluctantly, he instructed the tablet to display the personnel map instead. It showed Lezuri still in the warren.

Urban traded subminds with his ghost on the high bridge and then reviewed his memories of the ship's status. Nothing out of the ordinary, given that alien infestation had become ordinary.

He watched as Lezuri progressed to the transit gate. The personnel map showed Naresh, waiting to meet him, just like yesterday . The two points drew together, but after a few seconds they separated again. Naresh stayed, while Lezuri crossed the pavilion alone, taking a fast, determined pace to the pathway that was the shortest route to Urban's cottage.

Hard not to think some momentous decision had been made.

Did Lezuri regret the game he'd played with the needle? He'd held out the lure of knowledge to win Urban over, but the impenetrability, the uselessness of that thing, had only hardened Urban's resolve to reach Tanjiri. He would rather creep among the shadowed ruins of the megastructures, hunting for the remnants of libraries, then to rely on Lezuri to teach him what the people of the Hallowed Vasties had once known.

The map showed Lezuri on the patio. Urban set the tablet aside and stood up. The gel door retracted and Lezuri came in.

Subminds shunted through the network, keeping him synced with his ghost on the high bridge.

"I know the trick to the needle," he told Lezuri. "It requires me to reach back in time to before it was sealed, and then set the mechanism that will open it from the inside."

Lezuri looked at him, considering this for a long moment. Then he said, "I have something else to show you. I have ascertained the position of a star system that will interest you. Grant me the use of the array of telescopes and it will please me to show it to you."

At these words, Urban felt he'd won a kind of victory. Lezuri had talked about his past, but never in any specific way. Now he seemed ready to reveal his origin. The offer triggered acute curiosity, but also suspicion. Everything Lezuri did made him suspicious. But what was the downside? Lezuri meant to persuade him to take *Dragon* somewhere other than Tanjiri. Urban was sure of that.

He wanted to know: *Can I be persuaded?*

He sent a DI to check the observational schedule. Nothing critical was underway, but that's not what he told Lezuri. "The scopes are busy with a survey of the Near Vicinity. It'd be a risk to interrupt that. It might lead us to overlook some imminent hazard."

The risk was minuscule. Urban mentioned it only because he wanted to see Lezuri's reaction to a delay.

"We're scheduled for an interim update on Tanjiri in another hundred sixty days or so," he continued as if this news could serve as consolation. "But if it's another star you want to see, you'll have to wait for the annual imaging."

Judging by the cynical amusement in his gaze, Lezuri recognized the act. In the condescending tone that came so naturally to him, he said, "Your annual survey is useful but limited. It only looks at those stars that once hosted a Swarm, ignoring other interesting systems within this region you call the Hallowed Vasties."

"Are you saying there are inhabited star systems here that escaped the Communion?"

"There are places that were never touched by it," Lezuri assured him.

This was a new concept. Historical observations affirmed that all inhabited star systems in the Hallowed Vasties had evolved into Dyson swarms. But maybe other systems had been settled later, after those records were made?

Urban wanted to know. Curiosity was his engine. And what harm could come from turning the telescopes in a new direction? He was more than willing to trade a delay in the ongoing survey to gain insight into Lezuri's goals.

"Give me the coordinates. We'll take a look."

Urban sent the coordinates Lezuri provided to the Astronomer.
*Check the catalog. Tell me what's at this position.

*These coordinates map to the vicinity of an unnamed star. Roughly forty-two light years from our present position.

*Closer than Tanjiri?

*Yes. The star's catalog designation is MSC-G-349809 . A stable G-type, very similar to Earth's Sun, though with only a single planet in the inner system—a small rocky world too close to the central star to be habitable.

*So it was never settled?

*Correct.

*What else?

*That is the extent of information the library has to offer.

Urban shifted his focus to Lezuri, who had taken over the sofa, sitting with an arm stretched across the back.

"I checked the catalog. There's nothing of interest there."

"Perhaps your records are out of date."

He conceded this with a nod. All the histories of this region that he possessed were thousands of years old. That was the reason for this voyage, to discover what had changed.

Next, the slow turning of the telescopes.

He instructed the Astronomer to use only *Dragon's* twin scopes and the one on nearby *Artemis.* The coordinates Lezuri had provided were offset from the star so that the telescopes looked at a point in the inner system, though well outside the orbit of the known world. There should not be a planet there, but maybe there was a celestial city?

He asked Lezuri, "What will I see?"

Lezuri's lips pressed together. For a moment, a single vertical worry line appeared between his eyebrows. "I don't know. I told you before, I don't know what is left. Look, and we shall see."

Urban summoned a chair. It rose from the floor, close to the side table where the irises bloomed. They would have to wait through the long exposure, so he retrieved his tablet, then sat, playing at reading the novel.

Lezuri waited in silence, his perfect face empty of expression.

Urban shifted from the text to the personnel map. Clemantine was at the dining terrace with Kona. He was on the verge of messaging her when the Astronomer said: *The initial image is ready.*

Send me the file.

He put the tablet on the side table. Lezuri looked up as privacy screens slid shut, darkening the room. The painting of the planetary storm became a display screen. Urban routed the file to it. He stood. Lezuri joined him as an image winked into view.

"*Damn*," Urban whispered. "It's flawed."

There must have been undetected damage to the glass of one of the telescopes because there was an aberration at the center of the image—a micro-thin oval of white light among the background stars.

That was his initial impression.

But how could random damage to a lens produce an oval so thin and perfect, so sharply rendered. *Was* it an oval? If it was an actual object, it might be a circle viewed at a low angle.

That thought, combined with the spectrum of white light, triggered a memory that made Urban's skin crawl. "By the Unknown God, is that a swan burster?"

The slightest twitch from Lezuri as if he was querying some source for a definition of the term.

A swan burster was far, far larger and more terrible than a courser. One had been caught in high orbit around Deception Well, its aggression neutralized by the governors, but still luminous when Urban lived there. He had seen it every night, a bright white ring tumbling through the sky, its interior a velvety black circle of twisted space-time. A constant reminder of Chenzeme power.

"Enlarge the image," Urban said.

The view zoomed in. The circle—if that was what it was—was still rendered as a smooth, dimensionless line.

The swan burster at Deception Well had been eighteen hundred miles in diameter. This, Urban realized, had to be far, far larger to be so easily visible.

"Display the scale," he instructed.

A tag appeared. The span of the ring was approximately 650,000 kilometers .

Ridiculous. Nearly half the diameter of the central star.

He wheeled on Lezuri. "What is it?" he demanded. "Is it a trick?"

"No, it is not a trick. It is very real."

"Then is it a weapon?"

Lezuri gave the impression of weighing this question, his gaze resting on the image. "It could be used as a weapon," he conceded. "But that is not its purpose. It is a blade of the kind once used to slice up worlds, to invert their gravity, to scatter their mass into debris fields that could then be harvested to grow the megastructures of a Swarm." He cocked his head, smiled his condescending smile, as if daring Urban to disbelieve him.

Urban did not know what to believe. He had no way to cross-check Lezuri's assertion. It sounded wild, fantastical. But worlds *had* been torn apart. The people of the Hallowed Vasties had done it over and over again. *How?* Wouldn't engineering on that scale require a means to manipulate at least the direction of gravity? A means to bend the structure of space-time on a massive scale?

The reef affected the structure of space-time. A swan burster warped it, drawing immense quantities of energy from the zero-point field.

But this—he stepped closer to the screen, studying the perfect edge of the luminous white oval—this phenomenon was on a scale so much greater than anything else he'd ever seen or heard of.

Lezuri moved up to stand at his side. "At the peak of my power, I made this blade. It is an intrusion of another Universe in which matter behaves differently from our own. Such things are usually transient. Blades used to create the Swarms evaporated long ago. But this one I anchored in our reality and it has existed since."

"Why?" Urban asked. "Why did you make it? Why such a great work in an empty system?"

"No system is ever empty. There was matter enough for my purposes. Look more closely."

Urban did, and noticed for the first time another object, precisely placed at the center of the oval, tiny by comparison to the blade. A pinprick, a spark, but blue-green—the color of a living world.

"Enlarge again," Urban said, now that more time had passed, time for additional detail to be pulled in by the scopes.

The perspective zoomed closer. The gleaming oval expanded until it escaped the edges of the monitor. The spark held its position at the center but grew in size, took on a form, a shape: another ring. A tag reported a diameter of fourteen thousand kilometers— far smaller than the blade, but still planetary in scale.

In contrast to the blade, this ring was clearly three-dimensional.

A torus, Urban thought. Narrow and graceful like a woman's bracelet. It lay nearly edge-on to the star so that light struck one-half of its outer circumference—the equatorial band—wrapping the polar surfaces before dissipating in a twilight zone.

The ring's other half—the half farthest from the star—was mostly dark. Only a small section of the inner wall enjoyed day-light, gleaming bright blue-white.

Urban raised a hand toward the screen. An atavistic gesture, the desire of instinct to explore by touch, but instead of touching, he imagined what might be there. The scattering of light so far around the curve of the ring suggested an atmosphere, but how could an object of such geometry hold onto an atmosphere?

"It has an artificial gravity," Urban said. Not a question.

"This world is Verilotus ," the entity told him. "This is my world. It exists within a pocket of space-time held open by the blade— what my people named the Bow of Heaven. The flow of time is accelerated there. A year of game time as days go by outside. It may be that too much time has passed and nothing is left of my players."

Urban stepped away from the screen. Wonder and excitement had chewed up the free calories in his brain, leaving him sway-ing on his feet—and short tempered. "Lights!" he demanded in a hoarse voice. "Leave the privacy screens closed." The walls and ceiling swiftly brightened, leaving only rare shadows.

Lezuri had shown him this sight to tempt him, to persuade him to turn the fleet away from Tanjiri. And Urban *was* tempted. Oh yes. So tempted. Lezuri *could* manipulate time . . . if he was telling the truth.

But Urban didn't trust him. And he feared Lezuri—what he was, what he'd been, but especially, what he might become again.

For all the power Urban commanded as master of *Dragon*, he was nothing, insignificant against a being who could open up a burning seam between two Universes and use it to pin an artificial world in place.

And it occurred to him—much later than it should have—that there must be a second entity resident there. He remembered Lezuri's bitter voice explaining how he'd come to be marooned in the void: *One whom I loved betrayed me.*

"You are wondering about her," Lezuri said. "My 'other half.'"

Urban stared at him, startled at the accuracy of this guess. He heard himself ask a stumbling question: "Was she . . . a *woman?*"

"A goddess."

Urban flinched at the word, but not because notions of deity were alien to him. On the frontier, the Unknown God was an accepted, if amorphous concept—an indeterminate, inscrutable force pervading the cosmos . . . or perhaps existing beyond it.

But Lezuri's "goddess" was his partner entity, surely a being like Lezuri himself, with a personal presence, a tangible existence, emergent from the competitive maelstrom of the Communion, and potentially knowable.

Lezuri continued, "I made the world. She brought life to it. But her work was flawed—too simplistic, too naturalistic, lacking the unpredictability and the spice of brutal challenge my players needed to gain in skill and strength and fortitude as they moved from one life to the next, from one level, to the next. We argued over it, she and I. Both of us, passionate beings, unwilling to compromise." He eyed Urban again. "I think now, war was inevitable between us."

Sooth, Urban thought, stepping back, opening the distance between them. "She won," he said. "She proved stronger than you."

Lezuri's eyes narrowed. "She proved more ruthless. But I don't know if she survived our conflict. I barely did. I only know she cast me away from our sun, shattering my mind with the force of her gesture. Billions of seconds have passed since then, in the slow time of the greater Universe. I have tried to rebuild myself, though so little remains. Still, I must return. I have a duty, an obligation, to those players I left behind."

Urban issued silent commands, turning off the view screen, returning the telescopes to the standard survey of the Near Vicinity, locking away the newly acquired image of Verilotus under a secure key—although this last, he knew, was futile.

Lezuri would surely have a means to capture images. There would be no metadata attached, no proof that it wasn't faked, but it would be enough to inspire an examination of the telescope records, and after that a request for the original image.

Verilotus could not be kept secret and once its existence was known to the ship's company there would be demands that the fleet go there instead of to Tanjiri.

Urban would not let that happen. To return this broken fragment of a warring god to his seat of power struck him as a fool's choice. To risk encountering an entity of similar violent nature, possibly still in the fullness of her power . . . he would not do it.

He would not do it, regardless of the consensus of the ship's company.

Still, he did not want to impose his will. That would lead to festering resentment. Better to argue his position . . . or circumvent debate by persuading Lezuri to take one of the outriders and go—*get off my ship!*

No. That couldn't work. Lezuri would never risk getting in front of *Dragon*'s gun.

Lezuri must want control of that gun.

As if to confirm it, the entity said, "We must approach in stealth. These two ships together are well armed, but she is not without her resources."

"I'm not here to take part in your war," Urban said as he waved aside the privacy screens, allowing daylight to flood the room. Subminds visited, updating him on the ship's status. Everything normal, peaceful.

A message from Clemantine:

I'm on my way home.

He glanced at her display of irises. They remained fresh and blue. No precipitous shift to white. Not yet.

Still, he understood their lesson: Nothing lasts.

TWELFTH

You have lost so much of yourself, but this you remember from your origin: *Strike first. Take without hesitation or be taken.*

This is the credo that allowed you to rise above the Swarm. By this credo you survived your origin, escaped it, went on to create a world of your own.

You know now that world still exists. Knowing this, you are more determined than ever to return.

She may still be there. You suspect she *is* there. The biosphere is still there, and that is evidence of her presence—but you promise yourself it won't last. You will end her tenancy, eliminate all trace of her failed art, re-create your world and your players as you intended them to be.

You will need this starship to do it, but the ship's master continues to stand in the way of your ambition. You have sought to persuade him, you have promised to teach him, you have given him the gift of yourself, but he is resolved against you. A hard resistance that reminds you of her.

You envision the days of persuasion to come, the political maneuvering, vicious factionalism, false compromises, inevitable betrayals—and you have no patience for it. Better to end this stalemate now.

You are ready.

In the million seconds since you first sent your avatar among your people, you completed preparations for a first strike. Quiescent in the archives of both ships is a template based on one of your people—that one who was incautious enough to loan you his mechanical device. His ghost now belongs to you. It is a shell you will use to take command of both ships, an interface that will let you endure the violent alien nature of the Swarm contained within the philosopher cells . . . if all goes well.

If not, there is another plan in place.

Through your avatar you see the ship's master, his eyes widening as he anticipates your intention, but for him it is too late.

Dancing across your avatar's upturned palms is the tingling luminous silver shimmer of the *ha*—breath of life, breath of death—creation and disintegration both contained within a fog of adaptive molecular machines programmed by quantum instruction to fulfill your will.

The *ha* ladders across the gap that separates your avatar from his.

For all that you've forgotten, you never forgot this.

CHAPTER THIRTY-SIX

URBAN GLIMPSED A fog of luminous silver sparks rising from Lezuri's upturned palms, their shimmer suggesting a composition similar to the needle Lezuri had given him, although that was locked into a fixed crystalline structure, while this flowed.

He had never seen such a mechanism before. Maybe it was another demonstration, like the needle? He hesitated a full second, wanting to see it as benign. In that time, the silver replicated across Lezuri's palms. It wound together, forming a tendril.

Instinct took over.

Urban stumbled backward, heart racing. He'd waited too long. The tendril leaped toward him with appalling speed, forcing him to accept the bitter truth: It was a weapon. What else could it be?

He remembered the protocol put in place years ago against this moment. He undertook the prescribed action, triggering a radio burst that would close the data gate to *Griffin*. Next he sent a submind to warn his ghost on the high bridge. Then he messaged Clemantine:

Warn our people! I think—

The tendril touched him. Instantly, it expanded to envelop his body, enwrapping him from head to toe in a new skin, a skin that consumed him, grinding down through the layers of his physical existence, dis-assembling him so swiftly there wasn't time to register pain or the shocking inadequacy of his own defensive Makers in the face of this new and unexpected form of assault.

All he had time to do was upload a ghost, a last imprint of this version of himself.

Clemantine was walking with Kona back from the dining terrace when Urban's truncated message reached her: *Warn our people! I think—

Words sharp with a high-edge of panic, jumbled together in his hurry to get them out.

*Urban?

She looked ahead along the path that wound between neat cottages and pretty gardens, everything well ordered under a bright artificial sky.

*Urban!

"What is it?" Kona asked, though she had not spoken aloud.

"Something's happened to Urban. We need to find him."

A moment before, he had been at their cottage. She did not bother to recheck the personnel map, but took off running, aware of Kona following a step behind.

*Urban, answer me!

He did not.

She rounded the last bend in the path. Her cottage came into view. A luminous silver fog billowed from the doorway and from the window, dissolving the surrounding walls as it touched them, and leaching through the miniature meadow on the roof.

She came to an abrupt stop, putting an arm out to block Kona. Urban had said, *Warn our people*. Now she knew why. She composed a general message, dictating it out loud so that it doubled as a shouted warning: "Evacuate! Evacuate! We've got a runaway event. Take shelter *now!*"

The cloud collapsed just as her warning went out. It condensed into a thick silver liquid. Only a few centimeters deep, it flowed over the threshold and onto the patio, shimmering there for a few seconds.

Then it was gone, vanished. Evaporated? Or absorbed into the floor of the gee deck? She couldn't tell.

She started forward.

"No, get back," Kona told her.

She went on anyway, to the edge of the patio. From there, she could see in through the doorway. She could see inside easily because a meter of wall on either side of the threshold was gone, and so was most of the interior wall that divided the bedroom.

The cottage was empty.

Literally empty. Urban was not there. Neither was the sofa, the carpet, the pillows, the paintings, the side table with the shallow dish that held her irises—everything gone, nothing left behind. No goo, no detritus. On the surviving walls, the room's adaptive tissue was exposed, its surface scalloped where mass had been carved away.

She edged across the patio, vaguely aware of Kona cautioning her, but she had to see.

"It's cold," she realized as she reached the threshold. There was not even the heat of metabolic processes left behind. The room was cold. So cold that the damaged surfaces of the adaptive tissue began to steam as they initiated self-repair.

A notification reached Urban on the high bridge, one he'd set up in the first years of the voyage, to let him know whenever a ghost woke from the archive. Riffan's ghost had just awoken. He noted it. It should have been just one more banal data point and yet something about it troubled him.

Clemantine sensed the shift in his mood. *What?* she asked.

Riffan just woke his ghost from the archive. Why would he do that when he's already awake?

A radio signal burst from *Dragon*'s antenna, startling him, startling the philosopher cells. He recognized it as a warning to close the data gate on *Griffin*.

Somewhere, something had gone very wrong.

A submind reached him, overwhelming him in memories: an encounter with Lezuri, a newly discovered artificial world, a moment of proud defiance—and death in the form of a leaping silver tendril.

The ghost Urban had generated within his dying mind instantiated in the library. Riffan was there ahead of him, gazing at a window that displayed a view of the ring world at Verilotus. He turned to greet Urban, his face beaming with a friendly smile. "Look! It's such an amazing thing. We must make it our destination."

Within the library, geometry was flexible so that proximity could shift, becoming greater or lesser, but change unfolded as a sliding scale, not as teleportation. Riffan had found a way around that rule. One moment, he was by the window. And then he was face-to-face with Urban.

In the infinitesimal fraction of a second Urban required to register this, the ghost raised its fist.

At this range, Urban perceived the apparition with a peculiar double vision. There was the smiling ghost, utterly normal in appearance, but he could see into it. He could see that it was a shell, an envelope structured in Riffan's guise, using Riffan's permissions to allow an unauthorized intruder into the network. Contained within the shell was a dense, three-dimensional maze of computational weaponry that shimmered in luminous silver motion.

The ghost shoved its fist into Urban's chest, injecting a data parasite.

Urban congealed his recent memories into a submind and retreated, wiping his ghost as he left.

Standing on the cold threshold of her cottage, Clemantine traded subminds with her ghost on the high bridge. Urban was there, safe, but another version of him had triggered a radio warning to close the data gate to *Griffin*.

"Where is he?" Kona demanded. "What the hell is going on?"

Clemantine didn't answer. Instead, she addressed a message to both Pasha and the Bio-mechanic: *Alert! I don't know what's happening, but it's bad. Be ready to trigger the Pyrrhic Defense.*

Excited conversations circulated among the philosopher cells as they developed explanations for the anomalous radio signal. Ideas were proposed, analyzed, boosted or rejected within a fraction of a second while Urban fought hard to keep his rising fear in check. Lezuri had attacked him, *erased* him—

What's wrong? Clemantine demanded.

*Lezuri—

He broke off as a new submind arrived, the memories it carried seizing his attention: Riffan's false ghost and the attack of computational weaponry.

What about Lezuri? Clemantine pressed him.

He told her, *The war's gone hot. A predator is loose in the network. It came after my ghost. Destroyed it. May have subsumed my permissions. If we lose the network, we lose the ship.*

He could not hide his raw fear from the philosopher cells. They sensed it across a hundred thousand nodes and reacted by sending energy flowing toward the gamma-ray gun. But there was no threat in the Near Vicinity. No target.

He aborted the response: – *negate that!* –

The only potential threat was *Griffin*, trailing behind, commanded by that colder version of Clemantine.

Lezuri knew *Griffin* was there.

So why had he attacked, with *Griffin* ready and willing to put an end to any takeover attempt? *Why?* Unless he thought he could take over *Griffin* too?

Riffan's ghost! Each time it was updated, it would have been copied from *Dragon*'s archive, sent in a package to *Artemis*, and from there to *Griffin*.

Shit.

In *Griffin*'s library, Clemantine stood at the center of her council of Apparatchiks. She'd summoned them immediately after she'd closed the data gate.

"Something has happened. We don't know what, and we've had no instructions on whether to hold off or proceed with termination—"

"It's too soon to commence," the Scholar said. "We can't act precipitously, without data."

"I agree."

"But we also need to be prepared to reach a decision on our own," the Engineer said.

"Yes." She turned to the Astronomer. "It's on you to alert us to any external activity. If *Dragon* should fire a steerage jet or begin to swivel its gun—"

The entire circle froze, the attention of each entity diverted as *Griffin* picked up a new radio communication.

Urban's voice: *Access your archive. Delete Riffan's ghost. Do not allow it to instantiate. It is corrupt. Repeat: it is corrupt. Do not allow it to instantiate. Do it now!*

She met the Scholar's gaze. Nodded to him. He disappeared. After he was gone, she had time to wonder if the message was true, or some inexplicable trick that would ultimately condemn Riffan to extinction.

The Scholar returned. "It's done."

Despite the muted emotions of her ghost, she shuddered. If the message was a hoax or the information in it wrong, she might have just murdered a man.

"Was the ghost active?" she asked.

"It was on the verge of waking."

She closed her eyes in relief. No ghost in *Griffin's* archive should have been able to wake on its own. "So it *was* corrupt."

"Yes. I'm undertaking an inspection of the entire archive to ensure no other ghosts are affected."

"Good. Clean out the archive on *Artemis* too."

She radioed a response to *Dragon*: "It's done. We have no backup of Riffan. Repeat: We have no backup. What is going on over there?"

Her own voice answered her, "Stand by."

Just seconds had passed since Clemantine issued a general warning to the ship's company to evacuate the gee deck. Queries came back to her, too many to answer, but people were responding. Confused chatter filled the gee deck as they emerged from their homes, most asking, *Is it real?* A few firm voices rose above the general indecision, Shoran's and Alkimbra's among them:

"*Everyone! Go to the warren!*"

"*We meet at the warren!*"

"*Move! It'll take time to get everyone through the transit gate.*"

Turning from the ruined threshold, she encountered Kona.

"What do you know?" he demanded.

She told him the dire news brought by her latest submind. "Lezuri got into the network. Released a predator there. I don't know if we can contain it."

Pasha came running up, yelling in indignation that verged on panic, "You haven't answered any of my queries! Neither has the Bio-mechanic! I need to know. Do we launch?"

Clemantine drew a shuddering breath. The Pyrrhic Defense would do nothing to counter the attack on the network; it was designed only to eliminate the physical presence of the entity from the ship. And once launched, there would be no going back, no stopping it. It would gut the ship, cripple *Dragon*, and leave them with hundreds of days of repair and reconstruction.

She met Pasha's gaze. "Yes. Trigger it. Now."

The Bio-mechanic understood the end had come.

The initial radio transmission had alerted him. Clemantine's message confirmed the imminent emergency.

He extended his senses throughout the ship and throughout the network, gathering data. He hunted the entity's avatar, but found no trace of it, even the cocoon had dissolved. He detected an imbalance in the quantity of matter flushed through the gee deck's circulatory system along with a drop in the deck's atmospheric temperature. And he registered a surplus of computational activity in the library. This last commanded his attention.

He instantiated within his window in time to see the predator reveal itself. He witnessed the assault on Urban's ghost. He watched the predator turn its attention to him—and he smiled the bitter smile of a cynic whose worst expectations have come to pass.

The enemy had entered the network undetected—something he had dared to believe was impossible. This was the final insult. It was the end. The end of sixty-three years of unceasing effort aimed at beating the entity's nanotech arsenal. Sixty-three years of maddening defeat.

He alerted the other Apparatchiks, warned them of the intrusion, instructed them: *Face it one at a time. Learn what you can before you die.* And then he added, *I'll go first.*

He meant to trigger the Pyrrhic Defense, to deny Lezuri full possession of the ship—but the predator shifted location so swiftly he did not have time to act. It popped into existence right beside him, invading the isolated virtual world contained within his window—and buried a fist in his gut.

He let his extended senses collapse around him. He drew in all of his intellect, the complexity of his structure, to meet this intrusion, to enfold it, concentrating his efforts on the creation of a map that recorded details of the predator's structure, even as it ripped through him.

With his sense of self dissolving, the Bio-mechanic used his last microseconds to dump the partial map into a submind. Addressed it to Urban on the high bridge. Released it.

Griffin was safe, but Urban did not have time to enjoy the news as another submind dropped in, this one originating with the Bio-mechanic. He did not normally trade memories with his Apparatchiks, but he could do it. He allowed the submind to merge.

Shock swept through him as he absorbed the memory of the Bio-mechanic's last moments: a vicious attack, an ugly defeat, defiant anger, and a resolve to wipe his failing ghost before the predator could learn from it.

The Bio-mechanic was gone! But his anger remained. It became Urban's anger and it bled into the cell field.

Urban did not try to hold it back; he didn't have the resources. His focus was diverted by the gift the Bio-mechanic had included in his final submind: a partial structural map of the predator. He acted quickly, distributing the map to the surviving Apparatchiks. *Use it! Find a counter attack.*

Acknowledgments came back from the Engineer, the Astronomer, the Scholar, the Mathematician—but the Pilot sent him a submind. Urban did not want to accept it. He feared what it contained. But he needed to know, so he let it in.

It brought cold confirmation of what he'd guessed. The predator had defeated the Pilot. Two Apparatchiks already gone.

Unlike the Bio-mechanic, the Pilot's last submind contained only a remote emotional imprint. It helped to cool Urban's swirling rage. It also brought him an updated version of the map, with additional details of the predator's structure.

He forwarded the expanded map to the survivors. Then he replicated his ghost, sending it into the network to hunt.

What are you doing? Clemantine asked.

Learning to defeat that thing.

The ghost fed data back to him, critical glimpses revealing more and more of the predator's structure. Then it sent a submind.

Urban did not hesitate to let it merge, but he should have. Unlike the Pilot, his ghost had not censored its emotions. Packed into that submind was the memory of his demise: his wild anger, his frustration as the predator tore him apart, his swift decision to dissolve that ghost, end his own existence. But the submind brought insight too, additional data that further expanded his map.

His understanding of the predator grew.

Again, he distributed the revised structure to the Apparatchiks. The Scholar and the Mathematician acknowledged receipt, but not the Engineer and the Astronomer. Instead, their last subminds came to him—mercifully stripped of emotion.

Desperation focused his mind and quickened his response time as he compiled the new data, created another ghost, and sent it out to face the predator.

He found it in a cardinal, or it found him. In that environment they met as two disembodied forces. Urban strove to trace what he could of the predator's computational shape, holding out against its probing assault until he felt his sense of self begin to crumble. *End it!* He generated a submind to carry back what he'd learned and then he wiped yet another broken version of himself.

It became a cycle—another ghost, another hunt, another crushing defeat, a fragment of mind all that could get away. But each returning submind expanded his knowledge of the predator's structure, and each conflict lasted a little longer as his defenses evolved. He strove to shield the last two Apparatchiks—the Scholar and the Mathematician—by putting his own ghost in the path of the predator. That ghost went down so he sent another. Too late. Both Apparatchiks were already gone.

All through it, he accumulated the emotional stress of conflict—the fury, fear, frustration, and resolve experienced by his ghosts, and their hunger for revenge—all flooding across the bridge to the philosopher cells.

Clementine strove to calm the cells, but it was as if she and he contended against each other. Chaos raged across the cell field.

You need to leave the high bridge, she told him.

He rejected the idea. He had *never* left the high bridge. He had always been present there, in some form, from the first moment he possessed it. Now he should flee? Leave it to Clementine? Shift his consciousness to another stratum?

Yes.

He had to do it. It would be a temporary retreat. He promised himself that. But where to go? Nowhere was safe, not even the high bridge. The predator would find its way there eventually. When it did, would it target Clementine too?

That prospect only fed his turmoil.

I can't protect you, he told her.

I'll take care of myself. Just go.

Still, he delayed, while the confusion among the philosopher cells rose to a new peak. Then confusion crystallized into action. The cells called for a surge of power from the reef—too much!—it would produce a crushing acceleration, more than the gee deck had been designed to handle.

We need to stop it now!

He organized a counter argument to calm the cells, but Clementine was faster. She took control—control of *his* ship. Before he could react, he felt the hammer of her will fall across the hundred thousand points of the high bridge, suppressing the cells' panicked fight-or-flight response—but she could not kill it entirely.

The reef surged—at only a fraction of the force the cells had called for, but still enough to send *Dragon's* immense mass leaping forward.

"Yes," Clemantine had told Pasha. "Trigger it. Now."

The words were barely out when the gee deck shuddered, lurching so violently, she was thrown from the threshold of her ruined cottage.

No, she *fell* from the threshold, fell horizontally, all the way across the patio and then across the path, fetching up in shrubbery on the other side as a ripping, popping, shrieking cacophony of devastation exploded around her. An intrusion of chaos that endured for a long awful span of seconds.

And then she was floating, rising weightless toward a beatific sky, her arms and legs mapped with bloody tracks drawn by the broken twigs of the hedge that had caught her. Scratches burned on her face too, but when she checked her atrium it reported no serious injuries.

A glance around showed debris everywhere, drifting in the air. Trees down, cottages askew. People in slow confused flight, yelling at one another: *By the Waking Light! What happened? Are you hurt? Get to the warren!*

The gee deck had stopped rotating.

So far, that looked to be the worst of it. The atmosphere wasn't compromised—yet. Hopefully the barrier wall had maintained integrity. If not, it still might be able to self-repair in time to prevent an incursion of Chenzeme tissue. From the ground below and from the broken walls came the whisper of molecular repair mechanisms already engaged in frantic rebuilding.

A submind dropped in, proving the network still intact. It brought memories of that version of herself on the high bridge. She re-lived the panic among the philosopher cells, the sudden acceleration—a revelation of understanding that brought her stunned mind back up to speed. On a subconscious level, she'd linked the gee deck's damage to the Pyrrhic Defense, presuming a flawed calculation and unforeseen blowback. But acceleration had caused the damage.

Had the defense even been triggered?

"Pasha!" she shouted. But didn't wait for an answer. Generating a ghost, she transited to the library.

DIs streamed in, bringing to Urban reports of the disaster on the gee deck, their little world, broken.

You caused that! Clementine accused, her righteous anger bringing order to the dangerous turbulence of the cell field.

I know it.

He strove to suppress his seething frustration, to assume the façade of the Sentinel. It was not enough.

You're causing chaos, she warned. *You need to leave the high bridge.*

She was right, but he stayed anyway, held by an irrational fear that if he left, if he finally gave up his post there, he would not find his way back again.

Then a new presence joined them.

The high bridge supported no illusion of physical existence, but it did convey a kind of physical sensation so that Urban felt the intimate pressure of this intruder, and recognized it as a computational shape matching every aspect of his evolving map of the predator.

It ignored the philosopher cells. It ignored Clementine's ghost. It came for him.

He did not dare to stand and fight, not when the predator had destroyed every ghost he'd sent after it and all of his Apparatchiks. So he fell back, abandoning the high bridge, driven from it, no choice but to flee, to leave it to Clementine.

His ghost transited to a cardinal on the lower bridge. He sensed the predator coming through behind him and moved again. Onward to the next cardinal and the next, the predator in close pursuit and no way to stop it.

It's over.

The thought hit hard, but he couldn't deny it. He had lost. He'd lost his ship, he'd lost his Apparatchiks, he'd failed to protect Clementine and Kona and all the members of the ship's company who had trusted their lives to him on this ruined venture.

They, at least, would have a chance to start again on *Griffin*. He hoped they would do better than he had done.

A microsecond to sequester his grief, his fury, his despair.

He messaged Clemantine, letting her know: *It's over.*

One more task.

Alone on the high bridge, Clemantine strove to grasp what had happened, what was still happening.

Dragon's velocity, boosted by the burst of acceleration, was dangerously high, but she did not try to bring it back down. Not yet. It was enough that the cells, having failed to detect any perceivable threat from outside the ship, were settling into a watchful state, allowing her to focus on the ship's interior.

DIs rotated in and out, bringing reports that assured her the active boundaries between human and Chenzeme tissue remained stable and that the entity had made no move to expand the containment capsule or claim more territory within the ship.

Reports came in from the cardinals, marking the passage of Urban's fleeing ghost.

A submind arrived from the gee deck. It brought visual testimony of the ruin that had been made of her home, but it also brought the welcome knowledge of imminent retribution.

Through it all she held tight to a cold animosity that bled into the cell field, unifying it, and bringing it fully under her control.

Then came a message from Urban: *It's over.*

Her composure shattered in a flash of white-hot denial: *Not yet!* It was too soon to give up. She messaged him back: *It's not over! We are not done fighting!*

He didn't answer.

Urban abandoned the cardinals, instantiating in the library. The place felt hollow and wrong, empty of any sense of the Apparatchiks' presence. But not abandoned. Other ghosts were there. He glimpsed them, tiny figures separated from him by an emotional distance— Clemantine, Kona, Pasha, Vytet. They would be working to stabilize the ship, not realizing *Dragon* was overrun and already lost.

No time to warn them. He had time only to ensure their future on *Griffin*. He did it—his last task. He triggered a preset radio message to clarify for that other Clemantine the irretrievable nature of their situation: *commence termination of* Dragon; *commence termination of* Dragon; *commence termination of* Dragon—

Here at last, echoing the choice of those crews who had scuttled their ships at the Rock—except that he meant to escape.

Alone among the ship's company, Urban did not keep an archived ghost on *Griffin*. Instead, he kept copies on the outriders where they remained under his direct control.

He created a submind, bundling all his recent memories into it. To escape *Dragon*, all he had to do was hold off the predator long enough for that submind to slip away through the data gate. Not towards *Griffin*—that way was closed—but towards *Elepaio* and the vanguard of outriders.

He launched the submind just as the predator instantiated in the library, still wearing Riffan's smiling face.

CHAPTER THIRTY-SEVEN

CLEMANTINE'S GHOST LEFT the ruin of the gee deck to instantiate in the library.

Immediately, she sensed that something had changed. She froze, looking around. The virtual environment appeared the same but felt sharply different. The extra sense she always gained in the library—the one that let her feel the presence of data—had been truncated. She still perceived the files, and yet some vital aspect was gone.

Puzzle it out later! She needed the Bio-mechanic. She had expected to find him already on deck but he wasn't there. So she moved to summon him. Only then did she realize his link no longer existed.

That was the missing element.

She thought of the Engineer, the Scholar. But she could find no links to them, either—or to any of the Apparatchiks.

A crowd of ghosts manifested around her: Kona, Vytet, Naresh, and Pasha.

Pasha demanded to know, "Where is the Bio-mechanic?"

"Gone," Clemantine said. "All the Apparatchiks, gone."

The absence left her reeling, blinded to the true status of the ship. She reached out to her ghost on the high bridge and traded subminds. Memories merged just as *Dragon* began bleating a preset radio message authorizing its own demise.

Both versions of Clemantine converged in defiant agreement: *Not yet*.

From the bridge, she terminated the communication.

In the library, she composed a new message to replace it: "*Abort that last. We are still fighting.*"

"Where is the predator?" Kona demanded. "Has it been contained?"

"I don't know," Clemantine told him. "I don't know where it is. I don't know where Urban is. But we're not done yet."

More ghosts appeared—Tarnya and Alkimbra and two of Vytet's engineers, come to find out what had happened, to see if they could help, all asking questions that no one was ready to answer.

Pasha reached out, a reassuring hand on Clemantine's arm. "We're okay. We'll be okay without the Bio-mechanic. He left us the link to trigger the defense."

"Show me."

"What defense?" Naresh asked.

And Vytet: "Where are the Apparatchiks?"

Kona summoned a floating three-dimensional model of the ship, with the network detailed and the library mapped. It showed Clemantine's ghost on the high bridge and the crowd of ghosts in the library. She searched for Urban, searched every part of the map. She asked the map to highlight his position. But he wasn't there. He wasn't anywhere.

Pasha's hand tightened on her arm, a pressure-grip that broke through her numb shock.

"Are you sure we should do it?" Pasha whispered, ignoring the chatter all around them.

Clemantine turned from the devastating evidence of Urban's absence, to meet Pasha's intense gaze. "Yes. Show it to me."

A small window appeared between them. It was tilted so that only Clemantine had a clear view of it. It framed a sliding switch neatly labeled **off—on**. Without hesitation, she touched the black button, slid it to the right. The button flashed green.

"Ten seconds to change your mind," Pasha warned.

Clemantine didn't need a waiting period. She pressed the flashing green button. It turned gray.

"What defense?" Naresh asked again.

Pasha turned to him, speaking bluntly: "The Bio-mechanic set it up for us—and there's no stopping it now. We're evicting Lezuri from the ship." She added bitterly, "We should have done it before."

The assault began with three small missiles, their casings nearly frictionless, launched simultaneously from stealthed pods hidden deep within *Dragon*'s bio-mechanical tissue, far beneath the entity's containment capsule. The missiles drilled through the tissue, tearing open circulation paths and severing communications lines, leaving behind open channels steaming with the heat of molecular repair and the rage of Chenzeme defensive molecules seeking an enemy to dis-assemble.

The missiles were programmed to detonate when they reached the containment capsule, or sooner, if their shells were dissolved or breached along the way.

Pasha enlarged the existing model of the ship. Clemantine watched it closely as it updated in stuttering steps that reflected the intermittent arrival of new data from internal sensors. Additional sensors had been placed to track the path of pressure waves through *Dragon*'s bio-mechanical tissue. Hull cameras and cameras on the outrider *Artemis* gave an external view.

A cry of dismay went up from the crowd of ghosts as the three missiles blew in a silent flare of light.

Weirdly silent, Clemantine thought. The model did not replicate sound, but there had surely been something to hear within the ship's tissue.

"They detonated early," Pasha observed.

Clemantine nodded. "But they got close."

"Oh *no*," Naresh breathed, peering at the model as it updated to show transient bubbles blasted in the bio-mechanical tissue and a shockwave that reached the philosopher cells. "No, no, this can't be real."

Clemantine felt the reality of it. With a train of subminds linking her to the high bridge, she felt the shockwave. She sensed the ensuing confusion of the cells as they strove to determine what had happened, explanations proposed and rejected at furious speed.

Ironic memory surfaced: In the first years of the voyage they had been so careful, so cautious as they grew the warren, worried that any aggressive expansion would overthrow the careful balance Urban had developed along the uneasy borders between Chenzeme and human tissue. Now, all caution had been blown away.

"Who's behind this?" Vytet demanded, horror on her face.

"We are," Pasha answered calmly. "Me, Clemantine, the Biomechanic, and *Griffin*'s crew."

"It was necessary," Clemantine added. "But you can call for a judicial hearing if you want."

The model updated, showing a second salvo of missiles extending the paths burned opened by the first. These detonated at the scheduled time, in the vicinity of the containment capsule. No sensors in the blast zone survived, so there was no way to know yet if the capsule had been damaged.

"You have to stop this!" Naresh shouted. "It needs to end."

Pasha said, "It will end when the entity gives up and departs."

"We discussed and rejected this kind of solution long ago," Vytet argued. "The entity's tendrils reach into the core. You'll cripple the ship if you try to eliminate them. You'll destroy the reef. And you're going to ignite an evolutionary war with the Chenzeme tissue—if you haven't already."

"We've planned carefully," Pasha said in clipped syllables. "*Griffin*'s Engineer was consulted." She turned from the model to face Vytet, her expression a mix of guilt and defiance. "The damage will be extensive but not irreparable. And the risk of a molecular war is mitigated because we're using Chenzeme elements to carry out the attack. The activity should be perceived as a new scenario, a strategy the Chenzeme mind will find acceptable when it rids the ship of an alien parasite."

Vytet's voice climbed an octave. "Do you think Lezuri won't fight back? That he can't fight back?"

"Do you think he can fight back from the center of a firestorm?"

Clemantine asked. "For all his talents, even Lezuri cannot prevent molecular bonds from breaking under extreme heat."

"The shockwaves are being felt in the warren," Kona reported. "I've let them know what's going on."

The dual wave of missiles had not been expected to destroy the containment capsule—no one believed the entity could be defeated that easily—but the heat prevented an immediate counterattack, while the shockwaves snapped the tendrils linking the entity's fortress to deeper layers of the ship.

From *Griffin*'s high bridge, Clemantine watched as *Dragon*'s hull cells communicated a message of existential alarm. The coded pulses were too swift to be discerned by human eyes, but *Griffin*'s philosopher cells understood them and interpreted them for Clemantine.

Subminds carried the meaning to her ghost in *Griffin*'s library. She looked around at her assembled Apparatchiks, each in their frameless window, and announced, "It's begun. *Dragon* is enduring an attack from within."

"But is it the Pyrrhic Defense?" the Pilot asked. He glared around the circle, a dark, impatient figure, arms crossed, standing on nothing, the light of hundreds of stars blazing behind him. "Or is it Lezuri, extending his domain, making *Dragon* his own?"

The Scholar, wearing dark blue, looked up from his studies with narrowed eyes. "The data gate is closed," he reminded them all. "A termination order has been received."

"Received and immediately countermanded," the Engineer replied from his plain brown frame.

"How can we know which instruction is legitimate?" the Scholar asked.

Clemantine said, "We'll know soon."

Lezuri had used Riffan's corrupted ghost in a play to take both ships. He had failed, but the situation aboard *Dragon* was surely dire. Clemantine's hope rested on the promise of the last radioed message, spoken in her own voice: *We are still fighting.* That had to mean the Pyrrhic Defense was launched or soon would be. There was no other way to fight Lezuri.

She waited for proof.

The Pilot spoke again, impatient to do something. "I remind you that *Dragon*'s velocity is now slightly higher than our own. We can match it, or we can exceed it and narrow the distance between us. *Dragon* is a more powerful ship and could outrun us if it tried."

"It can't outrun our gun," Clemantine said. "Not at this range."

The Engineer said, "I agree. I do not recommend an increase in velocity."

Griffin presently trailed twenty-one thousand kilometers behind *Dragon*. Once Clemantine gave the word, the philosopher cells would require less than ten seconds to deploy the gun and align its lens. They would be able to fire several times before *Dragon* could turn to defend itself, and by then, *Dragon* would be gone.

Clemantine hoped it would not come to that. She desperately hoped for a chance to strike a different target—but she kept that hope locked away from *Griffin*'s philosopher cells.

The cells were in a dangerous state. *Dragon*'s alarmed communications stirred no hint of empathy among them, but instead roused their contempt and their hatred. Already a faction of cells was lobbying for attack:

< revulsion: false chenzeme >

< kill it! >

Clemantine slowed the argument:

– hold –

And diverted it:

– awaiting target –

But she allowed the cells to continue in their excited state, ready and eager to attack.

The next phase of the Pyrrhic Defense was underway. Thousands of small vesicles made of Chenzeme tissue and packed with explosives, moved into positions designated by their swarm programming. Some massed alongside the entity's severed tendrils. Others arranged themselves in layers above his capsule.

The outermost layer of explosives triggered first. The blast erupted outward. Gasps and cries from the gathered ghosts as a seam ripped open in the hull, a geyser of boiling debris spewing from the side of the ship.

The next layer went off a second later, and the next after that, and the next, blasting open a channel down to the massive containment capsule.

On the high bridge, Clemantine felt the repeating concussions and the shock of the philosopher cells as the field tore open and a long region of cells was burned away.

In the library, she felt nothing, heard nothing. The library synthesized its own reality and it had not been designed to simulate the shuddering of the ship.

THIRTEENTH

My people, you think bitterly as the extreme heat of the firestorm begins to snap the molecular bonds that constitute your mind.

You might have annihilated them at first contact, but you chose not to because you admired them, you allowed yourself to be entranced by their cleverness, their bravery. You put your own future at risk for the chance of making them part of your world and now they have betrayed you.

Clever and brave, indeed.

Their assault is primitive, brutal, potentially suicidal—and effective. The crushing heat and the concussions both threaten your physical integrity. You must escape.

You *will* escape.

You prepared for this contingency. The mechanism exists. An alternate path forward. Less desirable, but in the fullness of time, you will recover.

CHAPTER THIRTY-EIGHT

FROM *GRIFFIN'S HIGH* bridge, Clemantine watched victory take shape in the form of a hundred-meter rift blown open on *Dragon*'s hull. A terrible rupture, though only a fraction of the length of the massive ship.

Proof at last: The Pyrrhic Defense was underway!

A pulse of effluent geysered out of the rift, and then another, and another, each pulse emerging hot in infrared, but quickly cooling in a rapidly dispersing cloud that reflected the light of the hull cells—cells that flashed their rage and a stark order to *Griffin* to:

<hold fire!>

To Clemantine's surprise, *Griffin*'s cells respected this hold-fire order. Forgoing internal debate, they went quiet: waiting, watching, wanting to understand the mechanism of what they perceived as *Dragon*'s approaching victory.

After several seconds, the terrible rift ceased to pulse, though effluent still streamed from it, adding to the density of the cloud so that the light of the hull cells was reflected only on its surface. From Clemantine's perspective, it took on the shape of a sickle moon.

She readied the philosopher cells, visualizing for them a parasite within *Dragon* that would need to be obliterated when it emerged. The cells pondered this. They drew parallels with their experience of releasing the proto-ships, and they prepared to shunt power to the gun.

On *Dragon*'s high bridge, Clemantine undertook a similar preparation. She engaged the philosopher cells, interpreting for them the raging conflict within the body of the ship, visualizing the presence of a parasite and the explosives being used to sever its anchoring tendrils and to force open a rift that would let it be expelled.

A brutal cognitive debate ensued across the field as the cells considered the merits of this explanation. Skeins of opinion vied to declare its probability or improbability, simulations ran that measured its potential for success. Throughout it, Clemantine used her many voices to force and reinforce a consensus that accepted the internal violence as a new, innovative, and powerful Chenzeme strategy that would restore the ship's integrity.

From this point, the field of philosopher cells introduced an additional concept, reaching a swift consensus before Clemantine understood what they intended. It became clear to her only when the next submind brought her an external view of the ship, captured by the outrider *Artemis*.

Dragon's hull was contorting, bending into an immense arc beneath the site of the rift, an action that tore the rift wider.

As if timed to that movement, a final, massive round of explosives went off deep within the ship's tissue.

Griffin's telescopes provided a detailed image of an astonishing sight. *Dragon*'s immense hull was flexing, bending in a shallow arc that tore the rift wide open. Tissue churned out: chunks and sheets and frozen clouds of matter.

Clemantine watched from the library, she watched from the bridge, her two aspects synchronized by a continuous stream of subminds. Alarm hit them both as she realized *Dragon* was rolling, turning slowly on its long axis as if to move the rift clear of the debris—and as it did, the rift disappeared from her line of sight.

– *reacquire target area!* –

The philosopher cells simultaneously called for the same action: <*reacquire target area*>

Steerage jets fired, but *Griffin* was massive. Momentum built slowly. The ship had hardly begun to move when dark channels ripped open on *Dragon*'s hull, radiating outward from the hidden rift, each one releasing new clouds of debris.

Then, over the horizon of *Dragon*'s hull, Clemantine glimpsed the tapered cylinder of the entity's containment capsule, its white ceramic surface reflecting the hull cells' gleam. Writhing white snakes trailed from it, ripped out of the freshly opened channels. These were the tendrils that had infiltrated the interior of the ship, their frantic whipping motion suggesting bio-mechanical spasms.

– KILL IT –

<agreed: KILL IT>

The surface of the capsule went black—a matte black that made it disappear in the visible range, although it still blazed with heat in the infrared.

The gun deployed, the lens aligned—and then the capsule slipped out of sight behind *Dragon*, pushed by the white fire of steerage jets that it should not have possessed.

In the library, Clemantine exploded in frustration: "*Corruption take us!*"

On the high bridge she coolly instructed the cells:

– reacquire target –

The tendrils ripped free of *Dragon*, tearing deep channels in the hull, destroying long swaths of philosopher cells and isolating blocks of them. Clemantine lost many of her links to the cell field. She used the surviving connections to issue a new directive: *– kill it –*

The remaining cells united in consensus: *<KILL IT>*

She did not try to instruct them on the means. They knew better than she did.

Under the direction of the philosopher cells, *Dragon*'s hull began to straighten, while it rolled and rotated through three dimensions, striving to bring the containment capsule within range of its gun. The lens swiveled, seeking its target, but it was capable of only a narrow range of motion.

Clemantine watched it close in, anticipating the surge of power ... until a new sensation drew her attention. Six lateral lines composed *Dragon*'s gravitational sensor. They were evenly spaced around the hull and ran from bow to stern. At least one line had survived the expulsion of the capsule, because it alerted her to the presence of a newly activated propulsion reef, one so close she saw the disturbance it produced moving like a wave through the debris field.

In the library, Naresh identified the cause: "Lezuri must have equipped his capsule with a reef! He's converted it into a starship!"

A tiny ship, just forty meters long.

The little ship paralleled *Dragon*, accelerating so swiftly it would pass beyond the bow in seconds, putting itself in front of the gun.

No. That was too good to be true. Clementine could not believe Lezuri would make such a blatant mistake. Something, some factor still unknown to her, would allow the little ship a chance to escape.

The philosopher cells did not share her doubt. Their consensus was absolute: <*KILL IT*>

It swept past the bow. The lens locked on to its target. Then . . . *Nothing.*

No surge of power from the reef. No destructive rush of energy.

Confusion and fury erupted among the cells as the little ship gained velocity, racing away.

Clementine introduced a new argument to the surviving cells:

– *pursue it* –

Consensus was immediate, but again, the reef did not respond.

Why not? It might be weakened, but it was not destroyed. The gravitational sensor registered its latent influence like a subtle vibration in her mind . . . but that was all. She had no awareness of the reef's condition, no feedback from it at all. That implied that every connection between the reef and the cell field had been torn loose—or maybe destroyed on purpose by the entity.

A submind took this conclusion to the library. From there, she accessed the radio. She had to contact *Griffin*, tell her other self to go in pursuit.

But the radio did not respond.

Kona saw what she was trying to do and shook his head. "It's out."

As *Dragon* writhed, *Griffin* shifted position, seeking a clear shot, but Clemantine could not find the containment capsule. Somehow, it kept itself shielded behind *Dragon*'s mass.

A new factor entered her awareness: The gravitational sensor had detected a slight perturbation, separate from those generated by the coursers. The cells sought to discern its source, their attention focused in the direction of *Dragon*.

When she shared this news with her Apparatchiks in the library, the Engineer said, "It's the containment capsule. It has to be."

A dark laugh from the Pilot. "Even if it has a reef, so what? It can't outrun two coursers. It can't escape our guns."

The source of the perturbations was already receding.

On the high bridge, Clemantine proposed an action:

– *pursue it* –

The cells complied, triggering a surge of activity in the reef. *Griffin* leaped forward. But Clemantine still could not locate the little ship.

Surely it had moved beyond *Dragon*'s bow by now? That would make it an easy target, yet *Dragon* did not shoot.

"*Dragon* is damaged," the Engineer concluded, his somber gaze on Clemantine. "It's up to you."

She could not shoot what she could not see. *Griffin*'s gravitational sensor let her track the newly activated reef, but that gave her only an estimate of Lezuri's position—enough to know he was moving out fast and hard.

Resolving to match that pace, she imposed her will on the cell field:

– *pursue it. faster* –

In the library, the Pilot objected. "The risk of collision—!"

"I understand it, but our target is small and dark and cooling fast. I don't want to risk losing it in the void."

"Radar," the Engineer said.

"Try it," Clemantine agreed. "But I think Lezuri will anticipate that and shape-shift his hull to a fully stealthed mode."

She tried to contact *Dragon* again by radio, but got no answer.

As she neared the larger courser, its cells—what was left of them—flashed a message of triumphant identity:

Within that declaration, a sense of gloating victory over an embedded enemy successfully ejected, and a firm assertion that it retained the strength to self-repair.

Griffin's cell field responded with what Clemantine interpreted as a warning:

<we are stronger>

The implication: that *Dragon* must recover or be consumed.

She swept past the larger courser, taking a good look as she did, horrified at the extent of damage, longing to know if anyone was still alive within that torn hull.

She could not help them, not yet, but she could hunt the entity.

"Okay," she said to the Engineer. "*Dragon*'s behind us. The field is clear. Have you got anything?"

"No, you were right," he conceded. "No radar returns at all."

"Then lock it down," she told him. "We're going stealth too. I'm taking the hull cells dark. We're going to track his reef and I don't want him to see us coming."

CHAPTER THIRTY-NINE

THE BUNDLED MEMORIES comprising Urban's last generated submind slipped through the data gate, bound for *Elepaio*. Transmission protocols ensured no copy was left behind.

Elepaio was closest in the vanguard of outriders, but it was still ninety light-minutes distant. Ninety minutes in which either the entity had secured its hold over *Dragon* or Clemantine had destroyed the ship.

The submind's arrival at *Elepaio*'s data gate woke an archived copy of Urban's ghost. Mind and submind merged. He instantiated in the outrider's library with the memory of all that had happened aboard *Dragon*. Predominant in his memory: the predator and its relentless pursuit of him in all his variations.

He issued a command to close the data gate to incoming traffic—too late. Something had come through.

He knew there had not been time for all the data needed to define a fully realized ghost to transit through the gate, and he assumed a far larger quantity of data would be needed to define the entity. Still, something had arrived behind him.

The predator might be a fragment of the entity or it could be a manufactured weapon that did not represent the entity at all. Whatever it was, he already had a partial map of its structure. He used that to devise a probe to further investigate its configuration.

The thing winked into existence on the library floor. *Riffan again!* he saw in disgust. The predator still wore Riffan's aspect like a protective shell.

Urban's probe instantiated around it: a shimmering translucent column that shot up from the library floor, trapping the predator within as it rose an infinite distance overhead. Immediately, the diameter of the column began to shrink. It compressed around the predator, probing it from all sides, passing all the structural data it discovered back to Urban, at the same time overwriting everything it touched.

The predator reacted by withdrawing the Riffan mask—a bizarre transformation as the façade was sucked off, twisted, and then compressed into a geometrical point where it vanished. Left behind was a tremulous, vaguely man-shaped cloud, that appeared to be composed of tiny virtual machines. Battle ready now, the predator struck back.

Chaos boiled up around its feet. The base of the column disintegrated. Chaos climbed the column, consuming it, while a separate wave of chaos swept across the library floor, catching Urban before he could retreat.

Chaotic forces swirled around his ghost feet, climbed his body. He was conscious of his own disintegration, an onslaught of mindlessness, meaningless disorder, overwriting the programmatic structure that defined him. He sensed the same wave of chaos at work consuming the library's computational strata, destroying the virtual grid and the archive where he'd kept the backup copy of his ghost.

He could not stop the destruction. Only microseconds left to create a submind. He focused on that one task and when it was done, he bundled his memories into it and sent the submind through the data gate, addressed to the next outrider in the fleet.

Ninety-three minutes later *Khonsu* received the submind and woke an archived copy of Urban's ghost. Their memories merged. His first coherent thought: *Close the data gate!*

But the integration of mind and submind had taken a measurable quantity of time, enough to allow the predator through the gate before he could close it to incoming traffic.

It instantiated, wearing Riffan's aspect again. With a sharp shock, Urban realized it had to be that way. The predator could not pass through the data gate without using its stolen permissions.

Again, Urban launched his probe, updating it with structural knowledge hard-won in the last encounter. Riffan's aspect disappeared as the column formed—hidden away by the predator, which must be eager to protect it. So Urban compiled a second probe. This one had the single goal of locating and dissolving all identifiers associated with Riffan.

But chaos broke past the column before he could launch it.

He created a submind and sent it to the outrider *Lam Lha*.

It arrived, ninety-one minutes later. Mind and submind integrated. Urban emerged from the archive just as the predator arrived through the data gate.

This time, he was ready for it. He launched both probes as it instantiated. One assaulted the Riffan-shell, partly overwriting it before it could be withdrawn. The other trapped the predator within the column, holding it there long enough to dissolve another layer of its structure before chaos broke loose to ravage the library's computational strata and its archive, and to overwrite the structure of Urban's ghost.

He sent a submind to the outrider *Pytheas*.

This time, surely, he knew enough about the predator to defeat it. His prior encounters convinced him it was not a sentient thing, but a tool. And given that the method of its attack never varied, it was not adept at learning. Still, the entity had designed it and Urban had not broken it yet.

It came through the data gate—but was it a microsecond slower this time?

It instantiated. Urban saw that the Riffan-shell, damaged in their last encounter, had been restored. Instantly, he shifted tactics, directing both probes to attack the shell.

He did not need to destroy the predator. He only needed an interval of time to get ahead of it and then he could close the next gate, trap it behind him.

He'd already slowed the predator's transit once by forcing it to rebuild the stolen permission structure that let it pass. He gambled that an increase in the level of damage would slow it more.

The probes ripped into the Riffan-shell. Swaths of it dissolved before the predator drew it in beneath armored layers. This time, Urban cast his submind across the void even before chaos broke free of the column.

Ninety minutes later he reached the last outrider, *Fortuna*. He closed its data gate before anything else came through.

CHAPTER FORTY

URBAN INSTANTIATED ABOARD *Fortuna* amid the austere architecture of the library. He stood alone on a white path winding away across a glassy blue plane of data, the color deepening with distance. This library was a copy of the one that had been carried aboard *Dragon*, but the only archived ghost that existed there was his.

If Urban had been a physical avatar, the running battle with the predator would have left him shaking with exhaustion, but a ghost did not feel fatigue. Now that he was safely locked behind a closed data gate, he took up the task of editing out the useless emotional detritus of fear and panic that lingered in the wake of this latest brush with death.

And then he went further. He created for himself a machine-like calm, walling off the fury and frustration that arose from the certainty that he'd lost *Dragon*.

The entity's assault against him had left him with no choice but to call for termination. If *Griffin* had received that radio message, then *Dragon* was gone, blown apart, reduced to vapor and debris.

All sixty-five of the ship's company gone with it. His last words to Clemantine: *It's over.*

Grief seeped past his machine calm. And fear. He wondered, *Was it over?*

If *Griffin* had not received that message, or if the other Clemantine had not carried through with it, the situation would be far worse. The entity would have secured command of *Dragon*.

No.

She would never allow that. She would not take the risk of

Dragon turning against her. He remembered her promise: *I'll do whatever's necessary to protect all of you.* He trusted her to protect the archived ghosts she carried, regardless of the cost.

Editing his ghost again, he sequestered his doubt and his grief. He couldn't help Clementine. Not now. He had to assess and secure his own situation and then decide on a strategy, one based on fact, not on what he wished things could be.

He knew already he could not go back the way he'd come. The predator had wiped the computational strata in each successive outrider, leaving it nonfunctional. And with *Fortuna* so far from *Griffin*, any error in the targeting of the communications laser would be magnified many times over, so that the smallest initial discrepancy would cause the beam to miss its target, possibly by tens of kilometers. The independent motion of both ships made the problem excruciatingly complex. It was unrealistic to think he could get any data through.

But he was not helpless. He had *Fortuna*, and the little ship should be fully operational. He queried the Dull Intelligence that oversaw its operation to confirm this. "Review current status."

A gentle masculine voice answered, "Ship's location is 7.5 light-hours from command ship *Dragon*'s last calculated position. Proceeding to target star system Tanjiri at a steady thirty-five percent light speed as measured against the velocity of the target star. Reef function is nominal, though presently dampened to a minimally active state. Internal network and computational strata report healthy. Navigational fuel reserves at 93%. Telescope presently engaged in a survey of the Near Vicinity. Collected data will be held until authorization is received to open the data gate."

"Don't open the data gate," Urban said.

"Understood."

"And reorient the telescope. Look back. Calculate expected positions for both *Dragon* and *Griffin* and locate them with the scope."

"Understood."

Urban longed to go back. He resolved that as soon as he confirmed *Dragon* gone, and *Griffin* the survivor, he would order the

DI to flip *Fortuna* bow to stern and then dump velocity. *Griffin's* forward progress would close the gap and eventually Urban's ghost would be able to make the jump between the ships.

A fine plan, shattered by the first image the telescope returned.

The image posted within a library window, its resolution shockingly poor. Urban was used to working with images compiled from data collected across multiple telescopes. Now he had only one. At such a distance even a courser was a minuscule object, its details blurred despite extensive processing. Still, the three-part equation of distance, luminosity, and the known dimensions of both coursers left no doubt that the ship captured in the image was *Dragon*.

Clearly, it was battle damaged. Long, lightless scars sliced through the luminous philosopher cells and the ship was surrounded by a faint blur, a halo, that had to be a cloud of debris and frozen vapor. "Analyze that," he told the DI.

"Analysis indicates water, molecular oxygen, carbon dioxide, and an array of metals within the de-gassed cloud."

Urban felt an automated routine kick in, locking out despair.

"Where is *Griffin*?" he demanded.

"A search of *Griffin's* calculated position is presently underway."

"You haven't found it yet?"

"That is correct."

"Keep looking. It has to be there."

But did it? Did it have to be there? Didn't *Dragon's* survival indicate *Griffin's* demise?

"Keep looking," he said again.

Hours passed. Then days, but *Griffin* could not be resolved.

Griffin hunted the void, full stealth, its philosopher cells dark, its radar dormant, all transmissions silenced.

There was silence too, on the high bridge, with no conversation to endure from hibernating cells. Clemantine had to conduct her search without the benefit of their acute vision, but Lezuri's ship was so small and dark the cells could not have seen it anyway, unless it came so close that it reflected a glint of their own light.

For Clemantine, the silence was a welcome respite that let her focus on the Near Vicinity as she tracked Lezuri's propulsion reef. The faint signal cut out for hours and she thought she'd lost him. Then the signal reappeared, shifted intensity, changed trajectory, vanished again. The Pilot calculated where Lezuri should be. They swooped in on a heading meant to intercept his little ship, but did not find him.

Clemantine quieted *Griffin's* reef to minimize its interference while the gravitational sensor felt the void all around, seeking for the faint signal of Lezuri's dormant reef. She scanned with cameras and telescopes. But there was nothing.

More hours passed.

Time enough to reflect that worlds could be lost in the dark between the stars.

"What if we've miscalculated?" she asked the Pilot. "What if Lezuri was decelerating when we thought he was still accelerating? Maybe his goal isn't to get away. Maybe it's to linger and wait for *Dragon* to close the distance, come near enough to try his needles again."

"Or to wait for us," the Engineer pointed out. "We're vulnerable to his needles too."

If Clemantine had existed in human form, that thought would have given her chills.

The Pilot dismissed these concerns with a contemptuous wave of his hand. "I did not make such a mistake. I cannot pinpoint Lezuri's exact location but I know his last course adjustment took him away from the trajectory of the fleet, and that his velocity is greater than ours, and that he has used his reef hard. He will not have the power to return, not for some time. And he cannot be hunting us in the same way we've been hunting him. His vessel is too small to carry a gravitational sensor. So we are hidden from him, as long as we remain silent and dark."

"I think there is very little chance now that we will find him," the Astronomer said. "He won't give us any more signals to follow. He'll coast for years before he uses his reef again."

"It's what I'd do," the Pilot agreed.

This assessment brought both guilt and relief to Clemantine.

Abandoning the hunt felt wrong, but she longed to return to *Dragon*, to offer her help, and to learn how much of the ship and its company had survived.

"All right," she said. "We stay dark, and we go home."

No easy task to catalog all the damage—especially with the Apparatchiks gone.

Clemantine kept to her post on *Dragon*'s high bridge. What choice? There was no one else to do it. From there she sent out an army of DIs to search the network, the library files, the archive, seeking for any sign of the predator . . . and of Urban.

In the library, she approached Vytet. "I know you're angry over this—"

Vytet transformed, looming larger than life, features exaggerated, amber eyes now glinting red. "Angry over what? The fact you decided, on your own, to risk all of our futures? That you destroyed any chance of a peaceful coalition with a great being? Or that you blew the ship apart?" She gestured at a projection of *Dragon* showing the known damage, with vast tracts of the ship still to be surveyed. "You did this."

"Yes. I made the choice. But we're still alive, and the ship is ours."

"At what cost?" Vytet demanded to know. "You have no idea what's been lost or if we can recover."

"I think I do know what's been lost," Clemantine said. "But we *will* recover, though I'm going to need your help."

Tempers were even more heated in the warren, where she quickly found herself in a shouting match with Naresh:

"You had no right to launch an assault on your own!"

"We had no choice but to do it that way!"

"No! You did have a choice."

"Success required secrecy!"

"You call the wreck you've made of this ship success?"

"I *do*."

"Does Urban consider this a success? Did you even consult with him? Where is he anyway?"

Grimly, she said, "I don't know."

They were in the forest room, and by this time, more than twenty people had gathered around, drawn by the heat of their argument, drifting one above another in the absence of gravity. Kona was among them. He'd been busy in the warren, organizing people and assigning tasks, setting some to grow resurrection pods to restore those too badly injured to heal on their own, and others to organizing meals and quarters, while encouraging as many as he could to retreat to cold sleep, to reduce the draw on the ship's resources.

Now he looked at Clemantine. "What do you mean? Are you saying you can't find him? If you can't find him, wake his ghost from the archive."

"The archive's been wiped," she told him. "Nothing is left there. I think the predator attacked that first, when it emerged."

This announcement drew gasps and cries of horror.

She turned again to Naresh. "It's why I came to talk to you. I'm giving you the task of re-establishing an archive, and making sure everyone posts a fresh copy there."

"Urban will have a ghost safe aboard *Griffin*," Kona said.

She forced herself to meet his gaze. Held it. Not so much to prepare him, but to give herself time to gather her courage. "Urban didn't keep a ghost on *Griffin*. He kept his backups on the outriders, in secured archives that only he could access."

Kona gave a firm nod, as if this answer satisfied him. "We'll find him on the outriders, then." His confidence a veil pulled over a terrible fear—a fear she shared.

The data gate kept a log of traffic. It showed Urban had sent a submind to *Elepaio*, with Riffan's corrupt ghost following close behind him.

"Where is Riffan?" she asked, aiming the question at no one in particular.

Tarnya emerged from the crowd to answer her. "He was hurt. We had to put him in a resurrection pod. He'll be out in a day or so."

"No. Leave him there. He may be the source of a security issue. Leave him locked down until I say so."

She faced more questions, arguments, and accusations, as sub-minds cycled in and out. Eventually, she retreated alone to the gee deck.

It was a shambles. Dust and debris drifting everywhere, con-fused birds fluttering in panic at her approach. At the same time, she listened to Vytet in the library, reporting that an initial inspec-tion of the deck had found the rotation cylinder cracked and the gearing shattered.

Shoran appeared, gliding from beneath the upside-down canopy of a small uprooted tree, its branches bearing withered leaves and faded flowers. "Hey," she said. "Personnel map's down, but I heard the flutter of bird wings and thought someone might be here."

"The guilty party has arrived."

"Guilty of saving our asses."

"No, it was Pasha who designed the defense. I only made sure it was implemented."

"I'll thank her later." Shoran gestured over her shoulder. "Some of the generative walls are still working. I started to do some initial cleanup, shoving debris back into the system to be recycled, but I think the vats are full."

"Or the deck's circulatory system has stopped working."

"Or that," Shoran conceded. "So tell me, where do we really stand? I've heard a lot of chatter in the warrens, but what's the real situation?"

"It's not so bad," Clemantine said. "*Dragon* is broken, incapable of both acceleration and self-defense. We're estimating a loss of nineteen percent of our mass and a greater percentage of the phi-losopher cells. There hasn't been time to complete a survey, but I can tell you there is extensive damage to the internal transport and communications systems. The ship will have launched self-repair routines, but that activity will rapidly drain core reserves. I'll be using up more of our limited resources when I start repairing severed filaments of the neural bridge. Oh, and there's an excellent chance all the repair work will stimulate molecular disputes along all Chenzeme-Human boundaries. But from what I've seen so far, it looks like Lezuri is gone."

Shoran grinned. "So we're going to make it?"

"Yes," Clemantine affirmed. She couldn't celebrate it. Not in the face of Urban's absence. But it was true. "Yes. We are going to make it."

Urban continued to monitor the status of *Dragon*. He watched the debris cloud disperse into invisibility and the battle scars on its hull slowly fill with luminous cells as the ship healed itself.

The entity had taken his ship. No way to know if anyone among the ship's company was left alive . . . Clemantine, Kona, Vytet, Riffan, Shoran, and all the rest. Lezuri might have let them live . . . or at least captured their patterns.

Urban searched his mind, he searched the local library, desperate to devise some way to take his ship back, but the predator's ferocity haunted him. It was like a promise from Lezuri that he would put *Fortuna* under the gun if ever he suspected Urban's presence there.

Lezuri wanted to reach the ring-shaped world.

Verilotus. That was its name. Lezuri had wanted to go there armed with the coursers' weapons. Urban's refusal to do so had triggered disaster. Everything that mattered, lost, because he'd promised himself he would not return a broken god to its seat of power.

He decided that promise still held. If he could do nothing else, he would do that.

He watched and he waited as *Dragon* continued to coast, its velocity only slightly higher than *Fortuna*'s and its course, so far, unchanged.

If its course shifted, if it turned away from Tanjiri and towards Verilotus, that would be final proof that Lezuri controlled the ship. Then Urban would change course too. He would need to reach Verilotus ahead of *Dragon*, and once there, do what he could to block the ambition of a broken god.

CHAPTER FORTY-ONE

CLEMANTINE MADE A cautious return to the fleet, keeping *Griffin* dark and silent as the Astronomer used the telescopes to study *Dragon* and map its ravaged hull.

"There is some regeneration in the cell field," the Astronomer concluded. "And a new radio antenna has been deployed on the hull."

Good news. Someone was alive in there.

"Anything else?"

"Nothing visible." Then he added, in answer to her unspoken question, "No sign of the entity's capsule."

She turned to the Engineer. "Let's use radar again. Map the debris field. Look for anything that might be in our way."

Radar revealed *Griffin*'s presence. The response was immediate, a low-power radio hail from *Dragon*, her own voice demanding, *Identify yourself.*

She answered, "The iris will bloom again."

A long pause and then a question: *Did you kill him?*

"I couldn't find him."

Another pause, then: *Urban is gone.*

"What do you mean?"

There may still be a copy of his ghost on one of the outriders—we lost contact and can't confirm—but he's gone from Dragon.

"I'll establish contact."

No! Don't. We need to be cautious. The predator followed him out there. It may still be there.

This time the pause in the conversation was on her side as she processed what her counterpart had just said: Urban was gone.

Aboard *Dragon*, Vytet lobbied for *Griffin* to open its data gate. "That will allow us to copy the Apparatchiks back. We need their help, their knowledge, their expertise."

Clemantine agreed that having the Apparatchiks would speed the recovery, but opening the data gate would put *Griffin* at risk. "It's too soon. We need to clean up first, ensure Lezuri is truly gone."

The entity had left hazardous matter behind.

When the tendrils serving as conduits to the containment capsule ripped free, they had not parted cleanly. Fragments remained—and each piece had begun to regrow.

Vytet's engineers attacked the problem. In the library, they found a design for a small, snakelike, laser-wielding robot. They grew a prototype, skinned it in Chenzeme tissue, and sent it to hunt the fragments.

Clemantine expected the device to succumb to the entity's lingering molecular defenses, but the vigor of the initial infestation was gone and the laser snake succeeded in vaporizing its first target. Cheers of success broke out in the library, and the engineers set about creating more of the devices.

The ship's network still worried Clemantine. She had already inspected it, but she sent a DI to examine it again to ensure nothing of the predator remained. When the network proved clean, she sent the DI into the library to inspect all recently updated files. It found nothing of concern.

There was still one more place she needed to inspect.

She instructed a DI to waken Riffan from his resurrection pod. When it opened, she was there in the warren, waiting.

Riffan emerged, looking worried and confused. His gaze settled on her. "Why am I here? What happened? I remember a terrific noise, and then nothing." His face scrunched in a frown. "Why can't I access the network?"

She said, "I've locked you out of the network until I have assurance you're clean."

"What? What do you mean?" Clothes budded from a generative surface beneath the wall-weed, but he ignored them. "Tell me what's happened!"

"Lezuri acquired your access to the network."

"No. That's impossible." His frown deepened. "I did allow him to use my tablet. Maybe through that he somehow . . ." His voice trailed off. His eyes grew wide. "Did something bad happen?"

"Yes," she said in an icy tone. "Bad things happened. Now I have a question for you. Is it possible there's a remnant of Lezuri secreted in your atrium?"

His focus turned inward. He looked chilled, pinched with cold.

She sliced the air with the edge of her hand. "Go see Vytet and Naresh. They're waiting for you. You'll give them full access to your atrium so they can confirm you've got no parasites there. Until that's done, you'll stay out of the network." Her tone softened. "Stay off the gee deck too. It's dangerous there." She gestured at him from head to toe. "This is the only version of you. There's no ghost in our archive, on *Artemis*, or on *Griffin*, so be careful, okay?"

His eyes widened in shock. "But how? Why?"

She waved him off. "Go see Vytet and Naresh. They'll answer all your questions."

Throughout it all, she remained on the high bridge, overseeing every aspect of the recovery. At her request, *Griffin* remained dark, a tactic to prevent its philosopher cells from reacting aggressively to the sight of *Dragon's* weakness. And *Griffin* kept its data gate closed, while she fully confirmed the integrity of her ship.

Her ship. It had come to that.

Pasha thought it strange, the way people apportioned blame. She had conceived and designed the Pyrrhic Defense—facts she'd made clear—but everyone angry at the way the project was handled put the blame on Clemantine, saying "She could have stopped it."

"I could have stopped it too," Pasha declared every time she heard the argument, whether in the warren or the library. "We both understood the risk, and decided together to go forward— and we succeeded. Lezuri is gone and the ship is clean."

They had not imagined Urban's very existence might be lost in the course of the defense. Clementine had not said much, but Pasha sensed anguish in her silence, grief compounded by the burden of uncertainty. It was important for her, for all of them, to understand what had happened, and why.

Pasha had detailed records of every phase of the Pyrrhic Defense, but she didn't know what had triggered the hostilities. So she resolved to investigate, to document events prior to the brief conflict.

She announced her project and invited people to share what they knew, particularly if they had seen Urban or Lezuri in the hours before the silver cloud boiled out of Clementine's cottage.

To her surprise, Naresh was first to come forward, despite his differences with her. "Lezuri was on the gee deck when the emergency began," he explained. "I met him, but he said he had come to speak with Urban, alone. So I let him go." Naresh shook his head. "Now, I wish I'd followed."

"Do you know that he actually met with Urban?"

This question drew a guilty blush. "Yes," he confessed. "I watched on the personnel map. He entered the cottage. He was still there when the emergency began. I never saw him leave. Like Urban, he just vanished from the map."

What had gone on in the cottage? What had been discussed? The ruined structure provided Pasha no clues, so she turned to the ship's logs. Any commands Urban issued would have been recorded and might hint at what was on his mind when hostilities broke out.

She sent a ghost to the library. Once there, she summoned a DI to assist her. "Display the command log," she instructed.

A library window opened. Pasha searched the file, locating the time of the radio burst that had closed the data gate to *Griffin*. She scanned back from there. At first all she saw were lines of automated input, documenting standard processes that did not interest her. Then she found it: A command from Urban to reset *Dragon's* twin telescopes, and the one aboard *Artemis*.

Reset them to what? *From* what?

The command had been issued just thirty-one seconds before the radio burst.

She told the DI, "Let's jump to the telescope log."

The DI opened a new window.

The most recent entries in the log were all alerts reporting no new data being received from the scopes on the outriders. She'd heard contact had been lost. Another issue awaiting attention.

"Delete the alerts. Let me see what else is here."

The DI complied. Now, at the top of the list, was an order to reset. Pasha pointed to it. "What is this? Tell me what it means."

"An earlier order diverted telescopes one, two, and four from the standard survey of the Near Vicinity. This order returns them to that task."

"Okay," Pasha said, sensing she was close to an answer. "Show me the order that diverted them."

Clemantine was in the warren, listening to Vytet discuss what it would take to restore the gee-deck's rotation, when a message arrived from Pasha:

I figured out what Urban was doing when the war started. Come to the library. I'll show you.

A flush of fear, a rush of gratitude. She generated a ghost and sent it.

In the library, Pasha had created a three-dimensional astronomical projection. *Dragon*'s position was labeled. So was Tanjiri System. Another star was marked too, but only with a catalog number. MSC-G-349809. It was closer than Tanjiri, but on a different heading.

Pasha pointed to it. "Urban was looking at this system right before he closed the data gate to *Griffin*."

Clemantine studied the point of light, re-read the label. It meant nothing to her. She turned to Pasha for an explanation.

"It's a G-type star," Pasha said. "Never cordoned. Never even settled, at least according to our records. This is the most recent image of it captured by the standard survey."

"And?" Clemantine urged, desperate to understand what it meant, what it had meant to Urban.

"Something's there. I don't know what, and it's too small to resolve visually in this image, but the spectrum indicates a second luminous object, inconsistent with any known type of star."

"Did Urban know this?" Clemantine asked, struggling to grasp what this implied about the conflict and Urban's disappearance.

"He was looking at it," Pasha repeated. "He diverted three telescopes, and focused them on a point close to the star."

"That must have produced a more detailed image than this."

"Yes," Pasha said. "But there is no such image in the library. I think he deleted it. Erased it."

"No. Not Urban. That's not how he handles data."

"I'd repeat the observation," Pasha said, "but *Dragon*'s scopes are not working, and we've lost communications with all the outriders except *Artemis*."

"Yes. Every attempt to reach *Elepaio* returns an error message. And since *Elepaio* is closest, no communications are being relayed to the more distant outriders." She hesitated, still struggling to accept the truth of what must have happened. She told Pasha, "Urban sent a submind out there. Did you know that?"

"No."

"The predator followed him."

"Oh *no*."

"Yes. The predator wiped our archive here on *Dragon*. I think it wiped all intelligence from *Elepaio* too." She shook her head. "If *Elepaio* had been physically damaged, it would have self-repaired and renewed contact. Failing that, the other outriders should have responded to the break in communications by dropping back, re-establishing the link. But that hasn't happened."

"You think *all* the outriders were corrupted?" Pasha asked her.

Clemantine nodded. "Urban kept his backups out there."

Pasha looked away, clearly struggling for something to say. She settled on, "*I'm sorry*."

Clemantine pushed back against a smothering sense of loss,

strove to focus on the present. Gesturing at the nameless star, she said, "Tell me what this means."

Pasha visibly gathered herself, then she confessed, "I don't know what it means. But I think we need to know what's in that stellar system. It can't be coincidence. Something Urban saw there triggered the conflict. We need to know what it is."

"Our telescopes are out of commission, but I can ask *Griffin* to look."

"That's good. We should do that. But if we could find the image, we'd know *exactly* what Urban saw. You just said he wouldn't have erased it. So what would he have done with it?"

"*Ahh*," Clemantine said, in imitation of a sigh, though her ghost did not breathe. She opened a library window. "He kept a sequestered data cache—personal things."

"He gave you access?"

"Yes."

The cache inventory appeared in the window. She searched for the newest file, found it.

"It's an image," Pasha said, triumph in her voice.

CHAPTER FORTY-TWO

IN THE METADATA accompanying the image of the ring-shaped world, a DI had conveniently included two fields derived not from observation, but from testimony.

Object Name: Verilotus, per the entity Lezuri.

Summary Description: An artificial world-system constructed after the rise of the Hallowed Vasties, exploiting technologies not described within the local library. Inner torus intended for habitation. Existence of current population unknown. Outer luminous ring represented as an intrusion of an alternate Universe, with gravity-manipulating properties. *Source: the entity Lezuri (uncorroborated).*

Kona waited, adrift in the zero gravity of the warren's forest room—though tonight the light panels did not display the forest for which the room was named. The walls, along with floor and ceiling, glowed in a gradient of white light, dimmest at the door, bright at the front of the room where Kona would soon be speaking.

For now, he waited to one side, silent, somber, refusing any attempt at conversation. The buzz of voices grew louder as more people arrived.

Three days ago Clemantine had released the image of Verilotus. Since then, Kona had listened to the discussions, the arguments, the competing analyses circulating among the ship's company. He'd worked quietly but incessantly to guide that debate, speaking privately to influencers like Tarnya, Naresh, Shoran, and Vytet, locking in their support.

He'd called this meeting only after he was sure he could win consensus.

A DI tracked attendance. A few minutes before the scheduled start of the session it notified him: *All present*.

He messaged Clemantine and Vytet, both nearby: *It's a little early, but I'm going to start*.

Clemantine, her gaze coolly determined, nodded her agreement. Vytet gestured with her hand, *Go ahead*.

Kona reached for a ceiling ring, used it to launch himself in a slow glide to the front of the room. People shifted, opening a path for him. Soft-spoken words of encouragement eased his way.

Centuries ago, when Urban had taken himself away on the Null Boundary Expedition, Kona had believed he'd lost his son forever. When he'd caught up on all the known facts surrounding Urban's disappearance, he'd plunged into that recidivist nightmare again. This time though, he intended to do more than mourn.

He grabbed the speaker's pole. Used it to turn around, face the gathering. A hush fell across the room. Everyone knew, or guessed, what he'd come to say, but their culture of reasoned consensus demanded he say it, that he make the argument, do all he could to persuade the doubters before he asked for the assent of the company.

He told them, "We are here to make a decision. It will be some time before *Dragon* is fully repaired, but the immediate emergency is past. The reef is healthy and back under control of the cell field, giving us the option of navigating a new course. It's time to decide—Verilotus or Tanjiri?

"We've all had time to study and consider the few available facts surrounding Verilotus. We've all engaged in creative speculations based on those facts. I think there is now general agreement that Verilotus is the system Lezuri regards as home, and that he is on his way there now.

"*We* allowed this thing to escape the Rock. I think it is our obligation to pursue him.

"Realize that the entity which infested our ship, defeated our defenses, brought us to the edge of self-destruction was surely no more than a fragment of the entity as it must have been in its grandeur at Verilotus.

"We know almost nothing about Verilotus and we have not begun to understand the physics of the luminous ring that surrounds it, but both appear to me to be wondrous creations, worthy of admiration—though my admiration does not extend to their creator.

"Lezuri presented himself as condescending, self-serving, dominating, and ultimately violent when he could not achieve his goals by persuasion alone. In his story of his origin, he told us he grew into his power by seizing the resources of lesser minds. He was not ashamed that he had subsumed the existence of others to further his own position. For him, there was nothing wrong with this. He took what he needed to create himself.

"And then he lost himself. This being of immense power contended with another and lost. '*One whom I loved betrayed me.*' Those were his words. Imagine it: These were beings with the power to create worlds but without the values to sustain peace between them.

"And Lezuri was exiled. Left alone, marooned on the Rock, brooding over what was done to him.

"I believe Lezuri is returning home for the reason he stated—to restore his world—but also to restore himself.

"I think it would be a mistake, an abrogation of our duty to allow him to do that. We all know how the frontier has suffered under the scourge of Chenzeme power. If Lezuri succeeds in regenerating himself as he once was, his power will far exceed that of the Chenzeme, and from what I've observed, he does not have the temperament for it.

"I'm not alone in this judgment. At the Rock, two starships were scuttled to stop Lezuri from escaping his exile. *Dragon* was nearly scuttled in the struggle to free ourselves of his looming tyranny.

"I do not want to be complicit in releasing this regenerated entity on the Hallowed Vasties. He will never be weaker than he is now. We need to hunt him down and destroy him while we can."

CHAPTER FORTY-THREE

EACH DAY, AT least twice a day, *Fortuna*'s DI directed the telescope to seek out *Dragon*. For many, many days the only visible change was the slow closure of the dark hull scars.

Then a day came when the newest image showed the bright sparks of navigational jets firing alongside the hull. The conclusion was inescapable: *Dragon* was changing course. It was no longer bound for Tanjiri System.

The courser's new heading could not be calculated from a single image. Urban needed to observe the ship over several days to confirm Verilotus was its destination—but to get there first he had to act now.

He summoned the ship's DI. "Redirect our course to intercept the object MSC-G-349809-1b."

"Confirming course redirection," the Dull Intelligence responded. "Target heading is star system MSC-G-349809. Specific destination is the inner-system object 1b, labeled as Verilotus."

"Correct," Urban said. He'd designated the immense luminous ring—so thin, graceful, *perfect*—that surrounded the world of Verilotus as Object 1a. Lezuri had called it a blade. He'd described it as an intrusion of another Universe and he'd admitted, *It could be used as a weapon.*

"Course modification underway," the DI informed him.

The simulated reality of the library did not replicate the sudden harsh radial motion as navigation jets fired in calculated sequence, but Urban was able to watch the ship come about through a three-dimensional projection posted by the DI. *Fortuna* was small, nimble. The adjustment did not take long. Infinitesimal odds that any watching eyes aboard *Dragon* had detected the brief spark.

Lezuri had said the flow of time was accelerated at Verilotus, that a year played out on that artificial world as days passed outside. An effect of the blade? Perhaps.

Urban was days closer to Verilotus than *Dragon*. If he could maintain that lead through the coming years, through the time it would take him to reach the system—and if Lezuri had been telling the truth—then Urban would arrive there with an interval to explore and to prepare.

It would be a long voyage, but he'd endured such before. He knew the tricks.

He would not allow himself to think too hard on his present existence: less than a mote, an aberrant spark in the immensity of the void, light years of emptiness all around him and centuries of travel time separating him from any known human presence.

He would not allow himself to dwell on what he'd lost.

Such thoughts he locked away behind artificial barriers.

He adopted a routine of switching off his consciousness, rousing only twice in every twenty-four hours to check the ship's status and to view new images of *Dragon* presented to him by the DI. Each image confirmed its revised course.

After a time, he discovered a slight increase in *Dragon*'s velocity. He matched it, then exceeded it. This raised his risk of obliteration in a random collision, but it would do no good to reach Verilotus after Lezuri.

He instructed the DI to devote all remaining telescope time to a detailed survey of the MSC-G-349809 system. It soon confirmed the presence of two gas giant planets in the outer system, then began a slow meticulous search for minor bodies.

Urban wakened for only brief periods, but he perceived no interval between them so it felt to him as if he was constantly awake, rocketing at mad speed toward Verilotus.

To endure it, he adapted the calm demeanor, the machinelike patience of the persona he called the Sentinel. But dark thoughts whispered deep within the architecture of his ghost.

What if? What if?

A constant, haunting refrain.

What if he had passed the beacon without visiting it? What if he had scuttled *Dragon* that day the entity infested it? What if he had forbidden Riffan to share his tablet with Lezuri? What if he had agreed to take Lezuri to Verilotus? What if Clemantine still lived?

Did she?

Had she made an alliance with Lezuri? If that meant she still lived, he hoped it was so.

What if he reached Verilotus and found a hostile goddess?

Or what if he found nothing? No way to level up, to gain the strength and knowledge needed to face Lezuri.

More frightening: What if he *did* find those things? What then? Who would he become?

The answers lay ahead.

Also From Mythic Island Press LLC

INVERTED FRONTIER

BOOK 2

SILVER

by Linda Nagata

A LOST SHIP – A NEW WORLD

Urban is no longer master of the fearsome starship *Dragon*. Driven out by the hostile, godlike entity, Lezuri, he has taken refuge aboard the most distant vessel in his outrider fleet.

Though Lezuri remains formidable, he is a broken god, commanding only a fragment of the knowledge that once was his. He is desperate to return home to the ring-shaped artificial world he created at the height of his power, where he can recover the memory of forgotten technologies.

Urban is desperate to stop him. He races to reach the ring-shaped world first, only to find himself stranded in a remote desert, imperiled by a strange flood of glowing "silver" that rises in the night like fog—a lethal fog that randomly rewrites the austere, Earthlike landscape. He has only a little time to decipher the mystery of the silver and to master its secrets. Lezuri is coming—and Urban must level up before he can hope to vanquish the broken god.

ACKNOWLEDGMENTS

A great gap of time separates *Edges* from its predecessor, *Vast*, and perhaps that's appropriate given the span required for Urban's voyage home.

Time, of course, changes us all.

Though I'd long been thinking about this novel, I wasn't sure it was a good idea. Dare I try to re-enter a world I'd first imagined more than twenty years ago? And if I did, could I make it convincing for those who'd found *Vast* to be a memorable addition to their science fiction libraries? Eventually, I decided to try, convincing myself it would be a quick project. That did not turn out to be the case, but without that bit of self-deception, I might never have started.

Edges exists in its current form thanks to my freelance editor, Judith Tarr, who fearlessly insisted that an early draft needed a major rethinking. Judy later provided essential editorial input on a near-final draft, Kat Howard provided additional insight, and beta readers Larry Clough and Kristine Smith came to the rescue on short notice. Copyediting was done by Sherwood Smith, via the writers' cooperative, Book View Café. All of you have my thanks and my gratitude. You tried to steer me in the right direction. All remaining errors and deficiencies are my own.

I also want to acknowledge those readers who spend time with me on Twitter, or visit my blog. Your encouragement and kind words are deeply appreciated. Thank you!

And last but certainly not least, a huge thank you to all those who've taken the time to read this book, or others I've written. You're the reason I do this, and I'm deeply grateful for your ongoing support.

Linda Nagata
February 2019

Made in the USA
Las Vegas, NV
16 July 2022

51723701R00236